TIERNEY JAMES

Publishing Coordinator – Sharon Kizziah-Holmes

Owasso, OK

ISBN - 978-1-965460-22-1 (Paperback)
ISBN - 978-1-965460-23-8 (eBook)

DEDICATION

Dedicated to the men and women
who protect us from unseen dangers and corrupt governments.
Because of them, we remain free.

ACKNOWLEDGMENTS

This is when I get to thank all those amazing people who assisted in the transformation of an idea that keeps me awake at night and helps me turn it into another Enigma adventure. Invisible Goodbye took me to a land I've always wanted to visit; Russia. I learned so much in the process of writing this story for you. I hope you enjoy it.

Paperback Press – This is an amazing Indie-Assist company led by Sharon Kizziah-Holmes. Not only can I feel confident that the book will be produced in a beautiful and professional way, I know they will be there for me whenever I need some hand-holding with various vendors that sell my books. I couldn't do it without Sharon. Find out more about what they do at https://paperback-press.com/   Tell them I sent you!

Kate Richards – I had already written two Enigma novels when Kate became my editor. She pushed and shoved me into being a much better writer. Her witty comments and belief in my work has encouraged me to never give up.

Jaycee DeLorenzo – Thanks to Jaycee for always creating a beautiful book cover for me. She has this ability to figure out what I want even when I don't know. Sweet & Spicey Designs has never let me down.

Michael Byars Lewis – Now a military thriller writer, Michael was a former AC-130U 'Spooky' Gunship Evaluator Pilot. He spent eighteen years in the Air Force Special Operations Command. A twenty-five-year Air Force pilot, he has flown special operations combat missions in Bosnia, Iraq, and Afghanistan. He is currently a pilot for a major U.S. airline. Thanks to him he helped me fly an airbus into an Alaskan airport to save the Enigma team. Without his help, pilots everywhere would still be laughing at my feeble attempts at landing that big bird.

Mary Pat Kelly Tierney – When my characters have a medical emergency or I want to give them a medical complication, Mary Pat is my go-to gal. She gives me the courage to fix gunshot wounds, perform transfusions, and keep them alive long enough to fight another day. With 31 years as an ER trauma nurse and ED certified all that time, she became part of a pilot program for an advanced triage area needed due to the number of patients. Besides all that, Mary Pat spent14 years as a Family Practice Nurse Practitioner.

Lipstick & Danger Support Staff – These ladies have been with me almost from the beginning of this writing journey. They read advance copies to help me find mistakes, use social media to get the word out about a new release, help me decide on book covers, and encourage me to keep writing. What would I do without you guys?

Readers – Of course, you are the stars in my heart. Without you, I wouldn't have an audience to entertain. Thank you for believing in me and being patient between each new release. Your devotion and friendship mean so much.

Chapter One

Darkness always felt eternal flying over the ocean at night. The lights had been dimmed several hours earlier. Most passengers were asleep in spite of the twenty minutes of turbulence earlier in the flight. The occasional flash of distant lightning reminded him the plane remained at 34,000 feet. This comforted Joel Sandy as he clicked on the video screen embedded in the back of the seat in front of him.

He'd always enjoyed watching the flight path of the plane as it moved along the lines of latitude on the virtual map. Noting the wind speed, altitude, weather forecast, and various other statistics most of his friends ignored, gave him pleasure and a certain amount of comfort that all was right in the world.

Since he had an aisle seat, he stretched out one of his long legs then eased out to stand up and use the restroom one more time before slipping on comfy socks to put him in the mood. He could feel the antihistamine he'd taken an hour earlier start to take effect. When he returned to his seat, he fished out the sleep mask provided to all first-class ticket holders.

For a few seconds, he felt his body tilt to the right as if the plane made a turn. He glanced at the screen again to check their location.

The plane gently moved away from the route he'd expected in order to reach their morning stop in Dubai. He pushed the call button.

"Yes, sir?" The flight attendant had boarded the plane ahead of the passengers. He'd noticed her and how she didn't appear to resemble a citizen from Singapore but maybe Central Asia. "I didn't expect you to still be awake?" Her smile grew taut.

"According to the map, we are turning north. Is there a problem?"

"Not at all. Only an adjustment. There's a storm up ahead, and the pilot wishes to avoid any turbulence."

Suddenly the plane bounced as if it were losing altitude. "Something is wrong."

"Please buckle up. I'll go check it out."

He kept watch on the plane moving across the map while sleep caressed his fears until his eyelids began to feel heavy. He spotted the flight attendant talking to a man who sat up front. She pointed toward Joel, and the man dressed in a military uniform eased out of his seat, straightened his jacket then moved down the aisle and squatted down by him. The attendant followed.

"I think it is okay. He's almost out." The soldier stood and grimaced at the attendant. "This will soon be over. Maybe you can regain your place of honor in our glorious country."

"Nothing would please me more, General."

Joel tried to call out to the others, but his voice wouldn't work or the rest of his body. Had he been poisoned or medicated? With his sight starting to fade, he watched the small airplane on the map disappear before the screen went dark. His first thought was they were going to crash. When he awoke, he realized a different nightmare had occurred, creating real-life consequences.

~ ~ ~ ~

President Buck Austin sat down for a late lunch with a few of the ambassadors from Western Europe. He'd decided they needed a "Come to Jesus" speech about their support of NATO and their monetary contributions. The United Nations Ambassador, Talala Jamison, also attended to make her case for greater support for sanctions against Russia, Iran, and North Korea.

The president's chief of staff entered and bent down to whisper in his ear. He stood and motioned for everyone to begin eating. "A matter needs my attention, and I promise to return as soon as possible." The president rose from his seat, made a couple of jokes, and left with his chief of staff.

"Just give it to me straight," he ordered in his no-nonsense manner when irritated.

The chief of staff remained standing as the president leaned against his desk in the Oval Office and crossed his arms. "A plane went missing several hours ago on its flight from Singapore. About twenty of the two hundred passengers were Americans."

"Was it a terrorist attack?" The president knew he should be used to such incidents, but it never got easy, knowing precious lives were lost due to a crazed individual who had no respect for human life.

"We are still getting information. The Pentagon has been alerted, sir."

"The Pentagon? Why? What are you not telling me?" The president straightened and frowned.

"Those twenty Americans were some of our best scientists and engineers. They were working with DARPA and the Pentagon on a revolutionary cloaking device for our military aircraft and body armor for combat. The project was nearing completion. Several had traveled to Singapore for a conference, and afterward a few visited relatives in neighboring countries. Others were also guest lecturers at universities. All of them met up yesterday to return to the States and their work."

"Are they the only ones working on the project?" The president knew he should care more about the possible loss of life than a protected government project—but he didn't. "And did it not occur to anyone at DARPA sending twenty scientists and engineers to Asia was a bad idea? There are times I suspect they don't have enough sense to wad a shotgun," he drawled in his Texas accent.

"Yes, sir. They were working in conjunction with DARPA but not exclusively. Jango International Aeronautics out of New Mexico was contracted through the Pentagon for the bulk of the project."

"Then we didn't lose everyone?"

The chief of staff checked his notes. "We don't know yet, Mr.

President."

"Find the numbskull who does know," he shouted. "Whoever is responsible for the screw…" He gritted his teeth before continuing. "Here is what I want to know: what happened to that plane, who was responsible, and who the hell let so many brains leave the country? Am I clear?"

"Yes, Mr. President."

"And when you find the idiot who let them leave, drag his ass in here so I can rip him a new one. And I want this on my desk by tonight," he fumed as he walked to the door. "Now I'm going to have a nice lunch and suggest our so-called 'allies' get ready for trouble. Hopefully, the plane sank to the bottom of the ocean and not in a third world hellhole selling our people to the highest bidder."

"Mr. President, if they are still alive, what will be your orders?"

The president stopped as his hand squeezed the doorknob. He glanced down at the floor then back at the chief of staff. "The official report will be they all died. Do you understand?"

The chief of staff tilted his head and paled. "Are you sure, Mr. President?"

The president pulled back his shoulders and opened the door. "Do it."

CHAPTER TWO

The frigid air and clear sky reminded Darya Petrov of the Wakhan Valley in Afghanistan. With the snow piled along the curb and dim streetlights along both sides of the street, it took only a few seconds to remember home remained far away. The snow muffled the light traffic this time of night. It didn't compare with the quiet in the land of his mother or Montana where his Russian father had taken him for a better life and more opportunities.

He stood staring toward Lake Baikal as he adjusted his Siberian jacket and slowly let the flaps down on his ushanka hat of rabbit fur. Taking such luxury back to the village on the rooftop of the world, for the khan, might make the man's life easier, certainly warmer. Temperatures were dropping and soon it would be in the teens. The moon dipped behind clouds as a round of flurries dressed the scene before him to resemble a Christmas card. Tessa would love this, he decided.

He'd come here to gather intel for Enigma and the CIA, but he'd decided to abandon that folly soon after he arrived. Playing by the rules had never been his strong suit, and he thought making them sweat about where he had disappeared to and what he might be up to sounded a great deal more entertaining. To acquaint himself with his father's homeland, he took the Trans-Siberian Railroad and ended up in a place he never expected to find.

He'd left the train in Irkutsk and made his way east by whatever means he could find until he reached the Siberian forests around Lake Baikal. Although the land was covered in thick forests around most of Lake Baikal, it reminded him of both his homes, especially the one in Montana. His Russian sounded nearly fluent, and he met several families who took him in and fed him in exchange for him chopping wood and sharing chores with the men.

The decision to backpack into the remote areas around Lake Baikal helped put things into perspective concerning Tessa Scott. He decided to move forward with the information he'd come by accidently and eliminate the man called Robert. Captain Hunter would be next, and he would remove him from the picture with extreme prejudice.

He stumbled across what appeared to be an extravagant airplane hangar and a great deal of activity going on inside and out. Military guarded the area. From his position, Darya pulled out his binoculars and quickly ascertained something had gone terribly wrong. A soldier dragged a man in a white lab coat to an open area before giving him a hard shake. The intimidation started with yelling in his face as the lab-coat man cowered and tried to back away. Next came a blow to his head with the butt of the soldier's rifle. He slung his rifle to his shoulder and appeared to give orders to a few nearby soldiers who dragged him to a truck by the collar before throwing him in the back.

Darya decided to follow along the ridge. When he fell behind, their vehicle could be spotted heading toward a remote section of Lake Baikal. Even this time of year, without snow on the ground, it was still cold. Riding in the back of a truck, without protection, could kill a man if he got hypothermia before they had time to do whatever they planned for him.

They didn't waste time at the lake. He had circled around, hiding in the trees to avoid being spotted. Once they disappeared from sight, Darya made his way to the water's edge. He scanned the shoreline until he spotted a white lab coat floating in the water. Inching out of the trees, he spotted a half-naked man facedown against several large rocks.

He dropped his backpack and crouched to inch forward. His first impression was the man had already died either of exposure or a beating. Blood matted the hair at the back of his head. But a moan, followed by a slight attempt at pushing himself up, resulted in another collapse.

Darya checked the man's pulse then the bloody wound. He hadn't been shot, so maybe he could survive if he got him warm. "Hello. Can you stand?" Darya spoke in Russian as he rolled the man to a sitting position.

"I. I don't speak. I don't speak Russian."

Darya stood to survey his surroundings for trouble. "Are you an American?" he asked in English.

Would the man slip into shock as he shivered uncontrollably? "Yes," he said through chattering teeth. His lips were turning blue.

"I'll take you to safety so you can get warm. I have a camp nearby. Can you stand?"

Darya had found an abandoned one-room cabin when he'd first arrived. It was a ten-minute walk that turned into an hour. He gave the man his coat and hat but stopped short of donating his gloves. After taking care of the man's immediate medical needs and layering him with several blankets, he'd found in a wobbly, three-legged chest, he returned to the scene of the drop-off. Any signs another person witnessed their mischief needed to be erased. He brought several pieces of the man's clothing and shredded it.

After catching a rabbit, he butchered it and drained the blood onto the man's clothing. Cutting the animal into chunks and making a trail of the meat would attract a hungry wolf he'd spotted in the area. Russian wolves were known to be aggressive toward humans. If the soldiers came back, he hoped they might speculate the wild beasts enjoyed an easy meal.

"I've made you soup. Come. Sit up," Darya encouraged his guest later that night. He'd blacked out the windows but decided building a fire would be too big of a gamble. Luckily, the cabin had one electrical outlet and a hotplate that served as the stove. After he cooked some food for them, Darya cleaned everything up, hoping the smell wouldn't carry on the cold wind blowing across the lake and up to the ridge where they hunkered down.

"Who are you?" Darya inquired as he removed the tin cup he'd used for a bowl. "How does an American end up here?"

"My name is Joel Sandy." His voice sounded small and unsure. Darya understood his caution. Why should he trust a stranger who appeared to be part Asian, spoke Russian fluently, and dressed like a mountain man? And in Russia, you never knew who you could trust unless you were local.

"Were you a prisoner?"

Darya spoke slowly. He'd gotten out of the habit of speaking English. Living in Afghanistan with the Kyrgyz for so many years had caused him to become leathery tough and solemn; an expression Americans might consider intimidating. When Joel hugged his arms and rocked back and forth, he stood and moved to the window to check for trouble.

"Don't tell me. Makes no difference to me. I'm just passing through. I'll leave you money and see if I can find you a place to stay. I know a few people in the area. They were good to me when I first arrived."

Joel took a deep breath. "You speak English very well." Darya raised his chin in thanks. "You're not Russian?"

"I'm Russian," he confessed. He unrolled a thermal blanket from his backpack and spread it on the floor. "I've been away a long time."

"Why?"

"I have reasons." Darya yawned.

"Oh."

Darya wasn't sure what that response meant, but he didn't care. The less he knew about this guy the better, no matter if he was an American.

"Go to sleep. I'll find you a safe place tomorrow if you want."

"I-I need to get a message to the Americans in Moscow."

Darya stretched out on a blanket, folding his hands behind his head. "I think you might want to wait until spring. Moscow is 4342 kilometers. You have no money, and even if you got a ticket on the train, the police or military would find you."

"This is important."

He didn't respond. The day had taken a lot out of him physically. Usually he waited to think about Tessa as he fell asleep. Now he thought about those soldiers who carried rifles. He had set up along the perimeter rusty animal traps he found in a wooden cabinet. If anyone stepped on one, their scream would wake him. Fishing out tin cans from a trash pile behind the cabin, he fashioned a noisy trip wire to catch anything else.

"Please. I have important information that could affect the entire world." His voice bordered on panic.

"I don't want to get involved." Darya couldn't help but be curious though. "Tell me what is so important."

"I don't know that I can trust you." Joel took deep breaths, as if he might be hyperventilating.

"I don't know if you can, either. What I do know is I don't like soldiers pushing the little guy around. They remind me of people I knew in Afghanistan." He turned his head toward Joel. "Why were they so mad at you?"

"Did you ever hear of the plane that went down several years ago over the Indian Ocean?"

"No. I was busy fighting the Taliban and trying not to get my head shot off."

Joel studied him for a few minutes. "The plane had twenty scientists and engineers on board." His facial muscles relaxed when Darya sat up. "We were working on cloaking military planes and other equipment."

"If the plane went down, how did you survive?"

"The plane we were supposed to be on went down. Not ours. There was a switch at the last minute, I guess." He ran his hand over his head. "The Americans were brought here."

"How many were there?"

"The plane was full. I don't know. Ninety. Hundred."

"Where are they now?" Darya felt his interest piqued.

Joel shook his head. "I was knocked out with something. The Americans came here to work. The others must have gone down with the other plane. I never saw anyone else. The first thing I remember was when we landed in Vladivostok. We were forced into buses and taken to a hotel on the outskirts for a few days."

"How did you find out about the missing plane?"

There was an old television set in one of our rooms. It didn't work at first, but one of our guys got it working—or least part of the time. We didn't understand Russian, but it was obvious what happened. Our pictures were displayed, our grieving families paraded before the cameras." His voice cracked with emotion.

Darya waited. "I have not heard of this. Why did they want

you?"

"Cloaking. We figured out how to cloak an airplane and a number of other things."

Joel explained how the Russians feared Americans and their allies would use the new technology to gain the upper hand in military dominance once and for all. The Russians had spent the last twenty-five years trying to regain world power status after communism fell. The weapon would give them more power than they could have imagined. For the first time in many years, the Americans would fear Russia.

"But we had very little with us in the way of support, notes, etc. They weren't buying that. Several of our people were sick with heart disease and diabetes. After we were shipped here, there was little medical care at first. After the first three died, Moscow ensured we received medical care, more to eat, and some old American television shows from the sixties and seventies."

"Were you able to recreate the project?"

"Yes. At least we are close. I slowed the project down by sabotaging the software. Some of the others did their own kind of mishaps to keep things from coming to a conclusion. This could change the balance of power and not in a good way."

"Why did they beat you?"

"I had received orders to get the project done by spring so testing could begin on a plane. Engineers have modified their current Sukhoi Su-57 and several transport planes in order to begin testing. But then the timeline was moved up. General Oblonsky now wants it done by the end of January if not sooner."

If General Oblonsky was behind this, then nothing good would come of it. "What happened?"

"They realized I was stalling. The others had put me in charge and expected me to give guidance. Getting rid of me would be a warning." He covered his face with his hands. "They must be terrified. They'll be bullied into working harder and faster."

Darya lay back down and closed his eyes. "I will help you. But I will not take you to Moscow. I have a better idea." He knew the information would be too much to resist for the self-absorbed Under Secretary of State Bonnie Finley to resist. She owed him more favors than she'd ever have time to repay. Tonight, he would dream of Tessa and how it would feel to hold her in his arms again.

Soon she would join him, whether she liked it or not. All he needed was a little patience.

After the chance encounter, Darya worked on getting close to President Antonov. Part of that time he spent in a not-so-comfortable jail when he was caught snooping in the Kremlin. His claims of being the president's nephew fell on deaf ears until a General Oblonsky took an interest in him. From there, his life became a whole lot easier, thanks to President Antonov's unexpected welcome to a long-lost nephew.

There were national security issues to deal with and the relationship he now had with his uncle, President Antonov. He hadn't expected to feel anything but a kind of aloofness toward him since he had not been a part of his life. His father rarely mentioned him. The two men shared the same mother but not the same father. The president was the elder by ten years. At almost seventy the man remained vigorous and active. He had a wife, younger than Tessa, with a young son. The president could claim a great number of bragging rights on being fit and youthful. Although he'd learned the president indeed had an ego the size of Russia, Darya found him to be intelligent and hopeful for the future of his country.

Russia embraced him. He began to warm to the idea of being more than just the president's nephew.

CHAPTER THREE

Ambassador Finley glanced at the man in the shadows, known as the tribesman. She could feel his eyes on her when she tugged at the heavy doors to intercept the early evening visitor. With a slight nod in his direction, she watched him slip into the small alcove shrouded in complete darkness. From where he stood, she wondered if he took the time to admire the lights of Washington sparkling like diamonds through the large windows.

The ambassador understood the tribesman, or Darya, lurking in the shadows, didn't want to be here. And he certainly didn't want to be at her beck and call, no matter that she'd been given this new position of influence. These things did not impress him. Yet, his curiosity about the visitor entering the office got the best of him. The reflection in the windows might provide him with a clear picture to watch. She imagined him leaning forward to make sure he caught every word? Hopefully he wouldn't do anything stupid like confront the man he considered an opponent.

"Robert. How nice to finally meet you in person."

Bonnie extended her smooth hand and grasped his like a Baptist deacon. A moment of surprise flashed in his eyes. She knew men underestimated her strength both in person and the political arena.

That's why President Austin had awarded her with the ambassadorship to Russia. Scheduled to leave in a couple of days, this unexpected visit put her on edge.

"Thank you for seeing me, Ambassador Finley." He stammered. "Can I call you that yet?"

Bonnie revealed a warm smile and pointed to a leather chair in front of her desk. "Let's be less formal. How about you call me Bonnie. After all, we're practically family."

The sudden bewildered expression on Robert's face matched his fidgeting. "Okay, Bonnie. Family?" He nodded followed by a chuckle. "Oh, you mean because you and Tessa spent time in Afghanistan."

She couldn't resist letting a contemptuous smirk spread across her generous mouth. Making a man nervous gave her pleasure. "How is Tessa? We haven't spoken in a while. I'm hoping she'll tag along with me to Russia for a couple of weeks."

"Ah, that's a long time. She's pretty busy with the kids and—"

"Of course, she'll go. Trust me." She waved a dismissive hand at him. "Besides, it's only November. She'll make a couple of three- or four-day trips to help me get my bearings. Then, after Christmas, she'll go for a couple of weeks. It would be great for her career. I'm sure the president will have someone contact her. I mentioned this to him last week."

"What will she be doing?" He crossed and uncrossed his legs and rubbed his knees.

She hadn't expected Robert Scott to be so handsome and couldn't resist ogling him from head to toe. How did Tessa manage to snag good-looking men? The mildly attractive woman possessed a girl-next-door appearance and had a stubborn streak a mile wide, not to mention a thirst for the strangest adventures. Why Miss Perfect could calm the beast in men like Darya and Chase Hunter continued to be a mystery to her. Maybe that was the reason Robert came to visit. She wondered if he, too, had a rough side. If so, maybe the evening wouldn't be a total waste of time.

"Helping me get things squared away. Her recent Ph.D. in geopolitical conflict and resolution gave her expertise in the Middle East and Central Asia. She also brings a lot to the table concerning Eastern Europe. Since we shared a common experience, I felt comfortable requesting her help. I imagine she'll be surprised when she gets the call."

"That's part of the reason I'm here, Ambassador, I mean Bonnie." Realizing he watched her with interest, she walked around and scooted back on the top of her desk before crossing slender legs. A moment of interest sparked his expression to flirtatious. "Tessa has never really talked about her time in Afghanistan. She hasn't been the same since she got back."

Bonnie pushed her red hair away from her heart-shaped face and stared into the distance before speaking. "It was a difficult time, Robert. Horrible actually. I had nightmares for months. Still do, actually. I imagine she does, too."

"Yes, plenty of nightmares. She speaks a language I don't understand in her sleep, so I have no way of knowing what is going on. When I ask her about it, she clams up or gives me a benign story about one of those little girls she brought back home."

"I need a drink. Care for one?"

"I don't drink."

"Just like Tessa." She eased off the desk and went to pour a drink. "I can send for coffee."

"No thanks. Bonnie, I want to know what happened over there."

"If Tessa didn't tell you, I don't think I should."

He came to stand in front of her. "I'm losing her, and I don't know why. What happened to my wife over there?"

Bonnie downed the bourbon and set the glass down a little too hard. "Everything went to hell. That's what happened. We got stuck with a bunch of little girls and waited for a rescue helicopter. It crashed, thanks to the Taliban."

"Taliban," he snapped in horror. "I thought they were kept away."

Bonnie remembered how desperate she felt. Without Tessa, she wouldn't be standing here today. "Yes. Taliban. They overran the village and held us captive."

"Oh my God." Robert staggered a step back and rubbed his hand over his face. "What happened?"

"Are you sure you want to know?"

"Yes. I want to help her. Please, Bonnie."

"They planned to sell the girls as sex slaves or worse. Not that I can imagine what would be worse. We had a young soldier to protect us, but they dragged him out and beat him severely. He died." He'd actually survived and managed to get help for them. Robert didn't need to know that part of the story.

"I thought the villagers protected you."

"Is that the story they told you?"

He nodded.

She rolled her eyes. "Figures."

"What's the truth?"

"We were threatened. Intimidated. Usual Taliban crap."

"Did they—assault you?"

"Let's call it what it is, Robert. Rape."

He buried his face in his hands. "Dear Lord."

"But no, they didn't rape your wife. The leader saved her for himself after he got rid of the little ones. His men came to entertain themselves with me and Shirin."

He choked in horror. "She was a little girl."

"Not if you live in Afghanistan. The biggest hellhole on God's green earth. Thanks to your wife..." Bonnie needed to be careful here. She'd promised never to tell what she'd done. "Tessa beat them off and saved us. The leader, Masoud, threw them out when he heard our screams. He was furious Tessa had bested his men." She smirked. "But he admired a fighter."

"Did he..."

"No. To our good fortune, a mountain tribesman rode into the village with his men and scared the hell out of them. Thankfully, he ran them off and saved the day." Bonnie took a deep breath.

"I think I'll take that drink now." He poured himself two fingers of bourbon, gulped it down, and coughed. He spoke as if it burned his throat. "Were you finally safe?"

"Yes and no. They were drug dealers, and we were forced to go with them for protection. We didn't know if or when the Taliban would come back. The ride was hard, cold, and the children got sick. They were good people and tried to make all of us comfortable. We played a waiting game until the good guys could find us. The end."

"But you never were attacked again?"

"Not exactly."

She enjoyed that his face paled.

"The Taliban continued to hunt for us. They were bent on taking us back. Made the leader appear weak. Lucky for us, when they showed up the US Cavalry came riding in. God bless America." She glanced at the clock. "Robert, I have a meeting in twenty minutes. How about a late dinner?"

Robert straightened his tie. "I'd like that." He gave her the name of his hotel. "I have an early flight in the morning. My conference ended this afternoon. I rebooked my flight so we could talk. I'm glad you found time in your schedule for me."

She escorted him to the door. "So am I." He appeared surprised when she leaned in and kissed his cheek. "Like family," she insisted.

When the door closed, a shadow moved out from a small room in the rear of her office. "Why are you meeting him again?" a voice laced with a slight accent asked.

"What do you care? Don't you want him out of the picture?" Bonnie approached the man who had dark hair and almond-shaped eyes. Their paths had crossed in Afghanistan. "I gave you enough information to blackmail Robert from here to eternity." She squinted and formed a pooched smile on her mouth. "Clearly, your sweet Tessa doesn't want him to know about you." She patted his chest only to have him slap her hand away.

"Don't touch me. You are poison. Tessa doesn't know what she wants."

"I think she knows exactly what she wants. Apparently, it isn't you," she chuckled. "Roman Darya Petrov. Half Russian. Half-crazy Kyrgyz tribesman. I think you and I will work well together."

"We have a deal."

"Yes. Yes. I'll get your precious Tessa to Russia, and you can do whatever you want with her for all I care. I've had it with you and her. Keeping secrets and threats hanging over my head is compromising my plans to be Secretary of State under the next administration. Who knows where I'll go from there."

"I'm guessing hell." He moved to the door. "Just get her there and stay out of my way. I'll get you the information you need. Tell the CIA to leave me alone. I work with Enigma."

"We need those scientists back, Darya. Don't screw this up. I can easily call Captain Hunter and let him know where you are."

"Not if you're dead," he growled then closed the door behind him.

Bonnie didn't know whether to admire the Kyrgyz from Afghanistan or fear him. She owed him a great debt for getting them to safety. Tessa had compromised everything to make sure they were safe. Apparently, she'd moved on, but Roman Darya Petrov clearly had not.

She lifted her cell phone to her ear. "Tessa? It's me. Yes. I'm fine. Robert came to see me tonight." She listened to panic on the other end of the phone. "I told him nothing about Darya. I wanted to give you a heads-up we talked. He's worried about you. I gave him enough to make him sympathetic. He probably wouldn't understand what you did to save us all that time we were in the Wakhan Valley." She listened a few more seconds. "Talk to you soon, Tess. Sleep tight."

$$\sim \sim \sim \sim$$

The director of the Sacramento office of Enigma stood at his floor-to-ceiling window, peering out over the university campus. Trees, peeled of their green leaves, reminded him of how exposing the truth could resemble a cold winter's day. And on such a day, a person might cloak themselves in layers of warmth to avoid the cold hard facts of truth.

Whenever he expected Tessa Scott to visit him, Director Benjamin Clark waited at the window to watch her cross the campus grounds. She'd stop at times to speak to a student or talk on the phone, probably to one of the Enigma team. The carefree way she walked gave him a kind of hope the world wasn't such a bad place. Good people existed, and the sun would shine another day.

The other reason he watched for her created a habit of connecting in this manner. He'd stare down at her, stoic and sour faced; she'd look up and wave over and over until he returned the gesture. He would turn away and smile, knowing Tessa would rush to join him and tap lightly on the office door, after his secretary announced her appearance.

"Come in, Tessa. Please sit down." He stood and moved to take her leather jacket and faux-leopard scarf. Before he could step away and purposely would slow himself down, she'd squeeze his arm or pat his back. She'd ask about his wife and daughter, and he would do the same concerning her life.

"You wanted to see me?"

"Yes. I'm sure you already know Ambassador Finley has requested your help as she transitions to Moscow."

Tessa used a finger to shove a wayward curl behind her ear. "I heard. Spoke to someone from her office yesterday. I said I wasn't interested. An hour later I got a call from the Secretary of State."

The director compressed his lips together before staring down his nose at her. Tessa told him many times he resembled an American Eagle ready to snatch prey out of turbulent waters. He motioned for her to sit down on the leather couch, and he did the same on the other end.

"Why don't you want to go? Are the Irvins not available to help with the children?"

Francis Irvin worked for Enigma as a Biblical archeologist. His wife Martha assisted with his work from time to time, but when they moved next door to Tessa, her job became making sure Tessa had no worries at home.

"Bonnie Finley and I aren't exactly best buddies. I don't trust her." Tessa leaned back and inhaled. "Is that coffee I smell?"

The director stood and retrieved a cup of his favorite blend of coffee for her, a gesture he'd never do for any other Enigma people.

"Yum. So cold outside. This hits the spot."

"Why don't you trust her? Because she knows the truth about Afghanistan—or something else?" The director tried to not appear too eager to know the truth, although he had been informed of her relationship with Roman Darya Petrov a long time ago.

"I feel she holds Afghanistan over my head—like a threat." She informed him of her call several nights earlier. "I don't want anyone to know the awful things I was forced to do in Afghanistan. Especially Robert and my children."

"War has no saints, Tessa. But sometimes, and you of all people should appreciate this, God will send a guardian angel when we need it the most."

She observed him over the rim of her coffee mug in expectation.

He continued, "Which reminds me. Hear from your questionable angel lately?"

"No," she answered, a little too quickly for his taste.

"Tessa." He wondered why any time his name came up she either lied or avoided the subject. It was understood she'd keep tabs on Darya if need be and do whatever it took to keep him on the straight and narrow so he wouldn't go to prison. Whatever happened between them at their last encounter strained their relationship. Maybe the tribesman wanted her to leave Robert or turn on her boss, Captain Chase Hunter. "Talk to me."

"I don't talk to Darya—or at least he doesn't talk to me."

"You are the only one he trusts at Enigma. Maybe the only one in the government. I know the two of you have a special bond." He watched her blush. "No one blames you for the things you did to survive in Afghanistan, Tessa."

"The one thing I regret is hurting him after all he did for me—for the girls. Without him…"

"I believe he understood." The director reached out and awkwardly patted her knee.

"Yes. I agree."

"Do you still love him?" It pained him to see the anguish in her downturned mouth.

She sat her mug on the end table and took a deep breath. "With all due respect, Director Clark, that is none of your business."

He cleared his throat in the hopes he covered a chuckle. He admired many things about Tessa Scott. She could be all peaches and cream and possessed a quick wit that sliced like a papercut. Never any malice or contempt, just a belief some things were off-limits.

"With all due respect, Tessa, it is my business. I need to know I can count on you if that tribesman plays both sides against the middle and jeopardizes national security."

"What is this about, Director?" Her voice tightened, and her eyes did that blinking thing Chase Hunter took as a warning she was either about to tell a lie or was nervous about the truth. He'd tipped the director off to that trick a long time ago.

"Do you remember the plane that disappeared over the Indian Ocean several years ago?"

"Yes. All that happened before I joined Enigma." Tessa's expression changed from nervous to curious. "It was never found. Those poor families. I don't remember if there were Americans on board."

"Twenty of our most talented scientists and engineers."

"Ouch."

"Exactly. No trace of that plane. No ping from a black box or a debris field. Nothing."

"The Indian Ocean is vast. Didn't they speculate it might have run into bad weather? Wasn't there a theory it might have been a terrorist attack—maybe a passenger on board?"

"Yes. There were a couple of suspects but nothing concrete."

Tessa grew silent and waited patiently. He could imagine the wheels turning at race-car speed, as she tried to figure out how this new topic related to her.

"Does this have anything to do with Darya Petrov?"

"We believe your former lover has found the plane and our missing scientists. You are going to make sure he tells us where they are."

CHAPTER FOUR

Date night. Tessa had suggested she and Robert do this once a week, but it turned out to barely be once a month. With him setting up a new law office in Nevada City, a few miles from their home in Grass Valley, he often worked late, took clients to dinner, or fell asleep in his recliner. The romance between them had tanked, but they continued to pretend all was well.

After he was an hour late for their dinner date, Tessa left him a message she'd just pick him up at the office. He'd sent a text earlier there had been a last-minute client who wanted to put him on retainer. Time would get away from him and it would be ten o'clock before he realized he needed to head home.

Finding the office dark and locked up, she returned to her car then noticed a horse and carriage meandering her way. When it passed, she recognized Robert as one of the passengers. The other was a pretty brunette about ten years younger than her and, she could imagine, a lot thinner.

They hadn't gone much farther when the carriage stopped and let them out in front of Rocco's Restaurant. It had always been a date night destination for them. Robert held the woman's elbow and laughed when she leaned in and said something in his ear.

Things suddenly became a whole lot clearer for her. Their damaged marriage was on life support. Although it felt ironic, Enigma was the only safe place these days. Touching the call option for Director Clark on her dashboard, a familiar voice said matter-of-factly, "Tessa?"

"Yes, sir. When do you want me to leave for Russia?"

~ ~ ~ ~

Captain Chase Hunter tried to sleep for most of the flight to Moscow. He kept his earbuds in to avoid talking to his seat mate. He'd sprung for business class to accommodate his long legs and antisocial attitude toward commercial flights. When he switched from listening to a Tierney James book to soft jazz, he'd expected to fall asleep, but the image of Tessa Scott in a blue dress arriving at his door several months earlier, late one night, still haunted him with a missed opportunity.

She had been dressed to the nines in a formfitting blue dress her long black jacket failed to hide. The pearl earrings added a kind of elegance beneath her windblown curls. It made him a little crazy to see so much of her neck exposed. Coming to him in the middle of the night meant trouble, the husband kind.

Opening the door, he immediately regretted bringing the flavor of the month home with him after their fourth date. The usual tactic was to go to her place, but things had heated up pretty fast, and his condo was much closer. Tessa knew he rarely brought women home because it was too personal. Being personal eluded his DNA when it came to people outside Enigma. But with Tessa, his best friend, nothing seemed to be off-limits—except a physical relationship, which both claimed not to want.

"Aren't you going to invite me in?" She shifted her weight to one hip and exposed a pouty lip that drew his attention for a few seconds too long.

"I have company. What's going on?" Part of him felt embarrassed at having another woman in his condo, like he'd cheated on her or gotten in after curfew. "Have you been crying?" The bloodshot eyes and a smudge of mascara set off an inner alarm bell.

She waved a hand in objection. "No. Allergies."

"Since when do you have allergies? And it's November." This bewildered him. "Isn't this family night or date night?"

"Robert had a"—her voice sounded choked—"client to entertain. I decided to come into town and do some work since the kids were at the Irvins for the night."

Chase let his gaze caress her body and couldn't resist a wolfish smile. "Work? As what? Because you can sign me up."

A soft voice from behind him called. Tessa straightened and her face flushed with a pinkish glow. "Oh." She backed away. "I-I'm sorry. I shouldn't have come. This is embarrassing. Of course, you have a life." She stuttered when she got flustered, yet another thing he found charming about the Grass Valley housewife.

"Wait a minute. I'll get my coat, and we'll go get some coffee."

"But your—guest. I mean. No. Don't be silly."

"I'll call her an Uber. Wait for me downstairs." He laid a gentle hand on her forearm and watched her face slowly take on a frown. "Okay?"

She nodded as if in acceptance of his proposal but left without a word before he could take care of his guest. He decided to drive by her Sacramento place, a Victorian house chopped up into individual apartments. A light went out in her living room window just as he turned off the ignition. A text message followed.

"Decided to go to bed. I'm beat. Talk to you Monday. No worries. Sorry I interrupted your fun. Another brainy bimbo, I'm guessing. See you at work on Monday."

The following week, both of them had been in closed-door meetings over the Russian mission with no time to revisit her sudden appearance over the weekend. She'd slipped in and out of Russia twice to assist Ambassador Finley.

Once more, Enigma sidetracked his life to focus on the upcoming mission. Things needed to work like clockwork in order to keep from making any international headlines or tick off the trigger-happy Russians. They didn't appreciate being caught lying or stirring up trouble. What they did enjoy was taking advantage of a bad situation to advance their own agenda—like capturing a bunch of brains who knew how to cloak military weapons.

In the three years the scientists had been missing, DARPA and the company, Jango Aeronautics, had been playing catch-up. Although the work had been nearing completion, only the men on board that plane knew how to bring it to a proper conclusion.

Thoughts of Tessa always crowded out national security matters. He touched the spot on his chest that ached every time he saw her, smelled her, or breathed the same air as her. Without her, he wasn't sure where he would have ended up—prison, an alcoholic, dead—any and all were real possibilities a few years ago. Then she stumbled into his life swinging a rolling pin at a Libyan terrorist to protect him. He could feel a smile tease the corners of his mouth.

He decided to replay the last few years over and over in his head until the plane landed in Moscow. Just before he dozed off, he remembered the Enigma librarian stopping by his condo with a red legal envelope, before he headed to the airport, something to do with Tessa.

"I think you should read it," she said in her monotone voice. "It's about Tessa's husband."

"Does it affect the mission?" he quizzed, knowing she was apt to make things more important than necessary with her Asperger syndrome.

"No, sir," she confessed with a blank stare up at him.

"Can I wait until I get back, or is it life or death?"

"No, sir. It is not life or death. Just information as to the character of the man."

He grabbed the envelope and tossed it on the countertop that separated the kitchen and living area. "I'm well aware of his character. I'll read it when I get back. I'm in a hurry."

The librarian stepped aside as he exited his place and locked the door. He smiled warmly at her. "Thank you. I'll see you when I return." She pivoted and disappeared down the hall to her own condo.

Now he wished he'd taken the time to read it. Tessa had already arrived in Moscow under the watchful care of Ambassador Finley. All he wanted was to share a few quiet moments with her.

~ ~ ~ ~

Roman Darya Petrov walked several paces behind President Antonov as they passed through the crowds, shaking hands with supporters and students from a nearby university. Signs were lifted proclaiming love and ideals put forth by his administration. He waved, kissed babies, and posed for pictures from time to time. The snow was deep, yet the crowds came to see him and witness the rebirth of the greatness of Russia.

Entering through the grand doors, Darya helped the president remove his coat. He turned and patted him on the cheek. "You are a good boy. I am so glad you have decided to join me—us—in the quest for greatness."

Darya remained stoic and calm as he scanned the room for trouble. The genetics inherited from his Central Asian mother set his facial features apart from other Russians in Moscow. He represented a time when the country had failed in Afghanistan. Now here he was, living in the country of his father and assisting his uncle, the president of Russia. Russia and Afghanistan were light years from what he'd experienced growing up in the United States. He learned a long time ago to adapt to any surroundings he found himself. This was yet another exercise in mental camouflage.

"President Antonov, if you'll excuse me, it is time I go to the lecture."

"Yes. Of course. The American woman. Remember to be careful."

Darya bowed his head in respect then turned to leave. He had watched her for two days as she gave a lecture on the American West and environmental problems faced by Native Peoples. She didn't know he watched and waited like the patient snow leopards of the Wakhan Valley in Afghanistan. But soon she would not be able to leave him again.

The lecture had already begun when he entered the stadium-style auditorium. He had entered the doors at the top so he would be in the shadows. Watching her movements in secret prevented a certain amount of suspicious speculation from the Russian students who flocked to hear her speak. Her pale-gray suit and leather boots hid the beauty that lay beneath the clothing. With her hair pulled back in a ponytail, she appeared pale. This only reminded him of the sharp blue eyes that could turn violet when provoked. Would she be happy to see him again?

When he sat down, she said, "There are seats down here if you could move closer." She attempted to shade her eyes from the bright spotlights. Did she recognize him? No, surely not.

When he raised his hand in protest and remained seated, she continued with her lecture. Ninety minutes later, after a question-and-answer session, students filed out, some stopping for a word of praise or an invitation to join them for coffee.

She remained polite and smiled a great deal, something he enjoyed seeing. The last time they had been together he'd made her cry. He vowed never to do that again, fidgeting in his seat at the memory of her sadness.

The last student exited through the doors below as she collected her things. She glanced up in his direction and froze. Could she identify him after all? Her mouth turned down in an unattractive frown. He had no doubt she'd been warned about being watched, maybe recorded in case she was a spy. Instead of exiting through the closest doorway, she started up the stairs toward him.

Darya casually stood and waited only a few seconds, unable to resist her movements, before he turned and found his way out of the auditorium. He slipped into an office and partially closed the blinds on the window. With the lights out, she wouldn't be able to see him. To his surprise when she walked by, she stopped in front of the window and stared down the hall for a few seconds as if waiting for someone. Without warning, Tessa turned to gaze at the window and pressed her face against the glass. He stepped back further into the darkness in case she could see through the open slats of the blinds.

The urge to open the door and pull her inside, to start his plan now, no matter how much she protested, washed over him. The consequences of that rash decision could be a disaster. She moved away, a little faster than before and with a great deal more determination.

In the tongue of his tribe in Afghanistan, he whispered, "Soon, Tess-sa. Soon."

Chapter Five

The smell of Kazakhstan filled Carter Johnson when he stepped out from the Sputnik Hotel in Baikonur. Enigma had sent him here the week before Christmas in the States. His job was to get the ball rolling and work with his contact. Hopefully, if all went well, the captured scientists would be back home in a few weeks. He'd been here three days, and still no one had approached him. Missing his aunt's turkey dinner along with all the noise his nieces and nephews would make opening presents gave him a sense of loss.

He stood there, admiring the land before him then turned back to inspect the new paint job on the exterior of the hotel. Now a pleasant cream color with brown trim, it still resembled the plain, no-nonsense Soviet era style of decorating, a far cry from the vibrant colors of home.

The country had a relatively dry climate. Winters were very cold, but snow didn't pile up here like it did in the mountains. No attention had been given to planting decorative shrubs like in the States, so the patchwork of snow on the ground resembled a giant puzzle.

The sound of several flags flapping in the breeze caught his attention for a few seconds until he moved down the five steps to stand at the end of the awning stretched over the drop-off area. He inhaled deeply, loving the freshness and the cold. It was a far cry from Texas where he'd been raised.

A large tour bus, parked at the end of the driveway, belched out a puff of exhaust when it started up. He assumed the driver wanted the tourists to be comfortable on their way out to the Baikonur Cosmodrome, a trip that should take about forty-five minutes if the roads were slick, less if they'd been cleared. With the sun bright and the skies clear, he hoped for the best. During breakfast, he'd overheard two waiters say bad weather was expected in a couple of days. He was careful not to speak Russian or mention he'd been here several times in years past.

Baikonur Cosmodrome had become the only way for astronauts to reach the International Space Station since the Space Shuttle program had been scrapped. Playing nice with the Russians meant paying them eighty-six million dollars per seat on the Soyuz every time an American astronaut or supplies needed to be sent to the ISS. He wondered how long that would last if they got their hands on the technology to cloak aircraft, weapons, and maybe soldiers. It was very possible that the world could easily be held hostage to advance Russia to the world power they once were.

Moscow never liked to be beholden to another country and failed to rein in Kazakhstan when the Soviet Union started breaking apart. Under Soviet occupation, the people had been forced to speak Russian, but that changed once the Soviet Union began to break apart. The people took back their culture, wealth of natural resources, and their government. Now the Russians were forced to pay Kazakhstan 110 million dollars every year to continue using the Cosmodrome.

In Southeastern Siberia, Russia, a new spaceport had sprung up called The Vostochny Cosmodrome. This spaceport was under construction near Amur Oblast. It was intended to reduce dependency on Kazakhstan. The four out of five successful launch attempts had been met with optimism. How long would this place survive when Vostochny was fully operational?

Everything came crashing in on him when his affair with a Russian cosmonaut on the ISS became a little too public for NASA to handle. Served him right for trying to balance a high-strung Russian beauty and a crazy American astronaut who became a little possessive of his on-the-ground affection. When Svetlana decided to write a tell-all book about their fling in space, she got the boot from the space agency. Russia had enough bad press to control without a woman claiming she found romance on the International Space Station.

It all sounded like a bad romance novel now that he thought about it. There were no winners. The US president snatched him up and gave him a chance at Enigma. At least his appetite for thrills had been satisfied working with the secretive agency of President Austin.

But still he missed gazing at Earth from the ISS and feeling the wonder that made his heart pound.

Now here he was, not as Dr. Carter Johnson, astronaut, pilot, and engineer, but a tourist coming to see the Soyuz blast off to his faraway home among the stars. No one would recognize him. His life had become invisible to most people outside the space agencies. There remained a chance someone at Baikonur would recognize him, of course. But he'd muscled up and aged since those days, although he didn't want to admit that. The thickness blond hair had grown a little longer and showed signs of gray near his temples. He emitted a good-ole-boy charm when he spoke in his Texas drawl.

He put on his cowboy hat, which made his hair stick out in places. Slipping a piece of gum into his mouth, he chewed lazily. Other tourists he'd met from Europe and Japan started down the steps and moved toward the bus. Carter shoved his sunglasses on his nose and ignored one rotund man from the UK who tried to start up a conversation. He grunted a response to several questions. The man gave up and caught up with another excited tourist. He couldn't afford to get too chummy with these people. It was all part of the plan.

Today's trip would be nothing more than a tour of the facilities, most of which would be restricted for security reasons. The Americans could take a page from the Russian playbook when it came to being paranoid and overly cautious with their technology. The Russians didn't really believe in warning shots or the theory of innocent until proven guilty, which kind of took the enticement away from most of the would-be espionage groups or in-country hackers.

"We meet again," came a husky, feminine voice at his elbow.

Carter glanced sideways at the petite redhead smiling at him.

"Did you think a cowboy hat could hide that handsome face of yours?"

"Svetlana. You are a sight for sore eyes." Did his heart skip a beat?

"And you are here as what? A tourist?"

"Had a chance to come see the Soyuz blast off one more time." He grinned. "It's not like I had anything else to do, thanks to you."

She bit her bottom lip painted bright red. "Ah." She winked at him. "But wasn't it worth it?"

They stopped as the line of tourists slowly loaded onto the bus. He glanced over her from head to toe. "Parts of it certainly were worth it."

"Good. Because," she whispered, "you are going to be stuck with me for a few days. Maybe we can"—she smiled mischievously—"reconnect. You know, like old times."

"You are a dangerous woman, Svetlana."

"Hmm," she cooed. "Just how you like it, as I remember. What ever happened to that crazy woman who wanted to kill me?"

"Resting comfortably in some psych ward I'm told. Gets all the green Jell-O she can eat."

They were the last to get on the bus. Svetlana fanned her hand out toward the steps. "Please, go ahead. I am your guide to Baikonur Cosmodrome today. Perhaps we'll have a chance to discuss old times, comrade."

"Kind of like getting bitten by a rattlesnake, if you ask me."

She pursed her lips together, which turned into a frown. "Yes. Then you should proceed with caution." She examined her guest list. "I don't see your name on here. Traveling under an alias, I assume."

Carter took the sheet and scanned it, recognizing she posed a threat to his true identity. "Here it is. Carter Simms."

"And what do you do for a living, since you won't identify yourself as a washed-up astronaut?"

"I'm a project engineer for a mining company back in the States. Thought since I was here finding out more about the natural resources these folks are managing, I could learn a thing or two and take a side trip to Baikonur. Someplace I thought I'd always like to see." This was the place they first met.

"Interesting." Her voice took on that cynical vibe Russians were known for in the movies.

"Not near as interesting as you being a tour guide—instead of a washed-up astronaut." One corner of her mouth turned up. "Hopefully, some of that raw talent still exists."

"We are running late. You should get on the bus now before I alert the authorities you are an imposter."

"Are you threatening me, Svetlana, because I—"

"Relax. This time"—she leaned closer— "we are on the same side. I'm your contact on this mission."

~ ~ ~ ~

The hotel where Tessa stayed was frequented by Western tourists, especially Americans. Lots of tour groups had come and gone both times she'd visited Moscow to prepare for this mission. She accompanied Ambassador Finley on the previous trips to get things squared away at the American embassy. That trip lasted only a few days before she returned home for more meetings, plans, and statements of expectations. The second trip consisted of ten days being at the beck and call of the ambassador. Instead of staying at a nearby hotel, she'd been given a room at the embassy in order to work late.

Now, sitting alone in her room, she had time to reflect on a conversation she'd had with the ambassador.

"What do you think of Moscow, Tessa?" the ambassador asked one late night when they took a break.

Tessa sipped her hot tea before answering. "From what I can see from here, I love it."

Bonnie chuckled. "I guess that was a dumb question. I've given you no free time to explore. Why don't you take tomorrow off and be a tourist? I can arrange for someone to be your guide."

She set her cup down. "I'd rather tie up these loose ends and go home. I'll be back a few weeks after that. I miss my family."

"Of course. Speaking of which, did Robert ever mention he'd spoken to me?"

"No. I apologize for him putting you on the spot and grateful you kept your promise not to ever speak of what I did in

Afghanistan." The mention of those events caused her to shiver.

Bonnie stared at her before pouring herself a glass of wine. She offered Tessa a glass, but she shook her head no. "Afghanistan was a nightmare. I owe you my life. Robert seemed very distraught over what little I told him."

"Maybe that's why he's trying to work harder so I can quit this job."

"I take it things aren't going too well at home." The ambassador poured more wine and sniffed the liquid before taking a sip.

Tessa sighed and added a shrug.

"I'm sure Captain Hunter would have a lot to say about you quitting." Her smile resembled a spoiled feline. "I thought he and Darya would kill each other before we could leave that hellhole."

"Captain Hunter is protective of his people."

A soft laugh escaped Bonnie's lips. "I dream of that kind of protection, Tessa. You are blind as a bat. Anyway. That scruffy tribesman make contact with you yet?"

"Don't you think I would have said something if he had?" she snapped.

"No. I don't think you would have. Captain Hunter may be your protector, but I believe you're Darya's. The two of you got pretty chummy in Afghanistan as I remember. Oh, wait. He thinks he married you and now you're his wife."

Tessa took a deep breath and stared straight ahead at nothing.

"He's a dangerous thug, Tessa. You'd best remember that when he does come calling. You can't trust him, and he plays both sides. President Antonov is his uncle, and the apple doesn't fall far from the tree."

"Meaning?"

"Antonov is a vicious opportunist, or at least the people around him are and will do anything to make Russia a world power again. He struts around like a peacock and believes he is loved by all, but nothing could be further from the truth. He needs an edge, an ace in the hole. Wherever he's keeping those scientists, you can bet he's had them working on the cloaking project. That would be a way to intimidate the entire world, even the Chinese, who aren't afraid of anything."

"Do you have a point, or are you just flaunting your opinions that don't amount to a hill of beans?"

Bonnie gulped her wine. "Still the snarky little Grass Valley housewife who thinks she can walk on water." She stretched out her legs and leaned back in her overstuffed leather chair. "My point is, we both saw the side of Darya Petrov that can be like his uncle. Remember how he dealt with the Taliban? And it didn't matter that Chase Hunter was an American soldier, either. He was two breaths from slicing his throat, ear to ear."

"His kindness saved you and me, along with those little orphan girls."

Bonnie smirked and set her glass on the coffee table. "We both know your sacrifice had a lot to do with that. And, hats off to you, he fell head over heels for blue eyes and a stubborn personality, thinking you were in love with him, too."

Tessa could only glare at the woman. Everything she said was true. Darya could be a dangerous man to an enemy, but she'd never felt threatened by him after the first few days of captivity. "You don't know him," she whispered.

"Well, not in the Biblical sense. No. But, maybe if I'd slept with him, I'd feel different, too."

"You don't know what went on between Darya and myself."

"Something got him hot and bothered enough to return us to civilization. You turned your back on him in the States, and now he's turned rogue again. He knows where those scientists are, and you are the bargaining chip."

"I don't want to do this. It doesn't feel right."

"I don't care if you want to or not and neither does our president. Because of you, I'm going to have to make damn sure everyone is on script."

"Me?" Tessa huffed. "I'm a pawn in all this. And you don't have to worry about everyone at Enigma being on script." She leaned forward and offered a tight smile. "And just so you know. You're the one Enigma is concerned about. This goes sideways, and you'll take the heat for not doing your job. Enigma doesn't exist, so they won't be blamed."

"I have plenty of intel on Enigma."

"The quickest way to get caught in the crosshairs of a disgruntled Enigma agent's sniper rifle is to start hurling threats about things you know nothing of." Tessa reached for her cup. "Maybe we should get back to work before I start regretting having had Darya bring you back with me in Afghanistan."

"I only want you to be careful, Tessa," Bonnie offered calmly. "I care about you."

Tessa raised her gaze to connect with Bonnie's and squinted. "And I care about you, Ambassador Finley. I'm glad we had this chat. Now. Where is Darya?"

That conversation had occurred on her last trip. Now, here she was again, in a boutique hotel waiting for Captain Hunter and Agent Samantha Cordova. Both would be guest lecturers from the Sacramento University of Science and Technology, where she also taught. She had left California several days earlier and felt like she'd been followed the entire time. The university was a short walk away and the weather somewhat nicer since the snow had stopped, Tessa took advantage of the fresh air.

They had not had any time together for nearly three weeks. Both had been busy preparing for this trip, practicing their roles and being drilled on protocol and Russian law. Because she couldn't speak Russian, language lessons filled empty spaces in her schedule.

Then there were her children, who continued to adjust to the new normal at home. She and Robert had separated, or it felt like that. Most nights he spent at the tiny apartment over his office, staying at the house only when she had to be in Sacramento. The children had begun asking hard questions she wasn't quite prepared to answer yet.

Over the last year, her relationship with her husband had deteriorated. Was it because he'd been caught in several situations that nearly got him sent to jail? Thanks to Enigma, he came away unscathed. Just before Christmas, a certified red envelope had been delivered to the house. Robert managed to intercept it at the last second. She'd ask him about it and he shrugged to say it was important papers from a client and he needed to be sure it was secured. She thought Mr. and Mrs. Scott had been typed on the address label when she signed for it.

Now a nagging thought kept popping into her head that the red envelope involved her, not a client. Why else would it have come to the house?

A tap at her door vanquished the thought yet again and drew her to the chain latch. There was no peephole in this solid wood door, so she waited.

"It's me, Betty Crocker."

Tessa unlatched the door and let Samantha Cordova into the room. Disappointment washed over her, but she gave Sam a quick hug and stepped aside. "Hey, you!" she chirped loud enough for interested parties to hear. "Good to see you. How was your flight?"

Sam shut the door and eyeballed the room before addressing Tessa. "Did you have to touch me?" She dusted her arms off, as if she'd contacted head lice.

"Sorry. Trying to act like I'm glad to see you."

Sam gave a humph then walked to the window to check out the view. "Not bad. Any news?"

Tessa shook her head. "Darya has not made contact. Maybe we were wrong. Maybe he isn't here."

"You'd like that, wouldn't you?" Sam sighed flopping down on the edge of the bed and giving it a bounce. "Wouldn't want to tarnish your knight in shining armor." She locked stares with Tessa and pooched her lips out in a kiss. "My room is next door, cupcake. If your boyfriend shows up, I'll be close if you decide on a threesome."

Tessa huffed a groan of irritation and sat in the tapestry-covered chair near the window. "Where's Chase?"

"In the restaurant." When Sam stood up and stretched, Tessa was aware once more how tall the woman was and that, even after a long trip, she continued to be the most beautiful creature she'd ever seen. Too bad her personality didn't match her beauty. "Ahh. Were you hoping for a little reunion that involved—"

"Do you ever get tired of baiting me, trying to hurt my feelings, or showing how much you hate me?"

Sam put her finger on her chin, stared up at the ceiling, and responded. "No. No, I don't think I do."

"I'm starved." Tessa realized immediately mentioning food left her wide open for another insult, but Sam changed the subject.

"Satellite images haven't revealed anything yet. Russia has eleven time zones to cover. We are searching areas closer to the tundra."

"Talk about a needle in a haystack."

"Exactly. Intelligence thought we had something about a week ago, a runway, but then it disappeared."

"Could it have been cloaked, too?" If only Carter Johnson was here to explain it to her instead of her snooty companion. He, at least, didn't mind dumbing it down for her.

Sam tossed Tessa her purse laying on the bed. "Heard from him last night. He thinks it's possible. It could be the project has expanded beyond what DARPA and the Jango Aeronautics were doing." She put her hand on the doorknob. "You can find out all about it on YouTube. They have a nice little science show for kids you'll enjoy. That will save both of us a lot of embarrassing Q&A. Oh, and if you see a cockroach? Step on it. Chances are it's one of those spy drones. By the looks of this place, it will be hard to tell the difference." She pulled the door open, stepped into the hallway, stopped in front of her room, and unlocked it.

"Go on without me. If our boy is watching, seeing you with the captain will give him a little more incentive to speed things up."

Tessa nodded and started to leave.

Sam pulled her back. "Be careful. I don't trust the tribesman."

"You're wrong about him," Tessa whispered.

"You're so gullible," Sam cooed then shut the door.

Tessa hurried to the dining room. She surveyed the intimate space filled with small tables covered in hunter-green cloth. The hope was to see Captain Hunter sipping on a cognac or staring at a menu. Anytime he came into her life, things felt more manageable, safer, and friendlier. But he wasn't there. She could feel her shoulders sag in disappointment. Had he already left? Strong hands slipped around her waist, and warm breath touched her ear.

"Miss me?" Chase turned her around and kissed her on the cheek.

She fell into her role a little too easily by hugging his neck. "Missed you like crazy." His wolfish smile widened then he grabbed her hand and led her to the table.

"Maybe we can fix that later."

CHAPTER SIX

The hotel Tessa and her colleagues stayed had once been a small library downstairs and apartments upstairs. With the fall of communism, the property had been quickly snatched up by a man who would become a Russian oligarch, the new rich. The upstairs became guest rooms, and the library section transformed into a quaint restaurant. With the books still on the shelves, shiny wood floors, and small tables stuck in intimate corners, it was easy to feel like you'd slipped back into a time when things moved slower. An electric stove had been repurposed into a fireplace and took the edge off an otherwise cool room.

"You ever see this guy who shows up at your lecture before?" Chase forked the last piece of fish into his mouth.

"He comes in after I've started the lecture then slips out at the end. Always in the shadows."

Chase took a swig of wine. "Probably security watching you to keep track of your movements. The Russians are a suspicious bunch."

Dabbing at her mouth with the faded cloth napkin, Tessa realized she'd not eaten much of her dinner of pork and potatoes. At the thought of being followed, she lost her appetite.

"If you're not going to eat that—"

She shoved her plate up against his. "Help yourself."

"Travel makes me hungry," he confessed, scooping her portion onto the plate. "Can you describe this admirer of yours?" His infectious smile lightened her mood.

"Only you would think I have an admirer."

"Well, you are a babe, Tessa." He chuckled as she rolled her eyes at the suggestion.

"Maybe Darya." He let the words roll off his tongue like it could have been a slur.

"Then why didn't he just say something?"

"Maybe he's still pissed at you for leaving him." Chase finished Tessa's food before speaking. "Men like us don't forgive and forget so easily." He pointed his fork at her. "Best remember that. He's dangerous."

"Then you are, too," she offered as she glanced toward the row of large windows at the front of the restaurant.

Chase arched an eyebrow and scowled. "Are you nervous or scared to see him again—or have you seen him already and not told us?"

She shot him a narrowed gaze. "I'm neither. And I haven't seen him. It is insulting for you to think I'd…" She paused when Chase reached across the table and took her hand. His thumb moved back and forth across the back in a show of affection.

Such gestures were rare for him. It sent a signal of wanting to be personal. He'd made an exception with her on a number of occasions. Tessa knew it was his way of telling her whatever came their way, he'd stand beside her. There was never any doubt he found her company entertaining and special. But when it came to Darya Petrov, they navigated a slippery slope.

"Honestly, Tessa, I don't think you know what to expect. I understand Afghanistan changed everything for you. Things happen. My problem is not with how you survived but the way Darya got inside your head."

"Thanks for trusting me to come. I wasn't sure if I would ever get out from behind that desk again after all that hoopla in Africa."

He lifted her hand to his lips and kissed her fingertips, pretending to show affection. "Hoopla? Is that what they're calling it now? You know perfectly well we were—"

"Yes. Yes. You don't need to remind me. Thanks for throwing a bucket of cold water on my feelings." She pulled away. "I do kind of go for the strong-silent Neanderthal type."

"I've missed your sass." He grinned. "You might be interested to know I got rid of the last brainy bimbo."

Tessa sighed then shook her head. "Poor thing. Another broken heart to put on your shelf. Soon your reputation is going to catch up with you." She glanced again at the window. She'd noticed a man standing against a streetlamp seconds ago, staring into the restaurant. Was it the man from her class? Was it Darya? "I'm tired. Walk me to my room." Then she whispered they were being watched.

After signing the bill, Chase took Tessa's arm and pulled her after him toward the stairs. He touched her back as she went ahead of him. With a casual glance behind him and out the window, he whispered he'd spotted the man dressed in a heavy coat and traditional Russian hat. When they reached the top of the stairs, Chase slipped his arm around her shoulders. Tessa suspected he might be trying to lure Darya out with what appeared to be behavior of a devoted lover. She didn't like it.

Tessa opened her door, and he followed her inside and checked the room for listening devices. She waited at the window, trying to locate any signs of the man on the street, but he had disappeared. She remained standing in front of the window, hoping maybe Darya really was out there.

"Don't get upset with me," Chase said, casually coming up to stand in front of her. "This is only in case our boy is watching." He slipped one arm around Tessa's waist and pulled her tight against his chest then reached to pull the curtains shut with the other. Next, he moved away and turned out the lights, leaving only a dim one on in the open bathroom. "If he's out there, he'll be mad as hell I'm here with you."

He patted her cheek, grinning so wide his white teeth glowed in the dark of the room.

"Thanks. I appreciate you making me feel like I sleep around when I'm not home with my hardworking husband," she huffed, pushing him aside.

"Sorry, Tess. This is important, and he has gone silent for too long." He moved to the door.

"If he is as dangerous as you keep saying, then I'm the one in trouble. Don't you think he'd love to take revenge on me?" Tessa wondered if her eyes had sparked to violet like they often did when angry. He usually commented about it when it happened. He gazed a long time at her. In the shadows, she could see his jaw tighten and release and wondered if he was conflicted, but she stood her ground.

"He won't hurt you—at least not on purpose."

"And how can you be so sure?"

"Because he loves you, Tessa Scott." He pushed a curl from her forehead with his index finger, which she slapped away. "That does crazy things to men like us," he whispered.

Tessa felt her anger melt away. "And how would you know?"

The mood evaporated so fast, she thought the last few minutes were a figment of her imagination.

Chase opened the door and took a step backward out the door. "Just so you know, I'm establishing a little more insurance for the night."

"What?"

Before she could react, he forced her into his arms and kissed her with a hardness that showed irritation and frustration instead of affection. Either way, Tessa felt paralyzed when crushed against him and his lips found hers. When he released her suddenly, she staggered away and blinked back her confusion.

An impish smirk toyed at the corners of his mouth when he glanced down the hall then back at her. "Whoever is monitoring that camera at the end of the hall will most likely carry the image to Darya." He refocused on her mouth then searched her face. "I'll be next door if you need me."

Tessa bristled. "With Sam?"

He cupped her chin in his rough hand. "I sense jealousy."

She tried to push him away, but he only slipped a hand behind her neck, as if he'd pull her back into another embrace.

"No, you Neanderthal. I-I..." She hated when frustration made her stutter.

"The room on the other side of you. You are sandwiched between the two of us. Tessa, do not go anywhere with him if he tries to lure you away from us. Do. You. Understand?"

She nodded and tried her hardest to level a calm but irritated glare at him. He only smiled and patted her cheek.

"Good girl." He withdrew and backed all the way into the hall. "I don't want to lose you again. Remember. I'm the good guy." He turned away and went to his room.

Tessa closed the door and rested her head against the surface. "Dear God in Heaven. Help me get through this."

~ ~ ~ ~

"Do you have anything for me, Nephew?" President Antonov came from around his mahogany desk and went to the liquor cart. He held up the vodka to be polite. Although Russians considered it an insult if you didn't join them in a small sip of vodka when offered, the president knew Darya's mother had been a Sunni Muslim. He didn't insist.

"Thank you for seeing me so late, sir." Darya watched him gulp down the drink then stare at the glass as if contemplating another.

"Please. When we are alone, I would like very much for you to call me uncle. You are my little brother's son. I have missed him. I thought you were dead." He swung his arms out as if embracing the entire room. "And now you are here. So, tell me about the Americans. They have arrived?"

Darya clasp his hands in front of him. "Yes. The two who just arrived will begin teaching tomorrow."

"And who are they exactly?"

Darya gritted his teeth then relaxed his jaw. "Dr. Hunter is also Captain Chase Hunter. He teaches foreign language and literature at the university. He's friends with the American ambassador and a number of people in the government. Dr. Samantha Cordova teaches economics and has a romantic relationship with the prime minister of Israel."

"Really?" The president tilted his head and rubbed his chin. "That is very interesting." Darya was well aware of his dislike for the Jewish state. "And this other woman—"

"Dr. Tessa Scott. We were married in Afghanistan according to my mother's traditions."

The president returned to his seat. "Oh yes. I remember now. There was a problem with the legality of all that." Darya remained sober. "You might be interested in seeing this." He pushed some photographs across the mahogany surface.

Pictures of Tessa and Captain Hunter holding hands, talking intimately then touching as they walked up the stairs was something he'd witnessed himself. The next photograph showed him holding her against him and the next one kissing her. He stiffened, and his heart skipped a beat. The last picture showed him reaching inside the room, which hinted he might be touching her. Darya carefully returned them to the president.

"What do you plan to do about this, Nephew?"

"Kill him."

The president puffed out his chest then drummed his fingers on the top of the desk. "Are you asking for my permission?"

"Do I need it?"

"Let's speak of this another time. It is time to celebrate our Christmas holiday, a time for peace and goodwill. Besides, I need you to travel to Lake Baikal to check on a few things."

Darya remained tight-lipped. The picture of Joel Sandy flashed to his mind.

"Yes, sir. Soon?"

"In a few days. I wanted you to enjoy the holiday and maybe take your woman. There will be a large celebration here with all the new ambassadors, oligarchs, celebrities, and more. I want the visiting American teachers to come. I have already spoken to Ambassador Finley about this.

"Why Lake Baikal now?" Darya already knew of the cloaking project after rescuing Joel Sandy. Because of that encounter, he had returned to Moscow and sought out his uncle.

He'd posed as a tourist at first then began to listen to his uncle's propaganda. Viktor Antonov described the Americans as nothing more than a nation of *pindosys,* meaning stupid and ill-bred. It also meant cunning and dangerous, holding the same weight as a curse word among Russians. Darya pretended to agree from time to time.

"Your father was a double agent for us. Did you know that? The Americans placed him in Montana, but he was working for us all along." The president chuckled. "They thought putting him in a place like Montana he could do them no harm."

Darya knew the opposite to be true but he played along. The CIA helped with a start-up business so he could travel back and forth to Russia and other Eastern European countries. But his father had grown to love America. The country provided Darya with the freedoms and opportunities he'd never enjoyed. His father became as American as Chevys and apple pie.

"He would be very proud of you and I are working together for a better Russia. Soon we will be feared and respected as in the old days." The president stared off into space for a few seconds.

Darya wondered if he might be dreaming of how he could possibly bring all the other nations that had abandoned the Soviet Union back into the fold. If his father did know of his involvement with Antonov, he'd most likely beat him within an inch of his life.

"With your leadership, anything is possible," Darya said drily, and leveled a hard glare at the president. Russians didn't waste smiles for such announcements.

"I like your attitude. I'm sending you to Lake Baikal to make sure our revolutionary weapon is on track."

Darya felt his bottom lip jut out in objection.

"The Americans will stop these ridiculous and malicious embargos soon enough." A sinister chuckle escaped. "We'll see what President Austin thinks then. He will no longer snub us at world meetings."

"This will inspire the country." Darya remained doubtful but wanted to continue to stroke his uncle's ego. "And will you meet with the American ambassador before the celebrations begin?"

"I have invited her to coffee tomorrow morning around ten. Since you speak English, I would like for you to escort her to our meeting. Small talk while I make her wait. Wear a suit. You are dressed like a street thug tonight."

"Yes, sir. Will there be anything else?"

The president waved him off.

Darya exited the president's primary residence in the Senate building, sometimes referred to as the first building, in the Moscow Kremlin complex. The president would use the Grand Kremlin Palace for official ceremonies and meetings over the next few days.

Once outside, he spotted St. Basil's Cathedral. He caught a ride to Arbat, Moscow, where the streets had emptied. It remained part of old Moscow, full of wonderful stalls with tacky souvenirs for tourists. He enjoyed a stroll down the cobblestone street, which managed to retain rudiments of its once elegant past. He chose this section so the sounds of the performing artists and outdoor cafes would drown out any conversations he wished to keep quiet.

A bakery he frequented remained open with a number of tourists sitting at tables, sipping coffee the consistency of crude oil by this time of night. The owner stood telling a story that demanded wide hand gestures. He spoke English, French, and German and loved showing off his diplomatic skills whenever possible. The shop opened early and closed late.

Darya bought a cup of coffee then sat in the only corner booth. Since he'd left Afghanistan, he'd needed to make adjustments in his education, like how to use a cell phone, the Internet, and numerous other modern conveniences. He lived on the rooftop of the world for many years and avoided the trappings of civilization. Life was hard but a great deal simpler. He punched the numbers into his phone.

"It's about time you called," came an irritated female voice.

"Ambassador Finley, do not raise your voice to me." Darya switched the phone to his other ear before taking a sip of the warm coffee. "You need to keep Captain Hunter away from Tessa. Do you understand me?"

"And if I don't?" she snapped.

"Then you may end up at the bottom of the Moskva River with him."

CHAPTER SEVEN

Her heart hurt; a deep kind of hurt touched her soul. Tessa spoke to Robert on the phone, and the conversation was as cold as a Moscow winter, mostly because of her lack of understanding why he wouldn't discuss a possible move back to Tennessee. They could start over there. But he loved California and all the trappings of what it stood for. He enjoyed hobnobbing with the rich, going to fancy parties—Tessa did not.

The memories of her family's farm, riding horses in summer, canning fresh vegetables, and swimming in the creek was a dream she wanted for her children. Growing up around cousins, aunts, and uncles, to her, meant stability and a kind of familiarity which brought peace. Barbeques, honeysuckle vines, and church on Sundays with people she'd known all her life, felt like Nirvana. Maybe she and Robert would make their marriage work there. She wasn't in love with him any longer but hoped a kind of joy could be rekindled.

Was it her fault their marriage had unraveled? Had Enigma eaten away at her common sense and gotten her addicted to the rush of adventure and political intrigue? Or had it always been there and awakened by men like Captain Hunter and Roman Darya

Petrov. Moving to Tennessee, Robert would have a chance to be a hero, her knight in shining armor, and the kind of father she longed for to raise the children. Right now, he was none of those things.

Captain Hunter had become her best friend and superhero over the last couple of years. Although theirs had been a "hands-off" working relationship, the idea they might cross the lines of propriety was always in the back of her mind. She needed to get away from Enigma and him, to clear her head and give Robert a chance.

Then there was Roman Darya Petrov, the wild tribesman who'd saved her from a life of hell with the Taliban. He still haunted her dreams, and certain sounds brought his devilish smile into focus at the most inopportune times. The little girls he'd saved, along with her, remained in touch. They lived with Afghan families in California, and together they could revert back to their native tongue. She continued to practice the language in case—in case she was ever to see Darya again.

There was no doubt she'd fallen for his rogue persona and masculinity. She observed how he took care of the horses, whispering to them, training them, and treating them as if they were gifts from God. She soon realized he was doing the same thing to her and began to trust him much like the animals. His love overwhelmed her then and she'd escaped, afraid of who she would become without rules and the modern trappings of civilization outside of Afghanistan. Captain Hunter had saved her from herself.

A knock at the door brought her back to the here and now.

"Going down for breakfast. Chase is waiting. Coming?" It was Sam who watched her with curiosity. "Our boy get in touch with you?"

Tessa locked her door then dropped the key in her purse. "No. I don't think he wants to see me, Sam. Why would he?"

She offered one of her evil cat smiles and leaned down to whisper in her ear. "Revenge."

The thought chilled Tessa. She knew what Darya was capable of after seeing him deal with the Taliban. He'd hurt her once in order to save her or so he claimed. "And you think he'll hurt me?"

Entering the restaurant, Sam nodded toward a table where Chase sat. "I don't know the man. What do you think?" When Tessa didn't answer, Sam continued. "Not everyone has a good side to them. He lived in Afghanistan so long he became one of them. You were property. He may want you back to dispose of as he sees fit. Keep that in that Bible-thumper-love-thy-neighbor head of yours so you don't end up in a Russian brothel pumped full of heroin."

"I think you're wrong," Tessa mumbled.

"Russian brothel it is, then." Sam's light, amused tone irritated Tessa.

"Morning, ladies." Chase stood then pulled out a chair for each of them. "Coffee is strong but good. I ordered eggs and syrniki. Sorry, Sam, but the eggs are fried. Thought you might enjoy the syrniki, Tessa. The waiter says it's made with cottage cheese and flour. Kind of like a biscuit."

"You're in a good mood," Sam noticed.

"Slept great and having breakfast with two of my favorite people." Chase waited until the waiter set his plate in front of him. "How about you?"

"Good enough." Sam wrinkled her nose at the fried eggs.

"Had a little trouble. Couldn't shut my brain off." Tessa took her first bite of the syrniki and smiled as Chase observed her more closely. Was he wondering if Darya had made contact? "But nothing new," she said, trying to convey there had been no change in her status with Darya.

The message sobered him as if he didn't believe her. "Mind if I sit in on your lecture today? I'll have time between my own classes."

"Sure. But don't you dare ask me any questions or participate to make me nervous." She pointed her fork at him and pretended to scowl.

"Not me," he insisted. "I might learn a few things." Which meant he hoped to see her visitor.

Tessa could feel her stomach lurch at the thought of the two men meeting. It was fire and nitroglycerin when those two came in contact. She let the conversation continue between Chase and Sam. It all sounded so benign and academic. Chitchat didn't interest her as she tried to steal a sideways glance out the window to see if her mystery man waited for her. When she lifted her coffee, Chase was staring the same direction. He faced the window and had a much better view. Then his attention shifted to her.

Tessa shook her head, hinting she'd not seen anything, then stood. "I think I'm going back to my room to get a few things. A car is coming for me from the embassy. I have a meeting with Ambassador Finley. I don't want to be late. She's meeting President Antonov this morning."

Chase rose and laid the cloth napkin next to his plate. "I'll go with you."

Tessa raised her hand and frowned. "Stop it," she whispered. "Let me do my job."

Sam reached out and took his hand then cooed. "Sit down, honey, and enjoy your coffee. Maybe we can make plans for later," she flirted before cutting her eyes toward Tessa.

When he stiffened, Sam managed to tug him back down in his chair. Most of the time, Sam could be her worst enemy, but now the woman was trying to help. Or maybe she wanted to see Tessa land in a Russian brothel pumped full of heroin. Either way, Tessa couldn't help but soften her expression toward her.

"Have a good day, Tess. Maybe we can have lunch later."

Moving away, Tessa reached out and touched Sam's shoulder; such a gesture normally would get her shoved into a wall or an elbow to the side. This time, Sam reached back to touch her hand lightly then withdrew. The gesture stunned her, causing her to bump into the back of a chair at the next table where a pudgy German frowned at her.

Entering her room, Tessa closed the door and realized someone had been there and gone through her things. She remained still, hoping whoever it was had left. The room was cozy and the tiny bathroom small enough she could see that no one was there. The laptop rested on a tiny table that also served as her desk. On top lay a beautiful white rose with the earrings from Afghanistan she carried with her. She'd left them on the nightstand the night before.

Lifting the rose to inhale, she remembered the day Darya had bought those earrings for her. The world she'd always known changed that night.

She chose the earrings and decided to wear them, keenly aware there would be nothing to fear from Darya Petrov. Would the same hold true for Chase Hunter?

~ ~ ~ ~

"Is she lying?" Chase asked Sam as they grabbed a cab to head toward the university.

"No. I had my earbud in all night. Nothing. Didn't bother to turn on the television. She doesn't know I had her room bugged. When she went upstairs, she got her things and left."

"Thanks, Sam." Chase paid the taxi driver, and they dodged students to enter the university.

"She's gullible but not stupid, Chase. I put the fear of God in her about Darya. But you're going to have to deal with him sooner or later. Are you going to be able to handle his treachery?"

"If this is a double cross to get Tessa here, I'll break every bone in his body. We've done all this work to get our people back, and if he's trying to dish out payback for events in the past, then no, I'm not going to handle it well."

~ ~ ~ ~

"Darya told me last night he will be going to Lake Baikal in a few days to check on the cloaking project. I thought you might want to pass that along." The ambassador pulled on her leather gloves and grabbed up a thin burgundy briefcase. "He will touch base with Joel Sandy, the former lead scientist on the project. One of the workers has been slipping information out to Joel to help him ascertain how close the Russians are to completion."

"And?" Tessa walked alongside the ambassador as she headed outside to meet her driver.

The woman had transformed from a ragged hostage in Afghanistan to a stunning middle-aged woman. Every inch of her had been groomed, dyed, manicured, and dressed to the nines. Her auburn hair, pulled back to a bun on her slender neck, added a prim and proper air, something Tessa knew to be a ruse. The woman was a self-absorbed diplomat who thought nothing of stepping on others on her climb to the top.

Bonnie Finley stopped and faced her. "And the project is much further along than once believed. The plane rolls out in the next week to begin testing. Whatever obstacles were put in place have been circumvented by the Russian scientists who are also part of the project. They are ruthless in their push for perfection. Do you have your pilot in place?"

"Yes. Former astronaut Carter Johnson arrived at the Baikonur Cosmodrome several weeks ago. His contact is working to get him to Lake Baikal within the week. He doesn't appear to be concerned about being caught."

"That's what worries me. Not clear on the motivation of the contact. I do know Joel made sure the scientists know help is on the way. He could have left long ago but decided to stay, thanks to a Russian wife and the child he fathered. He felt it his responsibility to see the others had a chance to get rescued." Tessa watched the embassy sedan pull up to a stop. She added, "Promises were made."

"By who?" Tessa couldn't hide the panic in her voice. "What kind of promises?"

The ambassador opened the back door of the car as the Marine who would drive her to the Kremlin hurried around to assist her. "Come on. We'll drop you at the university." Once inside, she continued, glancing out the passenger window. "Something about relocation."

Tessa leaned back too fast, startling the ambassador. "That wasn't part of the plan," she snapped.

"Well, it is now. When the plane takes off, it will carry not only our American scientists, but Joel's family, who will most certainly would suffer a miserable death if left behind." The ambassador patted Tessa's knee. "Darya intends to be on the plane, too. Antonov gets wind of this, and he'll parade him around all the news outlets, making sure he comes across as a traitor or use him as leverage. Either way, Darya will probably get an unhealthy dose of nerve toxin."

She bit her bottom lip, thinking of the horrible outcome if one component went wrong. "Why haven't I seen him?" she whispered, heaviness settling in her chest.

Bonnie offered her a narrowed gaze then a sympathetic smile. "I think you are a distraction. Things are at play here. Big things at stake. No one trusts him, and Captain Hunter is partially to blame for that. You need to stop playing games to draw him out."

"Games?"

"Yes. Games. Pretending to be on romantic terms with the captain to get Darya to reveal himself."

She had been watched after all. "Not my idea."

"No doubt. If he didn't already know you were such a Girl Scout, I'm afraid the captain would have already met with a taste of Darya's ruthless sense of revenge. I'm warning you right now, don't be too chummy with the captain." The car stopped in front of the university. "It would be such a shame to lose such a fine specimen of a man. One of these times you're going to have to tell me how you managed to rein in the elusive bachelor." She chuckled. "And show me how you got that wild tribesman to fall in love with you?" She winked. "Because I was there when that went down. I'll have to admit I was a little jealous."

Tessa opened the car door and scooted out then turned to get the last word. "Sounds to me like you're still a little jealous. And when you walk into the embassy and start your psycho-deceiver speech to anyone who will listen, better take off those gloves. Russians find it insulting if you try and shake hands with them on."

The ambassador opened her mouth to speak, hesitated, and shut the door.

General Oblonsky watched the American woman who had been assisting the ambassador, off and on for several months. Now he'd heard she was involved with Darya Petrov. Suspicion welled up inside him. Why President Antonov trusted this nephew was a mystery. The man reeked of betrayal. Yet, the president had awarded him the title of colonel in the Army due to his service in the American military. The honor had rubbed the general the wrong way, considering how hard he had worked to obtain his position.

The thought of seeing the expression on Darya's face if he ever discovered it was him who'd sabotaged the plane his parents were on the day they traveled to see him graduate from West Point Academy gave him pleasure. But he wanted to save such a surprise for a later date. Knowing Darya was a coldhearted and dangerous man imprinted on him to tread lightly.

There had been several occasions when he'd tried to have his whores seduce the man. None of them interested him, much to his surprise. Until the American woman appeared, the general began to think Darya's interest lie elsewhere. He didn't begrudge a man taking pleasure to satisfy particular tastes. After all, he also had a few vices to protect. Perhaps he could use this American woman to undermine Darya's influence over the president.

General Oblonsky hated being replaced when it came to giving advice to the president.

~ ~ ~ ~

The lecture on the American West in the new millennium was well attended. All three of the Enigma agents planned a week of lessons on how the United States continued to change with the current geopolitical climate. There would be no mention of Enigma because it didn't technically exist and for the same reason, no discussion of how it had set up shop in twelve US universities and was funded by wealthy benefactors who had tired of government red tape and indecision. They weren't the only secretive entity of covert operations in the halls of homeland security, but they were the best funded. Enigma had been the brain child of President Buck Austin. Thanks to him, the wheels of change had begun to turn before he took office.

Chase found himself caught up in Tessa's lecture as did the rest of those in the half-full auditorium. He sat a third of the way down from the top in an aisle seat. The students had moved down to be closer to the speaker and hopefully have their questions answered. He'd noticed a man come in late from the upper area and sit close to the door. When the presentation concluded, students flocked around her with eager questions. And why wouldn't they? She was a pretty, well-dressed professor who waited patiently for each question to be translated to English then answered them with grace and stabs at humor. He heard the group laugh from time to time.

The man in the back stood and headed nonchalantly toward the door. Chase followed but let the door shut and counted to three before gripping the handle. Nothing happened. It was locked. He stared out the two-foot square window into the lighted hall and rattled the handle in frustration. Without warning, Darya stepped in front of the door window, showing almond eyes narrowed and a tight-lipped expression. This startled Chase enough he flinched, drawing a thin smile to Darya's thick lips. They glared at each other for several seconds before Chase heard Tessa call to him, drawing his attention. He lifted a hand in a friendly gesture and turned back to find Darya gone.

He turned the doorknob again, and this time it opened. Chase stormed out and saw the tribesman walking between two suits he surmised were bodyguards or partners in crime. They neared the elevator and didn't appear to be in any hurry.

"I see you're still slinking in and out of places you don't belong." Chase spit out the words as if they were poison.

Darya pivoted on his heel and barreled toward him, then halted inches away. Chase had forgotten how powerful his physique was and that he was a little shorter than himself. The memory of their physical confrontation in Afghanistan made him want to rub his jaw where the tribesman had slugged him. The man was a worthy opponent, and maybe under normal circumstances he might admire him. But the things he'd done to Tessa, he couldn't forgive. He'd messed with her head and, for all he knew, with her body, although she'd said otherwise.

"Stop stalking Tessa. You've done enough damage to her." He spoke in Russian through gritted teeth.

"Stick to the plan," Darya responded. "I know what I'm doing. You need to stay out of my way. Russia is a dangerous place, Captain Hunter."

"Sounds like my kind of country," he quipped.

The two bodyguards approached Chase as Darya returned to the elevator when it whooshed open. With the beefy Russians standing shoulder to shoulder, he thought of the former Berlin Wall and how much they resembled it. In unison, they turned and joined Darya on the elevator. When the doors closed, Chase heard the auditorium door open. He turned to see Tessa's smiling face. She carried her briefcase in one hand and her coat in the other.

"Where'd you go? Everything alright?" She approached and handed him her briefcase so she could slip into her coat.

"Yeah. Saw the guy you told me about in the back."

"And?"

"I think he's just someone keeping tabs on you." He leaned in and smiled. "You know. To make sure you don't give any students ideas about becoming a cowboy with your larger-than-life pictures of the American West."

Tessa exhaled and seemed to relax. "What a relief. Guess I should have you step in and talk about the plight of Native Americans since you know firsthand."

He took her arm in his. "Let's meet Sam for lunch. You can tell us how your meeting with the ambassador went."

"There's nothing to worry about with some guy following me?"

"None at all. Just a government jerk."

CHAPTER EIGHT

Christmas in Russia reeked of fairy tales and magic. It remained one of the twelve Great Feasts. Tomorrow would be Christmas Eve, January 6. Tessa planned to attend the service called Royal Hours where Vespers were combined with the Divine Liturgy. She read that following the service, families returned home for the traditional Holy Supper. There would be twelve dishes, one to honor each of the twelve apostles of Christ. It was all a part of the ten-day holiday celebrated since 1992.

Standing in Red Square, she gazed upon St. Basil's Cathedral, its colorful onion-shaped domes powdered with snow. Ornate trees standing twenty feet tall had been decked out in large jewel-toned decorations that caught the sparkle of white lights stretched to make canopies for vendors with food, gifts, or games for the children. Strolling musicians played balalaikas or a flute-like instrument called a svirel. This year because of the heavy snow, Grandfather Frost got to ride in the traditional sleigh pulled by two horses.

"I think Santa is a little early." Chase walked up next to Tessa and handed her a hot drink. "Who is the girl dressed in blue?"

"That is Grandfather Frost and his granddaughter the Snow

Maiden." Tessa couldn't help but smile seeing the children run along behind the sleigh. "Isn't it beautiful?" She felt the warmth of the drink seep through her gloves. The wind had died down and the few flakes of snow that fell reminded her of fairy dust. "I love this."

They walked through the crowd, examining the wares of vendors. Chase bought her a Santa stacking doll.

"Can't go to Russia without getting one of these." He smiled. "Besides, it kind of symbolizes our friendship, don't you think?"

Tessa nodded. "Many layers. We keep opening one after another."

"Each one a surprise but familiar." He refocused on her and sobered. "I've been wondering about Robert."

"It's too beautiful tonight to talk about Robert."

"The night you came to my condo—you came to tell me something, didn't you? You'd been crying."

"Chase, I know you want to help, but I'm not sure I should talk to you about this. And yes, I came to cry on your shoulder. Stupid of me. I depend too much on you as it is. I need to solve the problem all by myself. Stay out of it." She cast a sideways glance at him and took a sip of her drink. "You can't be the reason for whatever I decide to do."

He pulled her out of the way of several stampeding children and laughed before slipping an arm around her waist. "No, and I don't want to be the reason. But when you decide…"

"You'll be the first to know." She gave him a friendly nudge with her elbow. "But until then, I have big decisions to make. You're going to have to just continue being the—"

"Badass Neanderthal?" he laughed.

"Exactly."

They stopped to watch a puppet play. Chase translated it into English for her. She felt the weight of sadness about her failed marriage lift when she was with him. He didn't force her to make decisions or explain herself, or lay a heavy dose of guilt on her about being a terrible mother and wife.

Most of the time he was all business and watched over her training to make sure her skills as an Enigma agent were being fine-tuned. He'd stuck her on desk duty for months after their mission in Africa. Their feelings had become a little raw and exposed in near-death experiences. He claimed she needed more training before attempting field work and refused to let her tag along, except on a computer screen.

When this project came up, he had no choice but to let her go. No one at Enigma trusted Darya except Tessa. And he, in turn, trusted no one at Enigma except Tessa. He wasn't sure what would happen to her when and if they finally met. Would he take her and turn his back on the mission or see it through for her sake?

"There you are," Sam called as she strode up, hands in the pockets of her beautiful white rabbit coat. "Very festive." Coming from her red lips, it sounded as if she disapproved of such lightheartedness.

"Guess you're hoping for more lumps of coal from Grandfather Frost to throw at anyone with an abundance of joy," Tessa quipped with a crooked smile.

Sam leveled a stretched smile back at her. "One can only hope, Betty Crocker." Whenever she called her that, Tessa wondered if she needed to join a gym. "So, why are we standing out here in the freezing cold?"

"Admiring the Christmas decorations, of course," Chase said, lifting his cup of hot tea at the scene around him.

"Didn't we just do that a few weeks ago in the States? Humbug. Let's go."

They stood huddled up near a table of children snacking on a warm treat. Tessa could feel her mouth water at the delicious aroma, and she also noticed Sam's interested gaze.

"I saw the ambassador again this afternoon. She swung by the university to sit in on my lecture." The other two agents continued to stare out at the celebration, as if her words meant nothing. "Carter is in place, wherever that is," Tessa mumbled. Good to know. Apparently, he has a helper who plans to defect along with the family helping our guy in Siberia."

"He better have a big plane." Chase chuckled and pointed to children getting pulled along by their coat collars after trying to light fireworks. He continued smiling when his attention shifted to the fireworks exploding over St. Basil's. "I'm guessing it's a woman."

"Yes. Svetlana. I can't remember the last name." Tessa pointed at the fireworks and noticed most everyone stared up at the sky instead of at them.

Sam moaned. "Svetlana Iskakov?"

Tessa shrugged in ignorance.

Chase laughed out loud. "Probably not a problem, but she's the one who got him kicked to the curb at NASA."

Tessa cringed. "Geeze Louise. The six-month-affair-on-the-space-station Svetlana?"

"From what Carter told me, she got the boot as well or at least was barred from going back into space. They kept her on as scientist and test pilot. No loss if she crashed a plane, I guess. Maybe she's the one who will be testing the cloaking weapon."

"Well, maybe the old flame will be rekindled." Tessa elbowed Sam, noticing the intense frown on her puckered lips. "I can see it now—a ranch house in Texas, a bunch of little Carters running around—"

"Humph," was about as disgruntled as Tessa had ever heard from the senior agent. Sam didn't usually get jealous, because honestly, most people, especially women, swelled with envy each time she walked into a room. "I'll check her out." Sam turned to leave. "Are you coming?" Chase pulled her back.

"We won't be long. Stay. We need to come and go together. I know we're not far from the hotel. The fireworks won't last long."

She nodded acceptance and patrolled through the nearest vendors in an attempt at shopping.

"I don't know what those kids are eating, but I want it," Tessa confessed, pointing at the drips of caramel crème oozing out of the corners of their mouths.

Before Chase could step away to buy the food, Grandfather Frost approached, surrounded by excited children pointing and jumping up and down. He carried a blue robe-style coat with a hood, trimmed in white fur. He tried talking to Tessa and pointed back at the sleigh.

Chase intervened on her behalf. "He says the other Snow Maiden needed to leave with a love-struck finance. You remind him of the Snow Maiden with such long beautiful hair." This time he spoke to Chase. "He thinks a few more pictures with the families would make lots of Christmas joy."

Tessa clapped her hands together in youthful enthusiasm and shed her own faux-fur coat. The blue coat hit her above the ankle.

The weight of it surprised her as she secured the silver knot buttons. After removing her hat and tossing it to Sam, she pulled the hood up over her head to feel the warm fur brush against her cheek. The children sitting nearby gasped. Their parents smiled and applauded. She twirled around for Chase and Sam.

"There will be no living with you now," Sam snipped.

Chase walked around her and leaned in close enough the others couldn't hear. "Snow Maiden, can I tell you what I want for Christmas?"

She pushed him away and chuckled. "I'm thinking I need to give you a cold shoulder. How about that?" she teased, enjoying her new Russian Christmas role. "Get me that food while I help Grandfather Frost."

The old man and Tessa walked to the sleigh, and soon families were joining them for pictures. Her sadness and trepidation melted away in spite of the cold. The laughing children, spectacular fireworks in the sky, and thousands of twinkling lights wove a magical spell around her. Chase explained to Grandfather Frost she didn't speak Russian, so he did all the talking while she passed out sweets.

Tessa climbed up in the sleigh with several children when her Christmas partner motioned for her to sit. He pulled himself into the front seat, picked up the reins, and clicked his tongue at the white draft horses with bells and red ribbons woven into their manes, wearing black-and-silver harnesses. Children followed the sleigh, laughing and trying to throw snowballs, but were yanked back by parents. The sleigh circled back to let the children off. Tessa helped each one down and smiled at her new best Christmas memory.

She was trying to step down when he held up a hand to prevent her from leaving.

He stared at something past her. The next thing she heard was Chase yelling at her to get down. The sound of automatic gunfire, screaming, and the frightened whinny of horses, kept Tessa frozen in place for several seconds until the horses reared up and bolted toward the stands then swerved out into Red Square.

Falling back into the seat, she could barely keep from being pitched out of the sleigh. Grandfather Frost had also been thrown back and desperately tried to get control of the reins to slow them down. She heard a new sound. A snowmobile with a driver dressed in white, the face covered with a white ski mask speeded up alongside them. A rifle was slung on his back. He seemed to be trying to scare the horses in a certain direction.

Tessa elbowed her way up to see another snowmobile coming up fast. This time there were two riders. It pulled next to them, and the man on the back hopped into the sleigh and fell into her lap. In seconds, he'd jumped up and over the front seat to grab the reins. Grandfather Frost leaned away to let the masked man control the horses.

In seconds, they slowed to a trot. They were still frightened, and the new driver let them walk it out until they stopped in a dark place. Grandfather Frost took the outstretched arm to be pulled up. The man took a flask out of his coat pocket and handed it to Grandfather Frost. With a couple of quick swigs, he appeared to rally and turned to Tessa who remained in a haphazard position, sprawled across the backseat.

The other snowmobile pulled up. One man jumped off and came to hand Grandfather Frost an envelope with money sticking out. He shrugged and sat down.

Tessa stood on wobbly legs as the rescue driver walked around to the horses and spoke gently to them. It felt familiar to see him do such a thing. They quieted down almost immediately and took a treat he handed them. The other two riders pulled their rifles off their back and took up positions.

Scared out of her mind, she wondered if they were the ones who had shot up the celebrations, but flashing red lights were headed their way. When the rescue driver stomped toward her, she sat back down and scooted in the opposite direction. He stared at her a moment and motioned for her to join him.

"I'll stay right here, thank you."

The third man pointed a rifle at her and growled an order she couldn't begin to understand. She scooted to where the rescue driver stood and took an outstretched hand to assist her descent from the sleigh.

He motioned to the others, and they mounted their snowmobiles and sped off. Grandfather Frost seemed content to sip whatever might be in the flask. The rescue driver gave instructions to him, laughed, and received a wave of the old man's hand in what appeared to be a total disregard for their situation.

Tessa attempted to resist this last man who pulled her after him toward an area between two buildings. She dug in her heels, twisting and punching as he marched toward total darkness unaffected by the brightness of snow and Christmas lights. "I'm an American. Stop. Please. You are making a mistake. Stop."

But he dragged her far enough in that the sleigh now appeared to be illuminated with soft light. He pushed her up against a crumbling brick wall. When she landed a fist to his jaw, he grabbed both her hands and forced them behind her back. Pushing his body up tight against hers, he searched her face.

When she tried to wiggle free, he pushed harder against her. Tears cascaded down her face as she shivered with fear. Sam's warning of a Russian brothel, where she would have to parade around for men dressed like the Snow Maiden flashed in her mind. In spite of being terrified, she considered an idea in hopes of escape. She relaxed enough that her attacker did the same.

In a sudden move she tried to knee him, but he slapped her knee down. She realized too late it wouldn't have done any good wearing such a long coat.

"You still know how to fight," he spoke in Pashtu, the land of Afghanistan. He stepped back and eyed her.

Tessa stared in bewilderment at the man before her. Although they stood in darkness, she knew the voice. She took one timid step toward him and reached out to pull off the mask. He grabbed her hand and jerked her into muscled arms.

She stared up into the face of the man who'd saved her from unspeakable horror in Afghanistan. With her index finger, she traced the outline of his lips exposed by the cutout. It hadn't been that much different the first time they met.

"Is it good to speak in my people's tongue?"

Tessa nodded and found herself once more held captive by his touch.

"You understand enough?"

"Yes," she whispered as her fingertips moved from his lips to his face through the knitted mask.

"Then I will tell everything I know. But I must be quick."

Tessa found it hard to breathe and listen at the same time. The plans for the next couple of days were laid out so she could inform the others. The sirens grew nearer. Would Chase be close behind?

"I go now to keep you safe." He pulled her in even tighter, then rested his cheek against hers. "I have missed you, Tess-sa. Soon we can spend time together. Good?"

"Good. Be careful."

He raised the mask from over his mouth and grinned. Before she uttered another word, he kissed her with the kind of passion she now knew had been missing in her marriage to Robert.

"You need to hide," she warned as she stepped out in the open before glancing back again.

But he had already disappeared.

CHAPTER NINE

The police helped Tessa get out of their car and navigate through the crowd. Chase frantically elbowed his way to reach her. He glanced back at Sam who followed several steps behind, shifting her eyes side to side as they went. Vendors picked up strewn equipment, tables, and wares, to regain the kind of order present earlier in the evening. Families continued to file out, with a few needing first aid and headed to where several ambulances parked. Other than scrapes and bumps, no one appeared to be hurt by the gunman.

Tessa bowed her head when the officer spoke broken English to her. When Chase stepped forward and called her name, she jerked her chin up and ran into his outstretched arms. After a few seconds, he pushed her away to take a quick inventory of her appearance, making sure there was no blood. Although her eyes were red with a bit of smudged mascara, nothing indicated any injuries.

He switched to Russian to make sure he understood the information. "Thank you." Chase removed his glove to shake the man's hand. "Did you catch the shooters?" He pulled her in tight once more. She leaned into him and laid a hand on his chest.

"Nyet." The officer shook his head then put his hands in his coat pockets. "They were gone. One of them tried to assault your woman. But she fought and escaped."

Chase stiffened and glanced at Tessa who hugged him tighter. "Who were they?"

Sam laid a hand on her shoulder in sympathy.

"We are not sure. They left something behind that might help us."

Chase stepped closer to the police. "I used to be in the military and pretty good at identifying weapons. The one that shot this place up sounded like a machine gun."

The officer motioned for his partner to bring the weapon. "It was still warm." Chase reached for it but the officer pulled it back. "I do not think you need to do that."

He held up his hand. "Sorry. I have never seen anything like that. Homemade?"

"We think so. Resembles a weapon from the Chechen infantry. They adapted it from a Skorpion."

Chase nodded understanding. He knew the name but had never seen one.

The officer continued, "Now it is used mostly as a side arm."

"Chechens did this?"

The officer shrugged. "We took her statement. I don't think she really knows. Sounds like something they would do. We'll start turning over rocks to find out."

"What about Grandfather Frost? What did he say?"

The sleigh pulled up with a police officer and the man playing Grandfather Frost and struggled to stop the horses. He had to be helped off the sleigh and staggered before falling to the ground. Chase made an effort to assist him. Considering the overpowering smell of alcohol on the man, he doubted much information would be uncovered tonight.

"He won't be much help until morning." The officer who appeared to be in charge, frowned. "We have things to do here. Give me your location, and someone will come to talk to"—he glanced at Tessa in her blue coat—"the Snow Maiden." He offered a slight smile at her. "Tell her I am sorry. This is usually a peaceful celebration."

One of the police cars took Chase and his two agents back to the hotel. He talked to Tessa in the restaurant after he ordered hot tea. It didn't take long for the dining room to empty out. They headed upstairs to Tessa's room. Once inside, Tessa tossed the coat onto the bed and faced the drilling she knew would follow.

"What really happened?" Sam sat on the arm of the one chair while Chase peeked out the window and slowly closed the drapes. "If those were Chechens, you wouldn't have fared so well."

Chase stood rigid, legs separated and arms crossed over his chest. Smoothing her sweater, she eased down on the edge of the bed, which told him all he needed to know. She'd lied to the police. No more tears, or clinging to him the way she'd done in the past when scared out of her mind. He remained quiet until she cocked her head to steal a glance at him.

"Talk," he ordered. "Let's skip the narrative and tell the truth."

"No one was hurt, right?"

Chase noted the quietness of her voice. He shook his head and pursed his lips together to send her a message of impatience.

"It was Darya," she blurted out and stood so she could pace.

Chase moved to block her pacing. "Were those Chechens with him? If so, he's keeping some pretty rough company."

"They wore masks, so I couldn't tell much about them. Without Darya, that sleigh would still be going."

"Without Darya, the sleigh wouldn't have taken off in the first place," Sam interjected.

"Did he hurt you?" He wanted to make sure Tessa didn't feel threatened. He'd been through this before with her. She'd protect him, believing he was one of the good guys.

"No," she said quietly. "He wanted to tell me more information. In another week, they plan to roll out the new cloaking weapon. They have it installed on at least one fighter plane. It sounded as if the men with him are from Kazakhstan. They work here in Moscow."

"How did they hook up?" Sam seemed bewildered.

"I'm not sure. He wanted to let you know the timetable has moved up. Apparently, President Antonov is getting nervous about the project. But the whole idea was set in motion by a General Oblonsky. Darya said he was a dangerous opportunist who has convinced President Antonov this would be good for the country."

"What about the scientists? Are they in good shape?" Chase

knew the importance of those scientists returning home alive and in good health.

"For now. If the project is successful after the first test and the Russians have their people in place, then they plan to kill them. They will have lost their usefulness. Russians have been training alongside them all this time. It's imperative we get them out."

"Okay." He tilted his head toward the door, and Sam took her leave. When the door closed behind her, Chase sat on the edge of the bed and patted the spot next to him. She shook her head and moved away. Another sign she might not be telling him everything. "What else did he say?"

"That it was him in the lecture hall watching me. You lied to me," she growled.

"No. I told you it was a government jerk and there was nothing to worry about," he reminded her. "If he was interested in you—"

"Interested in me?" she fumed. "You think he's playing me? Why would he do that?"

"That's the million-dollar question, isn't it? Maybe to give me a little payback for interfering in Afghanistan. Or perhaps he's really trying to trap us here to use leverage against the US to get us back. Who knows? He's as shady as they come, and you buy into every little bit of drivel he hands you." He offered a condescending smirk. "What? Did he tell you he loved you?"

"Shut up," she warned.

"Maybe that he intended to pick up where he left off to prove what a great guy he is?"

"Stop it." Tessa doubled her fists at her sides.

Chase stood and gripped both her arms. Her muscles flexed beneath his fingers. "Don't believe anything he tells you on a personal level. Remember who he is, where he comes from. You aren't worth as much as a goat to him."

She jerked free of his grip and walked to the door. "I think you need to go. I am a professional just like you and Sam. I'm tired of being treated as if I'm a bumbling housewife who couldn't find her way out of a paper bag. I know to be careful, and I'm certainly aware of what Darya is capable of. But if you want him to stay on our side, you'd better let him get close to me."

"I'm willing to do that, but, Tessa, I'm going to be there every step of the way."

"You don't trust me. You think I'm still suffering under some romantic notions about him."

Chase opened the door. "Well, aren't you?" Her eyes had turned violet like they did when angered. Staring into their depths created a wave of regret at not having taken advantage of her hero worship on numerous occasions.

"Why?" Her voice cracked. "Why are you being so hard on him? What do you want from me, Chase?" she begged softly.

Chase took a deep breath and sighed as he expelled his frustration and temper. "Really, Tessa? After all this time, you still don't know?"

"Tell me, Chase," she encouraged. The tilt of her head and the raw emotion flooding her voice, as she stared up at him, caused that jab of pain in his chest. It was an ongoing problem where she was concerned. "I'm tired of guessing games and innuendos with us."

He turned to leave. "Another time."

She laid a timid hand on his arm. "No. I need to know."

Chase paused for only a second. "I'll see you in the morning, Tessa."

President Antonov rocked his son against his shoulder in the nursery near his master bedroom. His exhausted wife had played with the boy all day and acted as nursemaid since he was a little feverish and fussy. She never tired of being a mother and refused to let the boy's companion take care of him during times like these. This was his only child, and being able to step in to hold him awhile relaxed a mind full of anxiety and plans for the future. When one of his guards opened the nursery door and his nephew walked in, he lifted a finger to his lips.

"All went well at the celebration, I understand." The president shifted the child down in the crook of his arm and stared into the boy's face before turning his attention back to Darya.

His nephew stood, solemn and unreadable, with his hands folded in front of him. "Yes, sir. No casualties, but there was damage to vendor stalls, a few injuries—nothing major."

"And you went back on my behalf?"

"Of course. I talked to the police. They found the weapon I left. The blame is already being laid at the feet of the Chechens."

"Excellent. It is good to have a distraction for the world to be outraged enough to be looking in a different direction."

Darya only nodded and stared at him with his narrow-shaped eyes. Something about his composed personality unnerved him. Did he suspect him of having his parents' plane crash so many years ago? The deed had left him shaken at the time. Now he thought he was close to finding out who had compiled lies to target his only brother.

President Antonov wanted to trust his nephew since he had grown fond of him. But there were too many years of unknown experiences that may have shaped him into a dangerous opponent to fully embrace their new connection. Living with a tribe of uncivilized Sunnis in Afghanistan had changed Darya's father enough to work for the CIA and defect to the United States. Knowing Darya returned to his mother's people to become a drug smuggler and fight the Taliban gave him more than enough cause for concern.

There didn't seem to be any love lost between him and the US. Darya's plan to take that woman could become an international incident if his nephew's scheme failed. Either way, the president could easily eliminate the problem if it came to that.

"And the woman? Did that go as planned?"

"No. The police arrived too soon for that." Darya raised his chin and stared down his nose at the child in the president's arms. "I will see her at worship services tomorrow night and at your party. She was too frightened tonight." One corner of his mouth turned up in satisfaction. "But she is still a fighter. I admire that in a woman."

The president gave a slight chuckle. "You are like your father. I miss him."

Darya nodded then pointed to the child who rousted up and spotted him.

"Roman Darya," the boy called, reaching for him.

The president watched as his nephew transformed from a dangerous man to a protective guardian of his son. The two had made friends quickly, and little Yuri never missed an opportunity to enlist his new playmate to play hide-and-seek.

"May I, Uncle Viktor?" Darya dropped his hands to his side and took a step forward.

The president let the child sit up so he could hand him to Darya who wrapped his arms around him and kissed his warm cheeks.

"Are you sick or tricking your father?" Darya frowned at the child, who patted his cheeks. He shook his head vehemently and hugged the tribesman's neck. "You must get well, little one. Grandfather Frost comes soon. I spoke to him tonight."

The little boy's eyes grew large with interest. "Will he bring me a present?"

"Yes. But you must do as your mother tells you and not make her too tired. Can you do that?"

President Antonov stood and took the child and laid him in his bed, adding one final kiss to the boy's forehead.

"Thank you, for being kind to my son." He closed the nursery door behind them and started to walk toward his quarters. "Your Russian is much better than your English, Darya. I would have thought spending so long in the States it would be better."

"My father spoke only Russian to me, and my mother only Pashtu. At school I was quiet." He shrugged. "And the girls liked my broken English, so I didn't try to improve. In Afghanistan, it became a habit I found hard to break. I want to speak better for Tess-sa. I don't want to embarrass her. I am trying now to improve. Habits can be broken."

The president patted his back. "And so can a man's heart, Darya. Remember this as you move forward with the American woman. She may not feel the same as you once she knows you are one of us now."

"She feels the same as when we left Afghanistan."

"I hope so for your sake because, if she doesn't—it might become a problem. I do not want more problems."

"I understand." They stopped at the president's bedroom door. "Good night, sir."

The president watched his nephew stride away down the corridor and wondered how a man like Roman Darya Petrov could be a dangerous outlaw one minute and transform into a loving playmate for a little boy the next. Did he miss his own child that died soon after his birth? Could such a man be completely trusted?

A guard inched up to the president. "I want him followed." The guard nodded and took his leave.

~ ~ ~ ~

General Oblonsky opened his door just wide enough to speak to the man who'd followed Darya to his apartment. There remained nothing interesting to report back to the president. The news of the attack on the night's festivities surprised him. Where did these attacks originate? He already had sent his people to interview the police and the drunken fool playing Grandfather Frost. Nothing of any interest came of it. Darya had appeared on the scene quickly. Was it because the American woman had been involved? The general didn't like where this was headed, and he certainly didn't like not being in charge of the situation after finding out Darya was there.

He took out his phone, entered the number, and waited. On the third ring, a familiar voice answered.

"Have you located the American who is trying to find our project?"

"I am close, General."

"I grow impatient with your progress."

"Soon, sir."

He clicked off and dropped the phone on the nightstand. The woman in his bed cowered when he turned to her and removed his robe. "Now, where was I?"

~ ~ ~ ~

"Who was that?" Carter poured himself another cup of coffee as his companion joined him at his table.

Svetlana smiled coyly. "An old lover in Moscow. Wants to know what I've been up to. It is very late there."

"Tell him you were having breakfast with another old lover? Maybe we have a few things in common."

"I doubt it. He is a little too ruthless for my taste."

Carter gazed at her over the rim of his cup and wondered what she might be planning. If history taught him anything, it was to watch his back where Svetlana was concerned.

INVISIBLE GOODBYE

CHAPTER TEN

Since the university would be closed for a couple of days, Tessa decided to sleep in. Jumping time zones always cost her too much sleep, and she needed a good eight hours every night. After the excitement in Red Square and the appearance of Darya—it became impossible to fall asleep.

As she lay beneath the covers, memories of sleeping beside him to shelter from the cold of such a harsh land refreshed her tender love for him. The smell of him, and his touch in the middle of the night when he'd return from his watch, flooded her senses with the press of his lips against hers a few hours earlier in the shadows where he'd forced her to follow.

The clock showed ten when she decided to shower and slip into something relaxed and warm. When she pushed back the curtains, she realized a new blanket of snow had fallen during the night. Looking up and down the street, she cherished a faint hope she'd see Darya waiting to catch a glimpse of her.

People moved about with determination in spite of the cold, getting last-minute supplies for their Christmas dinner. The bakery bustled with clients, as did several other novelty stores. She wanted to get some gifts for the family and even for Chase and Sam. She remembered, too, there was a traditional gift you took when visiting a Russian home for dinner. Even though it might not apply for President Antonov, she wanted to make the gesture to show she understood the culture.

But it was Darya she wanted to please. What could she possibly get him? He wasn't a Christian and certainly not a good Sunni. What do you get someone who has nothing? Did he even care about such things? She didn't even know whether his parents celebrated Christmas once they'd relocated to Montana. Picturing such a scene was almost comical. Somehow it didn't fit the wild tribesman she'd known in Afghanistan. In that moment, she longed to hold him, to feel the beat of his heart and tell him how she regretted hurting him.

Could Chase be right? Did he want payback? Why else would he have waited to come see her?

This train of thought would do her more harm than good. She tried to focus on the problem at hand. The scientists needed to get out of Russia before orders were given to kill them. That had to be the priority, not whether her feelings were bruised because Darya had ignored her each time she came to Russia. The cloaking device needed to be destroyed somehow, and that would remain a complicated endeavor. Getting the remaining Americans out of Russia, along with the others who offered comfort and assistance could result in being discovered. If that happened, chances were good, she'd never see her family again.

After giving the Snow Maiden coat to the hotel concierge to return to the proper individuals, Tessa went to the restaurant for a late breakfast of crepes and bacon. Before she finished, Chase and Sam joined her. She couldn't help but wonder about their closeness of late and the way he listened so intently to her every word.

"Did you sleep in, too?" Tessa poured them each a cup of coffee then topped off her own. "With all the excitement, I had a hard time falling asleep."

Sam shifted her eyes to Chase and smiled at him over the rim of her cup. "Yes. Me, too."

Chase exchanged a glance with Sam and pursed his lips, perhaps to prevent himself from smiling. The thought had always been in the back of her mind that the two of them might have some kind of physical relationship going on from time to time, although he swore that was off-limits. After last night's final words with him, she now wondered if Sam was the reason he couldn't commit. She felt foolish at pressuring him to admit how he felt about their—whatever it was between them.

"I'm going shopping this morning before the shops close for Christmas," she said.

Chase shot her a narrowed gaze.

She went on, "I'm just going on this block of shops. I have a few things to get my kids. We should take a bottle of wine to the palace for the party day after tomorrow, too."

"Vodka would be better," Sam offered, looking over the menu then placing her order with the waiter. "I'm not sure that tradition holds when you go to a big party, Tessa."

Tessa agreed and decided maybe it wasn't such a good idea. "Anyway, I'm going out for a while."

"Wait, and I'll go with you." Chase set his cup down. "I don't think you should—"

Tessa stood up and slipped on her coat. "I'll be fine. Text me when you're finished with breakfast, and I'll tell you where I am. Sam, you're welcome to come shop with me, too."

Sam demonstrated her evil-cat smile. "Sorry. I think I have to clean the bottom of my boots or something."

Smiling sweetly, Tessa patted her on the shoulder and sniffed. "Oh, I see what you mean. If you weren't so full of crap, that wouldn't be a problem."

Batting her eyelashes like an innocent toddler, Tessa walked away, loving Chase's laughter filling the nearly empty restaurant.

The smell of freshly baked bread teased Tessa into taking several samples from a friendly shop owner until she caved to buying several kinds of his delicious concoctions. She could always share them with Chase. One look at Sam and you knew she put carbs and ISIS in the same category. A midnight snack with some hot tea would be just the thing on Christmas Eve after worship services.

She snatched up some Star Wars stacking dolls and a couple of wooden puzzles for the boys and a Russian doll and a snow globe of St. Basil's for her daughter. The shop owner agreed to mail them home for her. At another shop, she found a beautiful silk scarf for Sam and fantasized a moment about wrapping it around her neck to choke her but decided it would be a waste of a perfectly lovely gift.

A first edition book of Louie L'Amour's *Last of the Breed* was not only a perfect gift but ironic. The book involved a major, forced down in an experimental aircraft, over the Siberian wilderness and compelled to use the skills of his Native American ancestors to survive. It was one of Tessa's favorite Westerns, and she had often envisioned it being made into a movie. With Chase's military history and Cherokee background, she now could imagine him playing the lead. With packages wrapped, she headed back onto the busy street.

Checking her phone, she noticed a text from Chase. Part of her wanted to ignore his inquiry of her location so he could join her. The sensible side took over without much objection, especially when she spotted her protector stopping in front of several shops and glancing in. Tessa decided to connect with him.

"Sam decide not to tag along?" She shifted her shopping bag to the other hand. "Guess her boots were really in bad shape."

He chuckled and linked her free arm with his. "One of these days she's going to give you a thumping you won't forget."

Tessa shrugged and took the time to admire the hustle of the people on the street. Although it was Russian Christmas, expressions remained almost grim. She had to remind herself that here, people considered it insulting or thought you might be up to something if you smiled at a stranger. That was reserved for close friends and family. The Southerner in her wanted to say in each store, "Hi. How y'all doin'?" The absence of such warmth made her a little homesick.

"Maybe we can celebrate Christmas tonight—together," he continued.

"I'm going to church services. I've never been to an Orthodox church. I'm looking forward to it. You're welcome to come."

"The ambassador called and is sending a car. Apparently, the president has invited her to services as well and she, in turn, thought you might enjoy tagging along. She'll pick us up around 10:00. We've been invited to sit with the government delegation."

"We'll be sure not to sit too close to her. I wouldn't want us to be struck by lightning," she sniped sarcastically.

"She seems genuinely fond of you. What's the deal?" Chase

opened the door to the hotel for her and, together, they made their way upstairs.

Tessa stopped at her door and placed her key in his outstretched palm. "The deal is, when we were in Afghanistan, she let it be known how important she was after Darya and his men took us."

Chase followed her inside the room. "You've never mentioned that before."

"Another thing I didn't mention was she insisted I offer myself up as a willing sacrifice to Darya so he'd bring us back."

His expression froze in anger.

"And you know the rest."

"Tessa," he breathed. "I-I—"

"I refused—at first, but I had no idea about my past. Everything told to me came from her. My concern centered on those little girls." She removed her coat and set the bag of gifts on the chair. "I saved her life, and she saved my reputation from becoming tarnished…"

He invaded her personal space enough that she moved away only to be pulled back by Chase's firm grip on her hand. "I'm sorry about last night."

"Which part?" She spoke with such unconcern he released her hand.

"Tessa, I want us…"

"Yes?" Tilting her head, she glared at him harshly.

A tap at the door then Sam pushed in and flopped down on the end of the bed. "Am I interrupting something?"

"No," they said in unison.

Tessa said, "Come in, Sam. I got you guys a little gift for Russian Christmas. I wanted to give it to you before the ambassador arrives tonight. "

Sam sat down on the edge of the bed to unwrap the gift handed her and pulled out the scarf trimmed in gold. Christmas paper lay crumpled on the bed next to where she sat. Stunning, as always, she stood and thanked Tessa for the gift.

"You're welcome. I didn't see you over the holidays a few weeks ago to get you anything."

Sam arched an eyebrow. "Hope you aren't expecting me to give you a gift."

"I hope you'll think of me every time you wrap it around your neck and imagine me pulling it tight." She offered a mocking smile.

The tall beauty stepped next to Tessa and patted her on the cheek. "You see, Chase, all that syrupy sweetness is tainted with poison." She glanced at the captain then back at Tessa. "It's in these moments I almost like you, Tessa."

"I know the feeling," she quipped.

Sam coughed a half-hearted laugh as she reached the door. "I'll be back in a minute."

Chase shook his head in confusion. "It was a nice gesture on your part, considering what a hard time she gives you."

"In that case, I'll give you your gift since nobody gives me a harder time than you." She lifted the burlap-wrapped gift from her small table and handed it to him.

He untied the string and pulled the fabric away. "Tessa," he sighed. "This is a first edition of Last of the Breed by Louie L'Amour."

"The main character reminded me of you. Have you read it?"

"No."

"You'll love it. It's one of my favorites."

"Thank you. Really." He ran his hand over the faded cover. "I didn't get you—"

"Stop. Saving my life so many times pretty much gives you a free pass." Her mouth twisted in a forced smile.

"Tessa, there are things about us that I want to—" He hesitated and backed toward the door. "I'll see you later tonight. Going to be a long night. Take a nap."

~ ~ ~ ~

"Hey, I think we're being paged," Sam said, sticking her head into the room. "Looks like the wicked witch of the Ambassador Finley kind has arrived. Let's go."

The embassy car arrived on time with Ambassador Finley. She came inside the hotel restaurant where the three Enigma agents waited around a small buffet table set with sweets and other delights to accompany the hot tea, wine, and vodka for anyone interested. Both Sam and Chase tried the vodka and gritted their teeth afterward, followed by an "Aww" and a light chuckle.

There were times Tessa wished she drank alcohol to fit in better at social functions, especially on the international scene. But her strict upbringing had ruined that long ago. She wasn't embarrassed about her choice to abstain but had suffered rude comments over the years. Bible thumper, teetotaler, radical, too-good-for-us, ice princess had all been snickered where she could hear from the time she was in junior high school. But Enigma had given the impression they saw it as a plus rather than a minus. Even Sam didn't rub her the wrong way about never participating.

She'd asked the Enigma therapist, Dr. Wu, once about this, and his response was, "It is who you are. You have accepted them for all their quirks, so they have done likewise to you."

The fact that their quirks might involve killing, torture, stealing, or invading a small third-world country was beside the point, she guessed.

"This is perfect," Ambassador Finley offered to a waiter standing behind the white table. Her Russian language skills had improved. A few comments went back and forth between the two until she motioned them toward a table near the fake fireplace with an electrical insert. "We might as well sit. I believe we'll be standing for the whole service tonight."

"Will President Antonov actually attend?" Tessa set her teacup down. "Or is this a publicity appearance?"

"No, I believe he will be there. The service will be late. It's my understanding plenty of security will be present." The ambassador touched the faux-leopard coat collar that matched her hat. Auburn hair framed her face, softening the hard angles. "There is some concern about the whole Chechen attack, but my information says that may have been a couple of disgruntled rogue whack-jobs instead of an organized threat."

Chase's face showed no emotion. Sam took a delicate nibble of something on a cracker then leveled a warning gaze at Tessa, sending a message to keep her mouth shut. Was Darya not keeping the ambassador informed?

"I hope this isn't one of those long, drawn-out services where we have to smell incense and body odor for hours on end."

The ambassador's flippant tone irritated Tessa. It was a Christmas service after all.

Chase decided to pull up a chair between her and Bonnie. He focused all his attention on the ambassador, letting his eyes roam her face with a warm gaze and narrow smile, which she returned in a flirtatious manner.

Tessa learned early on the ambassador wasn't shy about liking men who could either help her politically or entertain her physically. If they were a mixture of both, all the better. She'd made comments about Captain Hunter on several occasions, indicating an interest. Apparently, he picked up on her interest and planned to follow through.

An overwhelming urge to gag at the thought of them being together only solidified her realization Chase was not the long-term relationship she craved. He came across as being interested, and caring for her, but to commit to anything other than a roll in the hay was probably not on his radar. Her thoughts suddenly raced toward Darya Roman Petrov.

CHAPTER ELEVEN

The air, cold and crisp, reminded Darya Petrov of his homes in Montana and the rooftop of the world in Afghanistan. He missed both. For the last year, his heart had remained frozen with regret and loss, after leaving Tessa behind in the States. The enormous guilt she felt for hiding their relationship from her husband, Robert, confused and frustrated him. Her religious beliefs prevented her from divorce. Then there were the children, both hers and the ones they'd brought to the United States. He wanted to become a father again.

He would have died in a confined place like prison. In order for him to remain free, he agreed to sell his soul to Enigma. That was the only way to make plans to rescue Tessa from herself and give her the life he knew she desired. This time Captain Hunter would not be able to circumvent his plans. Soon, if all went well, the Army captain would be history along with Robert.

He offered a slow smile as he stared at the Cathedral of Christ the Savior. Taking a deep breath, he walked across the bridge over the Moskva River. Services would soon begin for the people who continued to flock inside to worship their God of deliverance. Taking another deep breath, he locked his fingers in front of his body then exhaled slowly as he scanned the street nearby. The highway along the riverbank, leading to the church, remained crowded with approaching cars.

Two limos moved with the flow of traffic that slowed with the layer of new snow. Ambassador Finley would soon arrive. He wondered if she was irritated at the congestion and complained to her driver. Would she be exasperated about the lateness of the worship service? In the year or so since they'd met, he'd come to know that the woman took care of herself before others and demanded things go her way rather than to the rhythm of time and place. The thought of her possible frustration pleased him.

Standing on the bridge meant his presence would be visible to anyone who felt a need to know his movements. The man following him the previous evening had to be one of General Oblonsky's men. Knowing a nearby car with someone interested in his activities was enough for him to never let his guard down for more than a few seconds. Darya narrowed his gaze, as if by doing so, he might be able to penetrate the vehicle. Even at this distance, he could feel the general watching him, letting the hate well up inside him. Their relationship continued to deteriorate.

A nod to several of the president's protection detail let them know he would be joining the president and his family for services. In spite of his more Asian appearance, he managed to blend in with the throngs of people by keeping his head down. After all, the people of Siberia often came here as did the people along the Mongolian and Kazakhstan border. Border populations tended to be of several cultures and worlds. This had always played to his advantage.

The opulence of the cathedral took his breath away in spite of having seen it numerous times over the last year. It created a sense of standing in the presence of God. He'd never fully embraced religion but found a kind of strength through the spiritual realm it evoked.

Besides an overabundance of spunk, this had been what drew him to Tessa. She'd radiated strength through her faith in spite of having lost her memory. When it returned, her conscience gave up her heart's desire—him. He respected that kind of devotion but hated the outcome. The Robert problem soon would be solved, providing a path of surrender to him, once and for all.

He joined the presidential family waiting to enter off to one side. The smell of incense and burning candles teased his senses until he spotted the picture of the Christ. It was the kind of painting that wherever you moved, the Christ's eyes followed. It had always unnerved him. Tonight, he glared back, feeling judged for what he planned to do in the coming days.

A grim-faced priest dressed in gold robes stepped up and motioned for the president to follow. There was no excitement over his attendance. The government over the last century had not been a friend to the church. In recent years, the church had experienced a resurgence of freedom thanks to Mikhail Gorbachev. Now it was considered an unofficial state church, drawing people back into the fold without fear of persecution, especially since President Antonov's wife attended services each week, and he joined her at least once a month.

Solemn-faced worshipers patiently waited for the service to begin. Everyone remained standing, some with heads bowed in prayer, others casting curious glances around them, perhaps, like him, both inspired and fearful of the heavenly scenes and saints on the walls framed in gold. The heavy carpets spread across the complex tile designs throughout the sanctuary, possessed the power to overwhelm the humble servants of God with their intricate beauty.

He pondered again how this must be one of the reasons so many flocked to the early church, hoping to get a glimpse of their own future heavenly reward. The mosques he'd attended in Kabul, Afghanistan had the same effect on him as a child and later in life when he'd returned to his birth country.

A side door opened quietly, the gush of cold air causing the myriad of candles to flicker like tiny dancers. Two young men he knew to be Marines from the American embassy entered with Ambassador Bonnie Finley on their heels. Compared to the throngs of people crowded together in simple clothing, her black leather coat and fur hat gave her a kind of elegance that radiated importance. She turned back to slip an arm through that of Captain Hunter who had already started his security scan of the premises. The two women behind them followed, one also doing a security scan, and the other staring up at the walls in awe at the beauty.

Tessa. Dressed in a simple brown coat, with an ivory shawl over her head, she resembled many of the women gathered to worship. He watched her eyes grow round with the wonder the elaborate art dedicated to her God. Blonde curls fell down her forehead, and he could remember how they felt when twisted through his fingers on a cold night in the Pamir mountains. Buried desires rose seeing the look of holy distraction in her gaze.

They headed his way, intercepted by one of the protection details to be led to the president's group of guests. Together they joined the ring of worshipers. The ambassador stood behind the president and pulled Captain Hunter closer to her side. The Marines, one next to her the other behind, somehow represented security. Sam stood on the other side of the captain. Darya watched him glance over his shoulder at Tessa who still gazed at the surrounding art until one of the Russian security detail politely came to her side and spoke to her respectfully. A look of confusion crossed her face just as the captain turned around and responded to the man.

Darya had no doubt the captain quizzed him about moving Tessa to the front where she could see the service clearly. As she was led forward, the captain zeroed in on him, standing off to the side where he'd waited with the president.

The two warriors locked glares. The captain was a formidable opponent both in strength and cunning. This he admired more than he cared to admit. But Tessa would be one fight the captain could never win. He'd see to that.

He couldn't resist a smile as he squinted to see her through the crowds and enjoyed knowing the captain had already lost control of the night. The service began as he walked toward the president's entourage. Instead of standing next to the presidential family, he nudged his way down next to Tessa and stared straight ahead with his hands folded in front of him. The crowd jostled for better positions. She stepped closer to him until their arms touched.

Darya turned to the woman with the blue eyes, now staring up at him. He dropped his hand to touch hers and felt her fingers slip between his. When her face brightened, he squeezed her hand and received a smile.

In that moment, the world stopped being a terrible place to live. Tessa was finally here with him, the first step toward forever. When she broke her gaze to watch the procession of priests moving to the inner circle for the service, he took in her simple beauty a few seconds longer. Captain Hunter appeared to be on the verge of a stroke. This time his glee could not be contained before turning back to the service.

The time dragged on with the smell of incense and candle wax wafting through the cathedral. The president's little boy grew restless and escaped his mother to wiggle toward Darya who grabbed him up and whispered in his ear. The child nodded before laying his head on Darya's shoulder with a new calmness that drew a sigh and a nod from his exhausted mother. Tessa patted the little boy's back then met his gaze. The love they shared for a child in Afghanistan came flooding back to the tribesman and when her hand touched his that rested against the child, he hoped she remembered, too.

The service concluded when the midnight hour arrived, but the choir continued to sing. The crowd waited respectfully, and the little boy rousted up with a yawn before resting his forehead against Darya's cheek.

"You were a good father, Darya. That has always been one of the things I love about you." Tessa dared put her arm around his back momentarily before withdrawing, blushing.

He leaned toward her ear. "And other things, too, I hope."

She smiled then diverted her gaze to the floor. "Yes. Definitely other things."

"Who is she?" Yuri stared at Tessa.

"My good friend, Yuri. What do you think?"

"Pretty. Is she going to be my aunt?"

"Soon. Very soon." He hugged the child and set him down.

"What did he say?" Tessa asked. "My Russian is still evolving, it seems."

Darya laid his hand on the child's head. "My nephew thinks you are pretty."

The child looked at her with large round eyes. She chuckled and said, "Blagodaryu vas." Thank you.

"Go to your mother, Yuri." He set the child on his feet and gave him a little pat. "It is time to go home."

The boy staggered toward his parents when the sound of gunfire broke out.

~ ~ ~ ~

Earlier, Chase Hunter removed the ambassador's arm from his as he watched Darya Petrov slip in beside Tessa. The plan must have been to separate her all along. Did he also plan to remove her from the cathedral to keep her out of his influence and reach? Was it possible he had become a double agent and now worked for the Russians? Or did Tessa mean so much to him, he wouldn't chance jeopardizing the relationship, knowing she might bolt.

The man remained a worthy adversary and, under normal circumstances, he might admire the Kyrgyz tribesman who had tried to kill him. When Darya reached down and took Tessa's hand, he felt the reasonable side of him evaporate, especially when she smiled up at him with absolutely no fear or regard for her safety.

Clearly, she had forgotten what the man was capable of. He'd kidnapped her and gotten so inside her head, Chase now doubted her ability to resist the tribesman's lies and half-truths. The Enigma psychiatrist had called it Stockholm syndrome, where the captive comes to believe and respond to their captor's propaganda.

When the president's son ran to Darya, he wondered again about the family dynamics and if his allegiance toward the president would circumvent his loyalty to the United States. The man was a tribesman, so family and community meant a great deal.

At one point, Sam placed a firm hand on his and whispered, "Easy. You need to trust her."

He nodded and tried to relax.

The service concluded before he realized he'd missed most of it, stewing about the possibility of Tessa falling for the tribesman's baloney. He also worried whether the scientists could be rescued in time and if the cloaking technology could be taken out of the hands of the Russians.

"I thought this would never end," Ambassador Finley said through gritted teeth. "What was that?" She jumped toward Chase and caught his arm.

"Gunshots." He shoved her toward the Marines. "Get her out of here," he ordered.

Screams echoed off the lofty ceiling of the cathedral against the cries of frightened children. The throngs of people became a swell of panic, trying to move toward the exits. He pivoted to see the president's son bolt to the open area toward the center of the sanctuary, with Tessa hot on his heels. Seconds earlier, he thought he'd seen Darya move the child toward his parents when the first shot rang out, close enough he jerked the president down and lay on top of him and then scrambled up, looking around with a stricken expression.

He heard Tessa call out, "Yuri!" Another shot rang out as she reached the child.

Both Tessa and the child went down.

Chapter Twelve

People stampeded in the chaos. Bursts of automatic gunfire blended with the cries of terrified worshipers. The echoes bounced around the holy space, triggering a kind of confusion that drove people to hysteria. Several older people stumbled and fell, slowing the masses enough to prevent a speedy escape. There were people who tried to assist the elderly, only to find themselves jostled and knocked down, forming human barricades of squirming bodies.

Tessa gasped for breath. When she hit the floor, a sharp kick in the side knocked the wind out of her. Yuri cried out and grabbed the front of her coat to pull in closer for protection. Her mothering instinct kicked in, and she rolled on top of him to protect him from being shot. His warm breath against her neck gave a sudden rush of remembrance of her own children and a fear she might never see them again.

"God have mercy," she whispered before giving Yuri a kiss and stroking the back of his head. She tried to comfort him in English because every word of Russian she'd learned had flown out the window. His whimpers buried in her chest, she dared raise her head to scan the area and heard a familiar voice.

"Tessa!" Chase yelled. In a split second, he kneeled next to her, running his hand down her arm and hip, before trying to roll her over. "Are you hurt?"

Hearing his voice gave her strength. She shook her head but found she couldn't move with the little one hugging so tightly, and she had pain in her hip from hitting the floor so hard.

"I think I'm okay. Can you say something to Yuri to calm him down?"

Tessa had learned what Chase was capable of when he'd taken care of her own children a few weeks earlier. They adored him, even after he had been hard on them. In the end, he'd admitted the experience was one of the best times of his life.

He leaned over her, adding a layer of comfort to an overactive imagination. Another burst of gunfire filled the area. Someone jumped over them, and Chase covered her and Yuri's prone position with his bigger body. All the while, he spoke rapidly to Yuri and patted his back.

"Tessa, it's clearing out. We're sitting targets out here in the open." He pried Yuri from her arms. "Move it."

How he managed to pull the child up into his arms while standing and reaching down to jerk her to her feet remained a mystery. The Russian delegation was being led out by security with Yuri's mother screaming and reaching back toward them. Darya emerged from the group and barreled toward the Enigma agents with his gun drawn. He pivoted and surveyed the area around them to find a way to get them to safety. Once he reached their side, he eyed Yuri then Tessa.

"We're fine," she yelled above the screams.

"Come with me," he ordered Chase. "Can you keep Yuri safe, or do you want to take point?"

"Go. I got him. You know how to get us out."

Darya nodded and moved like the hunter and warrior she'd known in Afghanistan. His nearness gave her reassurance things would be okay. Although Yuri tried to go to Darya, one word from him and a nod toward Chase settled him down quick enough. Whatever the differences between the two men were, when it came time to act, they were on the same page.

Several other armed security men rushed out to assist Darya by surrounding them and walking backward as they entered a corridor. Doors opened to reveal the president and his wife, along with the American Marines and Ambassador Finley. The Marines had their weapons drawn and stood in front of the ambassador. The bored expression she usually wore had been replaced by fear.

When the door closed behind them, Yuri's mother pushed past her protection detail and surged toward Chase who set the child down. He ran to his hysterical mother and was scooped up and held so tightly, Tessa wondered if the child would be able to breathe.

She stepped toward Tessa, blabbering so fast, she couldn't possibly understand. But she assumed by the smile and tears, she was being thanked for protecting her child. Chase received a similar reaction, only he could respond in fluent Russian. Finally, she turned to Darya and gave him a kiss on the cheek and a one-arm hug. His expression never changed, but he offered a nod of appreciation.

Tessa realized the whole ordeal had taken less than a minute. Why did times of crisis always seem to go into slow motion?

Darya turned to Tessa and moved a step closer. Chase did likewise.

"Are you hurt?" Darya touched her cheek. "I will have the doctor come when the cathedral is secure."

All of a sudden, Tessa felt tongue-tied standing between two warriors who thought their job was to protect her from herself. Before she responded, Darya locked gazes with Chase.

"I think I'm okay," she said, drawing his attention back to her. One corner of his mouth lifted in a grin when he touched the back of her now-exposed hair then withdrew.

"I would feel better if you at least talked to the doctor. Okay?" When she didn't answer, Chase answered for her.

"When she fell, I think she may have cracked a rib. Probably should x-ray her arm, too. I saw several people stumble over her."

Darya's bottom lip jutted out, and his stare became hooded. To her surprise, he responded in a civil tone. "It was a dangerous thing you did, Tess-sa." She noted how he broke apart her name as he'd done in Afghanistan. It warmed her heart to hear him speak this way. He switched to Pashtu. "Thank you for sacrificing yourself to save little Yuri. As usual, you thought nothing of your own safety." He switched easily back to English when he spoke to Chase. "And I am grateful to you as well. It would be a great tragedy to lose the ones you love."

Tension rose between the two men.

Chase responded in Russian. Darya clapped his lips so tight, his jaw clenched over and over. Thankfully, Sam and the ambassador joined them, creating a needed distraction.

"I will find out what is going on." Darya met Tessa's gaze as if waiting for her to respond.

"Let me help, Darya." Chase spoke as calmly as Tessa had ever heard him.

"Not a good idea," he said slowly and glanced over his shoulder. "They need to believe you're only a visiting professor."

Chase accepted the decision with a nod.

"You and Sam can better serve by staying here and protecting the president and Tessa."

The ambassador's face soured when Chase spoke. "You're right. Do what you have to do. But I want a report what this was all about."

Darya sobered and stiffened. "You are not in charge here, Captain Hunter. Remember your place. I would hate to demonstrate your lack of importance to me and to this mission."

"Please be careful," Tessa warned.

Darya's face brightened, but he quickly turned away and joined several members of the security force at the door. He ordered the men left behind to barricade the door as caution guided him into the fray.

~ ~ ~ ~

"What exactly happened?" Ambassador Finley demanded when she moved toward President Antonov.

He had been with his wife and child when she intruded. At a snap of his fingers, one of the women in his group came to guide Nadia to a chair before he turned back to the ambassador. "We are working to find out. My people are very capable. We will leave as soon as we know it is safe to do so. Until then, you should be patient. You are under my protection."

"Thank you, Mr. President. I know you are doing your best to bring this to a conclusion. I pray there are no fatalities and that no one is badly hurt."

He turned to the other Americans standing nearby. "Introduce me to the others."

"Of course." The ambassador introduced them in Russian, but the president chose to speak to them in English.

He reached out to Tessa and lifted her hand to kiss before holding it with both hands. "Thank you for saving my son. My wife and I are eternally grateful to you. If there is ever anything, I can do for you, I am at your service. You showed bravery in the face of danger and possible death." He mumbled a command to his security standing at his elbow then addressed Tessa again. "My nephew mentioned you may have been hurt. I want my physician to check you over. If he thinks you need further attention, I'll see that it is taken care of immediately."

Moments later, the physician who kneeled by Yuri stood, patted him on the head, and offered reassurance to his mother before joining the president.

The president moved to Chase. "And to you, Dr. Hunter, I am grateful you were able to get to them in time. You, too, were in great danger. I suspect your military training helped greatly." He hoped to see a reaction from the American that he was aware of his military experience, but got none.

"Thank you, sir. You are welcome. Did you see if anyone was wounded?"

"I'm afraid they ushered us out quickly. I could hardly tell what was going on. My first concern was for my son, and that is all I focused on until my people forced me in here."

"I understand."

The ambassador butted in on the conversation with Chase. "President Antonov has assured me we will be brought up to speed as soon as possible."

The president glanced at her and frowned. "You will receive the appropriate information as it becomes available." With his curt response, he turned back to Tessa. "Please. Let Dr. Molotov do a quick preliminary exam."

"Thank you, President Antonov. Your concern and kindness is appreciated."

He nodded to the Americans and joined his family.

"Well that was rude." The ambassador fumed at being snubbed by the Russian president.

Tessa leaned in to her. "I think you've just been put in your place, Bonnie."

"Humph," she snorted. Not to be outdone, she squinted and looked down her nose at Tessa. "You seem to have endeared yourself to yet another egomaniac with an overabundance of testosterone. How do you do it?" Her lips narrowed in a snide smile. "Oh wait. I remember." She shifted her focus to Chase, followed by a glance over her shoulder to where Darya had exited. "And to think, you didn't even have to sleep with President Antonov."

~ ~ ~ ~

General Oblonsky smiled, watching the chaos unfold first inside, then outside the cathedral as throngs of people poured into the streets. Ambulances, special forces that were never far from the president, police, and the fire department had all responded quickly. The flashing lights splitting the darkness, screams, and the wounded being assisted, brought him a kind of arousal he usually experienced with a woman he chose to punish.

He'd waited in a hotel room not far from the Kremlin and enjoyed the video feed from different angles. After making copies to view again later, he'd make sure they were erased. He rewound the feed to see how the president fared and discovered how the American woman managed to save the president's spoiled brat. Thanks to Darya, the president remained safe and secure. It appeared that the American named Hunter also had some hand in the rescue.

No matter. Chaos bred confusion and indecision.

CHAPTER THIRTEEN

Russian security formed a protected circle around the president after his family was tucked safely inside the black armored car he'd arrived in for services. A line of soldiers surrounded the car as the president moved away. The chaos had been replaced by news outlets from around the world. First responders still attended the injured, lights flashed, and intermittent sirens blasted the crowds then faded into the distance.

President Antonov ignored the questions as he pushed toward the fallen, now on gurneys. The injured had bandages on their heads, collars around their necks, and a few had blood splattered across their coats or faces. A few of the reporters were allowed to follow if they kept quiet.

Darya remained at his side, constantly scanning the surrounding area for trouble. The attack took him by surprise. He didn't know who had stormed the services. Whoever it was, they weren't part of the original plan. These guys meant to do damage.

The president stopped next to an injured elderly woman who held the hand of a little girl. Darya guessed the woman to be her grandmother since the child kept calling her babushka and clung to her crying. President Antonov patted the woman's arm and told her she'd get excellent care then ordered one of his security details to make sure she was a priority.

When she shook her head and tried to get off the gurney to comfort the child, Darya lifted the child in his arms. "Do not worry, little one. Your grandmother will be taken care of."

The child sniffed and nodded.

"President Antonov, may I go with this woman to sit with the child until her family can be reached?"

Before he stopped speaking, another guard stepped forward to take his place.

"Of course." He turned his attention back to the woman. "Will that make you feel better? This is my best man. I trust him with everything, even my own child. I will take her to the hospital myself. She can ride with my wife and son." The woman smiled and told the child to be good. A hush fell over the crowd at the kindness of President Antonov and man with the appearance of a tribesman from another time and place.

In spite of being dressed in his best, Darya still looked rough around the edges. His eyes gave him a definite Asian vibe that a science fiction writer might describe as robotic. There were those who had called him Rasputin because of his almost mystic influence on the president. Others had made the family connection with Darya's father but knew nothing about his mother from the endangered Kyrgyz tribe of Northern Afghanistan.

The president moved on to the next injured person with Darya carrying the child who had slipped her arm around his neck. He continued to speak softly to her, especially when an injured person appeared gravely wounded. He would turn her away and point to something in the sky or ask her if the Snow Maiden would be coming to see her.

"I know the Snow Maiden. Do you want to meet her?" A spark of interest brightened her red face streaked with dried tears. She hugged his neck and nodded happily.

Darya quietly gave orders to a soldier standing nearby to get the American woman who had saved Yuri. He anticipated the action would create problems with the high-and-mighty Captain Hunter. He would deal with that later. For now, he'd enjoy a few more moments with Tessa.

In a few minutes, he saw Tessa emerge from the church. The

captain followed on her heels until he was stopped by two guards. Darya locked gazes with the man and knew his days were numbered before the captain tried to kill him, or maybe it would be the other way around. Either way, Tessa soon would be his wife, once and for all. There would be nothing Captain Hunter could do to stop him.

~ ~ ~ ~

"Why not come back to the embassy and discuss this new development along with the plan to get those scientists out of the country?" The ambassador laid a hand on the captain's arm as he exited the limo. Samantha had already slipped out and hurried toward the door of the hotel.

Captain Hunter stared down at her gloved hand and considered her real intention. Maybe if the circumstances were different and he hadn't already felt distracted, he might consider having a nightcap and see where the evening led them. He'd tangled with Bonnie Finley long ago and taken a pass. She was a conniving, self-centered woman who would do anything to advance her career or status to gain favor with President Austin. After Tessa told him Bonnie Finley was the reason she finally let her guard down around Darya, and that the woman had convinced her the only way out of Afghanistan was to play nice with the tribesman, Chase could barely stand to breathe the same air as the woman.

"I think"—he removed her hand from his arm— "I'm going to call it a night."

Bonnie leaned back against the seat, mouth pooched in disappointment. "If you think Darya is going to bring Miss Do-No-Wrong back to you at a decent hour, then you are delusional. He plans to make sure you're out of the picture."

"We'll see about that." He put one foot outside the car.

"He's already taken care of Robert. Not that she ever got over that brawny outlaw after returning home from Afghanistan. Honestly"—she pushed her hair away from her face— "I don't know why she kept pretending all was well between them."

"What has he done to Robert?" Chase did feel concern. The children were still at home, with the neighbors' and grandparents to help. But if Darya put plans in place to kill him, he wanted the folks at Enigma to intercede on the family's behalf.

"Nothing he didn't deserve." She started to smile. "Oh, get that look of revenge off your face. I know you have a thing for Tessa. I bet you've thought of pushing him off a bridge or giving him a poisoned apple yourself." A puff of discontent escaped her mouth. "For the life of me, I don't know why she attracts such lethal characters who adore her."

"Maybe because she is innocent and such a good person. People like us are the worst of the worst. Lots of skeletons and regrets in our closets."

She arched an eyebrow. "Speak for yourself. I regret nothing. Being a good person is highly overrated. Don't get me wrong. I'm indebted to Tessa. She saved my life. I'll never forget how she…" Her face went solemn before she stared down at her hands. "If it weren't for her, I'm not sure where I'd be."

Chase scooted the rest of the way out of the car and bent down to peer inside. "Most likely dead. I'm not sure even the Taliban would have gotten much pleasure from you. Good night, Ambassador Finley. Thanks for the ride. We'll talk soon."

~ ~ ~ ~

"You didn't have to walk me in, Darya. I would have been fine." She unlocked her door and wondered if Darya expected to pick up where they'd left off a year ago. He'd barely spoken on the way to the hospital or the ride back to the hotel. Besides taking her hand in his, he'd made no move to show his intentions until the car came to a stop and the driver stepped outside.

He'd explained the child thought she was the Snow Maiden, causing her to be smitten with wonder and nonstop chatter. Darya interpreted for the two of them. By the time family arrived at the hospital, the child had curled up in Tessa's lap and fallen asleep. She could hardly stand, needing Darya to pull her to her feet when the mother relieved her of the child. With a whisper to one of the guards who had accompanied them, Tessa found herself inside one of the black limos she'd ridden in earlier. It wasn't until they pulled up in front of the hotel, and the driver stepped outside, that the realization of being alone with the tribesman hit her.

"I should go in." She pulled her hand free of his. "I'm sure everyone will wonder where I went."

"We need to talk first. It is safe in here to speak." He turned on soft music to add a layer of noise. "If you don't mind"—he slipped an arm around her shoulders and moved his lips close to her ear—"I will whisper in your ear." But he took the opportunity to move her hair and nibble at her ear before kissing her neck. Goose bumps, followed by heat, spread across her neck and face.

She laid her hand on his chest. "Did you have anything to do with that tonight?"

"No." He pulled back inches but remained close enough she could feel his breath on her face. "This is what I know."

When he finished, Darya turned to examine her hair and face. He smiled before taking her hand and placed it inside the front of his open coat, on his heart. When she stared at her hand then up at him, her heart lurched inside her chest. This man loved her. She had nothing to fear from him. Gently, she did the same with his hand to her heart.

The movement was slow when he pulled her into his arms and held her. For the first time in a long time, Tessa felt safe, loved, and even treasured.

He pulled away and smiled. "My heart has been empty for too long. It is good you are here."

"I think I am an insurance policy to be honest. Enigma doesn't trust you."

Darya continued to smile and laid a hand on her cheek. "And what about you? Do you trust me?"

"Not completely."

This time his wide mouth let out a laugh. "Still trying to escape from what you truly feel." She wanted to protest, but, once more, he pulled her into his arms and silenced her words with a deep passionate kiss she melted into. "I will take you inside now before I decide to carry you off where we can be alone."

Once upstairs, Tessa pushed her door open. "Good night, Darya."

He nodded and stepped back, only to smile at her, narrowing his eyes to slits. Pivoting on his heel, he disappeared down the hall toward the stairs.

~ ~ ~ ~

The restaurant had closed several hours earlier. Only the hotel desk in an adjoining lobby remained open. Chase sat in one of the overstuffed chairs that appeared to be a holdover from an English manor. He sat calmly but prepared to confront Darya Petrov when he came downstairs. A fleeting thought the man might have intentions of spending the night with his junior agent toyed with his temper.

They lingered in the car long enough to give him the urge to drag her out onto the street. Tessa wasn't able to distinguish between being led to slaughter by a man or being manipulated by a man who played both sides against the middle. Darya could influence her with one look, one touch, as proof tonight, when he took her hand before little Yuri joined them. The expression on her face sickened him, and that ache in his chest had returned.

When they had spent time in Africa, it felt they finally had formed a personal connection. Had he been wrong? To keep her safe, he'd assigned her to desk duty for months. This formed a rift between them. A few weeks ago, he'd babysat her kids, turning the experience into one blunder after another. She'd kissed him for the very first time in what felt like appreciation. Finding out she and Robert were separated gave him hope that soon he could carry out his plans and let her know how he felt. Now, once again, those plans were put on the back burner. National security demanded he focus.

Darya hurried down the stairs and stopped when he saw him sitting in expectation. He strolled in and dismissed the clerk, who resembled a scared rabbit as he escaped. Chase guessed even he had heard that this man might be related to President Antonov.

He scanned the rooms and waited. A stubborn tight jaw flexed enough to alert Chase the man would not be intimidated. Raising his chin, he stared at Darya, feeling his nostrils flare in anticipation of a power play.

Chase rose slowly from his seat. "Never take one of my people again without letting me know what is going on. Understand?"

"I understand more than you think." Darya's bottom lip protruded slightly as he stared at Chase with a narrowed gaze.

"That was risky. What if I'd refused to let her go with you to the hospital?"

One side of Darya's mouth turned up in a smirk. "I guess it's a good thing you didn't try that."

"I want to clarify what side you're on, Petrov." Chase let the Russian name roll off his tongue like a slur. "You leave a lot to be desired in the trust department."

Darya pulled back his shoulders as he cocked his head to the side. "Then you'd better stay out of my way and stick to the plan."

"Tessa isn't part of the plan."

He turned to leave. "Tessa has always been part of the plan, Captain Hunter. It's just no one told you." Chase reached out and grabbed his arm. It was quickly shaken off. "Don't ever touch me again. I'll do my job and you do yours. Whatever happens between me and Tessa is none of your concern. If it were, you would never would have allowed her to come to Russia." He moved out into the darkness. "Good night, Captain Hunter."

~ ~ ~ ~

General Oblonsky hurried down the hospital corridor with several hospital personal who led the way to where the president and his family prepared to leave for home. He removed his hat and gloves and dismissed his security to wait outside.

"Mr. President. I came as quickly as I heard. Are you and your family all right?"

"Yes. We are fine. It was good of you to come."

"I, along with our intelligence people, am looking into this. We'll find these terrorists and put a stop to these attacks once and for all."

"There will be a meeting in the morning. Be there." The president lifted Yuri into his arms and kissed his forehead.

"Of course, Mr. President. Is there anything I can do for you now?"

"Thank you, old friend, but my nephew took care of everything."

The general nodded and stepped aside for the family to pass, hoping his resentment didn't boil over before he could let off steam.

CHAPTER FOURTEEN

After talking to Director Clark in Sacramento and informing him of his concerns for Robert's safety, Chase felt better about Tessa's husband not meeting with an untimely death. The neighbors, who unbeknownst to Robert also worked for Enigma, had the children for the evening. The director reconnected with his lead agent and assured Chase nothing was out of the ordinary, except for one thing: Tessa's husband was with another woman.

"When I get back, I'll deal with him myself. The dog."

Director Clark promised to put his people on protection detail. He also made it clear he didn't trust Darya Petrov as he read over the information about the evening's unexpected attack at the cathedral.

"Everything okay?" It was Samantha. She joined Chase in the hotel lobby. "I heard Tessa come in. Darya didn't stay long. You have anything to do with that?"

He shook his head.

"She's waiting for us. I think Darya filled her in what they know for sure."

Chase stood and took a deep breath before dragging his hand across his face. He needed sleep. "Let's get this over with." He was moving toward the stairs when Sam grabbed his arm and pulled him back. "She's not with him, Chase. You know that, right?"

"I'm not so sure."

Three taps on Tessa's door brought her straight away. She let her teammates in and went to pour them a cup of hot tea she'd brewed from the service cart in the corner of the room. She had been surprised to see Earl Gray tea and had enjoyed it each night before bed. Each took the cup and let the steam rise a few seconds before taking a sip. Tessa couldn't help but notice they never stopped watching her. The sinking feeling she was about to be chastised, forced her to throw out the information she'd gotten from Darya.

"What did the hospital say about your x-rays after the president insisted you needed them? " It was Chase.

"Might be sore in the morning, but other than that, I'm fine." He showed no signs of relief, so she continued. "The attack was unplanned at the church. He didn't know anything about it. President Antonov is furious his family was in so much danger along with the Christmas worshipers."

"Didn't know Darya or the president were such religious men," Chase quipped.

Tessa shrugged. "From what Darya told me, his father also attended services before ending up in Afghanistan where he met his mother. I know when they came to America, they attended services at a local church in Montana. Suspects have been rounded up already and, apparently, they are Chechens who took advantage of the staged attack the other night. There has always been bad blood between them and the Russians."

"Yes, but not much activity in the last couple of years." Sam set her cup down on the cart and sat in the one comfortable chair. Tessa couldn't help but think she resembled a spoiled feline when she crossed her long legs and leveled a look of contempt toward her. "Why now?"

"I've been wondering about that myself. Maybe they took advantage of the news from the market attack, conflict in religious beliefs, large crowds. Not enough to go on now. Darya also said we need to be extra vigilant because it wasn't uncommon for them to target foreigners in Moscow. It wouldn't be hard to figure out we were visitors since there has been plenty of interest in us at the university and a new ambassador. Maybe they were after her to get the US involved."

"That it?" Chase asked.

Tessa caught the impatience in his voice. "No. Nine fatalities, twenty injured, two of those critical, five serious, and the others may have already been treated and released. I went straight to the hospital when I left the cathedral." She knew he wouldn't ask, but his protruding bottom lip and military stance, as if he were inspecting the troops, spoke volumes. "One of the children needed extra attention since her grandmother was injured. She rode with the president and his family. Darya convinced her I was the Snow Maiden." She smiled. "She calmed right down when we met. Isn't that sweet?"

"Adorable." Tessa wondered how he could force the word to sound like an expletive.

"And you rode with her?"

"No. I rode in another car."

"With Darya?" Sam inquired with a snarky grin on her face.

Tessa bounced a glance off both of her teammates before speaking. "Yes, with Darya and two other guys who resembled bouncers who had been forced to stand naked outside of a bar in Siberia. What's the problem?"

Chase unexpectedly laughed under his breath, drinking the rest of his tea before handing the cup back to Tessa. "You have a flare for comedy."

"We don't trust Darya is all," Sam added.

"Well I do. And honestly, isn't that all that counts here? You need me to keep him reined in, not that he needs it. He's sticking to the plan. He also said we've got to be ready to move on this. The scientists are going to test the cloaking device within the week. After that he isn't sure what will become of them."

"Why? Surely, they aren't planning to kill them. They are too valuable," Sam asked.

"They've had to work side by side with other Russian scientists all this time. Now the Russians know almost as much about cloaking as our guys. Morale is low. Two are sick. Darya visited a month ago and got word to them Joel Sandy is still alive."

"How did he do that?" Chase inquired.

"A number of the locals work there, too. Food prep, cleaning, maintenance, those kinds of jobs. Joel Sandy married a local and now has a child. A relative is no fan of the government and delivered the message."

"How has he stayed off the radar of the government?" Chase inquired.

"Darya says the little village took him in. Kind of a culture all their own in that part of Russia. Anyway, he has been sending messages weekly to not give up, sabotage what they can, and to be sure they are ready to leave at a moment's notice."

"Is Joel planning on leaving?" Sam asked.

"About that? He wants to bring his family when it's time to go."

Chase's frown deepened. "No."

"You can't ask him to leave his wife and child behind. He's the reason we know about all this. If it weren't for him, we'd still be years behind on the cloaking project and the Russians would be ready to roll it out, scaring the rest of the world half to death. Can you imagine what they plan to do with it to further their dream of once again being a superpower?"

"Our time at the university ends in a few days. The guest lectures drew a lot of interest considering they were closed for the semester. Notice anyone a little too interested in you?" Chase shifted his attention back and forth between the two women.

"I got a marriage proposal," Sam admitted with a shrug.

"How many does that make for you?" Chase chuckled.

"I've lost count. Apparently, he thought we'd make beautiful babies."

He refocused on Tessa again.

"All I got was an offer for a free cup of coffee and a pair of leather boots." She wrinkled her nose and twisted her mouth to appear a little disappointed.

"The groups who want a freer and more open Russia don't strike me as people who would shoot up a church."

"I agree." Tessa returned the cups to the cart and came to sit on the edge of the bed. Chase tended to fill a room with his imposing presence. Moving away from him kept her levelheaded. "Anyway. That's all I got." She raised her hands as if surrendering. "Oh. And I will say that President Antonov was extremely caring for the people he visited and introduced me several times to the patients. He picked up the little girl and hugged her several times."

"It was a show," Sam groaned. "You're such an innocent. You'd think by now you could read people a little better."

"You mean like now because I'm sensing you're a little jealous he didn't take you with them instead of me."

Sam stood gracefully and moved toward the door. "Touché, Tessa. Nice to know you're developing claws to go with that chubby kitten look you love to sport." She laid a hand on Chase's arm. "See you in the morning." She glanced over her shoulder at Tessa. "If not sooner." And she was gone.

Tessa sighed. "Winning Sam over is a full-time job for me."

Chase stood like a military statue. "At least she hasn't tortured or killed you. I'd say that was as warm and fuzzy as it gets with her."

"Is that supposed to make me feel better?"

"Not my job to make you feel better or help you make friends."

Tessa slowly turned her head toward him and stood. "What's eating at you? Are you angry I left with the president without your permission? What choice did I have? It would have been rude."

"I don't want Darya manipulating you when we're trying to get this mission accomplished."

"He isn't. There was a child who needed calming, and he thought I could help."

"Convenient."

"You know, if you have a problem with Darya's methods, I suggest you take it up with him." Tessa stormed toward the door and was opening it when he reached over and pushed it shut. She glared up at him and realized his temper was about to flare once more. In spite of his mood, she still desired to please him.

He moved her away from the door. "He is up to something. I can feel it."

"And what would that be? You think he's going to turn on us and fall in with the Russians for good? Or maybe steal your thunder and get all the glory for a successful rescue? Oh, or worse, do exactly what he's supposed to do and he comes out the hero!" she growled.

He stepped toward her, and she fell back against the door in alarm. A chill creeped up her spine at the anger in his black eyes.

His breathing grew labored, and his nostrils flared as he stared down at her and pressed ever so lightly against her body while reaching around her back. Pulling her forward, he opened the door.

"I'm not always going to be around to pull off another Tessa rescue. And honestly, I'm getting a little tired of doing it. Follow my orders, now and always, or give me your resignation when we get back to the States. As to you and Darya, I'm starting to think you deserve each other." With that, he pushed her aside and left.

~ ~ ~ ~

Carter Johnson checked over the instrument panel on the Russian Yak-40 designed in the 1960s. It was the world's first turbojet for local airlines. This one had seen better days and needed some TLC. In recent weeks, he'd worked hard to see it was safe enough to fly. Strangely enough, these planes didn't have a luggage section, but he couldn't imagine they'd need one anyway. The cargo he'd be carrying was the human kind if all went as planned.

CHAPTER FIFTEEN

Darya entered the president's residence. He slowly unbuttoned his coat and removed both it and his hat before handing it off to one of the attendants following silently behind him. This was not unusual to be given the silent treatment by the staff. The whispers hinted that he was Rasputin incarnate, influenced the president too much, and had enchanted little Yuri. It didn't help that his Asian facial features and darker skin gave him a sinister vibe.

None of that mattered. The less they knew about him the better. It meant others kept their distance, and their distrust kept them guessing. Most of the time, he was spotted standing statue still, with little to no expression, near the president and his family. The two men who shadowed him were never far behind and made sure the curious didn't get too close.

A guard standing at the entrance of the president's quarters snapped to attention when Darya approached.

"Please let the president know I've returned."

The guard nodded and slipped inside the room then quickly returned.

"He requests a moment to speak to you."

Darya pushed past him and entered to see the president on the phone. He waved Darya a seat, but he remained standing. It was an old habit. Always be ready to bolt if necessary. Although the president was his uncle, it didn't mean he was safe.

The president hung up.

"What a night." He nodded toward the phone. "That was General Oblonsky with news. The Chechens they rounded up are sticking to their story about not being involved in the market invasion the other night."

"Which is true. But they are not innocent. Bombmaking materials, as well as maps, schedules, and objectives were found in their homes. Only the two of us know the truth of the other night. It was only to be a show of how fast we can respond. Tonight was a whole different matter. Innocent people got hurt."

"General Oblonsky assured me heads would roll over this. Russians need to feel safe at such gatherings. I am pleased he was able to find answers so quickly."

Darya's frown deepened. "I'm sure he is taking pleasure in extracting the information."

"Yes. He does take his job seriously in the most peculiar ways." He waved a hand in the air. "The media will be given an update tomorrow; it was a criminal element that led to uncovering a more sinister plan."

The president sat down in a nearby overstuffed chair. Nadia enjoyed all things English since she was educated there and loved to purchase such pieces for their residence.

The dark bags under his eyes alerted Darya to his uncle's state of mind. "Please, Roman. Sit down for once. Tonight, we are just family."

"Of course." He sat in the chair across from the president and wondered if this was the kind of furniture Tessa would want in their home.

"I still plan to move forward with the party tomorrow night. The Federal Protection Service is adamant about canceling it until they are sure the threat has been neutralized. But this recent bit of news should put their minds at ease."

"Are Nadia and Yuri resting?" Darya never spoke her name in public and rarely did in private. This felt like a good time to be familiar.

"Nadia insisted on having Yuri sleep with us tonight. The boy kicks like a mule. But"—he shrugged—"we were both shaken at how close we came to losing him. A few kicks does not seem so bad."

Darya smiled. "Yes, sir."

The president gave a tired smile. "And the woman, Tessa Scott, she is quite brave. I think you might have your hands full with that one."

"You have no idea." The image of her in Afghanistan, standing up to the Taliban, riding with him, the wind in her hair and telling him what a ridiculous Romeo he was, still made him smile. She wasn't what he expected to find in the most dangerous part of the world. Yet there she was, abandoned and sick but with the claws and fight of a snow leopard.

"Are you sure you want to go through with this?"

"I am."

"The US government will cry foul, and her friends may intercede to stop you."

"Not if you send them home."

"Why would I do that?"

Darya leaned forward in his chair. "Because they are American spies."

~ ~ ~ ~

Tessa slept fitfully after the confrontation with her teammates. Nothing ever went her way when it came to impressing them. Sam leveled enough doubt as to her judgment to put a kink in her self-confidence. She always felt like a limp rag doll after suffering her onslaught of questions, snide comments, and interrogation tactics. Maybe if she didn't want her approval so much, it wouldn't make any difference. But Tessa admired the brutal nymphomaniac who would have been perfect to star in an Amazon-women-rule-the-Earth kind of movie.

Then there was Chase. Just a few weeks earlier, he had been all smiles after taking care of her kids and saying how it changed his way of thinking about settling down and starting a family. He kept telling her what a great mom she was and claimed it was the best Christmas he'd ever had. She'd given him a picture of the kids after their night of mischief together, along with a round-trip plane ticket to visit his family on the Rez in North Carolina. She hadn't told him Robert showed little interest in mending the broken emotional fences between them.

It sounded too much like she wanted him to be her backup plan. By the time he'd returned after the holiday, she was on her way to Russia. When she'd met up with him, that warm, fuzzy expression had morphed into the hard-nosed captain she first met a couple of years earlier.

Deciding to pace herself, she got up and made coffee. The day ahead would be nonstop activity, thanks to Ambassador Finley committing the team to several parties at other embassies. Since facing Sam and Chase wasn't high on her list of things to do, she took her breakfast in her room. There was time to call home and check on the kids and hear all about school, hockey practice, and ballet lessons. At least their cheerfulness raised her spirits. Even Robert sounded halfway pleasant and interested in what she might be doing.

After dressing in slim black pants and a long ivory sweater, she added boots and pearl earrings and a matching bracelet. She glanced in the mirror and decided to pull her hair up in a twisted knot on her neck. Grabbing her coat and purse, she headed downstairs and noticed the embassy limousine parked outside with two guards in attendance. Voices from inside the restaurant met her when she entered.

"There she is. Sleeping Beauty decided to join us." The ambassador smiled.

Chase and Sam nodded a greeting and didn't weigh in on her absence at breakfast. There was little doubt they'd checked to see if she'd made other arrangements that morning, so she didn't try to explain. Both agents dressed business casual, but Sam had added a shimmering blue scarf and diamond earrings to glam herself up, not that she needed it. The woman could have worn a piece of burlap and walked the runways of Paris. Her boots with the three-inch heels would force many men to stare up at her, one of the things she loved most.

Each of them held a china cup of tea, and the waiter quickly brought her one. Since it was the four of them in the restaurant, his attention to detail added a feeling of importance. The ambassador quickly reviewed their itinerary for the day, explaining they would begin party hopping at the Swedish Embassy and conclude at about five at the Canadian Embassy. She planned to drop them off to prepare for the evening party with the president and reminded them it was a formal event.

"I rented everyone clothes for tonight. I doubted you packed appropriate attire for such a party. I'll send a car for you around eight." She shifted her gaze to Tessa. "Please be ready on time."

Tessa let the insinuation slide by her. Instead of responding, she yawned and covered her mouth before smiling. "Oh sorry. Kept waiting for Sleeping Beauty's Prince Phillip to join me. Finally gave up and came down here to find Maleficent." She appraised the ambassador coldly.

"Maybe we should go," Sam sighed then covered a smothered laugh. She slipped her arm through Tessa's and squeezed as they moved toward the door. A few whispered words of encouragement reached her ears. "There is hope for you yet, Betty Crocker. Well played."

~ ~ ~ ~

Svetlana helped Carter with some last-minute checks on the plane then adjusted her headset.

"You sure have been on the phone a lot." Carter taxied the plane out onto the runway. The airfield was in the middle of nowhere, but that was true of most places in this part of Russia. How Svetlana managed to commandeer the plane to here was a tribute to her influence and cunning.

"I called in a few favors," was all she had to say about the matter.

"Let's see what this bird can do."

"The beginning of a new life for me."

"When we get to the States, I'm treating you to one hell of a vacation." Carter grinned. "You'll have the gratitude of the American president."

"I'm counting on it."

~ ~ ~ ~

The intermittent streams of sunlight breaking through the clouds caused the snow to sparkle. Only a few people moved about the streets and traffic remained light. It was a day for families and friends to enjoy each other on this special Christmas holiday. She spotted a variety of media trucks still doing live interviews, and soldiers patrolled nearby.

Staring out the window, Tessa was slightly aware of the conversation between the other three, something about Christmas back home, favorite presents, family, and stockings. Ambassador Finley appeared to be dominating the conversation with an occasional comment by Chase. Tessa found the scene amusing since he had not experienced many holidays firsthand.

Sam mostly offered a, "That's nice," or "I bet that was fun." Tessa understood Sam stopped listening when the car door slammed shut. If the truth be known, she was probably devising a way to poison the ambassador with an Eastern concoction that couldn't be traced. This actually gave Tessa a reason to smile at her own reflection in the window glass.

The Swedish embassy was already crowded with other dignitaries. According to the ambassador, several guests were powerful oligarchs. Tessa moved about to survey the rooms of festive décor while carrying a glass plate of finger foods. She was drawn to the windows and stared out into what appeared to be a concrete courtyard furnished with little more than a few benches. If they had not been laden with fresh snow, it would have been void of character all together. Yet she stared with a rising pain of homesickness and a loss of a part of her. She wasn't sure what.

"Missed you at breakfast," Chase spoke calmly as he turned to give his glass to a waiter, along with her empty plate. When she didn't answer, he continued. "The info about moving the scientists turned out to be correct."

Tessa turned to him and frowned.

"I know you said as much—"

"No. I didn't say it. Darya did. You didn't want to hear it since it came from him." She shifted her gaze back outside.

"That doesn't mean I'm wrong about him being up to no good." He stepped up to the window and turned around to face her. "I want you to be careful. You believe the good in everyone, and that isn't the way the world works."

Tessa turned away, "And that would include you, Captain

Hunter. Let me do my job. I'll take care of Darya. You take care of everything else."

CHAPTER SIXTEEN

President Antonov kissed his wife on the back of her neck and admired her reflection in the mirror. The royal-blue gown from Paris fit her like a glove and made him desire her slim figure. Together they tucked Yuri in and gave instructions to the nurse to watch him closely since he'd been running a low-grade fever all day. Hand in hand, they entered the vast reception area and welcomed their guests.

He spotted Darya, aloof and eyeing the crowd suspiciously. The president wondered again if the evening would offer up more trouble than he bargained for by separating the American woman from her friends. The plans were not completely known to him. Darya insisted it would be wiser if he could claim innocence as to his nephew's extracurricular activities so he could express outrage and vow to assist the American ambassador.

The other part of the scenario would be justified after the revelation of evidence the American teachers were spies. There would be a volley of threats and insults by the American president. He anticipated getting a little down and dirty with the man. Darya had provided enough evidence to keep the spooks at Langley in denial and the Secretary of State busy tattling to other heads of state, for everyone to miss the bigger surprise in Siberia. Rolling out the superior military planes with cloaking devices would soon be on display for the world to see. Then he would decide how best to take back what Russia had managed to lose.

"Ambassador Finley, you are radiant tonight." The president held onto her hand with both of his and passed her off to his wife who made small talk. "Aw. We meet again, Dr. Hunter. I understand you served in the military. That would explain your show of courage last night." They shook hands briefly.

"Yes. Still in the reserves. Can't seem to get it out of my system," he responded with a crooked smile.

The president shifted his attention to the tall Dr. Samantha Cordova. "And you are also lovely tonight, Dr. Cordova. You may require protection from the way you are turning heads of the other gentlemen in the room. Let me know if you require anything at all." The woman flashed a brilliant smile that made even him, a little lustful.

"Thank you, President Antonov. But Dr. Hunter," she said, taking his arm, "is my guard tonight."

He nodded and reminded his wife of how Dr. Hunter intervened at the cathedral on their son's behalf. Next came Tessa Scott, a quiet flower who, in her own way, lit up the room. The president wondered if the blue eyes had been what first got Darya's attention or was it the pale delicate features that made her favor the Snow Maiden. The ivory gown and pearls exuded an elegance from a bygone era. This kind of beauty only improved with age.

"Dr. Scott," he said, lifting her hand to his lips. "I'm so glad you could come on such short notice. My son may insist on seeing you tonight. He told his mother this morning you were not the Snow Maiden but Elsa from the Disney movie, Frozen."

A soft laugh escaped her lips as he released her hand. "I would be happy to see Yuri. No lasting effects from last night, I hope."

"Not at all. He ran a low-grade fever today but seems to be fine now. His mother and I would be grateful if you'd speak to him."

"And the little girl? Any word about her and the grandmother?"

"The child is safely home, and I got word that the grandmother went home this morning."

Tessa beamed. "What a relief."

The receiving line was beginning to back up. "We'll talk in a while. Enjoy the evening." He grabbed her hand and kissed it once more.

As she moved on to his wife, he caught the eye of Darya and nodded. The man began to circle like a lion on the hunt. Tessa paused only a moment to say a few words and politely moved on, tagging along after Dr. Hunter who appeared to be dominated by the ambassador's undivided attention. Together they approached the bar, where Tessa split off and was stopped by a few college-age students who had been planted in her classes.

The president approved of her, and that wasn't true of most Americans he met. He wasn't sure she'd be a good match for his nephew, who was more than a little rough around the edges, having spent half his life in Afghanistan and the other half in the mountains of Montana. Darya assured him he would not force the American teacher to do anything against her will. Since she had saved his son, he now felt a certain obligation to also protect her.

Inwardly he smiled as he listened and nodded to those who paid their respects. Maybe he had it all wrong. Maybe it was Darya who needed protecting. That would be a pleasant twist of fate to witness. What was the old saying? Still waters run deep? Could be an interesting few days ahead.

* * * * *

Music played, masking the conversations Tessa couldn't understand. She identified a few Russian words, but stringing them together was impossible. There were other languages. She recognized the people she'd met earlier in the day who greeted her, thankfully, in English. Between exchanging comments on the stunning decorations and the abundance of food, Tessa pretended the smile plastered on her face was genuine.

Although she was excited to be invited to the president's party, the day of nonstop activities had begun to weigh on her. Added to that was the continued doubt Chase carried about her work. Did he expect her to resign when they returned home? Was that what he wanted? Did he have so little faith in her ability to hold up her end of the mission, he needed to second-guess everything she said and did? Did he hate Darya so much he believed he would betray them?

He had softened at her gift, and she felt he wanted to tell her something. The anger had evaporated between them for a moment, and things almost felt friendly.

The music in the next room called her to enter where tables were adorned with spectacular centerpieces of white roses and gold ornaments. Each chair had been wrapped in glittery toile and silver ribbons. The faint smell of incense, blended with the flickering pine-scented candles as she moved through the artificial white trees, standing tall and thin throughout the room. It gave her the feeling of being lost in an enchanted forest. With the waiters dressed in brocaded costumes trimmed in velvet and guests in beautiful gowns, Tessa wondered if she should have brushed up on doing the waltz. She definitely wanted to do that here. Tonight. With a person who could sweep her off her feet.

She felt a person at her elbow and turned to see Chase Hunter, tall and handsome. His skin looked even darker in this low light. Her heart raced when his eyes met hers.

"I forgot to tell you how beautiful you look tonight." She felt a smile spread across her face. "But I always think that. I'm sorry, Tessa, for doubting you." He offered his arm as Ambassador Finley walked past with the Swedish ambassador toward their table. "I'm afraid when it comes to you, my heart gets in the way of my brain. Don't give up on me."

Tessa slipped her hand through his arm and nodded. "You and I have become too complicated to continue this way. I'm hurting right now with the mess going on with Robert."

"I'll give you space and time to sort things out. But, Tessa—" he laid his free hand on hers where it grasped his arm—"you mean more to me than you know."

They moved toward their table where several people had already been seated. Sam now had the Iceland ambassador, who resembled a Viking, in tow. Just her type, Tessa guessed. The thought slipped in and out of her mind about where her teammate would be spending the night. Before they were seated, Tessa whispered in Chase's ear. "I want to know now, Chase. You need to stop toying with my affection. You use it like a weapon against me."

Chase sighed and stared straight ahead. "I know. And I will but not here. Not with all this hanging over our heads." She realized he was surveying the room for trouble, inconsistencies, people who didn't belong and, probably, Darya.

"Chase," she said as he pulled out a chair and sat down next to her, leaning in close, "I don't believe you."

He jerked his head up in surprise. "We'll talk later."

Tessa jerked her chin up in defiance, determined not to fall victim to his smooth talk and reasonable arguments to remain friends even though there had been something brewing between them almost from the moment they met.

CHAPTER SEVENTEEN

"Everything is ready." A man wearing a dark suit spoke quietly into Roman Darya Petrov's ear as he watched Tessa walk to her table on Captain Hunter's arm. Darya wondered what the captain whispered in her ear once she was seated. Whatever it was, she didn't appear to appreciate it from the way she jerked away. Those moments would soon be over for the arrogant captain. "Sir?"

"Yes. I heard you. Thank you." Darya nodded to the friend he'd made after moving to Moscow. Like him, he was of two worlds: the old maritime life of the north and the new Russia. The country was now led by a former KGB agent who promised democracy but continued to hold a tight grip on how everyone should think and respond to his policies.

"We have moved the woman's things to the monastery, and the priest is waiting."

"And the others?" Darya finally tore his gaze away from Tessa across the room to focus on the security guard standing stiff legged.

"A plane is standing by at the small airfield forty kilometers away, north of here."

"And radar?"

"Not a problem. A storm over the Gulf of Finland will work to our advantage. Our friends in Arkhangelsk are waiting to say exactly when they watched the plane crash into the White Sea. By the time the weather clears enough to send in a search party, it will be a recovery mission. The sea ice is constantly moving there."

"It might be spring before a serious search is carried out?" Darya refocused on the table where Tessa and her friends were being served dinner.

"Very possible. And the American ambassador? What do you want to do?"

Darya gritted his teeth. He'd never liked Bonnie Finley. Manipulation and deception filled her DNA. The only person who impressed her was herself. In spite of those being her better qualities, he had to admit, she continued to protect Tessa from anyone knowing about what happened in Afghanistan and with him. Without her, the ambassador would have died a horrible death. Maybe there was a spark of decency in her black heart.

"We need her. Do nothing. Her outrage will be enough to give me the time I need to do this." He pursed his lips together tighter with the image in his mind of what he wanted to do to her. "If she is a problem, I will handle it. Understand?"

Darya waited for a nod of approval from the bulky man before he moved away to attend to his duties. He found President Antonov still greeting guests and quietly mentioned that dinner was being served. The president smiled and waved to the those still waiting to shake his hand. Someone on his staff stepped forward to invite the remaining guests to find their tables for dinner.

"Thank you for the rescue. My face was about to crack from smiling so much." The president groaned as he took his wife's hand.

She smiled at Darya. "And we both know he doesn't smile all that much. He is out of practice."

Darya tried to appear pleasant but could barely raise the corners of his mouth. "I think it runs in the family."

"Yes. I believe you. Except I noticed you smiled a great deal when the American woman came to the hospital to wait with the child. Do you know her?"

The president glanced at Darya and raised one eyebrow before he addressed his wife. "You are a nosey woman. Leave him alone,

Nadia. Roman, be sure Dr. Scott goes to see Yuri. I promised him she'd make an appearance."

This order made Nadia smile mischievously.

"Of course, Mr. President."

"And," Nadia chuckled, "don't feel you must hurry back."

~ ~ ~ ~

The tinkling of china and crystal blended with the low rumble of conversations Tessa couldn't understand. Chase could see the interest and confusion in her blue eyes as she listened intently, absorbing the cultural geography of the night. She lived and breathed this kind of atmosphere. The candlelight danced off her gold hair that fought to be free from being pulled back into a braid then wrapped into a bun.

Russia could be such a fairy-tale place with magical onion-domed monasteries and landscapes a woman like Tessa would love. Maybe, just this once, he could forget who he was, and let go of all the rules and regulations that had dictated his life over the years. He thought about the ring his grandmother had left him. The ring of forever and a day. When would forever begin for them?

People began to leave their tables and move toward the open area provided for couples who wished to dance. Even Bonnie Finley took the arm of the Canadian ambassador and soon danced among the other partygoers. Chase reached over and took Tessa's hand, drawing her attention to him.

"May I have this dance?" He smiled. "I don't think we've ever done that."

Tessa stared at him straight-faced, but her eyes softened. She rose and moved to join the other dancers. It was a more upbeat tune, but he managed to not embarrass himself as he twirled her around then pulled her in closer, slipping his arm around her waist. She laughed unexpectedly; the kind of childlike laugh that always made him smile. Carefree. Innocent. All her optimism about life spilled out when she laughed. Those times when she grew snarky, combative, and batted her eyelids rapidly, indicating she was lying, caused him to second-guess everything. If he wanted her to love him, he needed to make a move and soon.

"Tessa," he whispered in her ear. He tightened his hold on her.

In that moment she looked up into his eyes. "I love…"

"Excuse me." It was Darya. Tessa immediately took a step away from Chase, but he didn't release his hold on her waist.

"I want to dance with you, Tess-sa." He smiled broadly at her, and her cheeks flamed. She glanced back to Chase with hope in her eyes.

"Chase? Did you want to say—"

He withdrew his hand from her waist. "It can wait."

"Yes. I believe you." She turned back to the tribesman who'd saved her in Afghanistan.

Darya lifted Tessa's hand to his lips and kissed its softness, never taking his eyes off hers. Chase watched helplessly and witnessed a change come over her. Whatever hold Darya had on her began to appear as the emotional tentacles he'd captured her with in Afghanistan drew her away from him.

He felt helpless to stop him. Darya was part of the plan to retrieve the scientists and destroy the cloaking technology before the Russians activated it on a full scale. The relative importance of his loyalty to country vs. what he witnessed now began to blur. Darya took full advantage of the celebration to lure her away from him so he couldn't protest and bring down security on him. He was up to something. But what? As long as important dignitaries and the president were present, Chase hoped Tessa would be safe.

If anyone could handle Darya, it would be her. Her instincts were good enough to suspect a betrayal—that is if she didn't succumb to some blind obsession she'd once had for the man. The Enigma psychiatrist had diagnosed her with Stockholm syndrome. Once Darya kidnapped her, she became convinced he was the good guy out to save the world. Chase showed up and took her from him, back to the United States, where he made sure she got the help she needed to forget those days on the rooftop of the world.

The slow music gave Darya the opportunity to pull her in tight against him. It pained him to see them staring into each other's eyes. Clearly, the man was taken with Tessa, and he wouldn't let any harm come to her. He glided her around the dance floor as if she were Cinderella at the famous ball in the fairy tales. The rough edge of the man had been replaced by a smooth operator. People began to stare at them, and he had to admit they made an interesting couple.

His heart sank. He'd waited too long. The truth was, he'd lost her.

"Stop staring." Sam walked up next to Chase and embraced him in a dance stance. "She's fine. You treat her like a child."

Chase relaxed and put his arm around his agent. "She kinda is a child at times."

"Well, that isn't the way you stare at her." She glanced over at Darya. "And he certainly doesn't think of her that way. Stop underestimating her."

"Since when are you her champion? The two of you drive me crazy sometimes. Are you friends or what?"

Sam stepped in closer and nibbled his ear, causing him to jerk his head away and scowl at her. "I'm not sure. Remember, my dear captain, that one of these days we're moving all the men underground and using you for breeding purposes." She offered him a feline smile.

"I imagine you would have a line waiting for the privilege." The woman remained a temptation, but he'd discovered a long time ago she would be poison. But, right now, it felt like the exact thing he needed. "What happened to the guy who could be Thor?"

"Turns out he's gay and not interested."

"Doesn't know what he's missing." He smiled.

"That's exactly what I said." She stroked the back of his neck with her fingers.

A commotion began at the rear of the large hall. Crowds parted, those still at their tables pointed and smiled as they watched a small child moving quickly between the tables with two security men in hot pursuit. It was Yuri, the president's son. He appeared to be searching for someone.

Chase strained his neck to get a better look when he heard Darya snap out a command in Russian.

"Boy! Come here."

The guests stopped on the dance floor, along with the music. Yuri peeked around people's legs until he spotted Darya. He ran to him at top speed. Darya bent down and lifted him into his arms but said nothing. The little boy hugged his neck tightly then extended one hand out to Tessa. She moved in to pat his back and let him run his hand up and down her face. Whatever he said to her made those around him laugh.

"He wants you to sing a song from a kid's movie, I think. I do not know this."

Tessa laughed softly. "I bet I can find one he'll enjoy."

Darya nodded to the boy, causing him to clap his hands before he laid his head on his shoulder.

"Darya, he feels really warm. I think he has a fever." She stroked his face and carefully put her hand on the back of his neck. "Let's take him to his room. Does he have a nurse or nanny to watch over him?"

"Yes. Come with me." He glanced back at the guests who moved to a slow tune. He caught the attention of Captain Hunter and watched the man's face twist in what appeared to be anger. Agent Samantha Cordova paused to watch them, too. The concern matched the captain's.

As they moved into an adjoining room, the president and his wife joined them. Nadia quickly took the boy into her arms.

"Darya?" the president snapped and touched the boy's head.

"He escaped his caretaker, Mr. President. Mrs. Scott believes the boy has a fever."

Nadia hugged the child, but he resisted and smiled back at Tessa, talking a mile a minute. His mother hugged him and shook her head, making eye contact at the same time with their guest. The boy puckered up his lips, and a tear rolled down his cheek.

President Antonov sighed and interrupted the boy's wishes. "I apologize, Mrs. Scott. My son thinks you are a Disney character who will sing to him. And now he is going to manipulate his mother into asking you to do so. Please." He fanned his hand back toward the ballroom. "You may return to the party."

The little boy wiggled free of his mother, wrapped his arms around Tessa's legs, and stole wishful glances up with pleading eyes.

She kneeled down by Yuri and received a welcomed hug. Darya knew the worst part about this job for her was having to leave her own children behind for weeks at a time. Soon those days would be over. He'd make sure they could be together and not worry about national security or world peace.

"One song, Yuri, then in the bed with you." Tessa beamed.

Darya translated for her, causing the child to land a grateful kiss on her cheek. He stepped back and waited. The child pointed to the ballroom where the musicians were finishing a song. "He wants them to accompany you, Tess-sa. Are you willing?"

"Well, Yuri, I see a piano right over there. Why don't we stay here and I'll sing my favorite Christmas song, just for you, instead of all those people. Okay?" Again, Darya translated for her. The child agreed and led her to the grand piano.

CHAPTER EIGHTEEN

General Oblonsky stood nonchalantly in one corner of the grand room where the American woman interacted with the first family. When he saw that the little boy had escaped his caretaker, he feared his plans might have failed. After listening to their conversation, he thought perhaps having them take the child back to their quarters would be an opportunity to lay blame for the impending accident at Darya's feet. The thought of his undoing gave him pleasure. He took a final sip of his drink before excusing himself.

~ ~ ~ ~

Tessa invited Yuri to sit next to her, which he did with eagerness. Tessa could see the fever in his eyes. She kissed his temple to confirm her suspicions. Her fingertips touched the ivory keys of the antique instrument, aware of the history, amazing musicians, and composers who may have performed breathtaking compositions in this very spot. And here she was, going to play a Christmas song from her childhood. When little Yuri stared up at her with anticipation, she realized, to him, her performance would outshine Sergei Rachmaninoff.

Taking a deep breath while letting both hands play a C scale to loosen up her fingers, she exhaled slowly and paused. There were so many wonderful songs he might enjoy, but a running list seemed to gravitate toward how she felt about running away and shedding the last ounce of self-respect she still possessed. Darya moved closer to the piano and watched with a kind of childlike curiosity, too. Another thing he didn't know about her. Stealing a glance over her shoulder, she noticed Chase and Sam push into the room, but they kept their distance.

She played a few bars, fumbled over the wrong notes, and stopped. She became aware other guests had meandered into the grand room. The notion *you could hear a pin drop* began to have new meaning to her. When she swallowed, it sounded like a loud gulp.

Yuri laid a hand on hers and smiled. She couldn't understand him, but by the encouragement in his tone, she felt he might be saying, "You can do this."

Once again, she let her fingers run along the keyboard, loving how familiar and dear the song felt to her. Her grandmother used to sing it to her when she was Yuri's age. There were three verses, and the notes fit her alto voice perfectly. When her own children were babies, she'd sung it to them to quiet and comfort restless moments. The thought of them, their love and mischievous faces, gave her courage. By the second verse, the only person Tessa focused on was the little boy with a magical smile. When she finished, applause broke out. She startled when Yuri hugged her.

"Oh my gosh," she said, returning the hug but staring at Darya who wore a kind of worship on his face as a smile spread across generous lips.

"Yuri says he is going to marry you." Darya patted him on the head. He spoke to the boy, who nodded before scooting off the bench. He cast glances toward Darya then Tessa and spoke in a serious voice. "I think I have serious competition."

"Yuri," Nadia said, taking his chin in her hand. "Time for bed. How did you escape your nurse?" She stared at Darya who frowned and took the child's hand. Whatever he said to her, she nodded and whispered to her husband.

"Darya, can you take care of this for us? I'm to speak in a few minutes. I want to know how he slipped away from the nurse and why she isn't tearing the place apart searching for him."

"Yes, sir. Come, Yuri." Darya extended his hand to Tessa who grasped it quickly and let him tug her to her feet.

The president bowed slightly toward her. "Thank you, Dr. Scott. Your voice is lovely. Once again, I'm appreciative of your kindness to my family."

"Of course, President Antonov. My pleasure."

He took his wife's hand and led her toward the gathering crowd and motioned them to reenter the hall where music had once more drawn people to the dance floor. "Go ahead, Darya. Duty calls. I'll wait for you."

Darya glanced toward where her teammates remained rooted and turned back to her. "It would please me if you came along. Yuri may go to bed a lot easier if you do."

Something inside her gut warned her that Darya used the boy to separate her from Chase and Sam. But she was tired of being the good girl all the time. The one who always repented at screwing up and taking too much time to make a decision forced her to admit being reckless felt a lot safer at the moment, maybe a new kind of freedom. She caught Chase's attention and wished he'd made the right decision earlier. When he raised his chin and frowned at her, she turned back to Darya.

"Let's go."

Yuri grabbed her hand and jumped along as she followed Darya out into the vast expanse of the palace. Tessa did not look back.

Watching them disappear from the music room, Chase rubbed that spot on his chest that always ached when Tessa drifted in and out of his life. Seeing her with Darya caused anger to enhance that pain. Once again, the tribesman had outsmarted and outmaneuvered him to get what he wanted. Tessa. "Excuse me, Mr. President."

"Yes?" He followed the captain's line of sight. "Oh. Not to worry. My son is rather insistent he be tucked in by Dr. Scott." The devilish smile spreading across his face gave Chase pause. "Not to worry. Colonel Petrov will take good care of Dr. Scott."

"Colonel Petrov?" Chase felt stunned.

"Yes. My righthand man was recently promoted." He chuckled

and moved away. "You'll excuse me. I have duties to my guests."

Chase and Samantha stepped aside and let the president and his wife disappear into the throngs of guests.

"Promoted?" Samantha fumed. "He's getting a little too chummy with the president, if you ask me."

"A doting uncle. Maybe that's all it is. I'll give it ten minutes before I go looking for them," he snarled and led his agent back onto the dance floor.

~ ~ ~ ~

Yuri faded fast as they entered the president's wing. "The boy says he's sleepy." Darya patted the boy's head.

"Where is the nurse? Maybe she can give him medicine for the fever," Tessa quizzed with concern. "Shouldn't his nurse have looked for him?"

"Yes," he snapped.

When they turned the corner at the end of the hall, Darya saw the nurse kissing and fondling the guard. He released Yuri's hand and stormed toward the two. They immediately released each other and fell back against the wall.

"Colonel Petrov," the soldier said in shock. "I'm-I'm."

"Shut up." Darya growled. "Why weren't you watching the boy?"

The nurse's eyes fell on him as Tessa approached. Yuri opened the apartment door to stagger in, turned, and motioned for her to follow.

"In a minute, Yuri."

The nurse fussed and was stepping inside the apartment when Darya grabbed her arm. He spoke in Russian so Tessa couldn't understand. "I'll deal with you when I'm through here."

Darya slowly turned back to the soldier, who had fear etched on his face. "You are dismissed from your post."

"But, sir, I—"

Before he could finish, Darya punched him in the gut, collapsing him onto the floor.

Tessa covered her mouth, suppressing a gasp.

"Give me your weapon. Now."

The soldier staggered to his feet and humbly surrendered his weapon.

"How dare you put the president's son in jeopardy."

"I thought he was asleep, sir."

Darya turned to Tessa. "Go inside." When she hesitated, he leveled a glare that could melt steel. She slipped inside and closed the door.

Tessa feared what would happen to the young soldier, but, knowing Darya, it would not be pleasant. She knew firsthand what he was capable of, having lived with him in the mountains of Afghanistan. He'd stolen her heart under those most dire conditions and circumstances.

Tessa pivoted to hear a child's sniffle coming from the next room. On tiptoe, she eased closer to see the nurse slap Yuri. In a couple of rushed steps, she pulled Yuri behind her, away from the nurse who should have protected him. The woman reached for him, but Tessa slammed her fist into the woman's jaw, knocking her to the floor.

"Never do that again," Tessa growled. She had no way of knowing if the woman could speak English, but her meaning rang clear.

The boy wrapped his arms around the back of Tessa's legs. Gently, she turned around and kneeled down in front of him, and he fell into her arms. She held him tight and kissed his face several times as he snuggled in close. When he stiffened in her arms and stepped back, she looked up to see the nurse had risen to her feet and now pointed a gun at her.

CHAPTER NINETEEN

"You silly, silly American. Now, send the boy over to me, and I'll let you go." The woman held the gun steady, her bottom lip curled out in disgust. "I mean the brat no harm."

Tessa reached back as if to reassure herself the little boy remained safely tucked out of danger of a wayward shot. "I don't believe you."

The nurse motioned for Yuri to come to her. Tessa could feel him vehemently shake his head. The nurse spoke Russian to him in a sinister tone. The boy trembled and stepped out from behind her legs, but Tessa pushed him back.

"What are you going to do?"

The corner of the nurse's mouth turned up. "What do you care? You are here only for a few days. The boy will give us leverage with President Antonov. Maybe he will listen to our people in the Chechnya."

"The child has nothing to do with that. Please. Just leave. I won't sound the alarm for a few minutes. There must be another way out."

"There are others who will take my place, when and if I die." Her eyebrows lifted in an amused expression. "Someone more powerful than me will make the world take notice. Even your cowboy president who looks the other way from our problems."

"You aren't taking the boy," Tessa warned.

In that instant, the nurse rushed her and tried to grab the boy. With all her strength, Tessa rammed a knee in the woman's groin, causing her to lower the hand holding the gun. In one fluid motion, Tessa twisted back her wrist, dropping the woman to her knees but not before she fired the gun. The gun hit the floor as the boy screamed. In the far reaches of her mind, she heard the large doors open and footsteps. But the scuffle didn't end.

The nurse, although crying out in protest, managed to snag Tessa's dress and jerk it with her free hand, hard enough to stagger her. When the woman tried to stand up, Tessa threw herself forward to flatten her on the floor. Thanks to her training, which she'd never used, she managed to roll the nurse onto her stomach. When the woman struggled, Tessa banged her head against the floor, followed by pulling her hands behind her back. Blood poured from what could have been a broken nose.

A hand pulled at her shoulder. Tessa looked up into the eyes of Darya, who helped her to her feet. When the woman pushed up, Darya slammed a leather boot to her back.

"You'd best stay down." Darya's growl brought to mind a hungry pit bull who hadn't been fed in a few days. The soldier from the hall handcuffed her and added a hard shake, perhaps realizing he'd been taken advantage of.

Several more security types stormed in, guns drawn, but at Darya's command, they holstered them.

Tessa gathered Yuri in her arms and went into another room to be away from the fray. He was burning up and went limp.

"Darya," she screamed. "I need help." His sudden appearance did nothing to calm the panic she felt, even when he took the child from her arms. "He's very sick. Get a doctor now," she ordered. Tears spilled down her cheeks. Nothing was more terrifying than having a sick child and not be able to fix it.

He laid the child down on his bed and shouted orders to the men outside the room. Tessa sat down on the bed to give her own orders. "Run lukewarm water in the tub, if there is one. I'll take off some of these clothes. We've got to bring the fever down, or he may convulse. Hurry."

When he disappeared into the bathroom, Tessa undressed the boy and whispered encouragement so he would focus on her. Once, she thought he tried to smile when his little brow wrinkled as if he were in pain. She scooped him up in his undergarments and carried him to the tub.

"I don't know if it's the right temperature, Tess-sa." Darya's voice now sounded heavy with concern as he touched the boy's head. Was he remembering how he'd lost a son years ago?

Tessa kicked her heels off and handed Yuri off to him. She pulled up the hem of her dress and stepped into the water. She adjusted the temperature by adding more cold water.

"I'm going to sit down in the water. Hand him to me when I say the water is okay." She eased down in the water and reached for the barely moving boy. Darya turned off the water and kneeled down next to the tub. "Drizzle the water on his shoulders, Darya." She locked concerned stares with him. "This will help. I promise."

Darya nodded. Knowing how he loved the boy; Tessa could see the fear in his eyes as he stared at the child. Gone was the ruthless tribesman who'd kidnapped her not so long ago and forced her to fall for his charm and mysterious secrets. Here stood a man, terrified for a sick child, similar to the one who had died in his arms on the rooftop of the world.

"Thank you, Tess-sa," he choked out.

$\sim \sim \sim \sim$

"Did you hear that?" Sam said, stretching her neck toward the foyer that led into the great hall.

Chase nodded and was moving in that direction when several security officers entered into the hall and surrounded the president and his wife. Nadia covered her mouth as one of the men whispered to the couple. They were ushered out with men talking into their cuffs and touching their ear fobs.

"That's not good," Chase mumbled in Sam's ear as if pretending to be endearing. She nodded and slipped her arm through his. "We need to find her."

Security approached another man whose expression sobered immediately. They escorted him out of the room, along with a few others who spoke in excited voices.

"Excuse me." Chase addressed the Canadian ambassador who had been standing next to the man who left with security. "What's wrong?"

"I'm not sure," he admitted. "Apparently, the president's little boy got sick. My friend is a doctor who is visiting me for the holidays. Not sure how they knew that." His voice sounded sarcastic enough for Chase to realize he was being flippant about the Russians nosing around in their business.

"Thank you."

The Canadian ambassador laid a hand on Chase's arm. "Tread lightly. I wouldn't be going out there in search of your friend."

"My friend?"

"I saw the blonde woman in your party leave with one of the president's henchmen. He's a bad one. The president's men stay clear of him. Only General Oblonsky is unaffected by the man's intimidation. People in the cabinet call him the new Rasputin because he influences the president."

"If you're trying to tell me something, Mr. Ambassador, just say it."

He leaned in closer. "You'd best get Ambassador Finley ready to pitch one of her fits to get her way. She's good at that. Then get the hell out of here."

Chase scanned the crowd until he spotted Bonnie Finley making her way toward him. He nodded in thanks and moved away with Sam at his side. The music started up again, and the confusion as to why the president left in such a hurry was replaced by a more festive vibe.

"Something is going down, Chase." Bonnie spoke through gritted teeth and waved pleasantly to a group of people at nearby tables then blew them a kiss. "I don't like it. Where the hell is Tessa?"

"She left with Darya to take the boy upstairs."

"Well, good luck getting her back." The ambassador calmly surveyed the room.

Chase bristled. "What's that supposed to mean? I didn't have a choice."

"It means if Darya gets her alone, our plans are going to implode. I'll do what I can to find where she went."

"Are you saying Darya is deviating from the plan?"

"For all I know, there is no longer a plan. Darya is a loose cannon. I'm not sure what side he's on anymore."

Chase glared at the ambassador. "What are you talking about?"

"The last time we spoke, he was cold and said we could take a page from the Russian playbook once in a while." She waved again at a nearby guest and made a reference to her watch and Cinderella. "Anyway, you'd better get Tessa back with you, or this whole freaking Russian machine will swallow her up and you'll never see her again—including Darya. We need those scientists ASAP. Next week they'll be gone for good."

"Where did that information come from?"

"I overheard high-level Department of Science and Technology guys talking." The ambassador continued to wink and wave to other guests. "They had already consumed enough vodka to sink a ship and were more than willing, with a little flirting and promises, to inform me of how important their work was going to be in a few days. Apparently General Oblonsky and Darya are quite chummy. Where there's smoke, there's fire."

"We're going to find Tessa. Be available and lay off the booze. You smell like a Russian yourself."

"I'll do my job. You do yours," she snapped.

CHAPTER TWENTY

Nadia burst into uncontrollable tears as Darya lifted the boy out of the tub, where Tessa held him gingerly. When he spotted his mother, Yuri reached for her and moaned. Although the bathroom was small for such an audience, he managed to wrap the boy in a towel as water dripped down Darya's front. He carried him to the bed where more towels and blankets were applied.

"I don't speak Russian," the doctor confessed as he peeled back the towels and demanded a thermometer and more room.

"Many of us speak English, Doctor. Please." The president nodded toward the boy. "Help us. We have requested a local doctor, but it will take time for him to get here."

Darya excused himself to find Tessa trying to get out of the tub with a soaking-wet dress. Her hair had begun to curl out of its restraints. He reached in and lifted her out onto the floor then grabbed a towel and wrapped it around her shoulders before staring into her eyes.

"Tess-sa." He pulled her closer and buried his face into her neck. "Tess-sa. I put you in danger. I am sorry."

She returned the embrace and ran her fingers down the back of his head.

"Thank you, for saving Yuri one more time." He touched her hair then held her at arm's length to survey the once beautiful, sparkling gown, now a ruined rag. "You need dry clothes." He stepped to the door and ordered another Russian into action as she began to shiver.

A blue robe soon appeared in the hands of the same guard who had been at the apartment entrance earlier. He was given more orders before Darya shut him out.

"Out of those wet clothes, Tess-sa."

Her eyes widened, and she took a step back, nearly falling into the tub, but Darya caught her arm and pulled her back. He couldn't resist smiling at her shyness, remembering they'd gone through this once before, the first time he'd forced her into marrying him for protection against the Taliban.

"Tess-sa. It is okay. I have held you in my arms naked before. Remember? You are safe here. I mean you no harm." She took a deep breath and lowered her gaze to the floor as Darya turned her around, unzipped her dress, and gradually pushed it down around her ankles. "Do you want me to help you with your undergarments?" She shook her head, so he turned to retrieve the robe and held it up to form a curtain for her.

When she turned around, naked and shivering, she dared meet his eyes. He gently helped her into the robe. Because her hands trembled, he carefully tied the belt. He ran his hands down both arms, feeling the velvety soft fabric.

"Come with me, Tess-sa." He now spoke in Pashtu, the language of Afghanistan. He could see her body relax and the fear vanish from her face. "I have sent for clothes. I ordered hot tea. I must talk to the president in his office in this apartment. Do you still understand all my Pashtu words?"

"Darya," she whispered and fell into his arms. "Yes. I understand."

"To hold you again, Tess-sa…" He let the words hang for only a second, before he kissed her upturned mouth, impatient to continue his plan to get her to safety and on the road to a new life with him.

A tap at the door broke the spell. He answered the door and turned back to her. "Come. I will take you to the office. A fire is ready. The tea should be ready, too. Please." He opened the door wider but did not touch her. She pulled the robe tightly around her neck and stepped out into a crowded room.

~ ~ ~ ~

"What are you doing?" Sam barked. "You can't just pull your gun and hold up the president. This isn't the Wild West, Chase."

"Give me a little credit." He led her out into the foyer. When a security guard eyed them, he pulled Sam into his arms and barely touched his lips to hers. He could feel her relax when he whispered in her ear, all the while running his hand up and down her back. "Let's head upstairs. We'll make it up as we go along if we get stopped."

Sam used the opportunity to get under Chase's skin and planted a hard kiss on his lips. She stepped away and led him toward the stairs at the end of the hall. Security might ignore them with the hint of a romantic interlude. The first-floor rooms were gathering places for a number of guests. The guards turned their backs as Sam continued her cooing and aggressive sexual attention to Chase. When they rounded the corner, out of sight, she turned off the flirting.

They slipped up the stairs and found the elevator to take them to the top floor.

"The president's quarters are this way."

Sam took a few steps backwards to make sure they weren't being followed.

The palace was a maze of halls and rooms, but thankfully their tech people had downloaded blueprints for these areas as well as several other important institutions to their phones in case of emergency. Chase scrolled through his phone until he found what he wanted and showed Sam. She tapped an area and pointed toward the stairs. He nodded.

~ ~ ~ ~

Tessa gazed out the window and realized how it reminded her of the snow globe she bought her daughter for Russian Christmas. She could see St. Basil's Cathedral in the distance. When she tightened her hold on the collar of the velvet robe, the sound of a door opening to the office diverted her attention from the outside world.

Nadia eased into the room, Darya at her side. She moved toward her to lay some clothes across one of the plush chairs. The president's wife appeared to evaluate her from head to toe.

"My English not good. I try now." She glanced back at Darya who stalked like a snow leopard to stand next to Nadia. "Roman will help me."

He nodded solemnly.

She went on, "I want to say thank you."

Her accent was so thick, Tessa found it difficult to understand her words at first. When she glanced to Darya for help, Nadia held up her hand and formed her words slower and clearer.

"You saved my son once again. Roman told me how you protected Yuri then tried to bring his fever down without any concern for yourself or"—she smiled weakly— "your beautiful dress." She pointed to the clothes. "I bring you a few things. It will be enough?"

Tessa forced a grateful smile. "Yuri is a good little boy. You are lucky to have him."

Nadia turned to Darya, who translated. Immediately, her smile widened. Before Tessa knew what was happening, the woman gave her a tight hug, followed by a gentle pat on each cheek. She spoke a rapid litany of words in Russian as she led Tessa toward the door.

"She says she will be forever indebted to you. Whatever you need or want, she can make it happen," Darya told her. Nadia patted Tessa's hair and pushed wayward curls behind her ears. "You have an ally," he continued.

"Hopefully, I'll not need one," Tessa said softly.

Darya spoke to Nadia in Russian.

"Did you tell her that?" Tessa gasped.

"No. I said you are pleased. You need to change into these clothes. Security and the president wish to speak to you. It will only be a few minutes."

Nadia spoke again then excused herself but motioned for Darya to follow her to the door. She wagged a finger at him before glancing back at Tessa.

Darya said, "I leave you now, Tess-sa. Nadia insists. I wait outside the door for you."

After they left, Tessa donned the several pieces of undergarments. She and Nadia were about the same size fortunately. A beautiful ivory lace tunic, embellished with pearls, hung down to the middle of her calves and made her feel like a princess. The long sleeves were sheer from elbow to wrist with an intricate design. The tan leggings were thin enough to be stockings. Her own shoes had been returned undamaged since she had kicked them off before entering the tub. When she opened the door, Darya's expression softened, and he took in a deep breath. He reached out to her then let his hands drop and stared into her eyes.

"Are you ready?"

She nodded and clasped her hands together, rubbing them nervously.

"This will be over soon," he reassured.

"Where are my friends? Ambassador Finley?"

"I sent for them." He spoke in Pashto which always had a calming effect on her.

"I want to go back to the hotel."

He laid his hand on her back to move her forward. "I need to make sure the family is secure before I take you to a safe place."

Tessa halted. "A safe place? You mean the hotel. Right?" A chill crept up her spine as she grabbed his arm. "Darya?"

"Ahh. There you are?" It was the president.

Tessa released Darya's arm and straightened as she bowed her head slightly in respect toward the Russian president.

He took her hand and kissed it. "Once again you are at the right place at the right time."

"How is Yuri, Mr. President?"

"Very sick. The doctor thinks he has Scarlatina. He's covered in red bumps and has a red throat. He thought he should go to the hospital, but we are making arrangements to do everything here since security will be tighter." He stepped aside and motioned for them to follow his security detail. "If you please, Dr. Scott. Let's take this into my work office outside the apartment. Yuri has fallen asleep, and Nadia is hovering like a helicopter. Best that we give them space. I do not want to get on her bad side."

"Of course." Tessa forced a grin at his quip, knowing how it felt when your child was ill. She glanced up at Darya, but his face was solemn and unreadable. He avoided making eye contact.

They stepped outside the apartment and shivered. How chilly the air was here. The nurse had been removed, and security appeared to be cleaning the mess they'd created. She wondered if it was a way to keep the mishap from getting out. The woman would probably spend a difficult night under the boot of a Russian GRU officer. Those guys weren't known for their patience and extracted information quickly when required.

~ ~ ~ ~

Spotting a couple of guards, Chase backed Sam into an alcove where a window looked out over the city. Any other time, he would have enjoyed the lights and decorations. Now all he could think about was Tessa being alone with Darya and what he might be up to. When the voices moved farther away, they slipped out and proceeded down the hall. A gathering of more security in suits talked among themselves. What had them upset?

"Can you hear what they're saying?" Sam glanced behind them.

Chase strained to hear them as he peered around the corner quickly.

"Something about the nurse having a gun and trying to shoot the American."

Sam rolled her eyes and puffed out a show of outrage. "How can one person get into so much trouble? That must have been the cause of the ruckus downstairs."

"And why security ushered the president and his wife out as if they were under attack."

"Anything else?"

"The doctor is treating someone." Chase tried to remain calm. Had Tessa been injured, or perhaps Darya? "Let's get closer. They're going inside the apartment."

They edged closer, holding hands and trying to appear involved with each other. A door swung open unexpectedly, and Chase jerked Sam into his arms where he began to kiss her neck and slide his hand up and down her backside.

A gasp forced him to peek at their audience. Standing next to Darya and several security men stood Tessa.

"Chase?" Tessa breathed with a sigh as her confused gaze went from him to Sam when she stepped out of his embrace. The shock on her face followed by hurt was almost more than he could bear.

"Tessa. Are you all right?" He pushed Sam aside and stepped toward her only to have Darya cut him off. He waited for Tessa to intercede, but the sadness in her face, wondering if it was finding him embracing Sam. Betrayal was a sword that had destroyed her faith in her husband and her worldview. He wasn't sure how much more she could take. "Tessa?" he repeated.

"I-I…" She gripped Darya's arm to force him to let her step forward. "Yes. I'm fine. Yuri is sick."

"Why are you wearing those clothes?"

The president slowly walked to the front of the group with hands clasped behind his back. "And why are you up in my private quarters and where my offices are located? I find that curious." At those words, four beefy security men swarmed forward and grabbed Chase and Sam by the arm. Another one stepped forward and searched them. Unfortunately, both of the Enigma agents had a small caliber gun made with a 3-D printer in an ankle holster. "This is very unfortunate, Dr.—I mean Captain Hunter." He nodded to Darya. "Remove them."

CHAPTER TWENTY-ONE

Security locked the Enigma team inside a holding area resembling a dungeon held over from the dark ages. The only things missing were a few rats, dripping sewage, and the smell of death. The cell did have a flickering lightbulb, enough to help Chase realize there were no windows. No chairs, cots, or facilities. The two women inspected the room as well. How would they fare in these conditions? Sam would deal with it a lot better than Tessa—a woman who thought staying at a three-star hotel without cable and a free continental breakfast was roughing it. Being prissy became more of a hindrance during these kinds of unexpected events.

"Do you have any idea why we just got thrown in here?" Chase demanded as he folded his arms across his chest to take a General Patton stance.

"No." She rubbed her hands together, eyelids fluttering. "And before you ask, I don't believe Darya would have done this to us."

"You mean to you. He would do anything to separate you from us."

"It has to be a mistake."

"Then tell us what the hell happened up there?"

She retold the story start to finish, including the part about getting in the bathtub with Yuri. Chase eyed her from head to toe, thinking she might be a princess from a Russian folktale in that brocade tunic. When she'd first stepped away from Darya, his impulse was to grab her and not let go. That would have been a quick death with the tribesman standing so close, wearing a dark expression that nearly closed his slanted eyes.

"Who was the nurse working for?" he asked. "Chechens?"

"I believe so. Background checks would have caught that. She mentioned something about listening to her people in the Chechnya."

Sam hugged her arms. "Could be part of the resistance. I would have thought the background checks would have picked that up, too. Of course, Russia is a bit behind on their intel capabilities. I never would have guessed this could slip through though."

"Which means she had help." Chase took his tux coat off and handed it to Sam. "Any ideas?" he asked Tessa. "Maybe you could ask your tribesman next time he decides to appear," he said flippantly.

"Go to hell, Chase." Her voice felt he'd been hit with ice water.

He straightened to his full six-foot-one height and glared at her. She'd never spoken to him in that way. When he stepped into her personal space, and she didn't back up, he realized she had truly become an Enigma agent. No nervous batting of her eyelashes, twitching her fingers, or staring at the floor like when she'd begun this journey several years earlier. Her fear of him had evaporated, and he hadn't noticed until this moment. She wasn't a scared little rabbit anymore. One thing she couldn't hide was her anger when her eyes turned violet. It used to amuse him, but now he wondered if he'd lost the ability to keep her reined in.

He stood there several seconds, glaring at Tessa who appeared unwilling to budge. Then the sound of keys in the door, followed by squeaking hinges opening it, caused both women to step closer to Chase. General Oblonsky ducked his head to enter the cell with two other soldiers waiting outside. A thin smile appeared on his narrow lips.

"Captain Hunter."

"General."

The three Enigma agents remained rigid under such a penetrating gaze. He circled them in a slow, calculated stroll before running his baton up Sam's back. She spun and landed a fist to his mouth, hard enough to stagger him backward. He ran his finger through the blood trickling from the corner of his lip and sucked it off.

"It is too bad I don't have time to explore your many delights, Dr. Cordova." General Oblonsky tilted his head before taking a deep breath he expelled slowly. "And you." He moved toward Tessa who took a step back. Chase stepped in front of her and pulled Sam to his side. The general halted and surveyed Chase. "Colonel Petrov told me to be careful around you."

"He should know," Chase spoke through gritted.

"To be honest, I trust him as much as I trust"—the corner of his mouth twitched upward— "you, Captain Hunter."

The general slammed his baton below Chase's chin. He slid it down toward his Adam's apple. Chase grabbed the weapon with a quick snap of his hand and jammed it into the general's gut, followed by shoving him with everything he had into the wall. For a sixty-year-old man, his body was toned and muscled. Before he could get off another punch, the two guards swarmed in and pulled him back with iron grips. He tried to shake them off, but the general lunged forward and landed several blows to Chase's chest and gut. When he pushed back, the general aimed for his knees and slammed the baton several times until Tessa threw herself in front of him, taking the final blow across her back.

The general stopped and turned his attention to Sam. He stepped back and jerked Tessa to her feet then shoved her into Sam.

"What do you want?" Chase choked as he struggled to stand. "We've done nothing wrong."

"From what I hear, you are American spies."

"Lies. We are teachers from a California university," Chase insisted, still trying to struggle free. "Who told you that?"

General Oblonsky turned his attention to Tessa. He reached out to touch her face, but she jerked away. Grabbing her by the chin, he squeezed hard enough to make her wince.

"Leave us alone," Tessa ordered and managed to push his hand away. "I will be sure to tell President Antonov how you have disrespected me and my friends. And right now, I am Nadia's favorite person. Wonder what she'd think if she knew you conspired with the nurse to hurt her son."

The general stepped back to eye her and smiled big enough his eyelids drooped. "Interesting idea."

Chase snarled. "Makes sense. You grew up in the Ukraine and Chechnya, but your father forced you to speak Russian, learn the history, so some day you could get revenge."

"Americans are good at storytelling."

When the general tried to reach for Sam, Tessa stepped in front of her "Leave us alone," Tessa said. "The American ambassador will have your head for this. We're under her protection."

"Yes. So, I hear." He paced while tapping the baton in the palm of his hand. "But perhaps you can be released to her protection by answering a few questions."

Chase managed to break free of the guards but didn't try and move away, knowing that next time they might use enough force to subdue him or even knock him out. "What kind of questions?"

"Roman Darya Petrov appears to have taken a special place in the president's life."

"Aww. Feeling a little left out, General?" Chase couldn't resist a smirk. "Guess Darya stole all your thunder. What do you want from us?"

"Information."

Chase shook his head. "Then you're asking the wrong people. Petrov means nothing to us."

General Oblonsky turned his attention to Tessa, and a crooked smile played across his lips. He touched the area where Sam had split it open and sighed.

"I think maybe Dr. Scott is closer to Colonel Petrov than you think. From what I hear, they plan to spend a few days in the country away from the demands of the Kremlin."

"You are misinformed, General," Tessa said then swallowed hard. Could that be a sign of her being found out or realizing Darya was up to no good?

"I think not, Dr. Scott. Isn't it true that the two of you have a history?"

It wasn't hard to fathom the general had been given instructions to find out everything about Darya when he showed up in Russia claiming to be the president's nephew. Chase didn't trust the direction of the conversation.

"Dr. Scott—" Chase cut in.

"I didn't ask you, Captain Hunter." The general turned to the guards. "If he interrupts me again, please feel free to silence him." When he refocused on Tessa, he tilted his head, his natural frown deepening. "Dr. Scott?"

"He saved me from the Taliban in Afghanistan and helped me get back to the States. I haven't seen him in over a year." Chase could hear the attempt at being stoic in her words.

"You must have made quite an impression for him to be willing to betray the US and keep you here with the help of President Antonov." He shifted his attention to Sam and snarled. "Is she telling the truth, Dr. Cordova?"

"More or less."

"Meaning?"

"Meaning, if I get the chance, I'm going to ram that baton up your ass so far you'll look like a ventriloquist's dummy."

General Oblonsky leaned forward. "I was thinking the same thing about you."

She squirmed under his penetrating gaze.

"No matter," he continued. "This is pointless. You are going home. Tonight."

"Tonight?" Tessa glanced over at Chase. "Yes, Dr. Scott. Your lover, Colonel Petrov, has convinced President Antonov your people are spies. Of course, he protected you, and, with you being the hero for Yuri, the president would never have harmed you or your friends. So instead, he has decided, over your ambassador's loud protests, that all of you must be expelled from our glorious Mother Russia, immediately."

"And we all know how Russia deals with protests," Chase growled only to get another punch to the abdomen.

"Yes. Your country should try it. I think there would be a lot less confusion and more harmony. That whole freedom-of-speech thing can be problematic."

"Especially if you don't appreciate the truth," Tessa dared interject.

General Oblonsky strolled calmly to the door and called to two more guards outside the cell. "Take Captain Hunter and Dr. Cordova to the airport."

"Dr. Scott is going with us," Chase insisted as he tried to break free.

"Other plans are in place for her." He took a deep breath and exhaled. "Colonel Petrov mentioned you might not be in agreement with that decision."

"Be sure to inform the colonel I plan to slit his throat when next we meet."

The general's laugh sounded like a pig squealing. "I almost want to be there to see who wins."

"I won't be left behind," Tessa snapped. "I'm an American citizen, and I will go with them."

"My dear Dr. Scott. American citizenship means nothing to me." He waved his men to move the other prisoners. "I'll be back for you soon." His stare at her drove Chase to try and break free, only to receive another punch to the gut.

When Chase and Sam were outside the cell, the bang of the door shutting and Tessa calling to him broke his heart. If he made it out of this alive, he would hunt Roman Darya Petrov down like a dog and end him. General Oblonsky would be next on his list of things to kill.

Chapter Twenty-Two

A dark cloud of indecision covered President Antonov's face. His nephew stood close by in his usual calm, stoic stance and waited for the information to be digested.

"Are you sure the American intelligence know of the location of the scientists and what we've been up to?"

Darya raised his chin. "Yes. It is only a matter of time before they have proof. They are very good at this kind of thing. You will be blamed and on the brink of war for an act not entirely your fault. You have been led to believe the cloaking device is the answer to all our problems."

"I will decide soon," he said, locking his hands behind his back. "A lot of time and money has gone into this project. I do not wish to think about it now. I have Chechens trying to cause unrest again, American spies snooping inside these halls, and an American ambassador I would love to drop in the Siberian Volcanic Traps. My patience wears thin with her temperament." He took a deep breath. "I'm not sure what President Austin was thinking when he appointed her."

Darya only nodded a kind of understanding and remained indifferent.

~ ~ ~ ~

"I insist on seeing President Antonov," demanded Ambassador Finley. "I'll not be kept waiting any longer. Get someone here now." The male secretary appeared a little taken aback by the ambassador's angry tone. "In five minutes, I'll be calling the US Secretary of State and he in turn will have President Austin call and ask your boss why I have been kept waiting. Do I make myself clear?"

"Yes, ma'am. Right away." He scurried off like a frightened rat.

She wanted to pace but decided that would show concern, so she stood stock-still staring out the window until she heard a door open. When she turned, President Antonov and Darya stood shoulder to shoulder.

"Ambassador Finley. I take it this is not a social call."

"It is more of a 'what the hell' call, Mr. President. Where are my people?"

"Your people?" he asked in bewilderment. "Your people are spics and were poking into my business."

"Where's the proof? You mean because they went looking for their friend when she left with your strong-arm here," she said, pointing to Darya. "She didn't come back. They were suddenly whisked away. No one would answer their questions or mine, as far as that goes."

"Did you encourage them to go exploring, Ambassador Finley? Maybe they aren't the only spies among us."

"With all due respect, Mr. President, there are no spies, to my knowledge, connected to me. These people are teachers from the United States." She noticed Darya hadn't so much as batted an eye and remained frozen in place.

The president moved to sit down on a leather couch. He spread one arm along the back. "My source is reliable. Even as we speak, they are being taken to an airport to begin their journey home."

"They are unharmed?"

"But of course. We are not the monsters your news media makes us out to be. I put one of my top men in charge. General Oblonsky."

Darya came alive at that moment and jerked his head toward the president. "General Oblonsky?"

"Yes. Why do you ask, Roman?"

He leaned closer to the president and spoke in a quiet voice to keep the ambassador from hearing. "Dr. Scott insisted on talking to her friends after being detained near your quarters. I left all three of the Americans in the care of one of my men, not the general. Given his reputation with…"

"Yes. Yes. I know. He relieved them of the Americans and took them for a brief interrogation. I thought it wise to keep you out of it. My instructions were to leave Dr. Scott in your care and no one else. I'm sure there is nothing to worry about."

"Sir, if I may go check on Dr. Scott."

"Of course. I know you've made plans for the evening with her. Please let me know how that turns out." A mischievous smile toyed with the corners of his mouth. "But you'll take care of the Americans, too, I trust. I wouldn't want anything to go wrong."

Darya nodded and excused himself with the grating sound of Ambassador Finley's voice continuing to ask pointless questions about loose ends and plans. The thought of the general being in charge of Tessa and Samantha gave him serious concerns. The man was a sadist when it came to women. The idea that Darya had started to nudge him out of favor also posed a number of questions about whether his plans had been compromised.

It took only minutes to discover where the prisoners had been taken. A security guard assigned to him ran up and paled when speaking. "I could not disobey General Oblonsky, sir. It would have meant being sent to an outpost at the Arctic Circle."

Darya nodded. "I know. Where are they now?"

"I followed them," he said, leading Darya down a series of stairs. "He had them thrown in a horrible place. I watched them leave about an hour ago with several of the general's men. But Dr. Scott was not with them."

"Where is Dr. Scott now?" The darkness swam up to meet them, split periodically with the pale flickering of an outdated lighting system.

"I don't know, Colonel."

Once on the level where prisoners had been kept, Darya began opening and shutting doors to cells. At the end of a corridor he heard voices and rushed to find one iron-clad door propped open. The familiar voice of General Oblonsky echoed down the damp corridor.

"Perhaps I should take you to my quarters, Dr. Scott, where you will be more comfortable."

Tessa cowered in the corner with General Oblonsky looming over her. She ducked under the general's arm, ran to Darya, and buried her face in his collarbone.

"Are you all right?" he whispered.

She nodded.

"Well, it appears I'm no longer needed here." The general's eyelids became hooded and the downward turn of a drooped mouth appeared more sinister than ever. "Dr. Scott, I regret we didn't have time to get better acquainted." He shifted his attention to Darya and arched an eyebrow of contempt. "I understand congratulations are in order."

Darya switched to Russian. "Thank you, General. And the others?"

"Taken care of. They were transported to the airport for their trip home. Due to the expected request, I'm afraid I couldn't provide anything comfortable." He lifted his watch closer to see in the dappled light. "They should arrive shortly. I'll inform President Antonov I have handed them off to you." He touched the brim of his hat and paused when Darya offered a steely-eyed glare and failed to return the salute.

Once they were alone, Darya gently pushed Tessa back to inspect her tear-streaked face. "Did he touch you?" When she didn't answer he repeated the question, more forcefully.

"No. I think he was afraid to do that."

Darya pulled her back into his arms. "Trust me. He was not. If I hadn't come down here when I did, I'm afraid…"

Tessa tightened her grip around his back.

"But you are safe now," he soothed, rubbing her back in slow circles.

"The others?"

"I believe them to be safe. But I will have to check. Do you trust me?" He held her at arm's length and lowered his head to stare at her squarely in the eyes. "Tess-sa?"

"Yes. Of course. Always, Darya. I believed in you when no one else did."

Darya ran his hands down her hair before touching the sides of her face, absorbing the memory of its softness. "I know. And now, you must trust me again. Greater than before. Can you? For me? For us?"

"I can." She took his hand and kissed the palm. "What did the general mean when he said congratulations were in order?"

The guard appeared in the door, breathless and keeping watch on the hall. "Sir, we need to hurry."

"The car is waiting?" The guard nodded and motioned for them to follow. "I think the general may return with his men. He stormed up the steps two at a time and shoved me into the wall."

"Come, Tess-sa." Darya took her hand and pulled her after him. He felt her place her free hand on his fingers as if afraid he might leave her behind. He stopped when they reached the outside and waited for the guard to motion him to the car. It didn't take long to put Red Square in the rearview mirror.

"Where are we going?" Tessa began to shiver. Darya pulled a down-like blanket over the two of them.

"A safe place."

"Are Sam and Chase there?"

"No." How much should he tell her? Time was of the essence, and he suspected she'd become hard to handle if the truth was revealed. He needed to keep a level head. Secrets brought her to him, and he didn't intend to jeopardize destiny.

"Why not? I should be with them. Are they all right?"

"For now. But you will not join them. They are in trouble. Oblonsky convinced the president they needed to be killed, but I offered another plan."

"Why not me? I was with them."

"You were working with Ambassador Finley. Trust me. She does not want anything to happen to you. She gave me her word."

"Her word? About what? This doesn't make sense. What is going on?"

"Saving Yuri gave you a free pass for a while. I don't know how long it will be possible for the president to continue to think of you in a positive light. There are many who poison him with their lies."

The driver slowed the car and pulled in front of a picturesque building with the traditional onion dome. The snow once again had stopped, and the moon came out from behind the clouds to bounce light on the gold domes topped with crosses. Darya knew Tessa well enough to know when she started to stare out at the building, for a moment she was lost in its beauty. Darya counted on her curiosity and admiration of the monastery to touch her in that spiritual place in her heart that separated her from everyone else he knew in the world.

"What is this place, Darya?"

A bearded priest exited the building, carrying a long monk's robe. When they left the vehicle, the priest bowed to Tessa and draped the wool robe around her shoulders. He gently lifted the oversized hood to cover her head. He greeted them without a show of emotion.

"Why here, Darya?" she asked.

"This is where we will be married."

CHAPTER TWENTY-THREE

Tessa grew weak in the knees as Darya slipped an arm around her. Ushering her inside, he stepped away and spoke to the priest, who continued to watch Tessa intermittently. She wanted to pitch a fit and stomp her foot. Darya had once again kidnapped her to mold her into his future plans for them. But the giant frescos on the walls and ceilings in all their glory took her breath away.

She moved on quiet feet, almost afraid of awakening the saints depicted on the walls and in statues. Turning in slow circles helped her see the magnificence of such a holy place. Candles flickered magical light patterns in the far corners of the church. Low, modern lighting had been installed where she stood so that the turquoise and cold décor formed a fantasy feeling of spiritual wholeness. Once at the front, she discovered a prayer bench and kneeled to ask forgiveness and safety for her friends.

Tessa found the quietness, broken only by the low voices of Darya and the dark-clad priest, overwhelming and laid her forehead against her hands, folded in prayer. Incense filled her with a dreamlike state as she reflected to another time. The images of Afghanistan—Darya carrying her away on a wild horse, sleeping under a yak hide with him pressed against her to chase away the cold—rushed in to soften her anger at him for this unexpected turn of events.

For the second time, he would force her into marriage and, even here, in a more civilized part of the world, she had no choice but to submit. But why in a Russian Orthodox Monastery?

"Tess-sa?" Darya stood next to her and extended his hand. "It is time."

Timidly, she took his hand and let him pull her up. "This is insane. You can't force me to marry you." Anger bubbled up at his insolence.

Darya's face grew solemn as he raised his chin and leveled a stern look of warning. "I can, and you will do as I say if you wish to remain safe and return to the US." His penetrating gaze alerted her to the level of determination in whatever plan was underfoot. "If you are my wife, we can move about freely."

"No." She narrowed her eyes from the rage rising inside her.

Darya grabbed her arm and pulled her to stand in front of the priest who stared at her when she shoved the tribesman's hand away. Another priest stepped up behind her and removed her monk's robe. He offered her a lacy red head covering. Tessa remembered how the women of Darya's village wore red head coverings after they married.

"Please allow me." Darya took the sheer covering and carefully placed it over her head. His hands slid down her arms, unnerving her. She remembered what they were capable of when he showed her his love in the mountains of Afghanistan. The way he gazed at her felt dangerously familiar. "It will be good, Tess-sa." His accent endeared her to nod acceptance in spite of herself.

The priest lifted a book of scripture and read quietly in Russian. It touched Tessa to the point where she felt tears might escape. The old priest turned his attention to her and asked a few questions. Tessa looked to Darya for assistance.

"He wants to know if you'll honor and obey me like a good wife." One side of Darya's mouth turned up in a grin.

"Absolutely not. Also tell him, not in a million years." She added a sweet smile and refocused on the priest. Out of the corner of her eye, she saw Darya nod. The priest spoke crossly to Darya and pointed to her. Darya chuckled and repeated one of the few words she knew. "Da. Da." Yes. Yes.

He drilled Darya with a series of questions to which he nodded or answered with "Da." He turned to her and took her hands. "I am to tell you I will take care of you the rest of my days."

"Considering the evening's events, you might be off the hook soon enough."

He lifted her fingers to his lips and kissed them. "However long I have with you, Tess-sa, will be a gift from God."

She blinked at the gentleness in his voice and gaze, took his fingers, and kissed them. "May God bless us on this journey, Darya." She sank her teeth into his fingers but didn't bite down. She met his eyes with her own to tell him she was furious.

Together, they looked to the priest, who nodded with pleasure and made the sign of the cross then said a few final words. Darya smiled and pulled Tessa into his arms. The strength forced her to melt against him. He lowered his head and kissed her warmly, lingering as she responded, experiencing that in-over-my-head emotion she'd nearly drowned in when they'd met in Afghanistan. And like there, she was powerless to resist.

The priest cleared his throat, and they separated but continued to hold hands. Another priest, also dressed in black robes, his beard nearly down to his chest, slipped in on quiet feet. Since his face was void of lines, Tessa guessed him to be about their age. He spoke in Russian to Darya then English to her.

"Your room is ready, Mrs. Petrov."

Tessa glanced around before realizing he was speaking to her. She tried to smile, in spite of anticipating what being married to a man like Roman Darya Petrov meant and how the night would surely progress. Their first wedding night had been in the tradition of the Kyrgyz tribe of Northern Afghanistan. She'd discovered things about him and herself that changed how she saw the world and had experienced love for the first time in her life.

The cold captured in the dimly lit hallway seeped into her bones and added to the chill and dread of being alone with her new husband as they were led to their room. Darya stopped and removed her monk's robe from the priest that followed. He placed it around her shoulders and whispered in her ear. "Don't be afraid, Tess-sa."

She squinted at him, trying to squirm away from his touch. "I'm not, but you had better be."

"The priest called you a shrew," he commented, withdrawing his arm and continuing to walk slowly. "I told him it was better than a stupid sheep who followed blindly."

"Being compared to animals is always a turn-on for a girl. Thanks for that."

Darya chuckled, drawing Tessa's gaze, and she loved seeing him smile.

The priest stopped at an arched door and unlocked it. Darya pushed down the lever and swung it open. Warmth poured out, and Tessa was pleased to see a roaring fire in the stone fireplace. She stepped inside as the priest handed Darya the key and disappeared like an apparition.

A window on each side of the fireplace drew her to examine the snow-covered garden. There were no curtains, and the frost on the panes nearly blocked the serene white world outside. There was a courtyard and more domed buildings that spoke of another time. When the door clicked shut, Tessa pivoted on her heels to see Darya staring at her. Was this how it would begin?

"Come here," he said in a low, controlled voice. She obeyed. He didn't try to touch her, although he was a breath away. "You are a beautiful bride, Tess-sa. I must leave now to check on the others."

A surge of panic washed over her. "You're not leaving me here alone."

"You are safe here. Only the priests know who you are and will not let anything happen to you if I am delayed." He took her arms in his hands. "When I return, we have much to say."

"I'm assuming 'no' won't be one of the things you'll want to hear." She couldn't help but feel abandoned and terrified of being left here.

Darya cocked his head and pursed his lips together as if to conceal a smile. "You are my legal wife now, Tess-sa. So 'no' will not be something I will consider."

"Just as a reminder, Darya, I'm already married to Robert Scott in the States. Just because you dragged me in front of a Christian priest doesn't change a thing."

"I must go. Time is of the essence. In the desk are papers in a red envelope. If you haven't seen them before, please honor me by reading them. I'm guessing you have not." He pulled her into his arms even though she tried to push away without much conviction.

The low sound of amusement in his laugh reminded her again of another time and place. With his passionate kiss, Tessa found herself helpless to resist and pulled him back for more.

"Darya," she moaned.

"Release me, woman, or I may forget my duty to your friends."

CHAPTER TWENTY-FOUR

Chase kept track of their route in case they needed to escape. The way Sam stared out the window, he guessed she did the same. In darkness, the world cloaked in winter's snow felt impossible to determine where they were. The cold gnawed at his bones, since he had not been given his overcoat. Thankfully, Sam had received a blanket to cover her evening dress that left parts of her olive skin exposed to the elements. After being on the road for several miles, he caved and moved closer to permit her to share the covering. Their combined body heat would sustain them for a while.

Their two guards in the front seat wore military uniforms and had taken orders from General Oblonsky like they were words handed down to them from God. They handcuffed one hand of each of them to their passenger door. The lights ahead indicated their destination. Would they be headed home or be diverted to another hellish place to be interrogated? How had this gone so wrong? And where was Tessa?

Without options, he'd been forced to leave her behind in that underground prison-like structure. She'd taken a blow from Oblonsky's baton, one meant for him, across her back and side. But the real concern, now, was the man had been left behind with her. His reputation with women painted a sordid, evil picture of what he might do to Tessa.

In spite of Tessa being whisked off with them to the holding area, he had to believe Darya wouldn't have let her fall victim to Satan's spawn. Whatever he planned, she appeared to be in the dark. She sucked in her breath in surprise and stiffened at his touch when he ordered security to take them away for President Antonov's safety. They were passed off to General Oblonsky. His men escorted them to, what turned out to be, a holding cell.

"Get out," one guard said in broken English as the other removed their handcuffs attached to the door.

Now he realized they were at a small airport. Could Vernon Kemp, their tech for this project, track them? Both he and Sam had a tracer thread run through their clothes, thanks to the ambassador's tech people. It was the same kind of mechanism used on the president anytime he left the White House in case of an abduction. Tessa had worn the same thing, but now she wore different clothes and couldn't be traced as easily. She was on her own.

Although polite, the two soldiers' no-nonsense tones and sour expressions left little doubt they could get physical if the situation required. The temperature, down around twenty degrees plus a windchill took his breath away. Fortunately, Chase and Sam had received a coat around their shoulders as they walked to a plane waiting in isolation. Lights from the inside showed no movement. The cockpit did have someone moving about there.

Chase had the overpowering urge to stop and stare at the Soviet era, Russian Yak-40 designed in the 1960s. Air safety had not always been a priority in the past and the joke in the States had been the Soviets fixed their aircraft with duct tape and installed screen doors for a quick getaway if things didn't go well on takeoff. However, after all these years, it remained an impressive aircraft. Hopefully, they wouldn't end up at the bottom of the Baltic Sea.

The cabin of the plane felt tropical compared to outside. They were ushered to seats across from each other and shoved into place. Sam spewed a series of insults concerning their manhood in perfect Russian, taking them off guard for a few seconds. The soldiers glanced at each other when Sam continued her rant. Did they worry they may have said something on the way that could have been vital information as to their destination.

"Didn't expect that, did you, assholes?" Chase also spoke in Russian and received a clip upside the head with the butt of a pistol. He could feel blood trickle down the side of his face but continued to grin in a display of disrespect.

Time drags on when you have no way of knowing what hour it is or where you're located. There remained activity outside near another hangar. People came and went on the plane, visiting with the out-of-sight pilot in the cockpit. The heat of the plane had chased the acute cold from his bones but managed to make him feel drowsy. He tried to focus on getting out of this latest mess.

What had Darya done to them? Had he actually crossed over to become a Russian agent? Did he sell them out? What would become of the scientists if they didn't get them out soon? If they didn't collapse the cloaking project, the Russians would have a much greater military dominance than the US. In spite of the US playing catch-up with cloaking, not having an upper edge to the technology would put them right back into a cold war.

Concern returned to Tessa's safety. If Darya had switched sides, what would become of her? Would he let her go as he'd done in Afghanistan or keep her prisoner until he'd tired of her? The trouble with that reasoning was although he hated the man, Chase knew Darya loved her. He'd watched her, drinking her in and mesmerized by each move. Unlike himself, Darya never hesitated at displaying that interest or admiration. Something about him influenced Tessa to submit to his dark aura and believe any damn thing the man said.

Dr. Wu had treated her in Afghanistan and after she'd returned to the States. He reported Tessa suffered from Stockholm syndrome, identifying with her captor. Chase believed it to be more than that. Roman Darya Petrov took advantage of her when she had amnesia, preyed upon her weakness to make rational decisions, and promised her a life of love she lacked at home. Although Tessa had said they had not been intimate in the Biblical sense, he doubted that with each passing day. She had only been with one man in her life, her husband. A man like Darya could easily sweep an innocent woman off her feet and make her believe black was white.

Over the last year, any mention of Darya had created friction between them. She would hear nothing disparaging as to his character, nor would she talk about him or her time in Afghanistan.

"He saved me from unspeakable torture and death, Chase. I'll never forget that. I owe him." This remained her line in the sand. If he crossed it, then he'd get the cold shoulder for a few days until they both pretended the conversation never occurred.

The jealousy that welled up inside him at those moments continued to surprise him. There had never been a woman who made him feel so helpless and desperate at times. He wanted Darya out of her life and out of her head. Was that why he hadn't confessed how he felt? Did he trust her enough to give his heart away for the first time? He'd hoped by giving her time, she would realize how dangerous her actions had been in Afghanistan and that Darya would only have ruined any chance she had at happiness in California. Maybe he should have confessed his true feelings instead of telling her over and over how much he admired her and that she'd saved him from himself.

He longed to rub the spot on his chest that ached every time he thought of her. The bright smile. The carefree laughter. Optimism and belief in divine intervention. Smart. Funny. She was also easy on the eyes. But mostly it was the way she made him feel when she entered a room that kept him being unable to resist grinning like a sixteen-year-old with his first crush.

A new man entered the front of the plane breaking his reverie of Tessa. He kept his back to them and spoke to the pilot in the cockpit. The two guards shuffled toward the exit and blocked the view of the newcomer. From what little Chase heard, they gave an update and were dismissed. As they exited the plane, Chase realized who stood at the front of the fuselage. Dressed in black, from head to toe, stood Roman Darya Petrov.

Chase's body stiffened and went on high alert. They locked gazes like battling gladiators. His heart began that adrenaline pump he experienced before a fight that helped find his path to victory.

Sam mumbled, "Don't get crazy, Chase. Remember there is a lot at stake here."

Rage overtook him and prevented a quick response. Darya moved slowly toward them then cut his stare to Sam for a split second. She remained a threat, in spite of restraints. Returning his focus to Chase, he studied the loosely attached cord that went from one wrist to the arm of his chair. It wouldn't be difficult to attack him if needed. Darya must have realized this, considering he stopped just out of reach but still managed to grab Sam's chin in his hand.

"Still beautiful and deadly, Dr. Cordova." He smiled and moved one step back when she jerked away from his touch. "I see these men have made you comfortable."

"Where's Tessa?" Chase growled through clenched teeth.

Darya arched an eyebrow, and a sinister smile toyed with one corner of his mouth. "Safe."

"Not good enough. Where. Is. She?"

"You are in no position to demand anything from me, Captain Hunter. But since I understand your concern for your team, I will tell you she is at a monastery not far from here. The priests are caring for her until I return."

"What do you intend to do with her?"

Darya's face morphed into a mask of icy calm. "I intend to keep her with me for a while. Congratulations are in order. We were married at the monastery tonight."

"In case you've forgotten, Tessa is already married. Another one of your lame attempts to circumvent the truth."

Darya took a deep breath and released it slowly. "No. I took care of that little inconvenient problem. The father of her children will no longer get in my way. Trust me when I say Robert Scott is no longer in the picture."

"If you have harmed him in any way, I'll make it my mission in life to see you pay for your actions." Chase restrained himself from lunging upward. "Tessa will never forgive you."

"I disagree. By the time I return to her tonight, she will be a very willing bride."

Chase jumped up and pushed forward at the same time Darya pulled out a stun gun and jammed it into Chase's chest. He fell back down in his seat, shaking violently.

In the recesses of his mind, he could hear Sam cursing so loud, it would have made a sailor blush. Darya pointed the stun gun at her to stop the insults. By the time his body returned to normal, Chase was limp.

Darya leaned over him and pushed out his bottom lip in mock

sympathy. "Sorry about that, Captain Hunter. You need to learn to evaluate your worthy opponent a little better in the future."

A tiny stream of drool exited the corner of his mouth as he straightened in his seat. "If you hurt her…"

"Hurt her? The woman is a snow leopard. I'm the one you should be concerned with." His low, throaty laugh unsettled Chase. "But you have never known what Tessa Petrov is capable of on a cold winter's night." Darya closed his eyes as if in nirvana then stared menacing at him. "Do you want me to tell you what I plan to do to my wife tonight?"

With every ounce of strength he had left, Chase pushed up out of the chair. Darya jumped back and avoided contact then punched him on the chin with a hammer fist. He quickly lifted the stun gun again as Chase fell back toward his seat and was in the process of jamming it into Chase's neck when a man came up behind him and grabbed his arm.

"We need to go, and we need the captain to be 100 percent."

Darya lowered the weapon and landed a punch to Chase's jaw hard enough, it knocked him to the floor.

"Stay down if you know what is good for you, Captain Hunter. I would love to finish this, but Tessa waits for me. Remember that as you're flying over icy waters tonight." Darya pivoted and stormed away, calling back to the pilot, "There are parachutes for you and your copilot."

He turned to offer another sinister smile to Chase then disappeared out the door.

The man left standing over Chase reached down and pulled him up then gingerly helped him back into his seat before removing the constraints. He stared into the pale eyes of his rescuer who patted his cheek.

"I swear, Chase, you make more enemies."

"Carter, thanks for havin' my six," he groaned as he rubbed his bruised chin, followed by the spot where he'd been tased. "I'm going to kill that guy."

"Not sure what Tessa sees in him." Chase leveled a sour frown as his friend turned to free Sam. "Sorry. He scares the bejesus out of me. No wonder they call him the new Rasputin." He helped Sam stand to stretch and tried to rub her arms to get the blood flowing. "I mean, Tessa is such a sweet little thing."

Sam pushed Carter's hands away. "Tessa is no sweet anything. I told you guys she was trouble the day she stumbled into our lives. Get a grip."

Carter smiled wolfishly. "No need to be jealous. You're still my go-to girl."

"Like hell I am," she barked. "I guess you've been playing house with Svetlana these last few days."

Carter turned to look back at the cockpit. "She's my copilot, so keep your voice down. This plane is not the best, but it can get us to where we need to be. We have another one taking off with us that will go down in the White Sea before morning. That will cover our tracks for a while."

"How did you manage that?" Chase struggled to form his words as he rubbed his shoulder.

"I didn't. Darya arranged everything. The guy is sneaky as hell. I kind of admire that."

Chase turned his glare up at him. "That's all I need. One more Petrov fan."

Carter laughed and slapped his friend on the shoulder. "Let's get this bird in the air. Buckle up, buttercup. It's going to be a bumpy ride."

CHAPTER TWENTY-FIVE

Tessa tried several times to open the door to no avail. Locked up and alone. Just another kind of jail, no matter it was in a Russian Orthodox monastery. She twirled around to scope out the room and found a few of her things carefully folded on an overstuffed chair with a worn brocade design. There were also clothes she'd never seen before: two sweaters, jeans, long underwear, like the kind her father wore on winter days to check on the cattle, heavy-duty socks, and a furry parka she might wear on a tour of Antarctica.

She fingered the flimsy satin nightgown, the color of champagne with spaghetti straps. She guessed it would reach to her ankles. It felt luxurious and cool to the touch. She lifted it to her nose and caught a whiff of rose petals. With the garment still in hand, she continued to examine her surroundings while frozen in place.

The flames in the fireplace popped and crackled without warning, causing her to flinch. Other than the light it emitted, there was only one other dim light coming from a lamp on a nightstand next to a bed with a brass headboard. The faded jade coverlet was tied in tufts with coarse string you might use in mailing a package from an era that was both simple and meager. She found it lovely, the kind of thing she'd want for her small apartment back in Sacramento. The dancing light from the flames highlighted a fresco-like painting on one wall of the Virgin Mary holding the baby Jesus, along with a small wooden cross hanging over the bed. Other than those two adornments, the room was void of décor.

Dropping the gown, she moved to the desk next to the door where Darya had instructed her to retrieve information. The drawer jammed, so she jerked it violently several times before giving up. But in the small crack that she'd managed, the edge of a red envelope became visible.

Running two fingers inside, she managed to pull one corner out but soon gave up and began jerking on the handle again. She could see the handwriting. It was identical to the one that had arrived at the house several weeks before Christmas in the States. Robert had intercepted it from her hands, claiming it to be from a client, and disappeared into the office with it.

Had Darya sent Robert something about her? Had this been the thing that drove him to lower her enough in his esteem, he felt comfortable seeing female clients for dinner? Is that why he'd decided a little time apart might do them good? She'd been so irritated with him, she'd agreed without hesitation. Their marriage was crumbling faster than it could be repaired.

The days of Christmas had been a sham for the sake of the children and her parents. He stayed at the house with no mention of them separating. They shared the same bed without the slightest loving touch. It had been a long couple of weeks.

But it had been a long year as well.

She gave the drawer one more tug, and it opened so quickly, the motion staggered her backward as the ivory pull fell to the floor. Without hesitation, Tessa grabbed the red envelope and tore it open. She carried it to the bed and sat down to read the contents. Page by page, she was trying to comprehend the information when tears began to streak down her face.

Lies. She'd been living a lie all these years.

Anger boiled up inside her, its heat evaporating the tears into desperation. She needed to get home. Shoving the papers aside, she jumped off the bed and slipped on the heavy socks and boots from her bag then the parka.

First, she needed to return to Moscow. The ambassador would

help her escape. Hopefully, she'd been able to secure the release of Chase and Sam. Heaven knew if they'd been able to carry on the job they were sent to do. Had Darya protected them or sabotaged the mission? She didn't know what to believe now. The information in the red envelope shook her to the core. Had Enigma known this information about her?

The lock on the door rattled before the iron doorknob turned. With a squeak, the door pushed open in slow motion. Tessa rushed the door, hoping it would be Darya, but found the young priest standing statue still. He folded his hands in front of him and smiled shyly.

"Would you enjoy a cup of hot tea or perhaps something stronger? I could also have a tray of sweets assembled for you. We made them for Christmas. The children of the village love them."

Tessa continued to stare at him, trying to decide how to circumvent any attempt to stop her.

He dropped his hands into a nervous twitch. "We have traditional gingerbread and pastila. Have you had it?"

"No. That would be lovely. Could you pack it to go? I need to get back to Moscow. I have a meeting with the American ambassador."

The pleasant expression on the priest's face faded when his eyes narrowed and lips thinned. "It is late for a meeting, Mrs. Petrov."

"I know." She pointed to her small clutch. "Fortunately, Darya left me my phone in case I needed to contact him. I've already reached him and told him. He's going to meet me there." She smiled and walked to the nightstand where she'd left her clutch. "You can call him if you like." She crossed her fingers he refused since she had no way of knowing if the phone would work here.

"What is this meeting about?" the priest asked, tilting his head.

"Sorry. Honestly, I have no idea. I suspect it has to do with my friends who got on the president's last nerve tonight. I'm her assistant from time to time. Probably wants to make sure I'm okay and that I'm in the loop."

"Loop? What kind of loop?"

Tessa again flashed a disarming smile and batted her eyelashes innocently. "What I mean is to keep me informed." She pulled the phone out and saw there were no bars and the battery was low. "Should I connect you with Darya?"

"That will not be necessary." The priest appeared to come to some kind of decision about her story since his eyes hooded and he dropped his chin to peer suspiciously at her. "You will need a car."

"Could someone drive me back? The American ambassador was adamant about me returning as soon as possible."

"I will see what I can do, Mrs. Petrov."

The way he said her name indicated he didn't believe her story. "Why don't I go with you to find out." She stepped forward, but he stood his ground until she came nose to nose.

"Mrs. Petrov, why do I think you are trying to leave the monastery?" His voice had turned icy.

"Maybe because I just told you I needed to. Perhaps your grasp of the English language is lacking."

"I assure you; it is not. You are trying to escape."

Tessa took a deep breath and leveled a confrontational glare to cover the jitters rising inside her. "You know what? You're right."

"I am?"

"Yes. Darya told me you were very trustworthy."

When a smile of content began to lift the corners of his mouth, Tessa jammed her knee into his crotch. The groan spewed from deep inside him as he bent double. Before he could recover, she locked her fingers into a fist and brought it down on the back of his neck. He fell to his knees long enough for her to rush behind him and give him a kick in the butt, which sprawled him face down on the cold floor inside her room. When he appeared to recover, she grabbed a small candelabra off the desk and landed a blow to the back of each of his knees, eliciting a cry of pain.

"I'm really sorry, Father. Seriously." She grabbed the door key from his hand and backed out. "Pray for me."

She slammed the door and locked it before turning her attention to the long corridor in both directions. Even before she continued her escape, the door began to rattle.

"Mrs. Petrov, I beg you to stop. It is not safe for you to leave."

"Whatever, dude," she whispered, and ran down the dimly lit corridor until she slid to a stop in a large vestibule where large double doors were between her and three more priests who stared at her in surprise. One of them was the man who had performed the wedding ceremony.

"Is my car ready?" she asked, making motions like she was

driving. She mentioned Darya's name, knowing they couldn't understand.

She could hear the young priest down the corridor yelling, what she imagined was, "Stop her!"

How did he escape? A Christmas miracle? Probably not.

The three priests surged toward her as if to capture her. Thanks to Sam's sadistic training in agility, they missed her at every turn. She maneuvered closer to the door, just as the young priest stumbled into the vestibule, panting and pointing at her.

A small window on each side of the double doors revealed a black sedan against the dark night. She smiled at the priests, jerked the doors open, and plowed into a strong body dressed in black.

"Where the hell do you think you're going?"

Tessa gasped and stepped backward into the light. "Darya," Tessa choked. He stepped forward, backing her inside.

All four priests talked at once while Darya cocked his head at her, removing his gloves one finger at a time. He laid a hand on his heart and sounded sincere in whatever he said to the priests before turning to Tessa with that cold, hard attitude that left little doubt at his rising temper.

"Darya. I can explain." She dug in her heels and bristled at a quick reach for her arm, which she shook off. Without another word, he picked her up, slung her over his shoulder, and marched back toward their room with a kind of determination that most certainly wouldn't end well for her.

CHAPTER TWENTY-SIX

Darya strode into their room and managed to shove the door shut with his boot before dumping her onto the bed. She kicked and crab crawled backward to put distance between her and his angry glare. With the slow removal of his coat, he hung it on a cast-iron hook beside the door before coming back and standing at the foot of the bed.

"Explain." He sounded tired.

Tessa scooted off the bed, not a place she wanted to make a stand since it would inflame an already smoldering situation. "I-I."

Darya narrowed his eyes as he became rigid.

"I mean, I'm going back to Moscow."

"No. You are not."

"Where did you go? Where are Chase and Sam?"

"I made sure they got out. They will be at their destination by tomorrow. The work will begin to destroy the cloaking device and technology. Hopefully they'll get the scientists out. They are in safe hands."

"How do I know that?"

His frown deepened. "Because I said so." He loosened the collar and began to unbutton his shirt.

"What happened to your hand?" Tessa spotted a cut across his knuckles and a bruise forming down several fingers.

He lifted the hand and pursed his lips together as if suppressing a smile. "I hit something."

"What?"

"Nothing important." He offered a lopsided grin. "Captain Hunter wasn't happy when I told him we married. He came at me—so I stopped him." He held up his hand and inspected it like a trophy. "I may have implied…" His gaze slid over her from head to toe.

"I can only imagine what you implied. Was that necessary? You are despicable." She moved around the bed and took his hand to examine.

He chuckled. "I am a man who loves you." He smirked. She dropped his hand when he slipped strong arms around her. "Tess-sa," he whispered as he searched her face and lifted a hand to remove a curl from her cheek. "I know you are afraid. But I will not hurt you."

"Then let me go. I should be with the team or least with the ambassador to finish this mission."

He released her and continued to unbutton the black shirt. "Neither of them need you. I made sure everything was in order so we could get reacquainted tonight. Ambassador Finley knows this."

"Ambassador Finley knew of your plan?" She pointed to the papers sprawled across the bed. "About that? I can't believe it."

Darya stopped and moved to the bed before picking up several papers tossed in disarray. "What don't you believe? That you were never married to Robert Scott or that he never told you the truth?" He dropped the papers and sent her a narrowed stare. "I am not making this up. The man who performed the marriage ceremony— who was he?"

Tessa could feel a tightening in her chest.

"An interim student-pastor who came to fill in while the search committee found us a full-time pastor. He'd just graduated from…" she tried to remember. "I don't know. A place in the Midwest. Robert found him. He said two other couples got married during the same time. What about them?"

"One couple died in a car accident the following year, another couple divorced, and then you. It was the divorced couple who stumbled across the truth and filed a complaint with the Tennessee Attorney General several years ago. Ambassador Finley came across it when she had you investigated."

"Investigated? For what?"

"She is untrusting and determined. She hoped to find dirt on you or Robert to make sure she could control any information that might come out about your capture in Afghanistan. Both of us know a lot about her and how she manipulated people, especially us." He eased down on the bed. "She wants to be Secretary of State and maybe run for higher office. President Austin won't be in office much longer."

"Why would I be a threat? Or you?"

Darya reached out and took Tessa's hand and pulled her closer. "In order to have her favor, get out of jail in Kabul, I had to do her bidding on a few nasty jobs."

Tessa imagined that might be connected to the death of the Afghanistan ambassador at the time. He was up to his neck in the drug trade and left them to die in the wilderness where he knew the Taliban would tie up any loose ends for him. Bonnie Finley was not a woman to be toyed with, and she certainly remained a vindictive opponent whenever someone got in her way on the ladder of political influence.

"Darya, I don't understand any of this." She nodded toward the documents. "If what you're saying about my marriage is true, why didn't anyone contact us?"

"It was twelve years ago. You moved around. Twice in Nevada and then California. Maybe they did and Robert never told you. Did he tell you when I sent the red envelope with the information? I sent one to you as well."

"I never got it." She sat down next to him. "How long ago did you send it?"

"After Thanksgiving, maybe first of December. When you didn't reach out to me in our usual way or contact Ambassador Finley about the information, I knew Robert had not shared it with you."

"Why would he do that?" Keeping the disappointment out of her voice proved impossible.

"I cannot say."

"When did you notify him the first time?"

"Before you ever went to Africa with Enigma." Tessa had traveled there to help a friend in Botswana. It had turned into a change of leadership for the country and, in the process, she'd nearly lost Chase to a Black Mamba attack. She didn't want to think about it, but it had been in those days she'd realized her heart wasn't in her marriage anymore.

"Does Enigma know about this?" It would be typical to keep information from her.

Darya shook his head. "Not unless they intercepted the information. I sent it to you at the university. Ambassador Finley and myself are the only two people who knew. She wanted you with her since I held the key to the cloaking mission." One corner of his mouth turned up in cynical amusement. "It was her way of controlling me. She has never trusted me because of my Russian background."

A tear squeezed out the corner of her eye as she tried to look away from Darya, only to have him lay a finger on her chin and turn her to face him.

"My life has been a lie. The man I thought loved me has been playing games. He knows the personal property laws in California would not be good to him if we married. He didn't want me enough to take a chance. That explains so much now. All this time I believed there was something broken inside me to cause him to pull away. That I just wasn't good enough."

"Do you love him?" Darya asked quietly.

"He's the father of my children. He'll hold a special place in my life because of that. But love? No. Not anymore."

Darya stood up and gathered his things together as if he were leaving.

"Where are you going?"

"You are hurting. I don't want you to feel I forced you into anything."

"A little late for that," she quipped and stood. "All this trouble you went through and for what? To hurt me? To show me what a fool I've been?"

Darya grabbed one of the papers off the bed that resembled a legal document. "Did you read this?" Tessa could feel her forehead pinch as she eyed the paper he held. She shook her head. "This is an annulment. The priest would not marry us unless I agreed to it. He wanted to know for sure you wanted to marry me. It was worth a gamble for me."

"So, what are you waiting for? You didn't need any of this to force me in your bed. We both know I'm powerless against you both mentally and physically. I promised you as much in Afghanistan. Clearly, no one from Enigma will bust down the door and rob you of what you believe I owe you."

"I will be next door if you need me. I will have someone take you back to Moscow in the morning since you are determined to go." He turned to leave.

"Darya," she snapped, causing him to freeze. "Why did you go to all this trouble? I need to know."

He slowly looked over his shoulder at her before turning to face her. "I love you, Tess-sa. In my heart, we were married in the mountains of my village. I thought when I showed you Robert was not your husband; you would feel free to love me back. And if I had a Christian priest to marry us, you would feel as if God sanctified our marriage."

"You do not believe as I do."

He took a small step toward her. "No. But I will believe whatever you want me to if it means we can be together. You are a good woman who stayed true to a man whom you didn't love. It was the honorable thing to do. I wanted to release you of that burden so you could love whomever you chose. If that is someone else—"

Before Tessa could stop herself, she ran to him and circled his neck with her arms before kissing him with such passion, she thought she'd been consumed by a wave of relief and desire. She could feel the clothing he held drop to the floor as he swung her up into his arms and carried her to the bed. They became entangled in their own desperate need to satisfy each other's desire as the night brought surrender to old lives made new.

~ ~ ~ ~

"Where are we?" Chase asked as they boarded a second plane. The newer plane appeared to be able to complete the grueling flight ahead of them.

"Arkhangelsk." Svetlana spoke offhandedly as she turned her attention to Sam who yawned and squeezed past them. She'd pretty much ignored the former Russian cosmonaut from the beginning. Chase figured it had plenty to do with Carter having had a romantic relationship with the woman at one time. Sam hated competition.

"And the other plane?"

"It flew out over the White Sea and initiated the cloaking device installed by Carter before you arrived tonight. Darya had it smuggled out weeks ago by a friend who works at the laboratory in the Lake Baikal region. It is not fully operational and will only last ten minutes. He is well connected there. The plane we came in on will crash in the water soon after we leave here. It has been fitted with remote control, and your people on the ground in Finland will see to it that it goes down in deep water. It will be spring before anyone finds it. Darya thought of everything."

"So it seems," he responded through gritted teeth. He didn't want to admit he might have been wrong about the man. "How well do you know Darya Petrov?"

"Well enough." Typical Russian answer, he surmised.

"What do you get out of this?"

Carter came onboard, checking information on a clipboard before noticing Chase and Svetlana. He gave a weak smile and escaped into the cockpit.

"I get even for taking me out of the space program to do meaningless work for the corrupt and egotistical government who ruined my career."

Sam kept moving toward her seat but offered her own snide remark. "I think you did that yourself when you told the world you were writing a book about a love affair on the ISS. Not Carter's fault his other love interest wanted to kill you."

Chase realized it would be a long flight with these two she-devils striving to win the most attention from Carter Johnson.

"Your actions will prevent another possible war."

Svetlana glanced into the cockpit then grinned at Chase. "Maybe I want to go to America when you leave."

A laugh that sounded more like a cackle came from Sam as she eased into a seat. "Oh sorry. I thought you were joking."

The two women locked stares, with Sam, clearly the winner on intimidation, before Svetlana huffed and returned to the cockpit.

Chase found a seat across from Sam and frowned. "Don't antagonize her. We need to get this done. I don't want any more surprises."

"You mean like Tessa sleeping with Darya tonight?"

"You don't know that," he snapped. "He could have been blowing smoke to get to me."

"One thing I know about Petrov is that when it comes to Tessa, he doesn't kid around. You better prepare yourself that he's done harm to Robert and now has Tessa under his thumb. He did it once before, and we aren't there to save her. The best we can hope for is that she knows how to play the cards she's been dealt and get out of this unscathed. Besides"—she paused, and Chase raised his chin in stubbornness—"if you'd romanced her like you do other women in your life, she'd be here with us instead of—"

"Enough," he snapped.

"Don't say I didn't warn you. Roman Darya Petrov is a fine specimen of a man. Maybe equal to you, Captain Hunter. Unlike you, he isn't shy about telling her how he feels. I bet he is proving that right about now."

CHAPTER TWENTY-SEVEN

Carter landed the plane on a remote airstrip about two hundred kilometers from Lake Baikal. Joel Sandy waited to drive them back to the place he called home so they could get some rest and catch up on the intel Vernon Kemp brought from Enigma headquarters in Sacramento. There wasn't much time left to dismantle the cloaking device and rescue the scientists. They were scheduled to be moved within the week. Whether that meant now or in five days, Joel couldn't speculate.

The airfield had been abandoned after the fall of the Soviet Union due to its isolated location and not enough traffic to justify maintaining it. After it became overgrown and neglected, the more ambitious and notorious opposition groups took it upon themselves to try and keep it in working order. The two metal buildings, although showing signs of age with its rusty patterns of neglect, was covered in a protective coating that sealed it from the brutal winters. The runway often had patchy growth that appeared to sprout up from cracks in the pavement. Because no one ever inspected the area too closely, the soldiers who dropped by unannounced to intimidate the locals never realized the plants were artificial and moveable in times of need.

This was one of those times. Winter brought challenges to maintain the airfield due to the snow. Luckily, most of the snow had fallen on the west side of the Sayan Mountain range in Southern Siberia. Even so, removing the snow with plows at the last possible minute caused concern. Joel knew the plane Carter flew had little fuel to spare to provide extra time for snow removal. The trick would be clearing the runway ahead of time while remaining ready to replace the snow before any Russian satellites took a swipe over the area. It needed to appear untouched and abandoned.

"Joel," Carter said, extending a hand as they disembarked the plane. He introduced Chase and Sam. "Appreciate what you're doing here. I know it puts you and your family in jeopardy."

"Family?" Chase asked.

"My wife and child." Joel fanned his hand out to guide them toward the open door of a van. "Come. We don't have much time. We need to get to safety and let these other men put the airfield back to its normal appearance." He sensed some confusion with the tall man named Chase. "The people who took me in had a daughter…"

Chase nodded. "Enough said."

"I'm planning to take her with us." Joel caught a disgruntled look from Carter. "If you don't agree, I'm not going."

"My orders are to bring all the scientists back. There was no mention of anyone else," Chase fumed.

"I'm the only one who married, Captain Hunter, because I escaped. The others have had little contact with the outside world. The government feared someone would start asking questions."

They loaded into a white van that appeared to be on its last hurrah. But it fired up like a new one after their equipment was loaded in the back.

"What condition are they in, Dr. Sandy?"

"Please, call me Joel. They are thinner, somewhat depressed they haven't been found, and showing signs of being suspicious of each other."

"Suspicious? What do you mean?" Sam said as she searched for a seat belt but found none.

"The Russians have applied a lot of pressure for the last six months to get the cloaking project completed. Took each person aside and promised to let them go as soon as they were able to get a reliable test. They also had to work with Russian scientists to fill in the gaps of what they didn't already know. As you can imagine, they have been working on the project longer than the US now but with little to no success. Strong-arming their own people filtered down to ours, and some have suffered abuse, both mentally and physically."

"Two years is a long time to be in captivity," Carter added, having gotten the information from Svetlana early on. "Most of them know as soon as the test flight works, they're of no use. So, they keep adding a misstep or virus into the program. It's easily solved, but the steps backward force them to start over on that section of the project. They are exhausted and discouraged."

Joel took a deep breath and let it out slowly. "Very true. They know their days are numbered no matter what they do. It comes down to putting in as many obstacles as possible or going ahead with the completion of the project. Either way they're dead. No way the Russians are going to let these scientists go home and say, 'Oh by the way, I've been in Russia for a couple of years building a weapon that will overpower us.'"

"It's my understanding"—Chase grasped the back of the seat as the van hit a slick spot then righted itself— "that the Russians have gotten clever at detecting false information and will right a wrong before our guys can sabotage any advancement."

"Correct. This led to medical attention being withheld from others. One man suffers from diabetes, so the threat of him not getting the insulin he needs is always hanging over their heads. Of course, being in captivity for so long, other ailments materialize such as congestive heart failure, arthritis, and dietary problems that normally would not have appeared at home. But here, needs are not met, and the absence of love ones and comfort can trigger lots of problems. They needed to be clever at not drawing attention to any sabotage they may plant."

"They know you're alive?" Chase inquired.

"Yes. Six months after I healed from their attempt to kill me, I managed to slip a note in with one of the food servers, a cousin of my wife. Knowing I was alive gave them hope they might survive." Joel slowed to take a curve. "If it had not been for Roman Darya Petrov, I would be dead. He saved my life, even though he had no idea who I was. He made sure I was taken care of before he left." Joel choked up. "I owe him everything. His kindness in spite of the risk will never be forgotten."

The group quieted down after he filled them in on a few more details. He suspected they were exhausted after their seven-hour flight. Carter had quickly fallen asleep in the front seat. Svetlana also closed her eyes, but the two Enigma agents stared out the windows as if mapping an escape route.

People like them never stopped expecting the worst to happen. He wondered about their experience, their past, and if they were friends with Petrov. The man called Chase had the same look as these two: steely-eyed calm, strong, observant, and unemotional. Sam reminded him of one of those video game heroes, where you remained clueless as to what she might be thinking.

After about an hour and a half, Joel slowed the van.

"What's going on?" Carter woke up instantly and straightened in his seat.

"Russian soldiers have a roadblock going into the village."

Chase reached inside his long coat to touch a Beretta M9. He'd stored two M4 carbine rifles under their seat just before he and Sam loaded up. Carter and Svetlana added their own M27 rifles, along with what looked to be 9MM Glocks. How they came in possession of Marine firepower was beyond his understanding, but now wasn't the time to ask questions. The big question was why Russian soldiers were combing the area and felt it necessary to set up a roadblock?

"Why would soldiers be here? How far are we from the airfield and developmental station for the cloaking project?" Chase reached around the seat to touch Joel's shoulder and met his concerned stare by way of the rearview mirror.

"Not sure. Maybe something has gone wrong. They've been coming around more in the last month but never a roadblock." Joel's voice caught in his throat. "Last time, they came to our house to look around."

Svetlana eased forward from the far back to wedge in next to Sam. "Someone is talking. I know it. They are checking it out."

The 1970s style truck ahead of them rolled through the checkpoint when one of the sour-faced soldiers motioned for them to pull forward. Joel put the van in gear and creeped to a stop as another guard came up on the passenger side.

"I see you have a lot of people with you." The soldier leaned down and eyed the passengers as the other man tapped on Carter's window to roll it down. "Where have you been?"

Chase had to admit Joel's Russian accent was good, and he sounded humble enough to not alarm the soldiers. "This woman"—he pointed to Svetlana—"is my wife's cousin. She and her husband work for the space station at Vostochny Cosmodrome. They came a few days early to visit family before heading out to the Siberia Aviation Complex. Orders from Moscow." Joel fished out paperwork and handed it to the soldier, who motioned for his buddy to come around and examine the papers with him.

"And the others?" Chase passed the papers forward to Joel. Reading the Russian language was not his strength.

"We are from the Engineering and Industrial Association outside of Irkutsk. Our visit is unscheduled and off the books. If you have questions, I suggest you contact President Antonov's right-hand man, Roman Petrov. He'll be happy to explain it to you," Chase offered flippantly. The Russian straightened and handed the orders to the other man. They stepped away and conversed for a few seconds.

Joel spoke out of the side of his mouth. "Dropping Petrov's name put the fear in the soldiers. He has a reputation of being Rasputin reincarnated and having an unholy hold on the president. But here, among these simple people, Petrov is respected. Part of the reason soldiers fear him is because that butcher, General Oblonsky, has poisoned their brains. The general is a jealous man and has lost favor with the president. Or so they say. Who knows when it is Russia?"

One of the soldiers took out a phone and made a call. In a few seconds, he pivoted to stare at the van, nodded, and disconnected. They started arguing between themselves while the travelers watched from inside the van.

"This is a risky move on the president's part. Even if the rescue mission goes off without a hitch, how is the Russian government going to explain having held our brightest minds for going on three years?" Carter asked as he cocked an ear toward the open window then pointed his chin. "Looks like they're a couple of scared rabbits."

Joel grasped the steering wheel. "Here they come."

They passed the papers through the windows. "You may go. Enjoy your stay. Do you need an escort when you go to the complex?"

"No. Oh. Why are you here anyway?" Joel added.

"Rumors of terrorists hiding in this village. We found nothing. No worries. We'll be leaving tonight."

"Thank you for checking it out. Probably those crazy hunters searching for wooly mammoth bones again."

The soldier gave them a two-finger salute and stepped back and waved them along.

A loud sigh of relief came from Joel as they wound their way through the small village, ending up at a log cabin with a long, extended front porch. It had wood stacked all across the front, almost to the roof and around both ends. Suddenly, Chase felt like he was in one of those survivor shows, where you had to live off the land.

The front door opened as they exited the van, to reveal a young woman and a small child. She ran down the steps and into the arms of Joel Sandy. The woman was taller than him and wore her hair in two long brown braids that fell to her waist. He was surprised at how much younger she was than Joel, but love had no age limit, he guessed. The freckles across her nose added to her country-girl appearance. The little boy waited on the porch and waved jubilantly at his father who wasted no time in running up the steps and scooping the child up in his arms.

"Do you understand now why I won't leave without them, Captain Hunter?"

Chase eyed them and nodded. He thought of Tessa and what she might be experiencing. What had Darya done to her in his absence? Was she injured and humiliated without him there to protect her? Or was Darya really like Joel, determined to make a life with a woman he, himself had always tried to avoid.

Watching Joel, he realized waiting on Tessa to leave her husband so he could romance her the right way left a huge gap for another man with less ethics to take what he, now, would never have. Whatever Darya had done to Tessa's husband would be to his advantage. Would he dare kill the man to be with Tessa?

Hadn't he considered doing as much on a number of occasions because the man was an idiot?

"Let's go inside. I have things to show you." Joel motioned for them to follow. "But first, Yelena has food waiting. You can rest then we'll work."

The others walked beside Chase, carrying the equipment they would need along with weapons. They brought them inside, quickly relieved of the burden by several rough characters who nodded a greeting.

Svetlana hugged them and talked rapidly before moving to the table where an older version of Yelena placed bowls of steaming food. She pointed a large wooden spoon at them like it might be a club and ordered them to eat.

"Do you know these people, Svetlana?" Chase asked.

"I grew up not far from here. Yelena and I attended school together. She is like my sister. My family moved away to help me in my education. But we stayed in touch over the years. We are safe here. No worries." She smiled at Yelena and her mother. "They are like family. When she told me she'd married, I had to meet the lucky guy."

Carter took a seat next to his former Russian cosmonaut partner and introduced himself only to receive kisses on each of his cheeks and a slap on the back by the burly father figure.

"Wonder what that's all about," Sam hissed.

"Maybe they are welcoming him to the family," Chase teased. Sam's crude response was spoken in English, so he hoped no one heard or understood the physical meaning of her threat.

"Seems to me you and I are in the same boat when it comes to chances missed." He smirked at seeing her snarled lips as she flopped down on the other side of Carter and squeezed in as close as possible. Chase joined her on the other side. "Behave yourself, Sam." He elbowed her gently in the side. "I don't trust Svetlana, either. Watch yourself. It is a little too convenient she came back just because Yelena had a new husband and rekindled their friendship."

CHAPTER TWENTY-EIGHT

Sunlight streamed through the frosted windows next to the fireplace that now needed stoking. Darya's phone had buzzed a few moments earlier, forcing him to leave a warm bed. A soldier from Joel's village had called to see if the papers they produced were indeed authentic. After reassuring them of their validity, followed by a promise of retaliation if they were not treated with the utmost respect, Darya accepted their apology. They insisted no harm would come to the visitors.

Clicking off, he laid the cell phone gently down on the fireplace mantel before turning his attention back to Tessa whose gold hair flowed across her pillow. He stared at her for only a few moments before crossing to the bed and lifting the covers enough to gaze at her nakedness. The cold air sent a shiver up her body so that she turned toward him as he slipped beneath the quilt and pulled her back into his arms.

"You are freezing," she moaned, trying to escape unsuccessfully.

"Then warm me up." He smiled as a lazy grin formed on her lips. He kissed her tender lips and felt her stir beneath his hands.

Her eyelids fluttered open wider before she kissed his chin and sighed. "What would my husband suggest I do? Do you want hot tea? I won't be able to find any yak butter to put in it like in the Pamirs of Afghanistan."

He brushed her hair away from her face and whispered, "No. That is not what I need to warm me up." For a moment, he observed her face then stroked it gently. "Did I hurt you last night?"

"Maybe a little," she admitted, "but in a good way. It's been a while since…" her voice fell, and she let her fingers trail over his physique under the covers. "I'm a little out of practice."

"If that is out of practice, then I am a lucky man. It had been a while for me, too."

Tessa propped up on her elbow and stared at him in amusement. "You haven't been with another woman since we parted?"

He rolled to his back and stared at the ceiling. "No. To me, you were my wife and I wanted to stay loyal and faithful. And I have, Tess-sa."

"Darya, I…I mean Robert and I…"

He pulled her on top of him. "I understand, Tess-sa. You went home to pick up the pieces and be his wife."

"There was nothing between us when I came home. We tried to go through the motions for a while. He treated me like I had PTSD."

"Did you?"

"Yes."

"I'm sorry I put you through all that."

"If you hadn't, I would be dead."

Darya rolled her off him and began kissing her neck and gradually working his way down. "Well I wouldn't want that to happen." He paused. "I love you, Tess-sa."

"Show me," she coaxed.

~ ~ ~ ~

Ambassador Finley tapped her foot, irritated that she'd been placed on hold. The director of Enigma, Benjamin Clark, had requested to speak to her ASAP. She couldn't be sure, but she suspected the Secretary of State or maybe the president would be listening in. Why else would she be on hold?

"Ambassador Finley?" It was Director Clark. She recognized his deep, no-nonsense voice easy enough.

"Yes, Director. How can I help you?"

"I'm assuming we're on a secure line."

"As secure as anything in Russia."

The director gave a snort kind of laugh. Did he find her snarky comment amusing? They'd never met in person, only on video conferencing. The man with a thick head of white hair and a beak-like nose failed to smile. Bonnie remembered how Tessa had described him a carbon copy of the American bald eagle. She never much cared for how he made her feel exposed when he glared menacing at her through the computer. If mind readers existed, one had to be Director Clark.

Tessa had said little about him over the time she'd known her. Typical Enigma agent mentality. Come to think of it, she'd never mentioned what she'd done for the agency. From what little she knew; Tessa was no more than a logistics or informational officer. Although those people produced a lot of grunt work for their teams, they faced little danger like most field agents.

"How can I help you, Director?"

"Just making sure you have what you need to deliver those Christmas presents I ordered."

Bonnie rolled her eyes and pulled her Sherpa cloth robe tighter. Could this get any more cloak and dagger? "Yes. Packaged and ready to make delivery. Sorry it took me so long. Had to find the size and number you wanted."

"I understand. When do you think I'll get them? Christmas is come and gone here."

"True. No way of knowing. Guess you can pretend they are an unexpected surprise. Either way, you'll have them before you know it. I made sure they were loaded onto a plane yesterday." Bonnie hated making double talk about something as serious as Enigma team members and missing scientists.

"Excellent. I'm grateful. I hope it wasn't too much trouble."

"I had a little trouble, but nothing I couldn't handle. From what I hear, the plane took off as scheduled."

"Rumors have it a plane went down in the White Sea last night."

Bonnie waited before she responded. "I hadn't heard that.

Hopefully it wasn't the plane that was to deliver your gifts."

"It better not be, Ambassador Finley," the director said flippantly. "It would make the Secretary of State feel as if he couldn't depend on your ability to get things done."

"I assure you, Director, everything is going smoothly here. Only yesterday, I spoke to a mutual friend who wanted to inform me the package was secure and ready to go before she got married last night."

The sound of dead silence followed by the extreme irritated voice of Director Clark caused her to twitch. "Married?"

Bonnie imagined the surprised expression on the director's face. "Yes. My assistant, Tessa Scott, fell for President Antonov's right-hand man and eloped. Could have knocked me over with a feather." She chuckled softly into the phone, wondering if there might be steam coming out of the director's ears.

Of course, it had been Darya who had given her the reassurance, not Tessa. For all she knew, the woman went kicking and screaming to the tribesman's bed last night. She couldn't resist bringing up that image, to her mind, causing her to be more than a little envious.

"I understood Ms. Scott was already married."

"The details are a little fuzzy, but I think Roman Petrov took care of that inconvenience."

The conversation took an ominous turn. "You listen to me, Ambassador Finley. If anything happens to Tessa Scott, or her family, I'll hold you personally responsible. You'd best get a handle on her location within the hour and contact me ASAP. Are we clear?"

"Careful or you'll have a brain hemorrhage, Director Clark. I suggest you search for a red envelope delivered to Tessa's office. I'm sure one of your snoops know where it is. If not, you might want to contact Robert Scott, you know, just in case he—needs assistance. One went to their house and one to his office. No problems here. I appreciate your interest in my work and my welfare. Perhaps if we both stick to what our job descriptions contain, things will move a lot smoother."

Before she could utter another word, the line went dead. She slammed the phone down and burst into laughter, knowing there remained a good possibility she'd thrown a curve ball to the high and mighty director of Enigma.

Her thoughts turned back to Tessa. Part of her wanted things to work out for her. Being feisty and cute might work to her advantage in California, but in Russia, and in the company of a man like Darya, things could go sideways pretty fast. Truth be told, he scared her with those cold dark eyes and the unemotional expression of apathy he wore. Only when in the presence of Tessa did he show any hint of being human.

Whatever the woman had to control the wild tribesman, Bonnie wished she had a few gallons of it to drink. With that kind of power, no telling what she could accomplish. Best to keep Tessa and Darya under her protection a little longer in case she needed a get-out-of-jail-free card. After all, the three of them had a deal to keep each other's secrets.

CHAPTER TWENTY-NINE

General Oblonsky paced slowly, resembling a caged tiger bored of the monotony of restraint. He had been summoned to meet with President Antonov. Their relationship, somewhat strained, had never been the same since Roman Darya Petrov entered the picture. They spent too much time together, and the man gained influence over the president in a short period of time.

After discovering Roman was the president's nephew and an American intelligence officer, the general realized the president had cultivated a double agent, similar to how his predecessor did with Darya's father. Such a shame the plane his parents used on the way to his West Point graduation crashed. Accidents happen, as Americans like to say. General Oblonsky was more of the thought, don't screw with Mother Russia or your plane will crash. After discovering the senior Petrov gave secrets to the Americans, the general took it upon himself to rectify the betrayal. That was early in his career and before Victor Antonov rose to power.

Chances were Roman had followed his father's footsteps into betrayal, although he had found no evidence of that. Because he looked more Central Asian than East European, the general had a hard time reading his body language and expressions. Roman didn't exhibit them. He was cold as ice, stealthy as a Siberian tiger, and strong as a Russian brown bear. He'd seen the man work out with his best men and defeat them with little to no effort on every occasion.

When the American woman showed up, he knew Darya indeed had a weakness. To see such an opponent, transform into a man, clearly smitten with a lovely teacher from the States, surprised him. After sending a number of women his way without success, the general had begun to think Roman's interest might lie elsewhere, but that also proved false. Discovering they were to be married with the president's blessing made him tread lightly. He needed to prove the man meant to undermine the president and their country.

"General Oblonsky, thank you for coming. I know it is early for you." The president rushed in and sat at his desk, still wearing a robe. One of the workers followed him in with a tray of sweets and coffee. The general nodded and stood at attention until waved toward a chair. "Please. Sit."

"How can I assist you, Mr. President?"

"Is it true the plane I sent the Americans on crashed in the White Sea?"

The general had forwarded the information to the president himself when he'd gotten word in the early hours of the morning. "I'm afraid so, sir. We began a search, but unfortunately, a storm has moved in and rescue efforts have been delayed."

"Has the American ambassador been notified?"

"No, sir. I wasn't sure how you might want to proceed on that news."

The president waited for his assistant to exit the room, lifted the china cup, and sipped carefully. A smile followed with experiencing the first jolt of caffeine to his system. "I'll summon her here within the hour and inform her personally. It is the least I can do." Another sip, this time, a little longer. "The American president will be furious, of course. He will probably go into cowboy mode and throw around threats for expelling Americans from the country, especially on such short notice."

"Sanctions will follow."

"Not likely. After all, these were teachers, not diplomats. They're not going to admit they were spies. We can't prove it, either. All we know is that they were snooping in restricted areas of the president's quarters and interfered with an investigation that involved an attempt on my son's life."

"What are your orders for me, President Antonov?" The general held his hat and began rubbing the brim impatiently with his thumb.

"We have a problem in Siberia, near Lake Baikal, I'd like for you to check on it in a few days."

"What kind of problem?"

"I believe Roman and his new bride might be headed that direction. I want to make sure they are safe from any further Chechen attacks. It is a long way from Moscow." His mouth revealed a thin smile. "It is also the location of sensitive research. Perhaps you could check on that while you're there. I understand we are close to testing one of the planes for the cloaking device."

"My informant should be there today or tomorrow to relay any concerns."

"I think if the plane went down, as you claim, we are probably good to go on the test, General Oblonsky. I want verification of the crash before you leave in a few days."

The general stood slowly and replaced his hat. "Of course. I'll keep you informed."

"General, if further action is needed, wait until I give you orders. Is that understood?"

"Yes, sir."

~ ~ ~ ~

The landscape continued to be draped in snow, some places deeper than others, as the Trans-Siberian Rail Train clacked rhythmically over mile after mile of emptiness. Tessa had dreamed of taking this romantic trip for years and had suggested it when she married Robert, or thought they'd married. But she'd caved to his desire to go to a beach in Florida. That was what they could afford after all. The desire increased as her studies in geography broadened her horizons, along with her work at Enigma. Now here she was with a new husband, traveling toward a rendezvous with danger.

Darya had slipped out of their compartment, instructing her to lock the interior top latch while he was gone. The bottom lock appeared secure but could easily be opened with a sharp knife from the outside. In spite of the fact that most of the compartments left their doors open during the day for socializing, Darya wasn't comfortable leaving her with the prospect of strangers dropping by. It would be obvious she was an American who couldn't speak Russian.

Although he promised not to be long, a person up to no good could take advantage of the situation and disappear quickly. She promised to keep the shade pulled until he returned and enjoyed the time alone while taking in the vast wilderness, villages, and solitude the trip offered.

There was a great deal to think about concerning this new situation. She'd surrendered her heart and body to Darya. Never had she known such passion and love was possible. She felt helpless with every touch and whisper. Not once did he force her to love him. It came so naturally, she amazed herself with how comfortable it all felt. The feeling of being lost in his arms since that first night continued each time they came together.

Now being on the train for the second day with him, Tessa realized there would be hard decisions ahead of them. Darya made it known he wanted to return to Montana, the land he thought of as home.

"I will teach your children many things. They will learn to hunt, ride, and live from the land. I will be a good father, Tess-sa. You will see."

"I'm not sure Robert will go for that. He is not going to want me to move his children that far away."

"I will convince him this is best," Darya declared.

"You can't bully him to give up his children." Tessa kissed him lightly. "I still need to confront him on the marriage."

"Will you tell him about me?" He pulled her into his arms and searched her face with concern.

"One step at a time."

"You do not have to do this alone. I will be with you."

"I'm more worried about what my kids will think than Robert."

Darya smoothed her hair away from her face. "We will take it slow. Whatever makes this work. I am willing. You and the children are my family now. I promise to be a good father to them."

Tessa knew he would be. She'd experienced his love of children firsthand in the wilds of Afghanistan. He'd protected a bunch of orphan girls from the Taliban and they, in turn, loved him like the fathers they'd never had. Maybe that was what drew her to him in the first place.

It wouldn't be that easy with her own kids who'd had every advantage in life. They already had a father, friends, school, and security. The only thing they worried about was whether or not they'd be able to outmaneuver their mother when they wanted to upgrade their computer games. From what Darya had told her about his place in Montana, it was not Internet friendly.

A tap at the door and Darya's voice had her scrambling to let him in with their meal. They'd decided to eat in this last night to talk about what to expect once they arrived at Lake Baikal. It was also a good time to spend their last remaining hours alone. Once they hooked up with the team, things would start happening fast. The thought of Chase had faded in and out of her mind over the last couple of days.

What would she tell him? Would he be angry she'd done such a reckless thing by marrying Darya? Not that she had a choice. She had surrendered to him with little objection after he showed her the evidence against Robert. Did she do it out of spite, relief, or loneliness? Having someone to love her felt good.

The consequences of her actions began to weigh on her now that she knew the others would find out about her love affair with the notorious tribesman none of them trusted. She had been warned not to fall for anything he said. Could the information about Robert be false? No. She'd gone over it thoroughly. What troubled her most was facing Chase Hunter.

Part of her had wanted to tell him he was more than a friend, that she admired him and wanted to see where their relationship would take them. However, whenever they had gotten closer, he backed off, isolated her, and worked her harder than the others on the team. Weeks earlier, she'd believed they were moving toward common ground. The kids admired him and still talked about how he'd taught them all kinds of things when would-be burglars tried to ruin their Christmas while she'd gone to pick up her parents at the airport.

Then Russia happened. Each time Darya's name came up, he got angry and doubted her ability to do the job assigned. Any romantic intentions he'd displayed in the last few months appeared to have evaporated. Maybe she and the children would cramp his style. One thing for sure, he didn't want Darya to encourage her affections. Too late for that.

"You have been quiet today." Darya poured her hot tea. "Are you having second thoughts about me?" His impish grin told otherwise.

"If I were, this morning put that to rest." She returned the light attitude before reaching for the bread and cheese.

"Ah. I will dedicate myself to your happiness."

She passed him some food. "You'd better keep up your strength if that is the case."

"I think maybe you are worried about what the others will say when they find out we are together." Darya glanced out the window at the fading light which showed his own concerned reflection. "They will not approve."

Setting her food aside, she poured more tea. "No. I may lose my job."

"I can support you, Tess-sa, if that is your fear."

"I'm not worried about that." She reached over and stroked his upper thigh. "I've worked hard to gain their respect. I don't want to lose that."

"When they find out about Robert, they will understand."

"Maybe. But let's talk about tomorrow. What will happen?"

"When we arrive, things will be ready to go to the research complex where the scientists are being held. I'm not sure if it will be one day or two before we escape. It depends on the weather and if the sabotage virus has been installed."

"What will I be doing?"

"You will help Joel's family get ready to move. But this is where Captain Hunter comes in. I believe he will give orders at that point. He may have other jobs for you. Any evidence we were there needs to be erased. I'm sure the team in place has already begun that sanitizing, but fresh eyes will be important."

"What about your President Antonov? You seem to have a good relationship with him. Won't this be hard for you?"

He took a deep breath and let it out slowly. "Yes. He is the last family I have. But we are of two worlds. I believe in democracy, Tess-sa. Even with all her problems, I believe in the United States."

"He'll come after you." It was hard to keep the fear from her voice. "This country has a long history of tracking down citizens who have opposed them. They often meet with an untimely death."

A sad smile played around the corners of his mouth as he laid his hand on hers. "If that happens, I want you to promise you'll bury me in Montana. Will you do that for me?"

"Don't talk like that."

"Will. You. Do. It?"

"Yes."

Chapter Thirty

The cabin where the Enigma team would spend the next couple of days was warm, thanks to a blazing fire in the cast-iron stove. A pot of food cooked on the top, filling the room with a delicious aroma. Loaves of bread piled in a basket lay on the surface of an old cabinet that would be considered a jewel of an antique in the States. A stack of chipped plates, stacked on the shelves, were in various shades of white and ivory, several appeared to have yellowed from age. Coffee mugs of various sizes were stacked on top of each other. Silverware jammed in a tin can reminded him of crowded soldiers confined in a small space and, like the other things, were all mismatched and clean.

Chase swung his knapsack and let it go. It landed on the floor next to a ladder-back chair that looked strangely out of place with all the rough-hewn furniture. Yelena spoke quietly to Svetlana but stared at him, Carter, and Sam suspiciously. He couldn't hear the conversation, but Svetlana nodded and smiled at Carter as if reassuring Yelena she vouched for him.

"Captain Hunter. My friend thinks you look wicked." Svetlana, petite and agile, grinned mischievously. He became aware of how much she and Yelena differed in appearance; she being tall and broad shouldered, similar to her father. "I told her you were one of the good guys and would get them to America."

"Carter, Joel, is there a place we can talk?" He didn't care for surprises. Taking these people to America might be impossible.

"Not until we eat," Svetlana declared as she motioned for everyone to the benches on each side of the table. "Yelena says her mother has been up since before daylight preparing this meal. She wants to please you."

The older woman, dressed in faded camo and boots, that looked warm enough to walk across the frozen tundra, put her hands on her hips and offered a big smile, revealing two missing teeth. The laugh lines around her eyes softened Chase's irritation and led the way to the table, signaling the others to follow.

The small talk around the table involved hunting at first then moved to the sudden appearance of the soldiers who had been patrolling their village for the last few days. They hadn't created any problems and left the villagers alone for the most part, especially if they were offered a home-cooked meal or vodka. Yelena admitted they'd had the soldiers in for hot tea and sweet bread a time or two, creating goodwill between them.

The soldiers didn't know Joel Sandy's true identity, only that he was Yelena's husband and worked with her father around their small piece of property. They didn't try to figure too much out about anyone in particular. Mostly they watched while carrying their menacing rifles through the two streets. The people here made their living from taking in summer tourists visiting Lake Baikal or giving them the cultural experience tourists believed to be true even in today's modern world.

In the winter they cut firewood to sell to other small villages closer to the big city of Irkutsk. If the weather wasn't too bad, and just enough snow, sleighs would bring day-trippers from the Trans-Siberian Railroad train to share a meal and listen to local musicians play their unique songs on instruments of yesteryear.

In warmer weather, they often pulled out the costumes for something extra to excite the tourists. Baked goods for the train passengers were popular, and small trinkets carved out of wood were good sellers for those who needed a souvenir to take home. The friendlier the reputation, the less likelihood of trouble from Moscow. It was a world away from them, and the locals didn't much care for all the politics and world drama that could easily overshadow their peaceful existence.

"Come. I'll show you our little secret."

Joel could hardly contain himself as he took them into one of the two bedrooms and tapped the nose of a ballerina on a Bolshoi Poster. It had been framed without glass. In spite of it being faded and watermarked around the edge, Chase guessed it had meaning to one of the residents. He stared at Joel as Carter and Sam entered the room.

"What are you doing, Joel?" Chase folded his arms across his chest. Patience grew thin when he didn't understand.

"This." He beamed. After touching the nose on the picture, he pulled out the handle on the bottom of a painted dresser which immediately rolled the whole piece of furniture to the side and the floor opened to reveal a ladder going under the house. "We were lucky enough to have a basement built here during the Cold War. It was also used when the old Soviets sent dissidents to Siberia for what they called re-education. Many a Russian made their way either back home or to a safer area by this gem."

Turning a surprised glance to the other teammates, Chase could see they were impressed, too. "Let's have a look."

When they climbed down the ladder, the sound of activity brewed, along with a voice Chase knew from home. Once back on solid ground, he spotted his favorite redheaded tech genius, Vernon Kemp. Even here, the guy wore a Hawaiian shirt. The flip-flops and shorts had been replaced with appropriate-weather attire, but he wasn't so sure how long that would last.

"Figures you'd have a setup like this, Vernon," Chase said, inspecting the latest technology toys.

Vernon assisted Sam and offered a sheepish smile as she turned her piercing stare on him.

"Ahh, my little tech hero. Have I told you how much I adore you lately?" she said, giving him a hug.

Carter pulled her away and hugged him, too, only to get a shove from Vernon who blushed. "What? I missed you, too, little buddy. Have you been down here all this time without getting one of these beautiful Siberian women to keep you warm at night?"

Vernon possessed a permanent crush on Sam and usually stuttered or turned crimson in her presence. But when it came to technology and national security, his fellow tech admirers called him the Terminator. The Pentagon had other names for him since he'd screwed with their firewalls and projects on a number of occasions. The NSA had a love-hate relationship with the young genius and decided it was better to play nice than to tell him not to do something.

"Welcome." He reached for Chase's hand when he finally extended it.

"I wondered where we'd meet up. Joel been taking good care of you?" He grinned, knowing Vernon waited for any crumb of praise he offered. "Not too late to call this party off if he hasn't."

A low laugh among the group rose as Vernon motioned them toward his computer toys. "I've been too busy to notice. Other than being cold as heck, I guess things are going good." Vernon took a seat at his work station and pointed to a number of items on the screen.

"The bad news is the Russians are closer than we originally thought to getting the cloaking device operational. I've hacked into their programs, and they've pretty much blocked our scientists from getting in. I compared their digital footprints for the last couple of years, and they don't match up now."

"Can you stop them once we have our people out of there?"

"Already in place, boss. Just need a distraction at the end so they won't alert whoever is helping them."

"Helping them?" Chase asked.

Vernon spun his chair around and frowned. "One of our guys has switched sides."

CHAPTER THIRTY-ONE

"We are almost there, Tess-sa. Are you ready?" Darya grabbed up the two small bags they'd packed at the monastery. "How are you feeling?"

Tessa believed she may have caught whatever made little Yuri so sick. She had snuggled and loved on him before getting into the bathtub with him to bring down his fever. Now her throat felt raw and, when Darya felt her head earlier, he thought her skin a little too warm. A cough had kept her awake for several hours during the night, but after he'd made her a cup of honey tea with herbs, the cough grew silent.

"I'm fine. Probably the same thing Yuri has."

"Then you'll need antibiotics. I'm sorry you're not feeling well." He leaned and kissed her cheek, causing her to smile warmly. "Let's be on our way. Perhaps you can get medicine at Joel's when we arrive."

She tried to step around him, but he blocked her path.

"I love you. You have made me happy."

Tessa touched his cheek with gloved fingertips. "I am anxious to start our life together." She kissed his wide mouth briefly and stared into his eyes. "Remember that I am yours now. There is no reason to believe otherwise. Understand?"

"You don't want me to fight Captain Hunter about our relationship now that we are married."

"Exactly. It will only delay the rescue and confuse the others."

He proceeded out the narrow door with Tessa following. "I admit in the past I was jealous of Captain Hunter. The two of you have a special friendship I feared might ruin our chances to be together."

She laid a hand on his back and couldn't resist applying pressure to feel the muscles through his coat. "A new life for both of us is exactly what we need. Thank you for saving me once again, Darya."

He looked over his shoulder and smiled easily. "You can thank me later if you are well enough."

A shiver of desire surged through her, knowing the strength and power he possessed.

~ ~ ~ ~

The next morning, after breakfast, Chase, with Agents Carter and Sam, returned to the spotless underground facility. Smaller than Tessa's thousand-foot apartment back home, everything fit tightly in this one room: computer center, four narrow bunkbeds, two cots folded in the corner, a couple of metal chairs on wheels, a small table for two, and a four-foot board with hooks to hang clothes. Cold from the rock floor permeated through the souls of their shoes in spite of an electric heater that took the edge off. It did keep the place fairly dry, but a slight hint of mildew clung to the air. Chase wondered how long it would be before all of them developed mold allergies.

"We keep extra supplies down here," Joel had explained the day before, pulling back a curtain where a wobbly metal shelf displayed boxes of various items, including a coffeepot, microwave, and first-aid kit. Chase wondered about the other nondescript boxes and their contents, but he'd check them out later. "We just got the uniforms in two days ago. Cutting it close, but our contacts came through. The black market can be a sweet thing at times."

"Please tell me we're not beholden to the Russian Mafia."

"Not here. Too remote to make a profit. Mostly everyone here is in survival mode and willing to help each other, especially if they can rub a bully's face, from Moscow, in the mud or, in this case, icy snow." He laughed as if he'd made a joke. "These are good people; hardworking, loyal and"—he nodded at the upstairs where his adopted family lived, "welcoming, or I wouldn't have survived. It still amazes me no one turned me in. I know Darya paid a few people off to protect me all these months and maybe still does. I don't know, but I'm grateful to them."

More praise for Darya. Chase twisted his mouth in a snarl. "Yeah. He's a real prince. Thanks, Joel, for doing the leg work here."

Joel excused himself to return upstairs while the others made themselves comfortable. Exhausted after taking a short drive then hike in the late afternoon to spy on the facilities where the scientists were being held, they took a few hours to rest before going over blueprints and tentative plans.

Things didn't feel so overwhelming today, after a good night's sleep and a couple of hot cooked meals.

"Boss, got an incoming call from the director." Vernon looked at Chase who nodded an okay.

The screen was surprisingly clear, and Chase refused to ask why, knowing Vernon would give him the long answer, one he wouldn't understand or care about. He trusted the kid to do his job.

Director Benjamin Clark sat at his desk, the surface void of any papers or mementos. There was a running joke that the forensic team would be hard-pressed to find so much as a fingerprint. Not known for displays of emotion or affection, other than an occasional outburst of anger, which could wither a seasoned soldier in a split second, the director also bore an unfortunate resemblance to an irritated bald eagle. A rare show of warmth was usually reserved for Chase. He had recruited him to join the Enigma fold as a young man to keep him on the straight and narrow.

The other person who could cause the corner of his mouth to lift into a grin was Tessa Scott. She took advantage of that leverage from time to time but knew when to step back. He'd been skeptical, at first, of her role in the Enigma family, but she'd worked hard to win him over and now endured him being overprotective from time to time. Chase let the director be the bad guy on those occasions, since, when he tried to argue with her, she'd use a kind of squirrely logic that got them all into trouble. In spite of that, or maybe because of it, he continued to be mesmerized and captivated by her innocent charm.

However, Africa had changed her pie-in-the-sky attitude. They'd almost died together, and a seriousness now gripped her. Something had happened between them. So far, he'd been able to keep his feelings and body in check where she was concerned. She was an Enigma agent and married. Things had continued to deteriorate with the husband, not that he minded, since he believed he wasn't good enough or appreciative enough to breathe the same air as Tessa. After he bumbled through a babysitting experience with her three kids before Christmas, she had genuinely displayed a willingness to get closer. Then Russia happened.

Now he had Darya to worry about. He was in her head. Stockholm syndrome, the Enigma psychiatrist said. Darya kidnapped her and carried her off into the wilds of Afghanistan. Whatever happened between them physically remained a mystery. The story she'd told him after he rescued her didn't add up, and she'd continued to be evasive, not to mention protective, of the man who came to be known as the tribesman.

"Director."

"Captain Hunter. I see your team is all there."

"Except Tessa."

"And Darya."

"Yes, sir. I'm not sure when they'll arrive."

Vernon spun around in his squeaky chair. "Oh. I can answer that. Should be here by mid-morning. I talked to Darya late last night."

Chase narrowed his gaze at the tech in front of the computer screen. Vernon's sudden fearful stare triggered his own brow to pinch in anger. One glance at the director revealed he, too, appeared surprised. "You've been in contact with him?"

"Ah, yeah." Vernon cocked his head one way then the another as if trying to pop the kinks out of his neck and rubbed it vigorously.

"And?" the director broke in.

"No problems. Getting off the train not far from here. Probably already on their way." Vernon stuck a finger in his shirt and ran it around the collar as if he were warm. "Haven't been here long so not aware of any updates." Chase refocused on the director instead of bringing the young agent to task in front of everyone.

"A plane went down in the White Sea as predicted, and there are search parties on the way. Ambassador Finley has registered her complaints on behalf of our government, but President Antonov isn't commenting yet. Sounds like you really ticked him off." The director smirked.

"It's a gift," Chase responded sarcastically. "What about Tessa? We had to leave her behind. Darya claimed he had her."

The director frowned. "From all accounts, she is in his custody and safe as can be expected, considering their history. They stayed in a monastery outside of Moscow where he is favored by the clergy."

"He's a Muslim. How can that be?" Sam stepped forward and leaned in.

Vernon chose to add his two cents' worth. "According to him, he's not much of anything or maybe a blend of that and Christianity. He's certainly had exposure to both in his lifetime. Anyway, he is the fair-haired boy to the Russian Orthodox priests." The attention given by the team to the new information caused Vernon to choke on a few words. "Why are you looking at me like I have two heads?"

"You'll be lucky if you have one head when the director and Chase get finished with you," Carter quipped as he landed a firm fist in the young agent's shoulder. "Holding out on us, Vern?"

The director cleared his throat. "Yes. I'm sure a come-to-Jesus talk is in order for Mr. Kemp, but, for now, let's get you caught up. Tessa is indeed with Darya, and they married at the monastery." He held up a hand to stop a bombardment of questions that jumbled together until nothing made sense. He quickly gave them the rundown of Tessa and Robert's fake marriage and explained she indeed was free to marry Darya. "Now, whether she married the tribesman of her own accord, it is difficult to say. No matter. That can be sorted out later. We need to get those scientists out ASAP. Chatter in Moscow indicates they are aware we are getting close."

"Think Darya is playing both sides?" Chase folded his arms

across his chest, trying not to imagine Tessa standing at the altar with the notorious bandit.

"No way," Vernon butted in, drawing more disdain from his boss.

"You've become quite a cheerleader, Vernon. Guess we have a lot to talk about later."

The director scowled. "I agree with Vernon. There is no indication he has played us. He is the one who discovered all of this cover-up and got the ball rolling. He served his country well and now is doing it again."

"Another fan," Carter snapped.

"Why do you think they are on to us?"

"General Oblonsky is scheduled to leave Moscow this morning with what we think may be elite special forces. Not sure how many at this point."

"You wouldn't need many of those guys," Chase added.

"Their State Department officials have been called in, and the downed plane with what they think are Americans onboard has never been mentioned. They are getting ready to explain this away if push comes to shove. And it will come to that. President Austin is circling the wagons in Washington. He's been stewing for a fight with Antonov for years. Their stealing American military technology and our most valuable people has got him in a gunslinger mentality."

"Any indication if the Russians now have the cloaking technology?"

"A real possibility. At the least, they are close. If they get this, the balance of power will shift pretty quickly. We lost time and technology due to these guys. Their being able to cloak ground weapons and transportation systems, airpower, and even uniforms for our people can revolutionize what war and peace looks like. Russia needs resources, economic strength, and, most assuredly, respect. Now they are considered harmless bullies with their fingers crossed behind their backs. They can't be allowed to get the technology, or life as we know it can change in a heartbeat."

"The Iranians, North Koreans, and Chinese would be promising the unthinkable to get on their good side," Sam interjected. "They don't mind doing a little damage to us if Russia promises to protect them. If ever there was a domino effect, this is it."

The director nodded his head in agreement. "So, let's get it done, and get the hell out of there. If you are caught…"

"They won't be," came a voice from behind them. Everyone turned around to see Darya Petrov and Tessa standing in rigid observation as if waiting to make their presence known. "I'll see to it, Director Clark," Darya promised.

The director nodded slowly then cut the live feed.

Chase pivoted to face the two but stared only at Tessa. "Nice of you to show up for the party."

CHAPTER THIRTY-TWO

Tessa could feel the electric tension in the underground room as the other agents left her and Darya to face Chase. Carter laid a hand on her shoulder and met her gaze with a conflicted one. She reached up and touched his fingers as he moved away to follow Sam and Vernon up the ladder.

The thought occurred to her if she fainted or staggered helplessly, Chase might withdraw his penetrating glare. The gaze reminded her of having a splinter removed from your finger with a rusty needle. His hooded eyes and a flexing jaw sent a warning of rage. All this made her shiver in spite of still being bundled up in her parka and thick clothing.

For the first time since she'd known Chase Hunter, she had to admit, she feared what was going to happen to her. Darya casually reached over and entwined her fingers with his and squeezed before drawing her attention to his solemn face. Now she knew him well enough to see comfort and reassurance in the almond-shaped eyes. With a hard swallow, Tessa dared speak. "I'm—glad to—see you all made it safely."

Chase unfolded his arms before shifting his attention to Darya. "Took you long enough to get here."

A snide smile spread across Darya's wide mouth. "I was preoccupied with—more important things."

"So, I hear. I want to talk to Tessa. Alone."

"No," he said flatly. "In case you haven't heard, she's my wife now, and I'll not have you throwing your weight around to intimidate her."

A surge of panic engulfed her to the point she feared she might vomit. It wasn't the first time these two had gone toe to toe.

Her boss switched his gaze momentarily to her like a swinging samurai sword then back to Darya. "She's still my agent and under my orders, not yours. Come to think of it, so are you."

"It's okay, Darya. I'll be up in a minute. Please." She laid a hand on the tribesman's forearm and felt muscles flex. His bottom lip jutted out slightly as he patted her hand and stared menacingly at Chase.

"We will talk later, Captain Hunter."

Chase didn't respond, except for raising his stubborn chin in an act of dismissal. A few moments of silence felt eternal as he refocused the attention back to her. Knowing to divert her gaze away was a sign of weakness or maybe fear, Tessa stood her ground and locked onto facial features instead of his eyes. Those eyes that had for the last several years, wooed, tempted, reassured, and demanded loyalty from her.

Somewhere along the way, they became best friends when not on duty or on a mission. They spent hours talking books, music, their past history, and future dreams. Moments snatched in secret and in innocence turned out to be more of an aphrodisiac than either of them expected, yet neither acted on the desire to explore a deepening relationship.

Tessa abided by her religious beliefs of being faithful to the man she'd promised to honor and obey. He held to the ethical conduct of an officer and a gentleman, refusing to cross the line to impropriety. Even when he'd flirted and gotten a little too physically close, Chase quickly retreated into his own world.

"Is it true? You married the tribesman?" His voice revealed nothing but the bark of a hard man to figure out.

"Yes." Her voice came out so softly, she noticed he cocked his ear toward her as if he thought he might have missed her answer.

For some reason, she wanted to cry and fall against him, to beg for forgiveness, but why? Not once had he ever told her they could have a life together. Other than saying she'd saved him from self-destruction, he had yet to hint his interest included anything more than getting her between the sheets.

She cleared her throat. "Yes. I married Darya. Turns out Robert and I weren't married after all. I saw all the documentation. It's true, Robert knew for some time, if you're thinking Darya tricked me. But if it makes you feel any better, I'll triple-check when we get back to the states."

"No need. It appears the director has already done that for you."

Somehow, she wasn't surprised. He'd always been two steps ahead of everyone else.

"General Oblonsky had plans to move me after you left, I think. Darya found me and took me to a monastery where I'd be safe."

"Then you already knew about Robert? The fake marriage?"

"No. I thought it was a plan to make me look like I was Darya's wife so the authorities couldn't touch me. Then I saw all the documentation."

He stepped so close, she could feel his breath on her face. "I bet you didn't ask a lot of questions to make sure."

"What is that supposed to mean?" She bristled.

"I think he got in your head again and this time you thought, what the hell. I'll just screw the bad boy because I don't have any other choice."

Before she could stop herself, Tessa hauled off and slapped his face with such force he staggered back. A red handprint appeared on his tanned cheek as a look of surprise flashed in his eyes.

"Don't ever speak to me like that again, Captain Hunter. I won't be made to look like a whore just because that seems to be what you are used to in the romance department." With fists doubled at her side, it was all she could do to keep from slugging him again. "I don't have to ask your permission to do anything in my private life. In spite of what you might think, Darya gave me a way out of the marriage almost immediately. The difference between you and him is that—he loves me enough to admit it."

He blinked and touched his face then stepped closer again and stared at her. "If he is threatening you or holding anything over your head because of me, I'll take care of it."

"Don't flatter yourself." Tessa stepped back from his close

proximity in order to breathe. Why did he still have such an effect on her? "Let me do my job." She continued to back up until her foot touched the ladder. The desperation in his eyes cracked her anger. "I never meant to hurt you," she whispered. "You've always been the one I…"

He moved toward her, but she quickly turned and scampered up the ladder, leaving him alone to decide what the new reality without her might look like.

~ ~ ~ ~

Darya turned Tessa around to inspect her military uniform. He wolf-whistled then pulled her into his arms, bringing a warm smile to her face, followed by a tender kiss. Not wanting to share the underground room with the others, they had been given the small attic for their room.

There was enough room for a full-size bed with a lumpy mattress, a wooden chair, and a floor-length mirror with spider cracks and a yellow hue that comes with age. Several nails hammered into the logs served as hooks for the owners' mementoes and a few extra supplies. There wasn't a window to get fresh air or have an idea of the weather. The floor had a hidden staircase that opened with a pull of the string, like the ones in the States. It had been left open for them so the heat of the fireplace would keep them from freezing to death.

"You are a handsome man in uniform, Colonel Petrov." Tessa smiled as she toyed with his collar.

He laughed and kissed her neck and mouth. "And you, in a drab Russian uniform, still take my breath away."

After Joel told the team they were leaving everything behind, no further preparation was needed. Underground explosives were set to destroy any trace of their presence when their escape was underway.

Since Tessa wouldn't need to help out, Darya had given her the job as medical assistant to Chase who had trained as an army medic for the Rangers then Delta Force. He could examine the scientists and determine their general health. He spoke fluent Russian as could Sam and Carter. In the event they were watched, and he had no reason to think otherwise, no one would know she was an American. It would be easy for Chase to play a chauvinist doctor if the need arose to protect Tessa from being asked questions.

Meanwhile, Svetlana and Carter would conduct experiments and gather further information as test pilots and hopefully be able to evaluate the ability to safely get the scientists out to the plane that would take off in a matter of days, if not hours.

Samantha would pose as Darya's assistant, logging notes into her tablet which instantly transferred to Vernon back at the cabin. Her fake pedigree included serving as one of the few female tank commanders of the Russian Army before being transferred into the Strategic Missiles Forces, where her superiors took notice. The woman continued to be an imposing presence wherever she went. With any luck, interested soldiers might follow her with carnal interest rather than consider security violations. Even the ice water running through her veins came across as sexual enticement.

Darya and Tessa joined the others who boarded several unmarked white vans. Joel had been instrumental in securing their rides. Wearing a Russian uniform and sporting a military haircut, Darya hoped no one recognized him. However, it had been a long time since the soldiers left him for dead. They probably didn't remember him, but fellow scientists certainly would. If one of them had switched sides, keeping him undercover remained a top priority. In the States, he had been the lead on the cloaking project. His vast knowledge of bending light revolutionized the advancement of such an endeavor.

Darya noticed how Tessa fidgeted against the cold. She'd hated this kind of weather. That had been one of the reasons he'd decided to return her to Kabul after he'd kidnapped her in Afghanistan. Her body didn't adjust to such extreme weather, and he feared he might lose her to sickness if the Taliban didn't catch up with her. In the process, he'd lost her to Captain Hunter who whisked her back to the States to resume a life she'd forgotten.

"It will be warmer in the car." Darya smiled at her rosy cheeks and longed to hold her one more time before heading toward danger. Captain Hunter pushed past them and held the side door open for them. He'd barely said a word since they had arrived, other than going over their plans and positions. In order for Tessa to be happy, he needed to clear a few things up or the man had the ability to make her miserable. Whatever had transpired between them the day before, Tessa hadn't felt it necessary to share, and he chose not to press. He trusted her.

"We don't have all day," Chase growled.

Darya stiffened and jerked his chin up in stubbornness as the two men locked glares. He helped Tessa inside and got in the front seat with Joel who was the driver. There had been room for all of them, but if someone needed to be evacuated, they'd be hard-pressed to have space to get them out. Sam got in with Tessa while the others followed Chase to the second van.

He glanced back at the two women, meeting the hateful stare of Sam. They had not hit it off on their first few encounters, and neither had done anything to change first impressions. The woman was all grit and steel, with the beauty of a mythological siren. She enjoyed being in control and knew her relationship with Tessa was tenuous at best. The woman also followed Chase's orders like they had been handed down from the Almighty himself. Her satanic snarled lips amused him enough to return the gesture before turning to Joel.

The vans roared to life, one backfired a puff of black smoke, and both rattled forward down the main street of the village. With a noisy engine and little insulation, whatever Darya and Joel discussed in the front seat couldn't be heard by the women.

Tessa glanced at Sam who frowned at her in return and jerked her arm away to keep from touching her.

"So, are you not talking to me, either?" Tessa asked.

Sam smirked at her before pooching out her lips in contempt.

"Sam, please."

Silence hung heavy for about a minute before Sam leaned closer to Tessa's ear. "What were you thinking? Darya Petrov is trouble."

"He'll complete the mission."

"I meant for you."

Tessa met her irritation with her own sour expression. "You don't know anything."

"I know Robert is home thinking you're a good little girl instead of playing with a notorious bandit," she hissed. "And before you get all high-and-mighty, the director told us about the fake marriage." Tessa turned away to watch the profile of Darya as he spoke to Joel. "That doesn't excuse you marrying him."

"I tried to get away. I really did," she mumbled. "He caught me trying to leave the monastery." Tessa turned back to Sam. "He only wanted to protect me. I was crazy with worry for you guys. He promised he'd taken care of it and not to worry."

Sam stiffened and puffed out cold air. She unexpectedly reached over and took Tessa's hand in hers. She tried to pull away to no avail. A spark of panic flared up inside her when she cast a timid glance at the senior agent.

"I don't pretend to know what is going on between you and the tribesman, but I guess"—Sam released her hand— "what is done is done. Clearly, he loves you. And"—she inhaled deeply—"thanks for protecting me from General Oblonsky. Why would you do that?"

Tessa grinned and bumped her shoulder with her own. "I was more afraid of you than him."

The corner of Sam's mouth turned up.

"And you're my friend, Sam." When Sam groaned her irritation and squinted, Tessa leaned in closer and made kissing sounds to irritate her. Sam gave a hard shove which caused her to nearly fall off her seat but reached out and stopped her in time.

CHAPTER THIRTY-THREE

The buildings housing the lab and living quarters appeared to be made of concrete, which emitted a sterile vibe from the bygone era of the Soviet Union. It blended with the snow-covered landscape and resembled a prison. Chase assumed the small windows prevented too much heat loss in the living quarters. The other part of the structure hinted it was of no importance, but Joel had assured them inside it was a state-of-the-art lab. Another nearby building, freshly painted, appeared to be new construction, considering it lacked the decades of grim and decay the other structure wore.

"That's the training and experimentation lab." Joel nodded casually as the others walked up beside them.

"Who are they training?" Carter asked.

Joel shrugged. "When I first came, there was no one. I've heard a group of ten pilots and support members have rotated in and out over the last couple of years. The last six months each group has stayed longer. They take what they've learned back to various military installations and become instructors for virtual programs our guys created. Even Svetlana has been here over the years, training."

Carter's head swiveled around to show more interest. "She never told me that."

"One of the times when Darya made an unexpected visit to our home, she was there. The three of us talked for a long time. She wasn't happy with her life here and believed she'd been given a raw deal when removed from the space program." He grinned. "As you know, she is a bit vindictive and temperamental."

"So, Darya made sure she was the contact for Carter?" Chase didn't like it and something about Svetlana being a part of this mission made him uneasy.

"That's right. He appeared confident in her ability to put some of the parts together in getting planes and other components together to make this work. They met several more times, I understand. But I wasn't there. I always felt like maybe she didn't trust me. Just my imagination."

"Do you trust her?" Chase grumbled.

"I didn't at first. My wife told me she was chummy with General Oblonsky. I even thought, at first, she was on the plane when it was taken. I've not seen the general up close since I escaped the research facility. But it was him on the plane. He never tried to hide it, either. There was always something familiar about Svetlana. The flight attendant didn't look Asian. But I had been drugged and can't recall much. I'm not very good at remembering faces, Captain Hunter. Why? Is something wrong?"

"The general has a pretty rough reputation with women. Can't imagine Svetlana would put up with him." Carter twisted his mouth to the side in contemplation. "She is the kind of person who would do anything to get what she wants or deliver payback."

"My wife has told me Svetlana is determined to escape to the US for a better life. They are very close."

"How near to completion is the cloaking project?" Chase asked.

"Just a little tweaking to do as of last week. You can only procrastinate so long with the Russians unless you want to sleep with the wooly mammoths." He raised his chin and nodded toward another Quonset-style structure near a runway. "That is what they use for their helicopters throughout the country. It's a portable building with two-axle bridge cranes. They have the lifting capacity of two tons. Impressive inflatable frames can hold up the entire building. There are no supporting columns inside the structure to get in the way of equipment, planes, or helicopters."

"Have the planes that will be cloaked arrived?" Carter inquired, clearly fascinated by the idea of an invisible airplane.

"Yes. Arrived two days ago. They've had to update the energy-efficient lighting systems. Our guys insisted on it in order to get everything up and running on time. We created a backup power system that can be controlled after we get in the air that will destroy any other systems they might try to use. I believe Vernon is monitoring it now."

Darya had disappeared inside, returning minutes later to motion them to follow him. Everyone fell into character and marched as a fine-tuned military group, their arrogance reflected in their lack of expression and interest in several of the men who rushed forward to greet them. Their presence appeared to put the Russians on edge from the way they jabbered nonstop about refreshments before taking them on the tour.

Removing his gloves, Darya surveyed the surroundings and nodded an approval of their hospitality. There were hot tea and simple breads with butter. They apologized for the lack of vodka but explained since the work remained sensitive, it was decided the risk of failure outweighed the Russian propensity to drink, even during work hours.

The hot tea was well received, but the guests remained silent for the most part. Tessa had taken up position near Chase as his assistant. One of the lab coat men tried to engage her in conversation, but he shut the man down before she had to answer.

"I think we'd like to get to work now," Chase snapped as he looked down his nose at the man. "Where are your medical facilities?" He frowned at Darya who was the ranking officer today. "We are wasting time."

"Of course, Doctor." Darya nodded and cocked his head at one of the Russians who had apparently been part of the welcoming committee. "We have little time before final preparations are implemented. My people are anxious to see this to completion. You understand."

"Most certainly, Colonel Petrov. If you'll follow me, Doctor, I'll take you myself." The Russian in a lab coat then gave orders to the other men to escort each group to their destination. "Your escort will be happy to attend to any of your needs."

"Thank you. I'll be sure to add your preparedness to my report," Darya voiced in a bored tone as he slapped his gloves against a leathery palm.

The Russian bobbed his head up and down, a pleased smile spreading across his face. "It is my pleasure to serve such a distinguished friend of our president, Colonel Petrov."

Darya grunted a "humph" and waved an impatient hand to proceed. Chase had to admit the coldness in such authority surprised even him. He played the part well, or maybe he was just a natural. Chase wondered what Tessa saw in the guy. All he observed most of the time was a drug dealer and a big ego. How could Miss Apple Pie think she could create a life with him?

The team of people separated into their various assignments while Chase and Tessa were led into a drab room with medical equipment from twenty years ago. He had brought a medical bag of his own with more up-to-date tools that could send vitals back to Vernon.

Both removed their outerwear and slipped into starched lab coats. Tessa helped him with the equipment in his black bag. He demonstrated how to use certain equipment and spoke quietly in Russian but periodically used English if Tessa used the phrase "YA ne ponimayu (I don't understand)." With the few words she knew, the chances of her tipping anyone off as being American were slim. They finished setting up quickly and waited for the first scientist.

"I'm sorry about yesterday," he said, zipping the bag shut. "It was a shock, and I'd been worried about your safety, even though Darya had assured me you were okay."

Tessa stared up at him with no expression.

"I shouldn't have called you a whore."

"You got that right."

"I don't know what you went through or what kind of danger you were in. I'm sure Darya tried to protect you. It's clear he…"

"Loves me?" Tessa sniped. "Because he does. I don't know what is going to happen back home. I know I'm booting Robert to the curb once and for all. I kept thinking things would change, but I knew weeks ago, even before our Christmas, it was over. I felt like such a failure."

"Just be sure this is what you want, Tessa." He reached out to touch her arm, but she shied away.

"I'm not sure what I want, to be honest. One thing I do know, Darya makes me happy."

Chase busied himself with setting up a kind of work station before speaking. "I heard you laughing last night. You haven't done that much lately. Didn't realize how much I missed it." He glanced sideways at her for a second before speaking. "I only want you to be happy and safe, Tessa. I got you into this life, and we've become close friends. It's hard not to be protective." He stole another glance and noticed her intense gaze had softened as she nodded her approval, wearing a half smile.

"You make me crazy, you know that, Chase?"

"Ditto," he confessed as Darya escorted a man into the room. "We've got company."

The man tagging along shuffled after Darya and kept his head down until introduced. His crown of brown hair peppered with gray appeared to have been trimmed, mostly likely for the inspection. Close-set eyes and a high forehead void of wrinkles gave him an almost cartoon appearance, especially with the pug nose and thin lips too small for such a round face.

"This is Dr. Miller, comrade." Darya locked his fingers behind his back as he addressed Chase in the native tongue. "He speaks no Russian, so whatever point you decide it is safe to tell him about moving him will be up to you."

"No idea who the traitor might be?"

"Not yet. I have been here only a couple of times and watched the scientists at a distance." His focus shifted to Tessa who fiddled with the instruments and seemed to ignore both of them. Chase followed his line of sight. The tribesman narrowed his eyes as they refocused on Chase. "We will speak of this other matter later."

"Count on it."

The morning passed quickly with each examination taking about thirty minutes. Russians typically break for lunch between one and two. The menu included soup, a main course of some kind of meat smothered in a gravy sauce, and a fruit drink, followed by hot tea and a gooey dessert. The American scientists sat at a nearby table and ate heartily, as if they weren't use to such a large meal. The effect resulted in smiles between them and overall well-being.

"For a bunch of guys, we were told had been taken well care of, they could stand sideways and stick out their tongues to look like zippers. They sure are gobbling this food down," Carter mumbled.

"They hardly said a word during the exams. We didn't speak any English, and I think they were told we didn't know any. I thought we'd learn something that way," Chase offered.

No mention of the rescue plan to any of the scientists. He thought it best to examine them for now.

Darya pushed his plate away and drank the hot tea. "Other things are happening."

"Like what?" Chase said casually as he eyed the other workers sitting throughout the dining hall.

"Not sure, but they are trying to make this place shine. It can't be for us."

"Maybe it's you they're trying to impress, since you have the president's ear."

Darya shook his head. "I thought so at first. But they were avoiding my questions about the timetable. I think they know their work could be in jeopardy."

"Joel, did you hear anything?" Chase asked as he picked at his dessert.

"Not sure. I stayed clear of my friends, except for one who knows we'll try to get them out. He says they got word from Moscow that a high-level person should arrive, maybe tomorrow."

Darya's face darkened. "General Oblonsky was behind the whole project. I couldn't prove he planned the taking of the plane the American scientists were on, but I'm sure he was behind it."

"Not your uncle?" Chase quizzed.

"I don't believe so, but he probably wouldn't admit it. He does know about the project. He's tried to stay clear to avoid admitting to anything."

"If he knows about it, then he must have issued the orders." Chase didn't want to give President Antonov any get-out-of-jail-free cards. "What makes you so sure about this?"

"Because I told him everything," Darya said offhandedly.

CHAPTER THIRTY-FOUR

The table of agents grew so quiet, Tessa did a visual count to make sure everyone was still there. All eyes were on Darya who waited for, what he must think, would be a bombardment of questions or sounds of outrage. The cold, dark expression on his face showed no emotion. She'd come to recognize that look when they were in Afghanistan.

Such intimidation tactics had served him well when dealing with the Taliban. Enigma agents weren't the Taliban, and all were a great deal smarter than the average person. Their experience and comfort level with lethal force made them a dangerous enemy to suddenly stop trusting you. The corner of Darya's mouth turned slightly up as he ran his gaze over the group, landing finally on her.

She sat across from him and couldn't help but feel both love and fear when he focused on her. The real man who he was inside could be seen in his almond-shaped eyes and had the power to keep her spellbound. Whatever he had set in motion, she believed to be an action that would get them out unscathed.

"Best not pretend I didn't know what was going on after they tried to kill Joel." Darya turned his attention to Chase, whose jaw tightened and released as if trying to control his temper. "Once I made my way into my uncle's favor, he let General Oblonsky take me under his wing. Coming here was one of those things we did together." Darya looked to Joel. "I would never reveal the man they thought they'd killed had actually become my eyes and ears."

Joel looked over his shoulder, obviously paranoid someone would still be able to recognize him. "Without Darya's help, I would be dead, and the Russians would soon be the world's superpower."

"You have been a brave man, Joel Sandy," Darya admitted as if impressed. "I know you could have left long ago with my help."

"Darya offered to get me out a few months after he found me. I decided I needed to make sure my friends and coworkers had a chance to escape. It has been a long process." Joel smiled at his champion. "Staying meant I could keep an eye on things. If I escaped, I wouldn't have had proof." He blushed. "By then, I'd already fallen in love. Does crazy things to a man like me."

Darya grinned over at Tessa. "It does to all of us."

Chase huffed out irritation before he twisted his mouth in a kind of disbelief. "And the president?"

"Once we began to form a bond, I told him the real work was being done by American scientists and engineers. Although he didn't seem surprised by General Oblonsky's treachery, he wasn't opposed to it, either, since his hands hadn't been on any of it."

"You're telling me a man like President Antonov had no idea about what was going on?" Chase quipped.

"He knew of the research. Just not about taking the Americans." He poured himself another cup of tea. "It's no secret that many countries are working on the same kind of research. The Chinese are not far behind. Ironically, the one good thing General Oblonsky did was have our people sabotage their research."

Joel chuckled. "That was something that made our people feel better about what they were doing, even if it was for Russia. They feared the technology would get into the hands of the North Koreans, who in turn would team up with Iran. The Russians were very convincing. One thing is for sure. They want to be the ones on top. Since the fall of communism, Russia has been in a steady decline."

"He's right," Tessa spoke, glad there was something she finally knew something about. "Population is declining. Couples are waiting longer to have children. Women are more educated and not sure they want to commit. Again, not so different than the US. Drugs and alcohol have been a problem like everywhere else."

Samantha taught economics and understood the components of their downward spiral. "But, economically, they have suffered. They do have a wealth of petroleum but are forced to compete with other world markets, especially Saudi Arabia. Chechnya also has given them headaches. Most young Russians have no idea what life under communism was like. They want a voice, opportunity. A recent survey suggested that half of the Russian youth would like to emigrate and never return."

Svetlana finally joined them with her tray of food and squeezed in between Carter and Joel. She smiled at her former astronaut partner then over at Sam who pretended not to notice. Tessa was pretty sure if the Russian wasn't careful, she'd end up a Popsicle in Lake Baikal.

Carter was attentive to her but carried a kind of reserve she'd never witnessed when he was with a woman. Did he not trust Svetlana, his wounds still raw from how she'd set his dismissal from NASA in motion?

"You all look like stoic Russians. I love it." She smiled. "I just heard day after tomorrow, General Oblonsky arrives." She elbowed Carter playfully. He didn't respond other than to cast a concerned glance at Chase, who apparently caught the discrepancy in time of arrival.

She continued, waving her fork. "We test the plane tomorrow and get in the simulator this afternoon. They weren't expecting anyone for a few more days, but Moscow is nervous. Your American ambassador is making a lot of noise about the downed plane with Americans onboard over the White Sea."

"Must be afraid something will leak about this operation if our intelligence people start taking a closer look at satellite images," Chase guessed. "They've got to know this place is here."

"It's been here since the Soviet Days. They haven't tried to hide anything. The only thing that has changed is the helicopter storage facility," Darya offered. "It has been a staging area for experimental aircraft off and on for twenty years. Nothing important ever came from here."

Carter pushed his plate away and skipped the dessert. "The plane that brought the scientists here is in that hangar. Svetlana and I will go over everything after the simulation exercise. But I'm thinking we need to start getting those guys ready to move."

"Agreed." Chase folded his arms across his chest. "They've got a makeshift infirmary. Tessa, I think you and I are going to have to create a distraction in order to get those guys onboard."

"I'll see what else I can find out." Darya pushed away from the table and walked around to where Tessa was sitting and extended his hand to her. She slipped hers in his, feeling the warmth and strength when he applied the slightest pressure. As she started to stand, he addressed Chase with more politeness than she thought possible. "We'll only be a few minutes, Captain Hunter." To her surprise, Chase nodded.

"Everything okay?" she asked in Pashto, a language they both knew. He led her into an empty corridor. With his hand now on her back, guiding her to a shadowy alcove, Tessa expected bad news.

"I needed to tell you something," he whispered in her ear as he pulled her into his arms.

A surge of warmth spread through her body as she returned the embrace. "I'm listening."

He remained silent as his wide mouth turned into a puckered smile. Letting his gaze run over her face, he touched her cheek then ran his fingers across her mouth. "I wanted only to make sure this was real. You. Me. Together, finally, even if it is in this place."

"I'm happy you found me, Darya, in Afghanistan, the States, and again here." She kissed him. "If you're worried I'll run away again…"

"I am not worried," he insisted playfully. "And even if you did, I'm not sure I would have the strength to chase you down after our love—"

"Shhh!" Tessa's face burned. "Someone will hear you."

"Let them," he chuckled. He released her. The team had entered the corridor and had nearly reached them when they stepped out.

It wasn't lost on her that as they stepped out of the shadows, Darya straightened his jacket and ran his fingers through his hair as if to put it back in place. His eyes locked with Chase's then turned to Tessa who could feel her face flush deepen. Darya slid his hand down her back until it reached her waist, but she stepped away, knowing the others got the message of possession and a moment of stolen passion.

Then she remembered Darya Petrov was now her husband and such moments belonged to them, no one else. They could think whatever they wanted about her relationship with the tribesman. He loved her and had promised her happiness. There would be no lies or half-truths to trick her to get what he wanted. Even now, standing next to him, she could feel his steady heartbeat, reassuring her of a better future and that her love would not be misplaced ever again.

Darya touched her fingers with his, causing her to glance up at him. The gentleness in his almost slanted eyes touched her like a velvet hammer. She wanted to fall into his arms again and tell him how much she loved him, but this wasn't the time. He moved toward the others, making sure he passed Chase, and bumped him with his shoulder then placed his hat on his head.

The others kept walking, but Chase stopped and glared down at her. "Are you ready to get back to work, or do you need a minute?" His snide tone irritated her.

She turned toward their destination and fluffed her hair then smiled. "Energized and ready, Captain Hunter." She took a few steps then turned back to witness his angry dark eyes and clenched jaw. "Coming, or do you need a minute?"

CHAPTER THIRTY-FIVE

With the third round of simulations completed, Carter and Svetlana were guided to the hangar to run system checks. The Russian in charge of keeping data on their progress had been surprised at how proficient Carter had been on the exercise. There was no way they could know the ex-astronaut had been practicing for several months back in the States, thanks to DARPA (Defense Advanced Research Projects Agency). The Russians made this one look like a first-generation Pac-Man game. Svetlana learned from his tricks to overcompensate for her lack of experience and quickly fell into the rhythm of flying a plane now equipped with cloaking technology.

Once inside the hangar, he became aware of several planes, one of which appeared to be the Singapore airliner. He stared in amazement that it hadn't been destroyed or broken up for parts.

"Why would they keep the plane?" Carter mumbled.

"This would be proof they were taken. Sounds risky." She put her hands on her hips and shook her head. "What were they thinking?"

Carter asked one of the mechanics working on a helicopter about the plane then returned to Svetlana who was going over a run-up checklist as if they were getting ready to take off.

"The mechanic said last week routine maintenance had been done, but it hadn't been flown in over six months. Probably a waste of time to fly home."

"We should stick to the plan, Carter. The plane we flew to the other airstrip is ready to go. I'm sure it's gassed up already. We need only to get these men there." The irritation in her voice drew Carter to notice her stiff stance and twitching fingers at her side.

"Feeling a little rusty is all," he quipped then winked. "Always wanted to fly one of these babies." He looked at the fighter jet. "But if you'd rather me fly our supersonic baby over there, I'm good with that, too. That cloaking device should be activated by now. If there are any bugs, I'd be able to find them."

Svetlana bristled. "No way. I'm a much better pilot than you," she sniped as she cocked her head. "Besides, I've flown it before."

"Not with cloaking. There's likely to be a bounce."

"I can do it. The device will shut down if there is a problem. Better to find it out now." She glanced at the Singapore airliner. "That's more your speed anyway," she teased sarcastically.

The sound of greetings alerted the two as they came around the plane to see Darya enter the hangar. He moved with purpose and the agility of a proud lion. Carter had to admit his narrow eyes shifting from side to side, taking everything in, caused even him to worry about getting on the man's bad side. The few people working stood rigid and either nodded or saluted. Darya responded by lifting his chin slightly and continued with a brisk walk toward them. Samantha followed on his heels, eyeing the men with contempt as they tried not to admire her form.

"I spoke to my assistant in Moscow. Day after tomorrow, we'll be getting company for sure." Darya spoke nonchalantly as he ran his hand along the side of plane. "It's to be expected, but I thought we might have more time to put our escape plans in motion."

"Does anyone in Moscow know you're here?" Carter came up beside Darya and spoke out of the corner of his mouth.

"Hard to say. It is Russia, and my uncle does keep tabs on me. He knows I'm on my honeymoon." Darya cut his gaze to him as if expecting a retort.

Carter decided to extend a hand in friendship. "Congratulations, by the way." Darya dropped a hard stare to his hand before he grabbed it in a vise grip. "She deserves to be happy."

"I will see that happens." Darya tried to release Carter's hand only to feel it tighten.

"I hope so, Petrov, because otherwise, I might get pissed off." He grinned and dropped his hand, made a fist, and gave him a friendly bump. "Quite a shock. I could have sworn she was in love with me." He grinned.

One corner of Darya's mouth turned up. "Perhaps if you had spoken up sooner…"

"Damn. You're right." He snapped his fingers and noticed Svetlana and Sam frowned, apparently not amused at their banter.

Darya shifted his attention to the two women then turned back to the huge plane before them.

"Is there any way we can get this baby up and see if she can still fly?"

Darya frowned. "When the time comes, they will expect you to fly that for a test flight." He pointed to the new Sukhoi Su-57 that had been in development for ten years. "You're on the schedule today. They're getting ready to roll it out.

Svetlana glanced over her shoulder and spoke with pride in her voice. "It is thought that this fighter jet will not only have stealth capabilities but will give us air superiority in attack operations. I was one of the test pilots during development. It makes sense that I fly her."

"I didn't think they liked their women pilots playing with these kinds of toys," Carter quipped.

"They were still disappointed in me for the ISS debacle with you, so if I got hurt or crashed, it wouldn't be a big loss." She gave a narrowed smile. "They aren't as forgiving as your NASA."

Darya's jaw tightened and released as he stared at the fighter jet, possibly considering her words. "Carter?"

He shrugged. "I aced the simulations. Been doing it for months. She's almost as good." He noticed her lips twist in irritation. "If anything were to happen to me, you'll need someone who knows how to activate the cloaking device and make sure it works. They're expecting one of us to do it. It's going to get crazy if they find out what we're doing."

"I know nothing of these machines, cloaking, or flying. You are the expert," he informed Carter as he turned and stared at the fighter jet. "If you are sure she should do it, then I will change the orders."

Svetlana slapped her hands together and smiled. Excellent. I'll go check it out and get ready." She moved away, followed by Sam who gave Carter a knowing glance.

When she walked away out of earshot, Darya turned back to Carter. "General Oblonsky is expected tomorrow. I have only told you since your job here is critical to the mission. Since the general supervises this project, I'm sure he'll be the one to oversee the test. No need to make people more nervous than they already are. The general will decide who ultimately flies her when the demonstration is presented to him." He turned back to face the plane. "What is really going on?"

"I'm thinking this big bird needs to be flown out of here with our brainiacs, not the plane we have hidden and ready to go. We'd have to stop and get gas before crossing the Pacific. On a full tank in this one, we could easily go nonstop to Alaska. No problem. Singapore has some of the best long-distance airliners. They can go 9,000 miles. This flight would be under 4,000 miles at best."

"This one has sat for a long time."

"All the more reason for me to work out a few kinks. She seems solid. Let me run a few tests and see how she does."

Darya glanced at the fighter jet being moved. "And the reason you didn't want Svetlana to know this?"

"Too many ways to leak what we're doing. She didn't like the idea when I hinted we should use it. Just being cautious."

"I'll arrange it."

"Any reason you didn't tell her the general would be here sooner?"

"I don't trust her."

CHAPTER THIRTY-SIX

The infirmary smelled of antiseptic and eucalyptus. Tessa let her mind wander to her children and how she rubbed a gooey concoction of eucalyptus on their chests when they were down with congestion or a cough. They often complained about the warmth as it seeped into their little bodies and claimed she applied it only because she loved the aroma.

"Why are you smiling? Something your new husband said—or did?" Chase said flippantly as he prepared for the next exam.

Tessa refused to be baited. The wall between them needed to disappear. "No," she whispered. "I was thinking of the kids, how they balk when I smear them with eucalyptus rub. I'm missing them."

"This won't be easy on them," he said.

She knew he referred to Darya. "I know. We'll work it out. He promises to take it slow and not push his way in."

Chase arched an eyebrow in skepticism.

"I believe him, Chase."

"Okay. Tess, I just want you to be happy—and safe. When Darya told me he had taken care of Robert, I thought he'd killed him."

"That crossed my mind, too. But he gave me his phone and allowed me to call home. My parents are still there and said they were all playing card games. Robert had taken the day off, and they were getting ready to go to the movies." She met his gaze. "Please, Chase. I hate this awkwardness between us. You are my dearest friend. You know that."

"Promise me you'll be careful. I'm still a little shell-shocked at the rash decision you made. Usually you're a lot more skeptical of relationships."

"You mean a relationship with you," she said flatly.

"Maybe. You never gave me a chance, Tessa."

"You of all people knew things were bad at home. Yet you still chose to stand on the sidelines."

"I thought you knew how I felt."

"Clearly, you were mistaken. I don't regret being with Darya, and I'm not worried about our future. But when we get home, I'm resigning from Enigma. My life has taken another turn. One I think will be for the better."

A Russian soldier strode into the infirmary with two more scientists in tow.

"Major Krupin, I wondered when you'd arrive with the next group. I'm afraid I have bad news." Chase let Tessa escort the two men to an examining table. They climbed on and sat with their hands folded in their laps.

The major pulled his shoulders back and tilted his head in confusion. "Bad news?"

"Yes. It appears that strep throat has infected five of the men we examined earlier in the morning. Several had low-grade fevers. We ran a strep test on each one."

"Strep throat? Isn't that just an inflamed throat?" His eyes went to the two men sitting on the table before running a finger under his tight collar.

"Yes. More or less. It is caused by a bacteria and has limitations, but antibiotics are given to prevent more serious complications like rheumatic fever. It is extremely contagious and spreads rapidly." Chase turned to Tessa who already knew what he was saying even though she couldn't understand Russian. "Please take their temperatures."

She did as he directed.

"If your people have come in contact with these Americans, then I need to give them a shot of penicillin immediately to prevent a possible delay on the testing of our new weapon."

Tessa cleared her throat and nodded affirmative on the temperature.

Chase sighed and shook his head before taking a closer look at the major. "And how do you feel, Major Krupin. You are a little flushed."

The power of suggestion could be a potent diversion. He cleared his throat and raised his chin in stubbornness. "I am fine."

"Come now, Major, there is no shame in admitting you don't feel 100 percent. As a matter of fact, there appears to be a slight rash on your neck. Or is your skin usually flushed?" He grabbed a tongue depressor and waved it at the major. "Open up."

The major did as ordered and let Chase examine him before tossing the tongue depressor in the trash. "There are a couple of white spots. And you say you are feeling unaffected."

"I am not sick," the major insisted.

"I have limited antibiotics, Major Krupin. Should I give them to your men and support staff or the Americans? Be quick about it. This is spreading and, by tomorrow, you're going to have people too sick to work. Up to you." Chase took a deep breath and let it escape as if he didn't care one way or another. "Or you can wait it out and hope for the best."

"My men then support staff. Will you have enough medicine?"

"Not likely. I will give shots to as many as possible. Maybe dilute them to go further. I have a few penicillin pills. I'll have my nurse divide them in half to stretch the doses. Would that be satisfactory to you?"

"Yes. Carry on." The major turned to leave.

"And, Major Krupin, I expect you back here to also get a shot. Full dose. After all, you are in charge after I finish. Colonel Petrov will have my head if I do not take care of you."

"Of course." He pivoted and disappeared out the door.

Tessa glanced back at the two scientists who appeared bewildered at the commotion. "Don't worry. You're fine." She smiled, making their eyes grow round with surprise.

"You're an American?" the older man quizzed.

"Apple Pie and the St. Louis Cardinals. That's me."

Chase stepped forward and stuck out his hand. "My nurse and I have a difference of opinion on which baseball team is better. I generally cheer for the Giants." The two men couldn't contain their relief and grabbed Chase's hand with enthusiasm.

"We are hoping you are pretty good actors. Think you can help us out?" Tessa asked.

~ ~ ~ ~

Carter Johnson landed the Singapore airliner after taking her for a short flight. There were plenty of reasons why the airline had one of the best safety and performance records. The plane handled like a dream, in spite of not being taken out in over six months, according to the flight log. At least the Russians hadn't let her sit idle for the last few years. He reasoned they took great care in trying to dissect information they could use for their own planes.

When he had insisted the plane be filled with fuel, the ground crew balked, saying it was for more important projects. Fortunately, Colonel Petrov showed up, snapping everyone to attention. Clearly, they were terrified of him by the way they avoided eye contact and lowered their voices in a kind of reverence. With eyes narrowed to slits as he lowered his chin, he actually did resemble a demon. Despite the short time he'd been in Russia, he'd established himself as a man you didn't cross. If someone has the ear of the president, then you had better step, lightly.

"Do whatever he asks," Darya warned. "He has my complete trust."

That got everyone hopping and fetching in short order. Once in the air, he used one of Vernon's fancy tech toys to contact him. "Were you able to find what we needed?" Carter asked.

"Yes. And it's a lot more advanced than what we've created back home. They have taken the weapon up a couple of notches. They are now able to install it on their tanks, body armor, and even created a light-bending fabric that will wrap a soldier to the point where you think a ghost is approaching you, except it blends with whatever surroundings it encounters. The enemy might think a breeze is moving through the bushes or jungle, but in reality, it will be a military force overtaking you."

"What are you doing to kill it?"

Vernon huffed his contempt. "I detect skepticism."

"Knock it off, kid. Just take care of it."

"Joel alerted several of his fellow brains to lock on to my signal. I've set loose a virus that will make the coronavirus look like a head cold." Carter could hear him laugh. "All I need is a time frame."

"Can you install it on this bird now?"

"Even as we speak. Child's play. Oops."

"Oops? No oops. What is going on?"

"Just messin' with you. Relax."

"Expect an ass whoopin' when we get back home."

"Noted." Another more measured laugh followed. "Give me a few more minutes for the plane, and you'll be good to go. The program wasn't designed for such a big beast. It might not cover completely. I'm not sure how it will do. I'll try and create a simulation when I'm done to see."

"But it will work, right? Won't affect the operating systems?"

"It will work. I'm saying I don't know if there will be side effects. Let me do my job. You do yours."

"You're pretty brave sitting miles away in a basement with a computer. You better make sure this works or else."

"Or else? If it comes to that, you won't be a threat to me anymore." Carter could imagine the kid smirking as he pushed his glasses up on his nose.

"Point well taken. Let me know when you have it installed. And bring Joel's family with you. Just tell them there have been some changes. We'll slip them aboard the Airbus we're using. Be sure Joel's wife stays clear of Svetlana, too. We don't want any leaks. I'll explain later."

That had been several hours ago. Vernon never ceased to amaze him. Although he wouldn't get to experiment with the downloaded cloaking device on the bigger plane, he had no doubt that the kid had worked his magic, and, with any luck, could get the device to help them evade trouble until they left Russian airspace.

Svetlana had been in the air longer than he expected. He waited for her to land and give him an update on the cloaking device already installed on the jet.

She exited the plane and came to his side. "You Americans

think of the best toys, Carter. There were a couple of glitches, but your people knew exactly how to straighten them out. The only problem that remained is when you roll to the right, the system flutters and goes back to normal for about fifteen seconds. They're working on that problem now. Shouldn't be anything to keep from doing the demonstration when General Oblonsky arrives tomorrow." One of the ground crew waved for her to join him. "Better see what he wants."

As she strode away, Carter squinted and turned his head sideways to watch her before he whispered, "And how did you know the general would be here tomorrow, Svetlana?"

CHAPTER THIRTY-SEVEN

The two scientists quickly agreed to help after being given a quick examination by Chase. Although he wasn't a doctor, he'd done enough battlefield medicine to pretend he knew what he was doing. He gave each of them a vial of liquid to use when they got a chance. They would also send the remaining people working on the project to them for their exams.

"What is in the vial?" asked one of the scientists.

"Poison ivy rash is a type of allergic contact dermatitis caused by an oily resin called urushiol. This resin is very sticky, so it easily attaches to your skin, clothing, tools, equipment, almost anything you touch. So be careful. You want to apply it where the Russians will get it on them. It is concentrated, so we hope anyone who comes in contact will suffer a quick reaction. I'm hoping you'll know where to apply it. Keep track of the places you put the liquid so your people aren't exposed."

After they left, Chase went over his notes.

As of now, there had been no indication of anyone showing signs of betrayal. One of the signs he'd watched for was less weight loss than the others. He'd studied each man's bio and stats before ever leaving the States. Vernon had everything downloaded to the tablet Chase carried with him into the examining room where he recorded the findings.

They shared a common sense of depression along with nervousness at being separated from the group. All seemed a bit suspicious of them and spoke as little as possible unless prompted to answer a question. Most failed to make eye contact and appeared to have taken up the Russian habit of not smiling at strangers. All the information was also being fed to doctors at DARPA who were on their way to California to take over their care if needed, once they escaped their prison of technology.

The State Department and the Pentagon were working closely with the president and the National Security Council on how to spin the event. This could easily become an act of war. Those Washington channels of communication had shut down in order for the team to protect the mission from being discovered. If they were caught, they would be accused of being spies. The US government would deny any knowledge of their presence on Russian soil. The possibility of Siberia becoming their new home was not a scenario Chase wanted to contemplate.

The afternoon group were let in on the true identities of Chase and Tessa without singling out the other team members who were a part of their rescue mission. Something told Chase not to reveal too much. He doubted they would be able to contain their excitement. The less they knew, the better. A suddenly gleeful bunch of scientists might be the one thing to tip off the Russians.

"You're going to have to trust me," Chase warned. "I want those men I examined this morning back here ASAP. Tell them nothing, except there was concern about their tests."

They eagerly gave a thumbs-up followed by another stern warning from Chase. "Don't do that. You look too happy. Soon you'll be home and have plenty of time to celebrate. We want everyone alive. Got it?"

They cowered, the look of unease seeping back into their wide eyes.

Chase patted them on the shoulder. "You'll do fine. Be ready to move tonight."

Tessa watched the two men leave, heads huddled together as they whispered, excited but skeptical of success. Everyone knew unless they escaped; their days were numbered. Now that the project neared completion, the Russians could easily take the technology and adjust it to their own needs. She breathed a prayer of protection for them. This kind of life, full of uncertainty and hardship, was laced with danger that had dangled over their heads for almost three years. Would they be able to complete the last exercise to save the world from a potential weapon that could revolutionize how wars were fought and won?

"Tessa?" Darya had led the others into the examining room while she had stood staring out the window of a small office, thinking about the coming hours. She flinched and whirled around, almost losing her balance. He caught her and narrowed his gaze in the way he used when trying to figure her out. "Are you well?" His hands remained on her arms.

"Yes." The forced smile she offered did nothing to erase his frown. "It's been a long day. I'll be glad to have this over. I'm worried these men won't be much help."

Darya placed a hand on each side of her face, drawing her closer. She placed a light hand on his waist. "They are anxious to leave. Everything is falling into place." He smiled and leaned in to kiss her forehead. "You are warm."

"I need you, Tessa, if you can tear yourself away." Chase loomed in the doorway, looking like a disgruntled Siberian tiger.

Before she could push past him, Darya grabbed her hand and led her to the captain. "Take her temperature. She is sick. I believe she might have the same thing Yuri had. I thought it was just a change in climate or food. But she isn't better." He quickly retold how she had protected him then gotten in the tub of water to hold him to help lower the fever. "Please," he added.

"Probably a cold. I'm fine," she insisted.

Chase reached out and felt her head then pulled out one of his disposable thermometer strips and laid it on her forehead. Jerking it off and dropping it in the trash can, his angry glare turned to concern. "You have 103-degree temperature."

"It's warm in here is all."

"Since when do you get warm?" Chase mumbled as he took the stethoscope and glanced at Darya before slipping it against her chest. "Turn around," he ordered gently. "Darya, can you help raise her lab coat and sweater for me?"

He nodded and followed instructions.

"I can't be sure, but you may have the start of pneumonia. You have a rapid heartbeat, and there does seem to be congestion."

"Can you help her?" Tessa knew the panic in Darya's voice had to do with losing his first wife and child years ago. In Siberia, reminders were everywhere of how fragile life could be.

"I have some antibiotics. If it is bacterial, it will help. If not, then we'll have to reach the States before we can do anything else. I'll give her something for the fever, too. I noticed earlier you were coughing. You didn't say anything, Tessa."

Tessa took a deep breath in irritation at the sudden abundance of attention, but the gesture only brought on a coughing fit. When Darya tried to comfort her, she waved him off, hoping he wouldn't be contaminated. Chase retrieved a bottle of water and urged her to drink it with the ibuprofen. He also carried a needle.

"I'm shooting this in your hip."

"No. You're not."

Darya reached under her lab coat and unfastened her pants. "Do as he says, Tess-sa. Stop being so stubborn. He is trying to help you."

Tessa stiffened and puckered her lips into a snarl.

"We are both much bigger than you and can easily remove your—attitude, if you get my meaning," he warned in a no-nonsense voice.

Tessa opened her mouth to protest then noticed the corner of Chase's mouth had turned up as if he was enjoying the confrontation.

"Please resist, Tessa," Chase said. "You've had a good ass whoopin' coming for a long time."

She pushed Darya back and lowered her pants in humiliation. "Fine. Do it," she demanded. "Ouch! You purposely jabbed me like I was a wild animal getting tagged." The smirk that passed between the two men at her discomfort irritated her. "I'm fine," she growled as she left them alone in the office.

"Fine. Just a heads-up, Darya, she says that a lot, and when she does—"

"She isn't," Darya completed the statement and watched her walk across to where a few of the scientists were standing.

"Captain Hunter, we need to talk about my wife."

"Not really the chatty type."

"I would do anything in my power to make her happy."

Captain Hunter remained silent.

"I know you don't think I am good enough."

"You aren't."

"True." Darya grabbed his hat off the desk and placed it on his head. "But it is what it is. I know our life will be hard."

"Because of you."

"Yes. I worry that might also be true. I need a favor from you."

Chase could feel his forehead pinch. "What is it?"

"Things could get messy here, and my job is to see it to completion. Tess-sa is a distraction I can't afford to have right now. Please. Will you see that she is safe when things unfold?"

"I always have," he said coolly.

"General Oblonsky will want me dead if he gets here before we evacuate. I fear he may try and use Tess-sa to get to me."

"Maybe you should have thought of that before dragging her to the altar."

Darya's eyes narrowed to slits of fire. "When I want something, I take it. You will have to accept that, Captain Hunter. We both know she will be a dedicated wife to me. It is who she is, and I think you know it."

He took a step closer, but Darya did not shy away. "This isn't over. When we get back to the States—I look forward to putting you in your place," he growled through gritted teeth.

The tribesman said nothing, but his nose flared, and his wide mouth thinned in anger. "Until then, Captain Hunter, see to it that my wife is safe, or I might find some radioactive sinkhole to drop you in."

"Noted."

CHAPTER THIRTY-EIGHT

Major Krupin entered the infirmary with a fast, irritated gait that got Chase's immediate attention. He surveyed the room with the same impatience you'd give a toddler throwing a tantrum. The frown he wore gave him an almost clown-like appearance. All he needed was a little white makeup around the mouth. With clasped hands behind his back, he raised his chin in a show of stubbornness. Chase decided to give him his undivided attention.

"Major Krupin." Chase made an effort to sound bored. "I have yet to see any of your men, and it is growing late."

The major waved at the beds where a number of scientists lay covered in clean but threadbare blankets. "What is all this? These men need to be at their stations. We have tests and last-minute programing to finish."

"They are resting for now. I've given them antibiotics. They all tested positive for strep. In a few hours, they will be ready to finish their tasks."

The major huffed his displeasure then cleared his throat. "I want you to examine four of my men."

"What seems to be the problem?" Chase asked, shoving his hands into the lab coat pockets.

"They have developed a kind of rash."

"Rash? What kind of rash?"

"I do not know," he snapped. "You are the doctor. May I bring them in?"

"Not here until I know what we are dealing with." He motioned him to escort them into an adjoining room, accessed from the hall. Once they entered, it was all Chase could do to keep from laughing at their red, swollen faces. One soldier's eyes had already swelled shut. "This is not good. Let me talk to my nurse." Major Krupin followed him as far as the doorway where Chase pulled Tessa aside.

"He's watching us like a hawk," Tessa said, glancing around Chase's large frame. "What exactly was in those vials you gave to our brainiacs after lunch?"

"A mixture of poison ivy and stinging nettle." He smiled down at Tessa.

"Ouch. Four soldiers aren't enough to take out of commission. I have an idea. Do you have more of that?" He looked over his shoulder and nodded. "Get Sam in here." She spilled her idea to him, which made him regret she might be leaving them soon to begin a new life. Maybe once this was over, he could eliminate the competition once and for all.

He sent one of the guards in the hall for Sam as he went to talk to the major.

"I can give them something to help with the burning and itching."

"Is it contagious?" The major took a step back and eyed the four men who fidgeted and scratched their necks.

"I suspect they also have strep throat. Not unusual to get a rash if they have had it a while without treatment. Someone here is a carrier most likely. It will not surprise me if this is widespread." Chase thought he heard a quiet groan emit from the major's throat, but the man quickly pulled his shoulders back and popped his neck, as if by doing so he'd get the situation under control. "It is already dark. Do you have a room here, Major Krupin?" The major admitted he had a sleeping room with the basics. His men had a bunkroom to use when off shift. "Good. If they are infected, the antibiotics should help. If they are feverish, I insist on a few hours' sleep, plenty of water, and I will stay the night to monitor their condition. Does that sound reasonable to you, Major?" Before he could answer, Sam marched in and snapped to attention when she saw the major. Chase went on, "I requested Colonel Petrov's assistant join us. With her helping my nurse, the job will be completed much faster. She is also a trained medical assistant and can easily spot strep throat or any other problem."

"Very well. I'll send in my men who are about to go on shift. Will that be satisfactory?"

"And make sure the others come when they've been relieved. But my nurse will check you out before you go so I can administer an antibiotic if needed."

The major tugged his jacket down and ran his hands across it to smooth any wrinkles. Chase wasn't sure if that was a habit or an attempt to impress the women.

One by one, soldiers appeared, whispering among themselves and casting glances at Tessa and Sam. He could only imagine the comments that might be passing between them and thought it probably best not to get involved. A Russian's expression of admiration for a woman's form and beauty were far different than in the States where he might receive a slap or a restraining order ASAP.

The major opened his mouth for Sam who smiled seductively and made what he guessed was a suggestive observation of her own. Whatever she said caused him to return the look of interest as she ran her fingers around his neck, checking his lymph nodes. Finally, she laid one of the temperature strips on his forehead, only to slowly remove it as she managed to slide two fingers down his jaw.

"Well?" Chase clasped his hands behind him.

"No temperature, but his throat is a little red."

Chase waved for a tongue depressor with impatience. Tessa was performing the same routine as Sam on another soldier who kept trying to engage her in conversation without success. Checking the major's throat for a second time, he sighed. "She's right. Probably nothing, but if you start to feel uncomfortable, you should return right away for a shot. It can happen quickly. I've been seeing this kind of infection in Irkutsk. Onsets fast with strep then pneumonia." Chase thought that probably was a gigantic reach in terms of possibility, but the major probably was clueless.

Major Krupin buttoned his collar and leveled a warm gaze toward Sam, who arched an eyebrow of contempt. The brush-off affected the major from the looks of his downturned mouth and stiff upper lip. "Very well. If there is a change, I'll call from my quarters, and you can send someone."

"Of course, Major."

Krupin's eyes never left Sam. Chase knew where that was headed. Poor sap didn't know what he was getting himself into. Death by Sam Cordova was not a pretty thing, especially when she seemed to take such delight in it.

Less than two hours later, Major Krupin didn't call but stormed into the clinic, demanding a shot for the rash around his neck and chest. His left eye had swelled shut. The poison ivy liquid concentrate had begun to work on him, considering how he twitched and rubbed his neck. Chase checked his temperature and throat again.

"I suspected this would happen. You have contacted this new bacterial infection. Your temperature is low grade, but your throat has gotten worse. How do you feel?"

"Just give me the shot."

"Very well. As you can see, your men from the first shift have begun to complain and have taken to their beds. A few are here, but I felt they would be more comfortable in their quarters."

"Yes. Yes. Fine. Just give me the shot."

Chase filled the syringe a little fuller than needed before injecting the Diphenhydramine into the major's arm. Over the counter name in the States was Benadryl, but this was a little stronger dose, often used before surgery to prevent vomiting and nausea.

"I suggest you get some rest, Major."

The major's eyes were already starting to soften as he nodded and lumbered out of the clinic.

"How are we doing?" Tessa asked.

"Great idea rubbing that poison ivy oil on their faces and necks. Planting the idea they may be sick also had a rapid effect on the soldiers. From my count, most are now in their bunks sound asleep." Chase grinned while letting his gaze run over Tessa's flushed face. "You ladies know how to distract. All they could think about was you touching them."

"Thank goodness we didn't have to say much." Tessa disposed of her gloves.

"If you had understood their comments, you may have not been so smiley-faced," Sam interrupted. "I'm sure that new husband of yours would have pushed a few of them into the icy waters of Lake Baikal buck naked."

"I almost did anyway," Darya said, coming through the door, leading the last of the scientists. "I reminded them I would not hear of talk about a fellow officer and a medical professional. If they expected fair treatment, they had best keep their comments to themselves." He joined Tessa and slipped an arm around her for only a moment. "How are you feeling?"

"I was about to take her temperature again." Once again, he became aware that staring down into her blue eyes was a dangerous attempt at connecting. She was another man's wife now, and he didn't want to tangle with Darya until later. "Down, but you need to take more meds. Sam, get that acetaminophen out of my bag. Give Tessa two," he ordered. "How about the local staff?" Chase wondered.

"All gone home for the night. They left soup and bread on the stove. Everything is locked down tight."

"And the planes?"

"The jet is back under cover in the hangar. The Singapore plane is fueled and ready to go. We need to get everyone onboard so we can leave by first light." Darya continued to survey the room. Chase got the feeling he was second-guessing him. "Vernon is almost here. He's going to do last-minute transfers on the cloaking device. I'd rather leave now, but we cannot be sure the technology would be completely destroyed."

Chase's cell phone vibrated. The screen revealed it was Vernon. Connecting, he listened, grunted a few acknowledgments before ending the call. "He's in the lab with our guys. They're getting started on the transfer."

"Won't someone be alerted to the intrusion?" Sam walked up and handed Tessa the acetaminophen without making eye contact.

"Vern created a Trojan horse that when activated will resemble thousands of spiders, spinning webs of confusion in all directions." Chase packed up the supplies they might need on the plane. "That's all I know. And even if I knew more, I wouldn't understand it. For now, we need to make sure security is getting their beauty sleep so Vern can get on that plane and work his magic."

Darya pulled out his phone and frowned. "Not good."

"What?" the others echoed.

"General Oblonsky arrived in Irkutsk an hour ago. If he and his henchmen can find their way out here, we won't have much time."

"Vern will get it done. He always does."

CHAPTER THIRTY-NINE

General Oblonsky regretted not spending the night in Irkutsk. Not only was he exhausted, but he felt irritated that his call went unanswered at the research installation. He'd been warned about the dangers of traveling at night in this part of Russia. In good weather, the trip could take two hours. With snow-packed roads, barely plowed, he expected the time frame to double. After their three vehicles had fishtailed and nearly ended up stranded in a snowdrift, the general made the decision to turn back.

Finally, when Major Krupin answered the phone, with slurred speech and nonsense about many of the people coming down with a bacterial infection, he decided returning to Irkutsk to be the best decision. According to the major, it was a very contagious bug, and his people had been given doses of antibiotics. The hope was by tomorrow, his men would be well enough to receive the general and not expose anyone else needlessly to the germs.

"Expectations are high we will be ready for the demonstration," the major promised.

After receiving communication from his contact at the installation, he managed to relax. Everything was on schedule. It appeared the one person he most wanted to see had arrived as well.

Roman Darya Petrov. Suspicions of a double-cross plagued him.

President Antonov had mentioned Petrov might be taking his new bride to Siberia. It sounded a little too convenient he would be visiting there without letting him know earlier. Then again, the president had withheld many things from him since the Asian dog appeared on his uncle's doorstep. If the project went well, the general expected a promotion and rekindled favor with the president until he could work on a possible unfortunate accident for the man. The mere thought of being rid of him brought a smile to his thin lips. The softening attitude toward the West repulsed him to the point of needing a drink as the car came to a stop in front of the hotel.

~ ~ ~ ~

"What made the Russians so sleepy?" Darya asked Tessa as they checked on the sleeping men in their bunks.

"Diphenhydramine," Tessa responded when he gave her a bewildered gaze. "Over the counter brand is Benadryl. This was a little stronger, and Chase made sure they had a heavy dose. They'll feel a little hungover when they roust up in the morning." She smiled and patted his arm. "Not to worry. They will sleep like babies."

"We should be long gone by the time they waken?" he asked.

"I sure hope so. That's the plan." She leaned into him, feeling a little wobbly and feverish. "See? They are dead to the world."

Darya turned her around and pulled her into his arms. "You are burning up. Let's find you a place to lie down. I want Captain Hunter to check you again."

Tessa complied by allowing him to loop his arm through hers and lead her back to the infirmary. By the time they entered, she'd had a coughing fit that lasted several minutes. He brought her a bottle of water then Chase appeared with a sour expression. Once more, he listened to her chest and back and took her temperature.

"Let me check you, too, Darya. It's definitely gotten worse. I'm betting on bacterial pneumonia, but I would have thought the shot I gave her would have slowed it down." A quick exam revealed he was okay.

"Can she have more medicine?" Darya asked as Tessa scooted

to the edge of the examining table.

"I gave all the scientists a half dose just in case they caught her bug. Be a shame to lose them after all this time because of something we could have prevented. I was hoping to wait if at all possible."

Darya narrowed his eyes as if to protest, but in the end, he nodded.

"I'll give her another one in a few hours when we're in the air. It should be comfortable enough since it's a passenger plane."

Tessa let her feet touch the floor and tried to take a deep breath, only to cough instead. She held up her hand for both men to back off. A feeling of helplessness washed over her as the room began to spin. Reaching out to Darya to reassure him, she saw the look of panic in his pinched expression. When he said her name, it sounded like a hollow echo. The room went black as her world closed in around her.

"Bring her over here," Chase ordered when Darya scooped her limp body up in his arms.

He believed the man was incapable of fear, but this had unnerved him from the look on his ashen face. He laid her gently on a narrow bed and kneeled down beside her, rubbing her delicate hand with his large calloused ones.

Chase hurried to get the last shot and returned empty-handed. "I was wrong. There is nothing left." He hooked her up to an IV. "She needs plenty of fluids. In two hours, we can give her ibuprofen and alternate every couple of hours with the acetaminophen. We do have plenty of that. It will help with any pain or fever she has."

"Is she going to die, Captain Hunter? Have I…" His voice faded as he leaned over and kissed her forehead.

"She's not going to die. We'll be on American soil this time tomorrow night, and she'll get the care she needs." He almost felt sorry for the tribesman.

"My first wife and child died without me being able to help them." The bloodshot eyes he turned on Chase resembled those of the devil himself. "You must do everything you can, Captain Hunter."

He raised his chin in stubbornness and pushed out his bottom lip. "I'm sorry. I didn't know. I'll do my best, Darya. But there are things that still need to be done."

Darya stood and gazed down at Tessa as if willing her to wake up.

"Besides, being her hero one more time will be sweet revenge for me. So, get the hell out of here and do your job."

One corner of Darya's mouth turned up in a grin. "It will be the last time, Captain Hunter. Enjoy it while you can." He bent down and spoke to her in Pashtu, the language of Afghanistan, and stroked her cheek. Chase put a hand on the tribesman's shoulder, drawing his attention back to the present. He took a deep breath and nodded to Chase then strode off. Watching him with Tessa helped him understand the chemistry between them. Although the man had a questionable past and could be a dangerous rival, the woman brought out the human and vulnerable side in Darya. Not so different than the effect she'd had on him these last few years. The difference was he'd taken for granted she'd always be there for him. Darya did not.

"I'm an idiot," he mumbled, checking her temperature again.

"No argument there," came Carter's voice as he entered the room. "Just saw Darya in the hall. He caught me up to speed." Sam joined them and spread a sheet over Tessa. For once, listening to Carter taunt his Enigma partner gave Chase a moment's peace. "Would you take care of me if I got sick, Sam?"

She arched an eyebrow and hissed in his ear. "I would certainly be happy to add whatever I could to your IV."

He jerked his head back and laid a hand on his heart. "Does this attitude have anything to do with Svetlana?"

"Go to hell," she growled before turning to Chase. "I'll watch Tessa. It's better than listening to Carter's display of neediness. Maybe you can reassure the brainiacs. They're getting nervous."

"Pack up any medical supplies you can find in case we need medical treatment on the trip back. Wipe anything down where we may have left fingerprints, etc."

"On it," she said, shifting her look of contempt back to Carter. "Where's your girlfriend?"

He leaned toward her. "Standing right here."

She stormed off toward the supply cabinets. "Humph," was the best she could give him as he chuckled.

"I don't want trouble between her and Svetlana. Got it?" Chase said, disposing of his gloves.

Carter shrugged and put his hands on his hips. "Got it. You really need to learn to have a little fun, Captain."

"You're going to get yourself killed one of these days."

"What a way to go." He grinned. "Relax. Sam is blowin' off steam. She's miffed about Svetlana—well for a number of reasons, but I can handle her."

"Really? You must have been one of those religious rattlesnake handlers in another life."

He pointed to himself. "Texas boy through and through."

"Let's get these guys on the plane before Sam and Svetlana decide to have a come-to-Jesus meeting."

"Yeah, well, I need to talk to you about Svetlana," he said between gritted teeth. "I think you're going to want Sam to have the Jesus talk before we start moving anyone onto that plane."

~ ~ ~ ~

Vernon exited the Singapore airliner with a big smile as Chase met him on the ground. He shivered against the cold then snapped his fingers like a little boy trying to impress his friends concerning a new accomplishment.

"Done?" Chase asked.

"Of course. I'm freakin' amazing if I do say so myself. I want a raise."

"I want a steak and mashed potatoes, but, like me, you'll have to wait." Vernon rolled his eyes and gave a thumbs-up. Chase realized the boy genius would probably never grow up.

"You mean it, boss? I could get a raise?"

He pivoted on a heel and started back inside. "No. Are you also finished in the lab?"

"Just a few more things to check and install." He tried to keep up with Chase's long strides. "Mostly double-checking the plane's installation."

"And the Sukhoi Su-57?" Chase halted so fast that Vernon tripped into his large frame, which resulted in the captain giving him a steely frown.

Vernon held up an apologetic hand and shoved his glasses

higher on his nose. "Not sure."

"Not sure?" he asked in a gruff voice.

"I mean, yeah, I've done something, but that bird has all kinds of safeguards and computer firewalls. Anything I do is going to trigger major alerts."

Chase continued to glare at him.

"Can we go inside? This godforsaken place is cold." Vernon shivered then opened the door. Together they passed into the dim light of the research section. "The best I could do was program in a spider."

"What the hell does that mean? And make it simple so I can understand," he warned.

They continued to walk until they entered the lab.

"Spiders use venom to immobilize their prey. Those enzymes are from their gut. After a few minutes, the prey becomes soft enough for them to suck in a tasty meal." Vernon chuckled. "Cool, huh?" When Chase only stood rigid with a deepening frown and squinted, Vernon continued. "In other words, my program activates when the plane vibrates, like a spider grinding its body against its prey. The program spits, or runs through the plane while it's flying, and when they activate the cloaking device, the body of the plane softens, and bam! It disappears for good." Chase arched his eyebrows. "Well, I mean it will be spread all over the ground, but it won't be invisible anymore for flying." Another proud chuckle followed.

"Can they trace the program?"

"Sure. But since the important schematics will either be distorted, fried, or gone forever, they'll think our boys found a way to destroy the research."

"Surely they've been making copies of the research. What's to prevent them from continuing the work?"

"You wound me," Vernon admitted, laying a hand on his heart.

"You found the copies of the research."

He rolled his eyes. "Are you trying to insult me, Chase? Of course, I did. Let's say someone is going to be in a lot of trouble down the road."

"Hopefully, we'll be gone and drinking a beer on the beach where it is a lot warmer than here."

He took a deep breath and let it out slowly. "There is one little

problem."
"Spill it."
"Svetlana."

CHAPTER FORTY

General Oblonsky watched the eastern sky lighten. Patches of fog floated in low areas or near the shores of Lake Baikal, slowing them down enough that he became obsessed with checking his watch. With an early arrival time, he could catch any misguided attempts to sabotage his project. The cloaking technology would give him the clout and respect he deserved.

President Antonov would once again see him as an asset instead of ignoring his ideas and suggestions. With any luck, he'd be able to catch the president's nephew in what he expected was an act of treason against Mother Russia. Pretending to be a loyal citizen would not sit well with the president.

The three cars turned onto the two-mile road leading to the research facility. Four uniformed men stepped out of the gatehouse when they approached and then stopped. A few pleasantries were exchanged while papers were checked. Two of the men examined the cars for explosive devices with their under-vehicle inspection imaging systems.

Soon they were waved through and given a casual two-finger salute as the gate arm lifted.

"When we get finished here, I want the names of those men.

Those uniforms were despicable. They have been in Siberia so long; they don't even remember the proper way to salute."

"Yes, sir," was all the driver could say.

The four men let the arm of the gate back down and stared after the cars headed toward the research facility. One picked up his walkie-talkie and called in.

"They are here. Yes. We were able to put the explosive device under the last two cars but not the first. Good luck."

The men pulled sock caps over their heads after tossing the military-issue one into the gatehouse. They picked up their weapons and disappeared into the forests to make their way closer to where the action would certainly happen.

~ ~ ~ ~

"Look alive, people," Chase shouted to the scientists. "We've got company. Relax. This is happening a little sooner than expected, but we can do this. Get to your stations and act normal."

The reluctant men turned their attention to Joel who posed like an awkward teenager next to the self-assured Darya Petrov who stood tall, shoulders pulled back and hands clasped behind his back. When he spoke, they all leaned a little forward to make sure they heard his every word.

"The workers who come each morning have been delayed or sent home with the story of an illness outbreak. They have been replaced by area resistance forces." When Darya spoke, it was with authority and a sense of calm. Chase watched Darya hold up a hand of reassurance as the men glanced at each other skeptically. "Not to worry. When we are finished here, they will melt back into the communities where they live."

Joel stepped forward. "I promise you; everything will be okay. We just need to do this last thing. Now please, go to your positions."

"How are we to get on the plane with new soldiers coming in and the ones you doctored starting to wake up?" one scientist asked.

It was a real concern since they would be out in the open.

Vernon dragged a box the size of a refrigerator in front of them.

"Fortunately, we have these. Great job by the way."

He smiled as he opened the box and lifted a garment out that appeared to be a large poncho. They all began to grin and elbow each other. He placed it over his head, folded the cloth around him, and totally disappeared. Seconds later, he unfolded the cloth, and stood among them. "I love this stuff," Vernon laughed.

Without another word, the men drifted off to their assigned duties while Vernon replaced the cloaking cloth. "I'll put this somewhere safe so we can use it if needed."

Chase joined Darya who moved toward the exit. The tension Darya exhibited in his gait and tightening and release of his jaw spoke of concern, maybe dread. He understood there was a contentious relationship between him and General Oblonsky.

"I'm going to need to stay out of sight when the general gets here. I'll take care of Sam and Tessa. We'll wait for your signal."

Darya halted and turned his head to stare menacingly at Chase. "I spoke to Tessa a few moments ago. Much improved. Thank you. I owe you."

"No. You don't." Their gazes locked for a few seconds before both refocused on the view out the windows.

Three vehicles were spotted coming down the winding road. Fortunately, the layer of snow had frozen and made the drive precarious enough to take it slow.

Chase turned to leave. "It's showtime. Good luck." He noticed the tribesman place a hand to his sidearm. "I need one of those."

"I left one for you with Tessa." Darya took a step away, but Chase reached out and grabbed his arm. The tribesman stared down at the gesture and shook him off. "You still don't trust me, do you, Captain Hunter?" When he didn't respond, a sinister smirk spread across Darya's wide mouth, followed by a low chuckle.

"Should I?" he quipped.

He leaned in closer. "Not for a second." He strode off toward the door leading to the outside.

Carter exited the plane onto the passenger-loading stairs and spotted Svetlana staring at him from the safety of the hangar. She'd managed the few maintenance and ground crew who had been held over and given the same amount of attention as the soldiers, but their dosage had been a lot less, so they would be up and about when needed. They didn't ask questions, which made working with them easier. However, the way she was watching him gave him pause.

"Morning, sunshine," he said with a big smile. "I see the crew is moving the plane into position."

"Why were you on that stupid plane again?" She shifted her weight to one hip as her scowl deepened.

He pulled out his phone. "Wanted to take a few selfies with this baby. Man, that thing flew like a dream." Pulling up the pictures, he offered to show her, but she huffed her disapproval.

"It's always about you, isn't it, Carter?"

"And you are pissed at me because…"

"Why are the Americans still here? I just saw them in the lab."

"Relax. Darya has it under control. We've got plenty of time. We can't walk them to the other airstrip you know. Waiting on the vans so we can get to that plane. You do remember it is at least an hour away." He tilted his head and eyed her curiously. "If they show up early, we'll leave when they head out. Either way, that plane is gassed and ready to go."

"I don't like it," she fumed and stomped her foot.

"You like having your own way, don't you, Svetlana?"

"I don't like changes to the plan."

"Well, you'd better get used to it because we've got company." He nodded toward the parking lot. "And here I thought Russians were incessantly late."

She looked toward the cars then back to him. "He's early." Her brow creased. "Why weren't we notified?"

Carter shrugged. "Maybe because we aren't in charge. Find Major Krupin. He might know." The urge to give her a wide grin was nearly too great when she stormed off to receive the guests. He mumbled, "Still trying to destroy my reputation, you lying Russian bitch."

~ ~ ~ ~

Tessa shoved a few more supplies into her backpack then chugged a bottle of water. The coughing started, followed by her throwing up the water in a trash can she almost missed. Her chest hurt, and her throat felt like it was on fire. The thermometer indicated her fever had dropped, but she knew it was the meds. Taking them for a prolonged period worried her, too. At least she felt well enough to help.

A few of the scientists who were slotted to be off duty joined her. They went to the box of cloaking fabric and pulled one out for each of them. Tessa gave them a flimsy bag containing two bottles of water, bread from the kitchen, and a few odds and ends she'd managed to find.

They did a lot of head bobbing when she warned them to walk slowly across the tarmac and board the plane. She helped them stuff the supplies into a makeshift backpack so they could hold onto the fabric. Vernon joined her and helped the men get dressed. He posed as a janitor and planned to lead them to the plane.

"We're ready," one man declared. He appeared to be the oldest, or maybe the long gray hair fooled them. His wrinkles deepened as he smiled, revealing a broken tooth. She wondered how he'd gotten that, but Joel had already told them a few of the men had suffered abuse. "Thank you," he said, grabbing her hand. He surprised her with a hug.

"I've been sick. You probably shouldn't do that," she warned and felt how bony his frame had become during captivity.

He nodded that he understood.

She peeked out the door. "All clear. You're the first. Take your time. Vernon will go with you."

"Line up behind me, and I'll walk you out."

As they left, Chase entered the room and, with Tessa, watched Vernon move the group away. The only thing visible were waves of bent light that blended in with the surroundings. If you weren't looking for it, you'd never know anyone was there.

"General Oblonsky has arrived. Darya went to meet him."

"Won't he be expecting to see me, too? Maybe I should be at his side."

He took several deep breaths and nodded. "Just be prepared if he shows up looking for you, or at least with Darya. Right now, Major Krupin will have a lot of explaining to do as to why the place is undermanned and in disarray. That might give us a little more time." Without warning, he reached out to feel Tessa's forehead, causing her to startle and step back. Instead of apologizing, he pulled her toward him with a firm grip on her elbow, and the other went to her face then forehead.

"Stop it," she fumed. "I'm fine." A push against his chest did nothing to get her released. He kept his grip on her when she tried to twist away.

"You are not fine. When did you last take fever meds?" When she shrugged, he clamped down harder. "Stop screwin' around, Tessa. This is serious. You can be fine one minute, and the next you could collapse."

Her eyes flashed violet as they usually did when he angered her. She pursed her lips together like a concrete angel. He came close to pulling her into his arms to force her to comply with his will. Those days were probably over. With a sudden release of her arm, she staggered back against the table. He dug in the to-go bag she'd packed until he found more ibuprofen and a bottle of water.

"Take it. Drink all the water."

Snatching the items out of his hand, she continued to glare at him. "Happy?" she asked, replacing the cap on the water bottle.

"No," he said, letting his voice go lower. "Pretty miserable if you must know."

The color in her eyes to faded to blue. "Chase, I never meant to—"

Vernon raced into the room. "You'd better get Sam and stay out of sight. Major Krupin and the general are on their way here. I overheard them talking. The general wants to see Tessa."

CHAPTER FORTY-ONE

Darya managed to level an unemotional stare at the men exiting the cars in the parking lot. It was a look that had served him well over the years. The first concern to leap to mind was whether Tessa would be safe. That faded to the nervous scientists who were more than a little anxious to be leaving Russia. Hopefully they had followed all of Vernon's instructions so he could finish the job after they'd escaped.

Out of all the Enigma team members, Vernon was the one person he knew he could trust. They had bonded when he'd first arrived in the States after leaving Afghanistan. He'd helped him assimilate and kept him informed about Tessa's well-being when he'd been sent back into the field. Out of the corner of his eye, he noticed Vernon strolling across the tarmac. A ray of early morning sunlight touched something behind him, revealing movement.

"General Oblonsky, I did not expect you until later today. I would have prepared warm refreshments if I'd known." Darya came alongside the stoic general who paused to inspect the surrounding area. Thankfully, he didn't spot the waves of bent light that formed around the scientists boarding the plane.

"I wonder how you expected me at all, Colonel Petrov." He

headed toward the entrance after Darya fanned his hand out in that direction. "My plan was to surprise you."

He opened the door for the general. "My uncle decided to let me know you were on your way."

This halted him as he leveled a bewildered gaze at him. "And why is that? Even he wasn't sure when I would be arriving."

"Ahh. Well, I wanted to let him know we left the Siberian Express train for winter tours around Lake Baikal. My wife became ill, so I thought while I was here, I'd see how things were progressing. I hoped there would be someone who could examine my wife to assure myself she was okay. Much to my surprise, my uncle informed me of the possible progress and tests concerning the cloaking project and your arrival. Surely you didn't think you could do anything without his knowledge?"

"Yes. Well, I am anxious to get on with it."

"Of course. This way."

The general gave silent orders to his men by lifting his chin then tilting his head. Darya wasn't sure what that meant, but the men dispersed quickly. Major Krupin joined them, tugging on his uniform coat and adjusting his neck as if to pop it into place.

"Sorry I didn't greet you, General Oblonsky."

"You look like hell, Major. What is going on around here? Where is everyone?"

"Sick, sir. Strep throat and another kind of virus is going around. Many of the men are still in their bunks. I can report that the maintenance force did not suffer the worst of it. They have managed to prepare Su-57 for the test. There was a preliminary test yesterday. The American scientists evaluated and made a few readjustments after talking to the pilot."

The general's lips pursed in irritation as he continued to take inventory of his surroundings. "Then I want to speak to the scientists before we do the test."

"A few are also ill, General. Perhaps speaking to the pilots would be best."

Darya lifted the walkie-talkie and called someone in the hangar to fetch the pilots. He hoped this didn't put Carter in danger. How much Svetlana had told the general remained to be seen. They arrived in short order, walking in with the strut and confidence God gave to pilots and astronauts. Darya introduced them in a no-

nonsense voice, Carter having been given a Russian name ahead of time.

"And I believe you know Lieutenant Svetlana Iskakov."

The general examined her from head to toe.

"The cosmonaut who disgraced our country." He smacked his lips as if he'd eaten a lemon. "And I don't know you," he addressed Carter with more respect. "What do you think of our little project?"

Speaking fluent Russian came in handy for him and so did the attitude. "Fantastic, General. However, I did not know that I would have to work with her." He glanced at Svetlana. "I am pleased to say, however, she has improved a great deal. She is almost as good as myself."

Svetlana bristled at the insult and doubled her fists at her side.

"I am ready to fly the plane, General Oblonsky," Svetlana blurted. "I have a great deal more experience and have flown her. He has not. I am ready at your command."

"Be that as it may, I want him to complete the test," the general announced with a wave of the hand.

Darya felt a slight uptick in his heartbeat, knowing he needed Carter to be on the airliner soon to do the final flight check. Before he could interrupt, Carter spoke up.

"It would be my honor, General." He grinned at Svetlana and winked, causing her face to flush.

Darya tilted his head toward the corridor that led to the hangar. "The test will be within the hour. Notify us when you're ready. I'm sure the general would like to see the new mission control room while you prepare." Darya narrowed a look of contempt as he spoke to Svetlana. "Assist him in anything he asks. Your sacrifice will be noted."

Without another word of instruction to the pilots, the general followed Darya's quick movement toward where he could see how his addition to the complex fared.

"Your wife. How is she?" The general turned to Darya. "You mentioned she was ill."

"Much better. Thank you." Darya's phone vibrated. He excused himself to take the call, leaving the general in the care of Major Krupin.

"I would like to tell her congratulations on her marriage to Colonel Petrov."

Major Krupin appeared bewildered at the conversation. "Married? To the nurse the doctor brought with him?"

"Nurse?" the general inquired. "Wasn't the doctor already here?"

"No. He arrived with the colonel and several other people. The other woman was the colonel's assistant and then helped out in the clinic when our men and staff started to get sick." The major turned his back to Darya. "What is the matter, General?"

"Were they Russians?"

"Of course. They spoke with me several times about the concern of spreading the illness among the men and brought supplies to leave for the future. Unfortunately, they had to use them in the end."

"And Darya's wife?"

"If you mean the nurse, very quiet. I never spoke to her. The doctor never allowed it. He liked running the show, as they say. If that was the colonel's wife, perhaps she infected my people," he said harshly.

"Or gave your people something to make them sick," he growled. "Take me to them. Now." He pivoted toward where Darya had been standing seconds before and discovered he had disappeared.

~ ~ ~ ~

"The scientists?" Darya snarled at Joel who met him in the lower level of the traffic control tower. "Where are they? Why aren't they loading on the plane?"

"Something went wrong with replacements. Several of the inexperienced controllers demanded they stay, especially after they heard General Oblonsky arrived early. If anything goes wrong, they know they'll be blamed. Since a few bugs showed up yesterday, they want to make sure the checklist has been approved."

"Get yourself to the plane. Tessa has the cloaks. Vernon will escort you out. I'll round up the rest of the men."

Joel rushed to find Tessa who waited for the remaining

escapees.

Darya entered the traffic control area where several replacements were being given final instructions by the oldest of the American scientists. He knew nothing about air traffic control, but the necessary instruments that could activate the cloaking device on the ground if the pilot couldn't get it done was here.

"What are these Americans still doing here?" he barked, causing the Russians to jerk to attention. "Do you want General Oblonsky to think you are unprepared and inept?"

"No, sir," one man dared speak.

"Are you ready or not?"

"Yes, Colonel Petrov."

"Then I will escort these Americans back to their lab." He glanced at the scientists with a sharp, narrowed gaze. "I expect you to monitor things there. But you are not to participate unless called upon. Is that understood?" He first spoke in Russian for the sake of the others, sighed, as if forgetting they couldn't understand him. This time he spoke in English before stepping aside for them to file out. "Carry on."

There was a great deal of head bobbing and trying to appear confident as Darya gave one long glance to each person. Stepping outside the control tower, he held up a gadget next to the code panel and scrambled the ability for the Russians to exit. The Americans smiled sheepishly as he jammed it in his coat pocket.

"Ready to go home, gentlemen?"

~ ~ ~ ~

The two pilots strode out into the hangar observation room, solemn and focused on their mission. Carter chewed gum and rolled his shoulders to relax then slapped his hands together in an attempt to appear ready. He grabbed his helmet up under one arm and smiled over at the perturbed Svetlana.

"Guess the general isn't all that into women's lib, huh?" He chuckled. "You're a fine pilot, Svetlana. You can be my wingman anytime."

Her frown deepened as her bottom lip protruded in a pout. "Go to hell, Carter. I'm flying that jet. This is my chance to get back into the good graces of my government."

"I thought you were going to the States with us? What are you talking about?" Carter rubbed his brow. "I'm flying that jet. You get over to the plane we flew here. We're leaving as soon as everyone is aboard." He glanced around her into the hangar. "Some of the scientists have already been driven there," he lied. "I'm flying that puppy out of here, all the way to the Aleutian Islands."

"You really think they're going to let you take a Russian jet?"

"Russian? That cloaking device is American technology your dunderheads couldn't figure out how to create without our Yankee ingenuity. Now that they kidnapped Americans and highjacked our technology, do you think I'm going to leave this behind?" His face was a breath away from hers.

"I'm staying. I hate you Americans. So pompous and rude. And you"—she jabbed a finger in his chest—"are the reason I got kicked out of the space program. I was their best, and it meant nothing."

Carter grabbed her finger and bent it until she winced. "Sweetheart, you got booted out because you had a big mouth. You weren't the only one who got their career sidelined." He gave her a gentle shove. "And if you were their best, we don't have anything to worry about."

Her eyes widened, and her face flushed crimson. "You are an American dog," she snarled.

"Bow-wow, my love," he mused.

Grabbing her helmet off the shelf, she moved toward the steel door. She pivoted back toward Carter who took a step forward. He halted when she pulled out a small pistol and leveled it at his chest. "I'm doing the test. Now, get in that closet." When he didn't move, she extended her hand toward his chest. "Now. I'm saving your life. There is a fighter jet on its way now to blow up that plane we were going to take. I'll let them know there are a few more scientists who haven't arrived. Then boom." She smirked. "No trace. And as for you, I'm sure we can make an arrangement with your government to get you back since you've been spying on our most precious research. You've been a bad boy."

With raised hands, he backed toward the closet. "It's what I do."

She motioned for him to get inside. She rushed to slam the door and locked it.

"You're making a huge mistake, Svetlana."

"My mistake was hooking up with you."

"Now that hurt."

The next sound he heard was what sounded like a chair being dragged over and shoved under the doorknob. The outside door whooshed open to heavy silence. A few minutes passed before he heard the closet doorknob rattle, followed by the latch being thrown. The door swung open, and light flooded in so that he had to momentarily cover his eyes.

"Bow-wow? Really?" It was Sam standing with her weight shifted to one hip and her arms crossed over her chest.

Carter stepped out of the dark. "Thanks for the rescue. Did you get all that down? I figured she'd not let me fly that plane. What a diva."

"Look who's talking," she said flippantly. "And yes. The evidence is stacking up. President Antonov will be hard-pressed to bring this to the UN Security Council. We just need to make it out of Russian airspace."

CHAPTER FORTY-TWO

When the major and General Oblonsky entered the infirmary, they found it empty. Chase could hear them talking in hushed tones. Tessa buried her face in his back and coughed. The heat of her feverish body impressed upon him the importance of getting her home where she could be taken care of properly. He had treated the symptoms but wasn't sure he had guessed correctly.

"Did you hear that?" asked General Oblonsky as he turned to survey the area.

Both men searched the area with no luck. "Just the wind," the major sighed. "I don't know where the doctor and Mrs. Petrov have gone. Are you sure this is the colonel's wife?"

"Tell me about the assistant you said the colonel had. I know of no assistant."

"Beautiful. Tall. Turned every head here. Had the look of the devil about her and cold as ice. But still, there was something about her that…" His voice faded as the general glared at him.

"And the doctor? Describe him."

Major Krupin complied and added, "Now that you mention it, he didn't so much appear to be Russian as from one of the old Soviet Republic populations. Not unusual in this part of Siberia."

Chase could hear the conversation move farther away from where they stood, cloaked in the fabric that rendered them invisible. Tessa's breathing had become labored, and her body had begun to sweat. One downside of the material was that it trapped heat. She leaned into him with all her weight.

With a slight adjustment, he could see through a small opening and determined the two men had stepped outside the infirmary. He unwrapped the covering he'd cocooned them in and let it fall to the floor as he tried to pivot toward Tessa. Her eyes were closed, and he caught her when her knees buckled.

He became aware of the ashen skin, and her wet hair stuck to her forehead. "Tessa." Grasping her arms, he shook her gently until she opened her eyes. "Babe?"

Her eyelashes fluttered, and a lazy smile toyed with one corner of her mouth. She tried to open her chapped lips with difficulty.

"I'm so hot," she slurred.

"The Inviso Blanket traps heat, and there were two of us in it. Better?" He leaned her against the cold window pane.

"Yes. Thank you." She ran her hands across the frosty pane then over her face. "It was so hot."

"I know. You'll be okay now, I think." He touched her hand and pulled her to stand straight. "We gotta go."

Darya entered with the remaining three Americans. "General Oblonsky is looking for us. We need to move. I saw him come out of here a few minutes ago." He walked over to Tessa. "Are you okay?"

"She got overheated under that blanket with me. I didn't have time to get an extra one." Chase felt like he needed to explain, but Darya didn't show he'd taken offense. Instead, he pushed Tessa's hair away from her face and cupped her chin gently in his hand.

"I'm good." She laid her hand on his and smiled. "We're going home."

He turned to Chase. "Do we have enough Inviso Blankets for everyone?"

"Not until Vernon gets back with the ones he has." He passed them out to the three American scientists. "I'll wait here for him. You can lead them out since no one will question you. Tessa, take the last one."

Darya moved toward the door. "The general is headed this way again. I'll distract him. Get everyone onboard. You may not need the extra cover if I can lead him away. Get ready to move fast."

"I'm waiting for you," Tessa insisted as she came up behind him.

"I can't risk it. Do as Captain Hunter and I tell you for once. You are the most stubborn woman I've ever known." He kissed her forehead. "And I love you."

From where he stood, Chase could see tears well up in her eyes as she laid her head against his chest. He joined them and took Darya's nod as a signal to pull Tessa's clinging body from his.

"I'll come back for him, Tessa. Let's go." The two men locked gazes for a few seconds then Chase stuck out his hand. "I had you all wrong, Petrov."

The tribesman glanced down at the outstretched hand and grasped it and lifted his chin in acceptance. He then disappeared into the corridor.

~ ~ ~ ~

"Everybody buckled in?" Carter asked as he moved down the aisle of the passenger jet. There was plenty of head bobbing and nervous smiles. "Sam, make sure the equipment and supplies are stowed away and secure. I need you to help Vernon. He's coming up the stairs now."

Carter made his way into the cockpit and finished the checklist he'd begun earlier to make things go faster. When he and Sam had slipped out to the Singapore airliner, he'd caught a glimpse of Svetlana climbing into the Sukhoi Su-57. The woman was determined to be the hero.

"Chase is bringing the rest now. Almost here." Vernon squeezed in behind him.

"I might need help in here. How are those flying lessons coming along?"

"Top of my class." Vernon clicked his tongue and snapped his fingers.

"Okay. Take a seat, and I'll fill you in on a few things. We are getting ready to taxi in five."

A quiet kind of commotion started outside the cockpit as Sam greeted the newcomers and gave instructions on finding a seat quickly. Chase joined him and Vernon, filling up the cockpit with his large frame. Tessa stood behind him.

"My favorite Grass Valley commando looks like hell." Carter grinned at Tessa, but she didn't appear to appreciate the usual attempt at flirting with her. It was a game they'd played for several years now. She'd become like a little sister to him after he realized his boss might kill him if he stepped out of bounds. "Ready? Lock 'er up!"

Chase shook his head. "I'm going back for Darya. He's all alone in there, and I'm not going to leave him with General Oblonsky who will kill him when we take off."

Carter came up out of his seat and grabbed Chase's arm. "Are you nuts? How do you know…?" He glanced at Tessa. "What do you say?"

"I trust Darya completely," she replied.

Chase removed Carter's hand. "So do I. Get this bird on the runway. I won't be long. If things go sideways, leave."

"No," Tessa cried.

Carter nodded and gave him a thumbs-up.

"I'm going with you," Sam declared. She pointed at a large box of weapons outside the cockpit. "We'll probably need those."

~ ~ ~ ~

Darya managed to intercept the general and major before they reached the infirmary. There was no mistaking the irritation and distrust in the general's stiff posture and vinegary pooched lips. The major scratched his neck beneath the tight collar.

"Where is your wife, Colonel Petrov? I would very much like to see her." The icy voice of the general only made Darya more aware of the danger if Tessa and the others didn't escape.

"I would like to know the same thing," he snarled. "She is not well. I left her here several hours ago, and now she's gone. You wouldn't know anything about that, would you, General?"

"Don't be absurd. I only wanted to offer my well wishes."

"I hope so. If anything happens to her because of your paranoid jealousies concerning me, I will most definitely speak to my uncle about your behavior concerning the present and the past."

"That sounds like a threat, Colonel. I don't like your

insubordination or your tone." The general took a step closer. His neck veins pulsed. "I'm also curious as to where your assistant might be and who she is. And the doctor. Where is he?"

"We both know I do not have an assistant. She is one of your own tank commanders on special assignment. I assumed you sent her to keep an eye on things. She arrived at the same time as myself." He squinted, giving him an already dangerous vibe. "I do not appreciate being spied upon. As to the doctor, I'm told he is local. I had no choice but to get my wife medical care when I heard no medical staff had been retained. Unacceptable, considering the condition of some of the Americans you kidnapped. Not that I need to explain myself to you." He let a sinister smirk spread across his wide mouth.

"You forget who you are speaking to, Colonel Petrov."

"Strange. I was thinking the same thing about you." His phone crackled to life. Slowly, he lifted it to his ear but remained fixated on the general. "We'll be right there." Slipping the phone in his inside pocket, he took both men in with a bored gaze and a deep intake of air. "Gentlemen, the test is about to begin." He stepped aside and motioned for them to follow. "Major Krupin, would you like to lead the way to the observation deck? I believe the jet has taken off."

Although the tension could have been cut with a knife, Darya found the flustered major amusing. He realized the man was trying to be obedient to two superior officers, but Darya had the ear of the president and a reputation just as sinister as the general. None of it mattered. Soon he would be gone and begin a new life with Tessa. Nothing else mattered to him. Finally, he would have the life he'd longed for these past few years. It was but a heartbeat away.

Upon arrival to the observation deck, he noticed three of the general's personal protection detail already standing at attention. They must have come up the exterior stairs that led from the open grounds surrounding the complex. An unease creeped into his radar as he locked stares with them, finding them unaffected by his presence unlike most other people he'd encountered in Russia. They were under the direct protection of General Oblonsky and probably feared little blowback from anything they did when given orders. He moved to the railing and noticed several other men below, cradling their AK-74M assault rifles, donning sunglasses that protected their eyes from the glare off the snow.

The tree line showed slight movement. He squinted and snapped his fingers at one of the Russians who worked at the complex then pointed to the binoculars hanging around his neck. Without acknowledging the quick handoff, Darya lifted them to his eyes. Lowering them, he suppressed a satisfied smile at what he saw.

The outside speaker crackled to life.

"You'll be able to activate the entire presentation from here." Again, Darya extended his hand toward the aide, and a laptop was brought, opened, and placed on the round table which had been set up for them. "There is a camera inside the cockpit. You should be able to witness the cloaking device activate after only a few minutes." Darya pointed to the jet taking off and hoped that Sam had intervened on Carter's behalf in order to get him to their means of escape. "It is only effective after reaching a certain speed. Our own scientists believe that can be adjusted in the future where our planes can cloak even on the ground, but that remains in development."

The roar of the jet taking off drew an intake of breath from the general. "Will we need to keep the Americans to further the work?"

Darya huffed an insulted response. "Of course not. We have everything we need. They are of no use to us now."

The general switched focus from the lifting plane to him. "And does your wife know of our plans?"

"I'm sure I don't know what you're talking about, General." Both men exchanged knowing smirks. "She thinks the Americans she saw here are guests on a tour that started at Vostochny Cosmodrome."

"Yet you let her assist the doctor in caring for my people and a few of the Americans I'm told."

"Yes. Well she wasn't allowed to speak to anyone on orders of a very stubborn doctor. Seems he likes Americans less than you, General Oblonsky."

"And she was okay with that?" he asked suspiciously.

"I doubt it. Then again, she has already learned to do what I tell her—if you know what I mean." He cocked his head at the general and smirked.

The general smiled sincerely. "Perhaps that is why she was feeling ill?"

Darya arched an eyebrow of contempt but didn't respond, portraying his usual dark mood to watch the plane.

"I think we have more in common than I first thought."

CHAPTER FORTY-THREE

The officers held their breath as the jet did a few flybys. The sound forced the Russians watching to shake their head or cover their ears. Darya remained stoic as if he were an unaffected robot. He could feel a tingling in his fingertips that often occurred before a fight. Every nerve in his body felt turbocharged.

This ability to draw strength and focus in such times had kept him alive for most of his life. During those years, he'd not been too concerned about anyone but himself. Now he had Tessa to worry about and wanted to make sure nothing got in the way of their life together.

An announcement that the countdown had begun to activate the cloaking device on the jet crackled on the outside speaker. The general and major lowered their binoculars and turned to Darya who stood unimpressed with clasped hands behind his back.

"Are you bored with this remarkable achievement, Colonel Petrov?" the general asked.

"I am only thinking about the possibilities that lie ahead, General."

"It has the potential of putting Russia back on top. Finally, we can rub the American noses in their own scientific discoveries."

"You realize it will only be a matter of time before they once again catch up with us. After all, this cloaking weapon originated with them."

"Yes. But we could do a lot of damage to their progress and technological advantage in the meantime. Our people, are working on sabotaging any advancements they have gained since their scientists have been missing."

"I think you may have underestimated their carelessness." Darya continued to stare at the tree line, noting how the undetected movement continued to press forward. "Sounds reckless to me."

"It's a good thing you don't have to make the tough decisions. President Antonov will be anxious to apply the technology to our entire military."

"So, you say, General." Darya turned his head slightly and let a thin smile spread across his mouth, causing the general to frown. "I'm sure he will discuss it with me when I return to Moscow."

The countdown continued on the speaker. The three officers lifted their binoculars.

The jet flew at an altitude that made observing the process of cloaking easy. Although the sound was deafening, excitement intensified.

"Activation in two minutes." The speaker voice sounded benign.

The pilot spoke for the first time, drawing the general to stare at the computer screen so he could see inside the cockpit. "That is a woman," he snarled. "Svetlana."

Darya sighed. "Another woman you can teach a lesson, General?" He shrugged. "What does it matter who flies the plane? She is quite capable." The general cocked his head toward Darya who had turned to observe him. "Or perhaps you know she has been playing both sides against the middle."

"What do you mean?"

"She has been working with the American government. They know we have the scientists."

The general paled. "How do you know this? I don't believe you," he snapped.

"I do not care if you believe me or not. The president is aware as well. If this project of yours does not go well today, you may be looking for another line of work, General." This time Darya could not suppress one corner of his mouth from lifting in mock amusement.

The speaker announced, "Five. Four. Three. Two. One."

The general rushed back to the railing and lifted his binoculars. One minute the jet was there and then it wasn't. Everyone on the ground and the balcony cheered, except for Darya whose eyes lifted in surprise for a second. There was a loud rumble, causing the jet to reappear.

"I can't control the cloak." It was Svetlana. "Ground control. Activate emergency protocols."

They responded by acknowledging her request.

The jet once again disappeared. This time there were no cheers as they held their breath.

"Something is wrong. My instruments are…"

The jet materialized just before it exploded into a fireball, sending debris over the nearby hills. The general leaned forward and gripped the railing. After the initial shock, he slowly turned to Darya and rested his hand on his MP-443 Grach sidearm.

"I am thinking you sabotaged the test." The general's voice had an edgy calm that alerted Darya his time was quickly running out. He motioned to his security detail. "Arrest him."

They rushed him, but Darya managed to take down the first two without much trouble. The third pulled out a baton and landed a blow to his gut, sending him backward and bent over. When Darya staggered to an upright position, the last man charged, emitting a loud growl of anger and waving the baton.

Darya grabbed the baton on the upswing and jabbed it in the man's mouth, causing him to choke as it was withdrawn. He then swung it at the man's nose with such force, blood splattered across his face. The second blow connected with his mouth. Teeth crumbled out when he whimpered defeat.

The first two rallied enough to stand and made a move for their weapons but not fast enough to keep the tribesman from doing the same. Two shots to the head dropped them before he aimed at the third, now backing up and holding up his hands. The man was backing toward Major Krupin, who bent down to pick up his sidearm that had slid across the floor, only to be stopped by the major's boot. The man reached back to receive the handoff of the weapon. Before the man could swing the weapon around, Darya pulled the trigger of his own gun and watched him collapse in front of the major.

The general's mouth twisted in irritation as he stared at the three dead men.

"I'm going to have to get a better screening method for my security detail." He rolled his shoulders and surveyed the area to see smoke curling up toward the clouds then sighed with boredom before focusing on Darya again. "You are a dangerous man, Colonel Petrov," the general said calmly. "You will pay for this. Not even your uncle will forgive you."

"Put your weapons on the ground and kick it over to me. You, too, Major," Darya growled, still feeling the punch to the gut with the baton. Both men complied. "President Antonov is a lot more forgiving than one would think when it comes to me. However, do not overestimate your importance or ability to undermine me."

"We shall see."

In that instant, the glass in a nearby window shattered. He glanced in the direction and saw a flash, just as something burned in his upper shoulder, causing him to lower his weapon. In that same split second, he managed to pull the weapon up and fired at the shooter, sending him falling through the jagged debris opening of the window where shards pierced his throat.

With the distraction, Major Krupin snatched up his gun and aimed at Darya's chest. The explosive discharge sound caught Darya by surprise as he blinked unbelief.

$$\sim \sim \sim \sim$$

Chase and Sam slipped back inside the hangar undetected then made their way to the observation deck. The plan had been to watch the demonstration there. If Darya made it that far, he most likely would come back this way. Knowing there were more guards below the deck discouraged them from an attempt to access from the front. The few locals who'd returned to work that morning, now stood outside, pointing at the debris falling from the sky. The breeze carried the smell of burning wreckage adding to the hysteria.

The distraction provided a safe way inside without being detected. The sound of gunfire hurried their movements toward the open door leading to the observation deck. The two agents swung the door open as the glass shattered. In the same moment, Darya staggered backward, lowering his gun to his side. But just as quickly, he lifted his weapon and fired. When the shooter fell through the window, Darya spotted Major Krupin lift his sidearm toward in his direction.

Stepping through the doorway, Chase fired his automatic rifle at the major, sending him back so violently, he flipped over the railing to the ground below. Sam ran up beside Darya and aimed at the general as Chase moved to the railing and glanced over at the ground below. The soldiers there were bending over the body and looked up as he pulled back.

"I thought you were dead, Captain Hunter," General Oblonsky said matter-of-factly.

"I get that a lot," he confessed. "Let's go." He pointed the barrel of his gun toward the door. "You'll make a dandy human shield."

Darya walked over to him and gave him a shove in the right direction. He appeared to droop one shoulder as they escaped through the door. His injury was not lost on Chase as he covered their exit. Soldiers were storming up the front steps of the deck. He bolted the door lock and motioned for Darya to drag a chair over to prop under the door handle.

"Are you okay?" Chase asked, noticing a slight paleness coming into the man's face.

"Yes. But we need to move. I have men ready to protect us as we leave."

"You're bleeding." Chase noticed blood soaking through the thick fabric of his coat.

"Took one in the shoulder. Not my shooting arm. I can still fight."

Chase nodded his acceptance and hurried with Darya to catch up with Sam and the general. They exited the hangar as the airliner moved out onto the runway. Russian soldiers materialized and shot several times before realizing their general was the hostage. They stood ready and circled around to get a clear shot, only to come under fire from Darya's men rising up out of the snow. Their white apparel made them almost as invisible as the Visio Cloth.

The Russian soldiers scattered to take cover as the Enigma agents ran toward the plane. A mobile stairway stood nearby. They shoved the general down on the steps as they tried to push it toward the door now opening to climb aboard the Singapore airliner. As the stairway bumped up against the plane, the door swung open. Tessa and Joel motioned for them to hurry before firing their weapons toward a few Russians who appeared to have a clear shot. The gunfire forced their opponents back long enough for them to scamper up the steps, dragging the general as he fought like a madman to escape.

When Darya turned to return fire, the general twisted and fell down two steps, far enough out of reach to hunker down and hop over the side rail. He rolled out of sight, so the rest of the team continued backing up toward the door as they fired their weapons.

Tessa and Joel backed inside to allow room for them to enter. Bullets could be heard pinging off the plane. Sam bolted through the door, turned, and aimed her weapon to cover the two men. The two cars fixed with explosives earlier burst into a ball of fire, giving the team a slight edge to escape. As the plane roared to life, Sam's warning became lost in the sound of the bombs.

General Oblonsky pulled a small caliber handgun from inside his coat pocket. He fired and hit the rail of the stairway next to Darya then moved the aim toward Chase who now tried to turn his weapon on the general, but the awkward position kept him from getting a clear shot.

Darya stepped down a step to let Chase get inside when the general fired and hit Darya, causing him to collapse and roll down the stairs.

Like a synchronized plan, Sam stepped out and fired, but the general had taken cover as more of his men tried to protect him. Chase tossed his gun to Tessa who had stepped out next to Sam and began firing to help cover him. He rushed down the steps to pull Darya up and sling him over his shoulder and lumbered up to the door as the women stepped out onto the stair landing and fired to protect their retreat.

Once they were inside, Joel slammed the door shut and helped Chase get Darya to a seat where he could be strapped in. Tessa pushed in beside him and grabbed his hand as he turned, eyes full of pain, and tried to grin at her.

Chase bent down to check both their seat belts. "As soon as we level off, I'll be back to check him over, Tessa." She stared up at him in fear when he admitted, "He took that bullet for me."

She turned watery eyes back to the tribesman. He pushed out his bottom lip and growled a response. "I guess you can kiss your hero status goodbye, Hunter."

CHAPTER FORTY-FOUR

Carter loved this part of takeoff: the acceleration, the roar, the heaviness, followed by the feel of the wind beneath the wings, and finally the thump of the wheels being retracted. He often told people it was almost a spiritual moment to him. It never got old. Except this time. Now he had the fate of mankind as his passengers and the lives of his best friends in the palm of his hands. The steadiness of his ability to fly almost anything in an untested plane with a cloaking device almost gave him pause.

At least it didn't appear the plane had taken any direct hits, thanks to Darya's friends on the ground. Whoever they were, the escape wouldn't have happened without them. The tribesman thought of everything. The man should get the Medal of Honor or a Nobel Peace Prize. Whatever the honor, he would stand with him proudly.

He saw Svetlana's plane crash, causing him to die a little inside. Part of him cared what they had been to each other and part of him felt disgust at her betrayal for a second time. That could have been him in the plane. Did she know the cloaking device had been tampered with by one of the scientists? Deep down, he believed the woman wanted to be the star, to get back on top and be the darling of Russia. That was the Svetlana he knew—ruthless, greedy, and self-absorbed. Still, it was a hell of a way to die.

They leveled off, and he unbuckled. "Can you take over for a couple of minutes? All you have to do is monitor. Nothing else. I want to check on the others."

Vernon assured him not to worry.

When Carter entered the passenger section of the plane, he saw Chase trying to lift Darya out of the seat. Every other row had been removed early into captivity, and the last four rows were completely gone. Carter pushed Sam and one of the scientists aside to help Chase. Together they carried the tribesman, now covered in blood, to the back.

"Help me with his coat, Carter. There are scissors in that black bag."

They removed the coat and uniform shirt to reveal the damage. Not only had he taken a bullet to the shoulder, but several to the chest as well, when he tried to protect Chase.

"God Almighty," Carter breathed.

Tessa fell to her knees and stroked his hair away from his face.

"Let's clean him up so we can see what we've got. Tessa, I'll have Sam help me."

"No, I want to help. Just tell me what to do."

"You are not well. He doesn't need your germs."

"Please." She grabbed a mask and gloves from his hands. "I'm not leaving him."

He agreed and gave her disinfecting wipes to clean him. Sam stood ready to remove any materials they needed discarded.

Carter felt sick to his stomach to have come so far and have this happen. The rescue wouldn't have been possible if not for the tribesman. "I gotta go." As he moved down the aisle, he warned the scientists they were not out of danger just yet, and if anyone knew how to help the team, they'd better get busy.

Entering the cockpit, he squeezed back into his seat.

Vernon grinned and sighed with relief. "Glad you're back. I need to check our computer."

"Good job. Those lessons paid off."

Vernon opened the laptop. "Oh, I didn't actually take any lessons."

"What?" Carter yelled.

"I found an aviator simulation school. Almost like the real thing. I mean, I did take ground school, so I kind of knew what to expect. They were pretty impressed. After all, I am a freakin' genius."

"You mean to tell me I left you in charge of this monster bird, and you didn't even know how to fly?"

He shrugged. "Guess so." He fist-punched Carter in the arm. "Surprise," he said, looking at his radar screen on the laptop.

"I hate surprises," he huffed.

"Then you aren't going to want to hear we're being followed by two really fast jets. And they are armed. They are veering away toward where you landed the other plane, Carter."

"I might have implied the scientists were on their way there to get on the plane." He grinned. "And here I felt sorry for Svetlana."

"She totally ratted us out, Carter. Sorry, dude."

Carter's frown deepened. "Guess she knows karma is a bitch."

"Whoa. They just let loose one of those hypersonic R-37M long-range air-to-air missiles."

Carter glanced over at Vernon's computer screen. "That was a little overkill, considering it has the ability to strike targets hundreds of miles away." He refocused out the windshield.

"Boom. Just activated the bomb at Joel's underground hotel. No trace of us there." Vernon gave an exaggerated impression of an explosion. "Okay. They are headed back to teach us a lesson."

"Are you sure about the cloaking device on this plane?" Carter glanced over at Vernon.

"Pretty sure."

Carter sent him a disgruntled glare. "Pretty sure?"

"Here they come."

"I see 'em."

~ ~ ~ ~

Chase removed the last bullet lodged in Darya's chest. One of his lungs appeared to be damaged, and any attempt to stop the bleeding remained lame at best. His breathing became shallow even after he covered it with a Vaseline-type seal. Every few minutes, he lifted the seal for the blood to escape.

"Come on, Darya. You can do this," Chase ordered. "Fight,

damn it!"

"Why is he still bleeding?" Sam whispered as Chase shook his head. "Could there be another wound we don't see?"

"Darya?" Chase asked, laying a hand on his arm. "Can you let me turn you over? I need to check to see if there is another bullet in your back."

By now the tribesman turned pale and found it difficult to speak, but he managed to nod that he would try. Both Sam and Chase gently slipped their hands beneath his back to turn him on his side. Tessa took his arm and pulled so he could hold on to her.

"Damn," Chase moaned and shook his head at Tessa. "Took a hit in the back, near the spine." Carefully, they lowered him back down. "Darya, this is when you need to fight like hell. As soon as we can get a message off, I'll make sure we have a team waiting for you in Alaska to fix this." He lifted the Vaseline patch again, and blood oozed out. "There's no reason why you can't survive."

Darya blinked a slow acknowledgement and turned to Tessa who couldn't keep silent tears from spilling down her cheeks. He managed to lift his hand to touch her face and tried to smile. "I love you," he whispered before his eyes closed.

"Darya?" she said frantically.

"Tess, he's unconscious. That's all. He needs the rest. We've done all we can do for now."

"It's a ten-hour flight. Are we going to get there in time?" she sniffed.

He glanced down at the man who had once been an enemy, now his hero. "I'm not hopeful, Tessa. You need to prepare yourself. Even if he does, that back injury could change his way of life. Do you understand?"

A nod and a choked-off sob were all she could muster. He realized how hard she tried to be brave. Something caught his attention out the window at the same time their passengers started nervous chatter. A fighter jet roared past on the right side of their plane, maybe 1500 feet away. He looked to the left in time to witness another jet that did the same.

"Tessa, I need you to go buckle in. Now."

The same movement caught her attention, along with Sam.

"I'm not leaving him."

Sam nodded toward the cockpit. "Carter might need you. I'll

stay with Tessa. Someone needs to keep the patch operating on his lung. This might all be over in a couple of minutes, so what the hell does it matter where we sit?"

Standing, he felt the heaviness of defeat crash over him. Was this the end for the Enigma team? When he started to turn away, he watched Tessa reach across Darya's chest and grab Sam's extended hand. Most days, the two women were oil and water, but a few times, like now, he caught a hint of friendship between them.

Inside the cockpit, Vernon continued to call out information as Carter gripped the yoke or control wheel to keep the plane steady. This is what Chase admired about the ex-astronaut—the more dangerous and impossible, the better he got. There wasn't a sweat bead on him or a lot of nervous conversation, just a question now and then, spoken with the calmness of an icicle.

"They're circling back, Carter." Chase felt a little unsure at the moment.

"Together they're going to create a wave to knock us out of the sky. If that doesn't work, they'll shoot us down."

"So, we're toast."

"Oh, ye of little faith, Captain Hunter." He turned his head to grin at Chase. "We are going to climb a few thousand feet and put the fear of God in those bad boys."

"Did the cloaking device get installed?"

Vernon looked up from his laptop screen long enough to smirk and click his tongue. "Installed it myself. Better go tell our esteemed guests we're going to rock and roll for about fifteen seconds. They should know this since they invented it, so tell them it's about to get real."

Chase hurried back to the others with the warning then to Tessa and Sam. He snatched a couple of seat cushions and kneeled down to give them the news. "We need to secure Darya's body so it doesn't move. I don't want that bullet in his back to cause any more damage when we accelerate to climb."

The voice of Carter came over the PA. "It's showtime. Hold on."

The whine of the engines being forced to climb sent the passengers farther back in their seats while gripping the armrests. The three Enigma agents did their best to hold Darya in place but struggled until Joel joined them to add an extra pair of hands as the plane shook violently. The sound of Joel's child crying, followed by his wife's comforting words to soothe him, mingled with the groans and prayers of the scientists.

A pop, followed by what sounded like a small explosion bounced the plane as it began to level off. Instantly, the plane flew as if soaring on eagle's wings.

Carter's voice came over the speaker. "And that, my friends, is how you fly an airplane." Cheers filled the cabin. "We are officially cloaked and will remain so for about an hour. We will return to our natural state at that point and will descend to a lower altitude in case we need to do it again. I'm guessing we'll be hunted until we leave Russian airspace. Hats off to you brainiacs back there."

Sam released her grip on Darya and stood. "I think I'll go tell Carter he's such a blowhard."

"I'll stay here. Go ahead."

Joel also stood and laid a comforting hand on Tessa's shoulder as he moved away to join his family. His in-laws had never flown before and were a nervous wreck.

Tessa continued to stare at Darya and barely noticed when Chase reached over to touch her forehead. She shifted her gaze to him.

"You're warm again. I want you to rest, Tessa. I promise I'll watch over him." He stood and retrieved a blanket from an overhead bin. He was surprised to find one after all this time. "You can stretch out next to him. But you need to sleep. Okay?"

"Okay." Instead of wrapping the blanket around her, she spread it over Darya, careful to leave the Vaseline patch visible to open and close. "He needs it more than me."

Chase removed the jacket he'd changed into before leaving the plane to find Darya. "Take this. I don't want you to get chilled."

She took the jacket and covered her chest and leaned against the wall. "Thank you for going after him. I'm so grateful."

"This time tomorrow, you two can tell your kids about the adventure you had on your honeymoon."

She smiled. "And how we became invisible. They won't believe it."

"Well, you can have them call their Uncle Chase, and I'll tell them you were right."

"I'd like that." She closed her eyes, heavy with fatigue. "You are the most amazing man, Captain Hunter."

CHAPTER FORTY-FIVE

Carter jerked himself awake and glanced over at Vernon who continued to watch his laptop, along with the instruments of the airliner. He rubbed his face and stretched.

"How long was I out? Just a catnap?"

"Maybe an hour. Sam brought us food and kissed the top of your head. You never budged, so it was hardly a catnap."

He fought the urge to touch the top of his head, and instead pictured her leaning over him to show a moment of affection. One of these days he was going to have to do something about her. Did he need rabies shots first? Body armor? Maybe a tetanus shot would suffice. Right now, he was competing with the prime minister of Israel for her affection, and that meant, if he wasn't careful, the Mossad would be dogging his steps. There were a few people you didn't cross.

"A kiss, huh?"

"I made that up," Vernon admitted as he sent an amused look to the ex-astronaut.

"Like hell. I can feel the burn of such passion even now."

"You're so full of it," came Sam's voice as she stood in the doorway. "That's the only burn of passion you'll ever feel from me. Chase wants to know where we are."

"An hour from the coast. Almost home-free." One other time they had to outmaneuver Russian aircraft by disappearing into areas where radar didn't reach and adding another hour cloak to the plane. There were enough deviations and blank spots on radar, they managed to not get caught. Vernon got a message off to the director of Enigma who made arrangements for an escort as soon as they crossed over into international airspace.

"How's Darya?"

"Hanging on. Doesn't look good. I've seen wounds like this before. Usually they survive maybe an hour. Tessa is back there talking to him in Pashtu. He opens his eyes and tries to smile sometimes."

"How's Tessa?"

"Pretending to be brave, like always."

"Chase?"

She shrugged. "Stoic. Hard. Distant."

"Guess he'll never change."

"Your dashboard just did. What is that flashing light?"

"Whoa. We're running low on fuel." Vernon sat his laptop aside. "We aren't going to make it."

Carter straightened and did a quick system check. "Damn."

~ ~ ~ ~

Tessa forced a smile when Darya appeared to be alert and took the hand she offered. "We're over into international waters."

He squeezed her hand.

"Almost home. Vernon got a message off, and medical help will be standing by for you."

He licked his lips before trying to speak. "Captain Hunter?" he whispered.

Chase kneeled down and opened the Vaseline patch again and checked his weakening vitals. "I'm here. You're one tough son-of-a-gun, Darya." The tribesman coughed, a trail of blood trickling from the corner of his mouth. Chase gently wiped it away before checking his wounds.

"I did not want to die in Russia."

"Me, either. Thanks for saving my life."

He closed his eyes and grinned. "That was an accident."

Chase chuckled. "I figured as much, but I owe you."

"Tess-sa, you made me a promise if I should die."

"Stop that talk. Didn't you hear what I said about medical help standing by?"

"Tess-sa, you must say goodbye."

She forced back tears and tried hard to keep her voice steady. "Never."

Darya tried to reach Chase's hand but lacked the strength. She watched Chase take his hand as it dropped. With feverish eyes turned in his direction, he jutted out his bottom lip then pulled the captain's hand over Tessa's that lay on his abdomen.

"I know you tried to save me, but Tess-sa did that long ago." He turned back to her. "Now you must save him. You have given me happiness. Come whisper goodbye to me in Pashtu and then you must live, Tess-sa. It. Is. What I. Want."

She bent low to his face and whispered words to him in Pashtu. Finally, she gazed into his eyes and whispered, "Goodbye. You are forever in my heart. I won't let you down."

He smiled and took one last breath.

A dam of sobs burst in Tessa as she begged him to wake up and breathe. Reasoning evaporated as she pleaded with him to return. When Chase squeezed her hand, she stared across Darya's body at him, shocked to see tears welling up in his eyes. He tried to speak but couldn't, but she knew, he, too, was sorry to see him leave this world. The sound of soft crying and awkward silence filled the cabin. Everyone onboard had in some way been touched by Roman Darya Petrov.

Tessa became aware Sam had come to her side to kneel down and cover Darya with another blanket she'd found in his backpack. The design was the American flag. She slipped an arm around her shoulders and helped her stand.

"I need to buckle you in." Sam guided her to a seat and fastened the belt before turning back to Chase to help secure Darya's body. He stood tall and stared down at the man he'd once hated. "Carter needs you," Tessa heard her say. "I'll stay with Tessa."

He nodded and started down the aisle but stopped and squatted next to her. "I'm truly sorry, Tessa."

While tears continued to cascade down her cheeks, she

managed to give him a half smile and lay a hand on his cheek. "I know."

~ ~ ~ ~

Carter frowned. "This is when I wish I had a regular crew to assist me on this big bird."

"What's the big deal. You got me," Vernon mumbled as he focused on the instruments. "I can do it. Who else do you need?"

"Usually besides the pilot, in this case, me, who loads the flight plan and flies, there's a pilot monitor who does the interior inspection of all the systems and instruments. He even works the radio inflight stuff."

"Sounds like me. Anyone else?"

"Yeah. A relief pilot who backs up the other two on the ground and in-flight."

"Guess that leaves me out."

Carter leveled a disgruntled glare at his genius. "Ya think?"

"Well it's not like we originally planned to take this plane. Besides, what about the fuel?"

"Even on a plane like this, the gauges aren't that accurate. We really don't know how much fuel is in the lines throughout the manifold and engine. Maybe we can ask Tessa to say a prayer that we have more than we think. She seems to have the ear of God most of the time."

Chase squeezed inside the cabin.

"Update," Chase demanded as he struggled to balance himself against the sudden wind turbulence. "What's the plan, Carter?" Chase bent down a little closer to his ear.

"Since the engines are fed fuel through the manifold, they'll run out of fuel at the same time. Good news is this airbus has a RAT system."

"Speak English."

"Ram Air Turbine. It's a small propeller that extends in the slipstream. The hydraulics will be able to extend the landing gear. Takes a little longer, but hey, we got time, right?"

"Hell if I know. Doesn't sound good to me."

"We're at a higher altitude right now. We can convert that into airspeed and fly farther, and longer. I've estimated the lift over drag speed for this aircraft and—"

"Are we going to make it or not?"

"Well…" He glanced down at his instruments and back at Chase. "We got company. The Russians are determined to drop us out of the sky. I can't cloak this plane again."

"Why not? Give it to me straight," demanded Chase.

"We won't have the power. Too dangerous. We'll be out of gas by then and coming in fast to compensate for no power. We'll have to lower the landing gear at the last possible moment." He turned to Vernon. "Tell them what I wrote down for you. And that we have company. I want to know where that escort is."

Vernon nodded. "Anchorage Center, request direct Adak Airport for visual straight-in Runway 5." Radio silence felt eternal while they waited." Vernon fidgeted. "Adak has given us a red light not to land because of the snowstorm."

"Well, we're landing whether they like it or not."

Vernon relayed the message with the number of people onboard, the injured, and how much fuel they had left. He also suggested they might have Russian company on their tail.

A quick response followed this time. "Anchorage Center. You are cleared direct Adak Airport. You'll have a pair of F-22 Raptors from Elmendorf AFB in Anchorage intercepting said aircraft well before they reach American airspace."

Vernon looked at Chase a little white-faced. His freckles were nearly invisible. "We're coming in fast. My math says ten more minutes until we have a visual. Fuel starved now."

Carter rolled his shoulders and let out a cowboy yell. "Gonna feel like you signed up to be in the rodeo. Better find you a safe place," he ordered. "It's about to get interesting."

"Get us on the ground in one piece, Carter," Chase ordered before leaving.

"If I don't, there won't be much you can do about it, my friend." He let loose a jovial laugh and refocused.

The loss of power happened ten minutes earlier than predicted. Carter felt a wave of doubt wash over him as he mentally pictured himself landing this plane. He did everything he could think of to push her harder before it was too late.

"A little closer," he mumbled. "Be good to me, baby." He made the dreaded announcement. "Brace for impact."

The storm cleared enough for him to see a narrow strip of land that sat between two small hills. The winds had increased, but he managed to keep control.

Carter felt that old exhilaration grab hold of his heartbeat and focused on the runway covered in snow looming ever closer. When he lowered the landing gear handle, his worst fear came true. The three green lights, indicating his landing gear was down and locked revealed only two lights. A loud ting sounded in the flight deck. He cross-checked the altimeter—seven hundred feet above the ground. He was running out of time and altitude.

"What is ECAM actions?" Vernon shouted.

"The onboard computer identified there's a malfunction. We have a checklist for this but don't have time for normal procedures."

"What are we going to do?" Vernon gazed down at the approaching runway.

"Manual gear extension. Now!"

Carter deviated from the standards, but that judgment came from decades of experience. The aircraft could land with no nose gear, but the snowy runway conditions could send them into a slide off the runway and possibly into the water.

Vernon reached up and manually extended the gear. The mechanical up locks that held the gear in the belly of the aircraft were released. "We're three hundred feet above the ground."

The onboard computer announced, "One hundred feet."

Carter's glance darted from the altimeter to the airspeed indicator and back outside.

"Fifty feet," the computerized voice continued.

He felt a slight thump underneath him. A quick cross-check showed three green lights now. No one said a word except the computer that continued to count down.

He could already see flashing lights of the first responder vehicles as the weight of the plane dropped closer and closer to the runway.

The jet touched down firm, just like he wanted. Since the thrust reversers were inoperative due to engine failure, he only had partial spoilers to help slow them down. Finally, it began to slow, only to slide sideways toward the end of the runway because of the ice and snow until it came to a complete stop.

Carter grinned and gave Vernon a high five before picking up the mic. "This is your captain speaking. Welcome home. You're now on American soil." A loud roar of cheers could be heard from his passengers. "Damn. I'm good."

~ ~ ~ ~

Chase hurried back to check on the passengers. Although relief showed on their faces, it remained a quiet and respectful atmosphere for Tessa's sake as she grieved for the man who made their escape possible.

She fumbled with her seatbelt until he reached down and released her. Pulling her up, she fell against him and sobbed softly. The only thing he could do was hold her until her pain ebbed away. Everyone stood in silence and waited, with heads bowed.

"Tessa, I'll take care of Darya for you." He looked to Sam and raised his chin in a nonverbal command. "Sam is going to take you to get some medical attention. You're burning up. Will that be okay?"

"Yes," she mumbled, then pushed away from his embrace to wipe her tears away. "Yes," she repeated.

Moving to the back of the plane where Darya's body lay, Chase stood at attention until the plane emptied of passengers, except for Joel Sandy. He watched the scientist whisper in his wife's ear. She laid a hand on his cheek and glanced back at Chase, her face contorted with sadness, then exited the plane.

"I owe Darya this. Let me wait with you," Joel said quietly.

Chase nodded.

Kneeling down, Chase pulled back the sheet one last time to gaze at his former enemy. He folded the tribesman's hands across his chest and wondered why they weren't colder.

Careful not to disturb his body, Chase reached to touch his neck with two fingers. Then he felt it.

"Well, I'll be damned, Petrov."

~ ~ ~ ~

Tessa had never imagined how beautiful Montana would be this time of year. A warmer-than-usual winter and little snow had made it possible to bury Darya's body on his land. The casket stood ready to be lowered into the ground as the Enigma team stood by watching Tessa lay her arms across the shiny surface.

Each person had shared a memory of Darya, from their first encounters to now. It was a balm to her soul to have her work family here. Director Clark, head of Enigma, had spoken last saying that due to Roman Darya Petrov's selfless actions, the world would be a safer place, and that the president would never forget his sacrifice.

She removed the sheer red scarf he'd given her as a wedding present and laid it on the top of the casket, kissed her fingertips then laid them on the surface. "Goodbye." She turned to the others. "Would you mind if I had a few moments alone?"

They moved away, except for Chase, who backed up to stand ten feet away with his hands crossed in front of his body. He had barely left her side since they'd returned home. Joel Sandy came alongside him and waited to be acknowledged.

Chase slipped on his sunglasses. "Well?"

"I'm sorry, Captain Hunter. Tessa doesn't need to know now."

"Thank you."

The wild horses that lived on his land thundered into the field ahead of them. Several ventured closer, but the stallion drove them back before he approached cautiously but remained at a safe distance. Tessa felt frozen in place as she watched the beautiful animal stop and stare at her then bob his head. A sudden gust of wind toyed with her hair as it snatched up the red scarf and sucked it up into the air. Both she and the horse watched it twirl aimlessly until it fell across his back.

She lifted her hand to her heart as Chase walked up beside her.

"He's here." Tears welled up at the corners of her eyes, but she forced them back.

"Are you ready to leave?"

Tessa turned her back to the horse as he pounded the earth toward his herd. "Yes. I have unfinished business at home."

Chase shook his head in acknowledgment. "And I have some in Russia."

EPILOGUE

President Antonov moved through the airplane hangar after he disembarked from his helicopter. He'd spent the night in Irkutsk. President Austin was making his life a living hell in the world news media about the missing scientists found alive. Fortunately, his nephew had put into place a cover-up for him to fall back on, much to his surprise. The Chechens were blamed once again, and they were happy to take credit.

The Russian government promised a thorough investigation, considering it took a lot of working parts to hijack the airliner in the first place. Claiming that he knew nothing about the project would only make him appear weak and uninformed. He promised to find those responsible for the kidnapping and hijacking of the airliner, which he profusely denied knowledge of while admitting to the research.

There was a lot of rhetoric about the Cold War starting again, economic sanctions and losing their position on the Security Council at the United Nations for a period of time. Threats were exchanged of military retaliation. After vowing to turn over any information concerning the events leading up to and after the taking of the airliner, he decided to also abandon Crimea and return control back to the Ukraine. That appeared to take the American president by surprise, and he praised President Antonov for doing the right thing.

President Antonov entered the building and moved up the stairs to find the observation deck. General Oblonsky took the steps two at a time to catch up in time to open the door for him. As he moved out onto the deck, the warmth of the sun, which had finally broken through, touched his face. The brightness caused him to stop and take a deep breath and lock his fingers behind him. The thought of Darya standing here, involved in so much treachery, nearly broke his heart. Little Yuri still asked for him.

"Mr. President?" came the gravelly voice of his highest-ranking general. "Beyond the woods is where the plane went down. We now believe the pilot, Svetlana, crashed it on purpose."

"So, there was no tampering with the systems?"

"Our people say the system worked perfectly the day before." He stood at attention with his head slightly cocked to the side.

The president raised his eyebrows suspiciously. "Why do I not believe you, General Oblonsky?"

"Sir?"

"Whether she did it on purpose or not is irrelevant. All of this is your mess that I am having to clean up."

The general's eyes widened in surprise. "Excuse me for saying so, Mr. President, but it was your nephew, Colonel Petrov, who sabotaged the work here."

"Not true," came a familiar voice in English.

The general pivoted to see Captain Chase Hunter holding him at gunpoint.

"Guards!" yelled the general in alarm as he paled.

The president moved toward the exit door. "They have all been sent away, General. You must pay for this mess and for the death of my last living relative." He sighed and nodded to the American captain and walked out but couldn't resist waiting on the steps until he heard three shots. In a few seconds, the door creaked open, and Chase joined him.

"Thank you, Mr. President."

"Do not ever let me catch you on Russian soil again, Captain Hunter. I will not look the other way next time."

~ ~ ~ ~

Only the tick-tock of the regulator clock hanging in the office broke the silence. A fire blazed in the fireplace which had only recently been installed. The sound of children's voices had evaporated when Tessa's parents took them to the movies for the Saturday matinee. They had stayed on when she went to Russia to help with the children. Robert would be gone for the last part of her trip, so they'd decided to treat themselves with spending more time in Grass Valley.

She'd come home exhausted. Antibiotics had kicked the strep throat almost overnight, but the pneumonia lingered. What she had been taking in Russia hadn't worked. Then there was the funeral to deal with both physically and emotionally. Once home, she told her parents about the marriage being in trouble and that everything had just been a sham. Their grief at losing a man they considered a son devastated them. The truth about Darya she kept to herself. There was no need to share yet another tragedy. Chances were good they would not understand.

Robert had been staying in the house while she was gone to hide the truth of their partial separation. Now several suitcases, propped against the bookcase, waited for his ultimate return within the hour. She sat in the glider rocker and stared into the fire, trying to find a reason to forgive him for all the lies.

The sound of the front door unlocking stopped her therapeutic motion in the chair. She stood up to brace herself against any more lies.

"Tessa." He smiled when he found her in the office. "Good to have you back. Did you have a good trip? Your parents here? Where are the kids?" The smile faded as he noticed a red envelope with the contents spread out across the cherry desk. "You've been going through my desk?"

She let her hands fall to her side. "That's what you're concerned about? That I've been going through your desk?" The icy tone in her voice made him fidget.

"I wanted to tell you, Tessa. I was so ashamed and embarrassed. So much happened with work, a new job, and you flying to parts unknown all over the world."

"You lied to me."

"I was actually protecting you," he insisted. "I'll fix this. I promise." He stepped closer and tried to touch her, but she sidestepped the move. "Don't be like that. I've missed you."

She nodded toward the packed bags. "I want you gone before the children come home. They don't need to know we don't even need a divorce."

Robert soured and squinted. "You are the most stubborn woman I've ever known. How in the world do you think you're going to manage without me?"

"I've been doing that almost since we got married. Sorry. When I thought we were married."

"You are in Sacramento all the time, at least when you're not playing diplomat with the president's people. You've gotten a big head and an inflated opinion of yourself."

She responded coolly. "I've taken a leave of absence from the university. I'll be working from home and consulting for the State Department when needed. My traveling days are over for quite a while, maybe for good. The junior college has asked that I teach a class."

"You think I'm going to support your lifestyle, this big house, and your shopping habit?"

"If you paid the bills, you'd know that the house has been paid off and has been in my name for some time. I have saved almost all of my money I made at the State Department. There are no outstanding bills for you to worry about."

"I want my kids." He appeared to be breathing harder.

Tessa moved to the desk and lifted a folder. "My attorneys have drawn up papers for visitation and other matters concerning our assets. Look them over and, if changes need to be done, I'll put you in touch with them." She walked over to the suitcases.

"This isn't over, Tessa. Just another one of your ridiculous moods I've had to deal with over the years. You think you're such a badass." He grabbed up the suitcases.

"You have no idea, Robert." She smiled victoriously. "Now, get out. I have a new life I need to get started."

In moments, she heard the front door slam. She moved to the window draped in sheers to watch a few snowflakes begin to fall. The weight of the world lifted, causing her to place her hand on her heart in relief. Now the chance to be herself was really possible.

No more hiding what she'd become because of Enigma.

Her phone buzzed on the desk and she turned to pick it up. Recognizing the number, she answered and listened to the voice on the other end. "Thank you, Chase. I'm glad you're home."

~ ~ ~ ~

Joel Sandy walked quickly down the corridor to the intensive care unit. The swish of the doors opened after he punched in a few numbers and hurried through to a private room where he was met by the Director of Enigma, Benjamin Clark. He stared at the patient who remained in a coma.

"Director, I'm surprised to still see you here."

He frowned at Joel and sat in a nearby chair. "Do you have everything you need for him?"

"This is the best place he can be. Thank you for helping me get him here."

Director Clark turned his eagle eyes to him, causing a chill to run up his spine. "No one must know about this. Not even Captain Hunter."

"Of course."

"The Russians are looking for him. You see my concern, I'm sure."

"I understand, sir."

The director stood slowly and reached out to place his hand on Darya's arm. "May God heal your dark heart, Petrov."

THE END

INFORMATION ON MALAYSIAM FLIGHT MH 370

On March 8, 2014, Malaysian Airline Flight MH 370 headed for Beijing then disappeared off radar. What happened to the missing plane? As of this writing, the plane has not been found. The official investigation concluded that the wreckage is at the bottom of the southern Indian Ocean. One theory is that the plane was hijacked and then flown out over the ocean until it ran out of fuel and crashed into the sea. All 227 passengers and 12 crewmembers were presumed dead after data showed the Boeing 777's last recorded position. Most of the passengers were from China (153). The twelve crewmembers were Malaysian. Other countries represented were Australia, Canada, France, Hong Kong, India, Indonesia, Iran, the Netherlands, Russia, Taiwan and the Ukraine.

Onboard was an IBM executive from Texas, who had been living in Beijing. The flight was supposed to mark his last trip to China before relocating in the Malaysian capital of Kuala Lumpur. The other two Americans were sisters, one just 4-years-old. Besides the three Americans, Freescale Semiconductor of Texas, confirmed that twenty of their employees were on that flight. An engineer working for Eastman Chemical Co. in Pittsburgh in Pennsylvania, was returning to the US via Beijing. Another passenger worked for Halliburton.

The many other passengers included artists, travelers, engineers, a doctor, hospitality workers, teachers and more.

This unsolved mystery helped me imagine the story you have just read. What if the truth was never told? For more information on flight MH 370 I would direct you to the many interviews and documentaries on YouTube. The science behind "cloaking" is real and you'll be surprised at how far science has taken us in using this technology for military superiority.

MEET TIERNEY JAMES

Tierney James decided to become a full-time writer after working in education for over thirty years. Besides serving as a Solar System Ambassador for NASA's Jet Propulsion Lab, and attending Space Camp for Educators, Tierney served as a Geo-teacher for National Geographic. Her love of travel and cultures took her on adventures throughout Africa, Asia and Europe. From the Great Wall of China to floating the Okavango Delta of Botswana, She weaves her unique experiences into the adventures she loves to write. Living on a Native American reservation and in a mining town, fuels the characters in the Enigma and Wind Dancer series.

After moving to Oklahoma, the love of teaching continued in her marketing and writing workshops along with the creation of educational materials and children's books. Try some of her other books to bring a little adventure to your life. http://www.tierneyjames.com Speaking at book clubs, school functions, church and community groups are a few of the things Tierney enjoys doing when not writing her next adventure. She also helps beginning writers in their quest to becoming a published author through her workshops and classes. Family, two adopted dogs and gardening fill her life with plenty of laughter to share with others.

Tierney has won multiple awards for her writing and is an Amazon #1 Best Selling Author.

Enigma Series
- An Unlikely Hero
- Winds of Deception
- Rooftop Angels
- Kifaru
- Black Mamba
- The Knight Before Chaos

Stand Alone Novels
- Turnback Creek
- The Rescued Heart
- Dance of the Devil's Trill

Wind Dancer Series
- Dark Side of Morning

Education
- African Safari

Education for Marketing
- How to Market a Book Someone Besides Your Mother Will Read

Children's Books
- There's a Superhero in the Library
- Zombie Meatloaf
- Mission K9 Rescue